Distant Dreamer

Barry J. Dalberto

*to Sharon
We had a wonderful time with Mr. Ray Marinai at that ~~great~~ great Purnneseo School.*

Barry D'Alberto

Distant Dreamer
Barry J. Dalberto

All rights reserved. No part of this book may be reproduced or transmitted in any form or by any means, electronic or mechanical, including photocopying, recording, or by any information or retrieval system, without the written permission of the author, except where permitted by law.

Copyright © 2017 Barry J. Dalberto
All rights reserved.

Cover painting by Peter Paul Dalberto
Cover design by Patrick J Harsch

Printed by CreateSpace, An Amazon.com Company
Available from Amazon.com and other retail outlets

ISBN-13: 9781975947101

ISBN-10: 197594710X

What Readers Are Saying

In "Distant Dreamer" Barry Dalberto weaves a luminous tale of Mark Fisher, a young teen, who by day serves as a summer wilderness guide to persons with physical and sensory challenges. By night Mark is so attuned to the thrumming of the distant past that, as the veil of sleep descends, he experiences an alternate life as "Marq" among the legendary voyageurs. The parallel narratives at once shine a light on persons, who challenged by injury, physical, emotional or sensory needs, strive to test themselves in the wilderness much as the voyageurs tested themselves in the dangerous race in the transport of furs across vast distances to the great inland sea. Dalberto reminds us in this tale that no matter what burdens we carry through life, we are all voyageurs.

Diane M. Sainato, Ph.D.
Associate Professor, Emerita
The Ohio State University

Barry takes us to the North Country where living with the land is revered. Having grown up in Michigan's Upper Peninsula, I was immediately drawn back to my home, my town and my woods. As seasoned campers, my husband and I were impressed with the detailed descriptions of how to set up a campsite, how to properly erect a tent, how to prepare for and survive storms, and how to make a mouth-watering blueberry cobbler from fresh-picked berries.

Barry's lyrical descriptions of nature will inspire any reader to become a more observant person. He describes watching a mated pair of loons fishing: "Upon spotting prey they dove and each surfaced with a fish which they swallowed head first. Their beautiful backs were coal black with white diamonds. They popped to the surface like corks, beaded with water."

A wonderful read for outdoor enthusiasts, young readers looking for an outdoor adventure story, and fireside lovers of good writing.

Dorothy Pritchard,
Retired City Regional Planner

DEDICATION

To Ray Mariucci, my favorite teacher, role model and hero at Quinnesec Junior High School. His innovative teaching, humor, emphasis on being physically and mentally fit, and zeal for sports left enduring marks on all his students.

ACKNOWLEDGMENTS

Many thanks to several dear classmates from Quinnessec School are in order. They freely offered critiques, asked questions, and exhorted me to continue when I grew overwhelmed and discouraged over the years. Patrick (P.J.) Harsch, my old friend and a character in the book; Pam Person Edens and her sister Diane Person Schumacher; and Billie Johnson McCandless read through painfully written early versions of *Distant Dreamer*. They graciously shared their own memories and times of those golden childhood years.

My daughter, Amanda Jagla Nimz, transferred my original manuscript from its word processor format to Microsoft Word and did some editing.

Peg, my sweet wife of 23 years, did her best to drum computer savvy into me and stuck with me to the end without losing her mind. P.J.'s talented wife, Wallis, cheerfully tackled the daunting job of editing the final version while also managing to create a smoothly flowing read. She was incredibly helpful and never faltered.

William J. Cummings provided me with historical information on the Iron Mountain/Kingsford area, including Quinnisec School and its ties to Henry Ford's Woodie factory in Kingsford. William's father, nicknamed "Dutch," was our physical education teacher at Quinnesec and also taught math courses at Kingsford High School.

My old pal, classmate and fishing partner, Patrick (P.J.) Harsch was always a constant help and source of support. He checked my history and offered suggestions, asked questions and did research. He converted the manuscript to the required format for publication and designed the cover using my Grandpa Pete's painting.

The cover is now a fitting tribute to the amazing self-taught painter whom I learned to love and appreciate more as I matured. Soon after Grandpa Pete gave me the painting, he died at age 84 in 1968. I miss him still.

To The Reader

This is a work of historical fiction. Much of it focuses on the author's home turf in the Iron Mountain/Kingsford and Quinnesec areas where it happens. The names of its principal book characters were changed, as parts of the story are fiction. The timeline was also advanced 20 years, from the 1950s to the 1970s.

A central theme runs throughout the entire book: an abiding respect for the majestic beauty and mystique of nature and its Creator. This theme meshes closely with the Canadian fur trade era of the 1700s and 1800s and the marvelous antics and hard work of the French-Canadian voyageurs, as well as the Ojibway Tribe's contributions of trade routes, birch bark canoes and handiwork.

The book's characters' names were changed. Ray Bond is their teacher, Ray Mariucci. Mark Fisher is a pseudonym for the author. The story is seen through the eyes of Mark. P.J. Hars is Patrick J. Harsch, Bob Forge is Bob Forgette, Marla Perkins is Marsha Perkins and Mike Hohl is Mike Hohol.

Mark shares the author's early childhood and exemplifies the author's love for wilderness. The author uses flashbacks to his family life, friends and classmates to bring his story to life. Dream sequences take the reader into the historical, fascinating fur trade era and the lives of the voyageurs.

The author compiled his notes while he portaged, paddled and fished through many of the locations described in the Sylvania and Boundary Waters Wilderness, following old voyageur routes.

Fifty plus years have passed since the author's time at his beloved Quinnesec School. Memory can play tricks, so any errors are solely his, with his sincere apology to all concerned.

French Words and Phrases

adieu	goodbye, farewell
allons-y	come, let's go
allumez	light up
aller	get up, go
alors	so then
ami(s)	friend(s)
après-midi	afternoon
avec	with
bien	good
bon appétit	good appetite
bonne chance	good luck
(le) beau pays	the beautiful country
bonsoir	good evening
bienvenue	good day
bonjour	good morning
bonne	good
campement	camp
capote	long coat
c'est fini	it is finished, done
c'est magnifique	it is magnificent
c'est moi	it is I
chanson	song
chanson d'amour	love song
coup de grâce	final blow, finish
d'accord	I agree, all right, OK
déjeuner	lunch
dépêchez-vous	hurry up
difficile	difficult
donnez-moi	give me
donnez-moi du feu	give me a light
ecouté	listen
engagé	contract worker
en garde	be on guard
entrée	main course of meal
esprit de corps	team spirit, morale
et	and
faire	to make

feu	fire
fille(s)	girl(s)
fini	finish, done
fleche	arrow
hivernants	voyageurs who over-winter
homme du Nord	man of the north
idée	idea
il pleut beaucoup	it's raining hard
jeune	young
jolie	pretty, très jolie (very pretty)
le fait	fact
le travail	work
levez-vous	get up!
mais oui	but yes
mangeur de lard	pork eater
magnifique	wonderful, magnificent
merci beaucoup	thank you very much
merde	poop
mes amis	my friends
métis	half breed
mon dieu	my lord, god
patois	mix of languages
petit déjeuner	breakfast
piece	bale of goods (90#)
pomme	apple
pomme de terre	potato (apple of the ground)
pose	rest
pour	for
reposer	to rest
rubbabo	voyageur supper
savoureux	tasty
s'il vous plaît	if you please
souper	supper
tour de force	a test, a strong showing
très bien	very good
trois pipes	a distance of three pipes (smokes)
une	one
voilà	behold, look
vrais	true, fact

CONTENTS

1	Wilderness Survival Class	Pg. 1
2	Solo Three-Day Practical Survival Test	Pg. 9
3	Day One	Pg. 11
4	Dawn of Day Two	Pg. 22
5	Dawn of Day Three	Pg. 30
6	And the Winners Are	Pg. 45
7	Going Home	Pg. 49
8	P.J.	Pg. 64
9	Preparing for the Trip to Ely	Pg. 69
10	Leaving on a Greyhound Bus	Pg. 72
11	Memories of Home and Family	Pg. 87
12	Preparing for the Boundary Waters	Pg. 90
13	Into the Boundary Waters The First Day	Pg. 102
14	Boundary Waters The Second Day	Pg. 129
15	Boundary Waters The Third Day	Pg. 149

16	Boundary Waters The Fourth Day	Pg. 165
17	Boundary Waters The Fifth Day	Pg. 178
18	Boundary Waters The Sixth Day	Pg. 190
19	Meeting Sigurd Olson	Pg. 208
20	Wenonah Canoe Factory	Pg. 219
21	Camping With Ray and Ange	Pg. 234
22	Mark's Solo Camp	Pg. 247
23	Going Home Again	Pg. 261

The movement of a canoe is like a reed in the wind. Silence is part of it, and the sounds of lapping water, bird songs, and wind in the trees. It is part of the medium through which it floats, the sky, the water, and the shores..... A man is part of his canoe and therefore part of all it knows.

Sigurd Olson

Chapter One

Wilderness Survival Class

Mark sat in his eighth grade math class at Quinnesec Junior High School. He watched as sunbeams filtered through the windows and illuminated dust motes. A warm, late spring day beckoned to him. The snow had melted and lilacs bloomed and perfumed the air.

His thoughts kept returning to daydreaming about his heart's desire: to be out roaming the wilderness back in the day of the fur trade. There he stood dressed in buckskins while paddling a birch bark canoe. He was free to camp, fish and explore. It was heaven.

Suddenly he felt a sharp nudge from across the aisle. He turned to find his best friend P.J. grinning. Their teacher, Mrs. Ryan, had just called on Mark to solve a problem at the blackboard. He flushed a deep red then stood and walked up and gave it a try. Math was not his best subject. Mr. Ray Bond taught the best class Mark had. Mr. Bond was one of two male teachers in the school. The other was the principal, Mr. St. Louis.

Ray Bond taught a course titled Wilderness Survival and Lore. It involved lecture and independent research, as well as several field trips. The course stressed becoming self-reliant competent woodsmen (and women) with emphasis on using wild edibles, camp cookery, making shelters and first aid.

Mr. Bond had been a military Special Forces Ranger in WWII. He had relied on his training and wits for self-defense, foraging for food and making improvised shelters while evading capture by the Imperial Japanese Army on tropical South Pacific islands. After the war, he returned and pursued a college degree and earned a teaching certificate. He was Mark's hero.

The day that Mr. Bond announced the new survival test was still fresh in Mark's mind. The wilderness Survival and Lore course had become his chief motivator to attend school. Ray Bond was in his mid-fifties with a muscular build. He wore glasses and had dark brown hair combed into a wave in front. His wit and sense of humor were paired with a quick smile. He used innovative methods that made his class fun and interesting.

He began the announcement by saying:

"There will be a very special event offered for the first time, to this class. A solo survival test will be held in early June, right after graduation. It will be located in the Sylvania Primitive Area, near Watersmeet, MI. It is open to the top five students who have earned the highest combined scores in the final written exam and during our field trips. Other criteria will be based on my observations of each person's desire to excel and survive under extreme conditions. It will be a real test of what you have learned in this class. It well test your ability to handle making shelter, finding and cooking food, making fire and dealing with weather, on your own. A school bus will be provided for transporting the five finalists and all their gear from the school to the Sylvania Primitive Area Headquarters. It is important to show up at the school on time and get your gear on the bus. Leaders will be on hand to help you pack. There will be an equipment signup sheet posted in this room the last week of school. You will need to check out any gear you lack and sign for it. Please return all gear to the school after the test.

"There is also an exciting bonus to be offered to the top two finalists in the Solo Survival test! My wife and I will sponsor a week's canoe camping trip to Northern Minnesota's Boundary Waters Canoe Area Wilderness. It will take place in early July. Travel dates and arrangements will be available later.

"The survival test includes the five finalists who will be transported by canoe with all gear necessary for spending three complete days solo in a remote area of the Sylvania Primitive Area. Basic items required are a good fillet knife, length of fishing line, hooks, hatchet, shelter cover, food and cooking equipment. Finalists need to have their own packs to carry their supplies which will be examined before leaving base camp. They could choose to take some food and equipment items not on the required list, but they also have to carry in everything on their own backs. There also are some forbidden items: radios, tape players, musical instruments or any other electronic gear. Reading material is encouraged as long as it's appropriate. All permits and fees for camping will be handled by the Quinnesec School."

Mr. Bond continued, "The present Sylvania Primitive Area contains more than thirty-four lakes with good numbers of fish. It once was privately owned and contained several cabins and a large, exclusive lodge. In 1967 the National Forest Service purchased the eighteen-thousand-acre Sylvania Tract, removed all buildings and opened it for public use. Ottawa National Forest personnel currently manage it.

"The finalists will have to construct their shelters and furniture using only dead trees and using the eight by ten-foot nylon tarp as a shelter cover. Special permission has been received from the Sylvania Headquarters to keep and eat any fish they could catch, including bass."

Mark recalled how the class gave each other wide-eyed looks as Mr. Bond continued.

"Each finalist will be escorted to their assigned test area by a leader in a large tandem canoe. They will be dropped off near their test area. Each test area has specific colored and numbered flags at its boundaries. Finalists are free to explore and plan their days as they desire as long as they stay within the boundaries and make their morning and evening check-ins. At the end of the test, each finalist will be evaluated by two leaders, the morning of the fourth day."

Late in May, Mark heard that a list of the five students who qualified as finalists had been posted outside Ray Bond's Room. He hurried upstairs, taking three steps at a time until he reached the second floor. He slowed as he approached Mr. Bond's doorway, which was mobbed. He tried to be patient but was quite frustrated. Then P.J. tapped him on the shoulder. He shook Mark's hand and with a wry smile whispered, "You're at the top of the list, my man, congrats! What's more, I'm going too! We need to get our solo test camp assignments from Mr. Bond."

He and P.J. knocked on the room door and heard a loud, "Come in." They squeezed past the group and stood at attention in front of "The Man's" desk. Ray Bond sat surrounded by stacks of paper that hid the top of the massive solid oak desk. He made one final note on a page, pushed his eyeglass frames back on the bridge of his nose and leaned back, smiling. He looked up at them and held out his hand. Mark and P.J. took turns shaking their mentor's hand.

"Congratulations to you both!" Ray said in greeting. "I think you're going to like your camp locations for the solo test. Here are your assignment briefs for your camp areas. I have to go to a meeting right now. Take these home and let me know if there are any questions, OK? See you lucky lads tomorrow."

Mark and P.J. took their sheets, saluted and left, with beaming faces. They shook hands and headed to their first class. Mark hoped to examine his brief during study hall. He folded it carefully and tucked it into his shirt pocket. After enduring long math and science classes, he finally sat in study hall and opened the camp assignment.

He was to be placed in a remote area near a small, elongated lake with a primitive campsite that included a cast iron fire grate with a cooking surface, a vault pit toilet and a shelter space. Mr. Bond would brief all five finalists the next day, during class. The rest of the students would watch the movie *The Call of the Wild*, hosted by Mr. St. Louis.

Mark told his family about his qualifying for the solo test. They were happy for him and thought it was an honor. They also liked the idea of all costs being paid by the school. Mark went up to bed early that night and spent a while reading the solo camp assignment brief. He concentrated on the site map on the bottom of the sheet. It was neatly done and included important details such as the site's north- south orientation and a distance scale of the lakeshore and trails, marked in rods. Mark finally shut off the light and drifted off. The next thing he heard was his mom's voice as she shouted up the stairs.

"Get up Mark, breakfast's ready!" He jumped out of bed, dressed, ate some cereal and fruit and walked down the highway to Brin's Store to catch the school bus. He chatted with P.J. about it on the way to school. The day dragged until it was time for Mr. Bond's class.

As soon as class began and attendance was taken, Mr. Bond asked Ricky and Marcia to pull down the window shades. He told the class to enjoy the movie and let Mr. St. Louis take over. The five solo camp finalists were asked to follow Mr. Bond out into the hallway. He led them down to a conference room in the library and seated them at a round table. While he gave them a brochure and handout sheets, he shook each finalist's hand and sat back down. All eyes were focused on him. Besides Mark and P.J., the other finalists were Bob Forge, Mike Hohl and Marla Perkens.

Ray Bond began by saying, "Congratulations to you all for your hard work and demonstrated proficiency in this year's Wilderness Survival and Lore Class! You all picked up your campsite assignment yesterday, right?" Everyone nodded and held them up proudly.

"Good," he continued. "The brochure is courtesy of the Ottawa National Forest and has all regulations and maps pertaining to the Sylvania Primitive Area. Please look it over before we leave for the test. Now listen up while I briefly outline it. Take notes. No time for questions today, sorry. We'll have time at base camp for that. This will cover hand tools and supplies you need, expected behavior and procedures to follow in case of an emergency. Each of you has his small lake or stream and is required to stay within site boundaries. They will be marked with bright colored flags and a number at the four main directions on your compass.

"Your first priority after finding your camp area is to begin making a shelter in case bad weather moves in. Wilderness etiquette requires you refrain from unnecessary loud noises and to use all your senses to appreciate and respect the natural solitude. Three days being totally alone might be a blessing or a curse. It depends on the disposition of the individual. If any finalist isn't comfortable spending three days alone, this will tell the story. The campfire will be the heart of the camp. It will provide heat, light and a huge sense of comfort. If tended faithfully, it will give you hot food and drink. It can be your best friend at night and especially after a storm."

Ray Bond paused to take a drink of water and continued: "The only exception to the 'no electronics' rule is the small, battery-powered radio which you are required to use to check in with base camp each morning and evening at designated times, using a special call name. Radio procedure will be covered at base camp. Each radio also features a waterproof clock with a lighted dial and a compass. If anyone fails to check in at designated times a response team will be sent quickly, depending on visibility and weather. They will arrive and determine the reason for the missed check-in. If it was due to something beyond the finalist's control, such as a malfunctioning unit or an emergency, aid and/or replacement of the radio will be made. The finalist would continue the test with no penalty. If the failure was the finalist's fault, either deliberate or by negligence, he or she will be disqualified and removed from the competition. In case of accident or illness, contestants would be treated with first aid. He or she would be allowed to resume testing, if it is a minor incident, or would be evacuated to base camp or medical facilities if severe."

Mark watched the blood drain from the finalists' faces after that cheery note. He hoped his own skin didn't betray him. P.J. began furiously cleaning his glasses as a way to cover his nervousness. It definitely was food for thought. After Ray Bond gave the warning, he paused to let it sink in. With just a hint of a grin, he continued his monologue.

"Now I'll run through a list of necessary tools and other supplies. Please note that your handout contains this list, so follow along. The list will also be posted in my room in a few days. Use it for checking out gear from the school. You will need to have the following items packed before you leave for Sylvania. Notice that most items are available from the school. I'll read down the list. Please follow along. You'll need:

one 8x10 foot nylon tarp with grommets*
one 8-inch fillet knife with belt sheath*
one small hatchet*
one sharpening stone*
100 feet nylon parachute cord*
fishing hooks, sinkers*
one folding camp saw with Swedish steel blade*

one kitchen kit consisting of pots, utensils, plate, bowl & coffee pot*
one headlamp or flashlight*
one canteen with cup*
one first aid kit with instructions*
one box waterproof matches*
one journal*
one sleeping bag and ground pad*
one towel and a change of clothing*
one rain poncho*
toilet paper*

Note: asterisks* mark gear available at the school.

Bring flour, brown rice, pasta noodles and sauce, spices, baking powder, dried fruit and nuts, cooking oil and shortening, sugar, chocolate bars, oatmeal, etc. Note: your food choices may differ from this list. Bring what you need to prepare wholesome, nutritious meals.

"Well, that's all I have time for today. The rest will be up to you guys and gal!" He grinned at Marla. "It will be a tough test, but you are equal to the task. The bell is about to ring, so you can wait here and proceed to your next class. See you all in class tomorrow. Bonne chance."

After Mr. Bond left, the five classmates sat around groaning, but they were also charged up with the heady experience awaiting them. The bell rang and everyone scattered. Mark left for his last period, study hall. He clutched his handouts and began to daydream.

Mark Fisher was his full name. He was fit, weighed 135 pounds and was 14 years old, due to starting school one year late. He lived on three acres of land at the west side of Iron Mountain, MI, with an older brother, Pete, a senior at Kingsford High School, and a set of twin toddlers, Frank and Wendy. His father, Frank Sr., was a house painter. His mother, Lee, was a homemaker and restaurant worker and tended the family fruit stand in summer. Hunting and fishing were sacred activities and all participated. There were always chores to do at home. In summer, it meant row crops to weed and pick, including red raspberries, strawberries, beans and peas. Wild berries were picked also. Much of the crop was sold at the family's fruit stand. There were old growth red and white pines at the back of the property which butted up to state land. Mark and brother Pete had a rabbit snare line in winter that provided an occasional bunny for the stew pot. Mark made stick forts and pretended he was a frontiersman with chipmunks and birds as his friends. Any time he could, he would grab some worms and a fish pole and head for a nearby lake.

Sometime around fifth grade, a new kid moved into the area and rode his bus down through Iron Mountain to Quinnesec, MI, and Quinnesec Junior High. His name was Pat Hars, nicknamed P.J. He and Mark were fast friends and shared a love for fishing. P.J. lived in a house that had frontage on Moon Lake, so it wasn't hard to figure why they spent so much time together. Mark loved fishing and exploring and was at times P.J.'s mom's "star boarder!" Pat spent more time fishing Moon Lake and knew it well. He wore glasses that always needed cleaning or repair. Mark used skill and muscle while Pat applied patience and thought to solve problems.

Mark and other neighborhood kids walked to the bus stop at Brin's Store a quarter mile west on U.S.2. It was a combined grocery, home supplies and live bait store. In the basement were large concrete vats full of fatheads, shiners and suckers. Mark made many trips there, sometimes for groceries, but more often to stand in front of the wonderful display of candy and comic books. It was rare he had more than a dime to spend which usually meant an agonizing choice between candies or the latest Tarzan comic book. In winter, he and his brother Pete bought suckers that they used to bait tip-ups to tempt Moon Lake's pike.

The rural school buses gathered in the large driveway to load, unload and transfer kids. The bus Mark and P. J. took carried them through Iron Mountain to Quinnesec, since they lived outside the Iron Mountain city limits. Quinnesec was a small town near the Menominee River and Fumee Falls, a beautiful park within walking distance from the school. Mark looked forward to the May school picnic. Right after attendance was taken and a short lecture about required behavior and penalties for being bad, all students went outside and lined up behind their teachers. They would then march through town in formation. Traffic guards would stop highway traffic, allowing the classes to cross and continue down to Fumee Park. There they would spend the day climbing up the trails above the falls, wading in Fumee Creek and eating lunch, ice cream and cake. Several picnic tables were shaded by tall pine trees.

Quinnesec Junior High School was a solid brick two-story building with three large playgrounds with swings, monkey bars, slides, teeter totters, three baseball diamonds, and acres of grassy fields to run wild on. Along the west side was a thick forest of red pines with branches to the ground. The forest was supposedly off limits to students, but some regularly dove into its dark domain. If one was caught exiting the trees, punishment was waiting. It would begin with a stern lecture and end with a paddling at the expert arm of Mr. St. Louis, the principal, one of the few men in control of the school.

In winter, snowball fights and "King of the Hill" ruled. Spring brought boys and girls to the warm south wall where they played marbles, which required digging holes in the sand with their heels to act as marble pots. Terms like "draggies" and "trysies" echoed along the wall along with much arguing over who won the marbles named purees, cat eyes and steelies.

The marble pot holes were dug by planting a sturdy shoe heel on its back edge and moving in a circle while applying enough pressure on it to dig a suitable hole. It would be wider at its top and needed to be deep enough to hold up to 15 marbles of various sizes.

Each pot could handle a minimum of two and up to four or five players. It was also necessary to decide how many marbles each player would shoot, with two to four being the normal range. After the players used their heel to mark off a "shooting line," they would flip coins to decide who had the first toss. They stood about ten feet away and took turns tossing one marble each until all were thrown. Each player had to know where their marble landed. The first shooter was the player whose marble was closest to the pot. The shooter could keep shooting until he shot all the other marbles in and claimed the lot or missed. The second closest player then took his turn. Sometimes only one or two exceptional players did all the shooting. The only acceptable shooting style was to press your thumb against the inside of your index finger and give the marble a push towards the pot.

The one who got the last marble in a pot won them all. The recess bell signaled all games were done and broke up some games unequally. Everyone had cloth or leather marble bags that were a proud possession and guarded closely.

As May approached, other pursuits called. The most popular was baseball. It was called workups. A hardball was thrown overhand with no protective gear but leather baseball gloves.

Another more interesting game, called Stretch, matched two boys facing each other. It was played around the back end of the school. Each would draw their pocket knives and attempt to throw their knife so it stuck in the ground to either the side of their opponent's feet. He had to stretch his foot out to the knife. When one player couldn't reach the opponent's knife stick, he lost the game. Most boys packed pocket knives. It was a special place and time.

"Kill" was another rough and tumble game which any number could play. It had no rules, only penalties. All that was needed was a rubber ball that was kicked into the back playground whereupon someone yelled, "Go!" Whoever grabbed the ball would run from the pack until caught and either surrendered the ball willingly, or was gang tackled and had it torn away. It was the most savage game at school. Mark relished the rugged game.

Chapter Two

Solo Three-Day Practical Survival Test

It was early June, just two days after graduation. An early morning ground fog created an eerie scene. The parents of the five finalists saw their kids off after helping them load their packs onto the bus. Mark sat chatting with P.J. on the bus. Suddenly a car horn blew right next to his window. There was his mom and the twins, waving at him. Mark opened the bus window and waved as the bus left the school.

"Nice of your mom and the twins to stop by to see you off," P.J. said.

Mark smiled and answered, "It is, especially since she had to take my dad to work first and needs to hurry back to open the fruit stand!"

P.J.'s mom, older brother and sisters had previously been there to see him off. It was comforting to have their families' support. Mark's mom told him not to get hurt.

Some instructors, called leaders, helped with last-minute packing and rode with the finalists on their bus. Most of the other leaders were in a larger bus with all the base camp tarps, tents and gear that had already left for Watersmeet. It also towed a big double-decker trailer full of tandem and solo canoes. It was a long ride to the Sylvania Primitive Area. The anticipation was almost more than Mark could bear. On arriving, there was much excitement and confusion before everyone found his assigned canoe and paddled and portaged their gear to base camp.

Finally, he was riding in the bow of a big tandem Old Town Royalex canoe and approaching his test camp. The leader, Mike, was in the stern while Mark's mountain of gear rode amidships. It was a perfect day: cool and sunny, and the lake was dead calm. Faint ripples fanned out ahead as the first rays of the sunrise illuminated the high tops of pine, birch and poplar. Loons were calling in that quasi-jungle sound and had done so since they had left the base camp. It almost sounded like a warning of some dark trouble, but the day looked perfect.

Mr. Bond had given the five finalists a last-minute talk, including tips and warnings. The radios were checked and put in waterproof bags. Then they all left with their leaders in tandem canoes and headed in different directions.

When they next met, the lucky two top scoring finalists would take away the honors and the right to the big prize. Mark's leader, Mike, suddenly jolted him out of his daydream by announcing:

"Well, here's your new home!" Mark gazed at his area and spied a faint portage landing leading to a trail that disappeared around a turn. Mike gestured toward the shore and spoke:

"Your camp area is marked with a boundary flag that is red with a white number one. Follow the trail to the right side of the lake about fifty rods distance. Do you know how long a rod is, Mark?"

"A rod is an old surveyor's term and equals sixteen-and-a-half feet," Mark replied.

Chapter Three

Day One

As the canoe kissed the beach, Mark jumped out and unloaded his gear. With his heavy Duluth pack hoisted, he waved goodbye to Mike. Mike waved back, turned around and was out of sight in seconds. Mark stood watching him leave, with a mix of loneliness and excitement. After hoisting his pack onto his back, he leaned forward and let the tumpline settle on top of his head. It was similar to what the fur trade voyageurs did when carrying heavy loads, except theirs were longer, extending from the top of their head down to their butt. It took some of the weight off his hips and transferred it to his neck and upper back. Due to its remoteness and lack of use, the portage trail was littered with trees that he detoured around or stepped over. Then as he crested a hill, he glimpsed a flash of reflected sunshine on blue water through the thick trees.

It energized him, as he realized that he was beginning an adventure that could lead to an exquisite prize, a Boundary Waters Canoe Area (BWCA) back-country trip! He began looking carefully for the red flag and was rewarded as he neared the shore of his lake. It sat at the intersection of a trail and was framed by a healthy patch of wintergreen and ground pine. Bending low, he popped a few fat, red wintergreen berries into his mouth and chewed slowly, enjoying the sweet, minty flavor. Picking a double handful of the wintergreen leaves seemed logical. He was fond of the tea made from them. He was careful to not pull out the plant's roots, so it could grow new leaves.

He stuffed them in his pocket, re-shouldered his pack and followed the trail. In a few minutes, he was at his camp. The fire pit was nearest the lake and sat on a massive rock shelf that overlooked and gradually descended into the lake. He dropped his pack and made a quick perimeter check.

He found the pit toilet that was a square wood box with a hinged cover. It was nicely hidden a short distance away. There was a fairly level shelter area close to the fire pit. It was close enough to the fire pit so his lean-to shelter front would face the fire pit. Its light and heat would reflect into the lean-to while sheltering him from wind and rain. He could stay warm and dry near the fire. Mark extracted his camp saw, hatchet and cordage for lashing.

His first job was to cut poles and erect them to form a sturdy shelter frame that would use the tarp as a roof. He had noticed some nice standing dead cedars that were a good size for support poles. Some had grown nice strong forks at their tops. Mark dragged several poles back after using his folding saw to cut them down and "limb" them. He chose four that had nice forks near the top and made the front forks equal at about five feet. Then he did the same for the two back poles at four feet long. Before he could erect the four corner support poles, he needed to create a heavier log base in a rectangular shape to give the poles a strong base to lash to. The topsoil was thin and wouldn't allow him to dig them in. He located two solid, dead maple logs and cut them into two equal lengths for side base logs and two that would fit inside and flush with each end of the rectangular base. He raised each corner slightly to allow space underneath the logs for lashing by inserting flat rocks until it was fairly level.

Wrapping parachute cord multiple times around adjoining logs made a strong structure. Mark then stood the corner poles upright. Each corner pole was lashed until each corner was secure. He also placed four heavy rocks, one at each corner to give the frame extra strength. Since the tops of the corner posts had forks, he laid a crossbar connecting the forks and lashed it tight on both sides. He repeated the procedure with the rear posts and also lashed side poles to the corner tops and crossed them, letting the pole bottoms rest on the ground. Once more, he secured the bottoms with rocks and lashed the side support poles where they crossed. The shelter frame was as sturdy as he could manage. The last task was to use cord to tie the 8'x10' tarp overhead. Threading the cord through the grommets and encircling the crossbar in front, he stretched the tarp as taut as possible and repeated the lashing on the back crossbar. It was now a sturdy shelter that should hold fast despite even nasty weather. This type of shelter was similar to one the class had made together during a class field trip with Mr. Bond. They had also constructed other survival shelters such as tipis and a lean-to by using only sound, dead wood, bark and other natural materials. They were taught how to lash sticks together and tie various knots using parachute cord. Mr. Bond was a walking storehouse of survival knowledge, thanks to his military training and experience in WWII. Mark was glad he remembered the excellent instruction in what Mr. Bond called "field expediency."

Mark quickly moved his bedding and other gear inside the shelter, placing his sleeping bag and ground pad at the back. He would weave branches and bark into the sidewalls later to provide more protection. First, he needed to cut a good supply of firewood and kindling. He cut more dead cedar poles and dragged them to camp. He set up a firewood cutting area near the fire pit. After cutting a stack of small cedar branches, he gathered an armload of dry birch bark and placed it under the tarp. Mark knew from his prior experience that nothing was better for starting kindling than dry birch bark. Its secret ingredient was resins, which not only resisted water and insects, but also created a hot flame and black smoke when lit. Even if the firewood was damp, the birch bark would burn hot enough to reach its kindling point and ignite the firewood.

Memories of past encounters with fire suddenly flooded his mind. One night years earlier, Mark had just gone to bed. A fire lit up the woods behind their house. He ran to tell his dad, who verified it and called the fire department. The fire trucks filled their yard and the chief thanked him for spotting the fire. They put out the small fire that night and left a tank with a hand pump in case embers reignited. Another time Mark had been playing with a fire in the outside fieldstone fireplace. Suddenly his pant legs were on fire! He ran screaming and crying to the back porch. His dad crashed through the door, jumped down and rolled him on the ground, smothering the flames with his bare hands. His mom helped hose down his burned legs with cold well water, rubbed in vegetable oil and made him wear shorts.

Another narrow escape happened when he and his older brother Pete were home alone. A fire from a neighbor's burn barrel began slowly burning towards their chicken coop. Pete told Mark to run up to their house and call the fire department, while he set a backfire between the oncoming fire and the chicken coop. When the firefighters arrived, the fire had nearly burned out. They dampened down the spots still smoldering and checked with the neighbor's hired man who had lost control of a trash fire. At first he lied and accused Mark and Pete of setting the fire, but later relented. He confessed he lied to save his job. Unfortunately, it came too late to stop the blame from landing on Mark and Pete.

Another scary incident happened one winter night when fuel oil flooded their home's oil burner in the living room. The stove began to burn red-hot. When their dad tried to close the fuel shut off valve, it failed. He told everyone to dress and hurry over to the neighbors. As Mark and his mother were leaving, they saw the stovepipe was smoking and glowing cherry red and with white hot spots! It made a scary huffing noise as though it would explode. As they left, his dad hollered, "Go, she's going to blow!" Fire shot out of the chimney as they ran next door to Ella's and

Jim's to call the fire department. In the meantime, Pete once again saved their lives. He fought panic and, as a last resort, grabbed a box of baking soda and dumped it into the hot stove. It quickly snuffed out the fire. The firefighters arrived and put out the chimney fire. The next day the stove was replaced. Mark had always feared and respected fire since those hard lessons.

It was nearly noon. His camp was almost set up. He sorted out his smaller food pack and munched a bag of mixed nuts and dried fruit. There was still much to do, but he needed some quick energy and protein to continue. He remembered that Ray Bond always stressed avoiding dehydration. He raised his canteen to his lips and took a long swallow of cool, sweet water. It was all the water he brought with him. Boiling lake water would supply his further needs. Mark sat on a log and studied his lake. It was unnamed except for being listed as #14 on the map. It was crystal clear with many tree trunks lying on the bottom. Its shoreline dropped off into black water at the rock ledge in front of the fire pit. There were many mature trees along the shore. Lofty white and red pine reached up 150 feet into the sky.

Walking along the shoreline was easy since there was minimal undergrowth and largely unobstructed views of the lake. He was fortunate to have such a fine camp area. It seemed to be a good time to cut a fishing pole. A nearby, flexible cedar branch was just the ticket. After attaching ten feet of fishing line and tying on a hook and sinker, the search for live bait was on. Not far up the shore a black ribbon was swimming!

It was a leech! Perfect bait. He dove for it and trapped it against a rock near shore. It was tough to hang onto. He fumbled it a few times before getting it impaled on the hook. He grabbed a big rock and returned to the rock ledge. Once the pole was fishing for a meal, he wedged the pole's butt end into a crack in the rock shelf with a rock on top. This lake was said to contain pan fish, including bluegill, sunfish, perch and crappie, as well as largemouth bass, small mouth bass and northern pike. A few of the larger, deep lakes in the Sylvania contained lake trout. With the setline working on dinner, Mark turned his attention to making some camp furniture and possibly a luxury fixture.

He needed a simple table that would give him space near the fire pit under the shelter front. He decided on a rectangle about 2 x 3 feet. He placed the two longer side sticks on the ground. Next, he laid the shorter sticks so they crossed near each end of the parallel side pieces. It created a rectangle with the sticks extending a few inches beyond the frame. He lashed the four sticks where they intersected, pulled them tightly together and tied them off. Next, he took two beaver chews and attached them in an X that connected the four corners. He then lashed and tied them off where they crossed to form the X. It made the rectangle much stronger by essentially bracing it with two triangles, which were very stout.

Beaver chews are sticks of green wood branches that beaver had stripped of their bark and were left near shore. Beaver work from dusk to dawn when they are safer from predators. They tend to any damage to their dams or lodges by using their own discarded beaver chews that they weave together and pack with mud into their dams and lodges. They often chew the bark of their favorite tree, the poplar or aspen, at the shoreline, discarding the "beaver chews" that can be used by savvy campers for construction of camp furniture, or if they have dried out, as firewood.

Next, he flipped the table frame over so the X was underneath. It was there for strength on the bottom. To finish the table top, he wove some more beaver chews close together across the narrow sides. Lashing each tightly and tying them to the side pieces at the X made it tight and strong. Any wide gaps might allow utensils to fall through to the ground. It wouldn't be perfect, but would be adequate to hold his plate, utensils and hot pads. The last step was to raise two forked sticks that were lashed to the front two corners while the other end would rest on the shelter base log. It was done.

The last piece of furniture was a chair. It would need to be mobile and comfortable. Mark cut two short log chunks about 8 inches in diameter and 18 inches long. Each of these chunks was flattened using the hatchet so they would not roll. Another log chunk the same size was notched on both ends so it would fit the tops of the other two base chunks. It was nearly complete. Mark used the hatchet to scallop a more contoured seat. He now had a serviceable, mobile chair.

Having been so busy, he had forgotten his fishing pole on the rock ledge. It was past time to check it. He began walking down, but stopped when he came upon a big flat rock. Turning it over yielded two fat angle worms. He knew from experience that one could never have too much bait. As he approached his fish pole, he found a slack line. When he pulled in there was no bait! Either the leech had wriggled off the hook or some crafty fish stole it. He quickly threaded the worms on the hook and cast it in. After holding the pole for a few minutes without a nibble, he stuck the pole's butt back in the rock crevice and replaced the hold down rock. He made a mental note to check it soon and returned to his camp. After another drink of water and a few bites of jerky, he felt refreshed. He was pleased with his morning's work, but in the words of poet Robert Frost, he still had "miles to go" before he slept.

Mark decided his luxury item was to be a Native American sweat lodge. It would be a fresh learning experience. He'd never attempted one, but had read about their construction and history and had seen pictures of them. It would be similar to a tipi. A circular base of sticks would be tied at the top. He took his hatchet along and gathered a large number of stout, flexible beaver chew sticks that were lying near shore. A sand beach close to camp would make a good site.

Mark chose eight stout beaver chews about one inch thick and cut them five feet long. He arranged them in a rough circle and brought the tops together. He lashed them together using strong cord and wrapped the cord on both sides of each support stick. He kept tension on the cord as he worked until he made a full circle. He then spread the base out to allow enough room for him to sit inside and pushed them down to the same depth for stability. A vent at the lodge's top would dissipate excess heat. An entrance needed to be cut near the bottom. First, he lashed a sturdy two-foot long stick to the front two legs about two feet above the ground. Then he cut the base sticks off between the horizontal door top. This formed an entry 2x2 feet. He would be able to squeeze through and then pull a slab of birch bark across to close the entry once he was inside. A good supply of large birch bark slabs was needed to attach to the sidewall support sticks. They would overlap and hold the steam in.

Mark found the perfect source when he stumbled on a wide, dead birch that had hung up on another downed tree. It allowed him to score the suspended trunk with his hatchet held at a shallow angle and strip big curved sheets of sound bark onto the ground. He stacked as many slabs as he could carry and took them back to the lodge. Slits were cut near the bark top edge with his fillet knife. Cord was passed through the slits and lashed over the overlapped slabs to the stick supports. He also cut a bark flap that could be pushed aside to enter or exit. A shallow pit was scooped out just inside the entry. He squeezed inside and sat back. It would be tight quarters, but he hoped it would work.

Mark was pleased with the design and was anxious to try it, out but it would wait until later. It had been a hard day and the setline should be checked. He also needed to get a fire started and make supper. In an hour he'd have to check in with base camp. His check-in times were set at 6 a.m. and 6 p.m.

His stomach growled its displeasure at being starved as he hurried toward the lake. As he neared the massive rock ledge, a sharp "kiri- kiri" startled him! He gazed up as a large shadow passed overhead. A magnificent bald eagle made a steep dive toward the lake surface. It leveled off and began skimming the surface. Its whole body tilted back as its deadly talons were brought into play. With a powerful thrust, it struck and captured a careless bass. With its catch wriggling, the regal predator beat its powerful wings to gain altitude. Pure white head and tail feathers flashed against an azure blue sky. Mark was entranced. His eyes tracked the eagle until it landed in a large pine tree on the opposite shore. He felt privileged to witness the primal feat. It was his reward for being in the right spot at the right time. It required being tuned to nature's marvels that await those who are vigilant. He was learning that nature revealed its secrets and life and death sequences to those who are patient and watchful.

Mark turned away from the eagle and returned to his own fishing. As he neared the rock ledge he saw that the fishing line was taut and the pole tip was jerking. He grabbed the pole with one hand, lifted the rock free with his other and began walking backward slowly. He couldn't see what it was yet. There was just a green flash as it made a strong run, bent on escape. It was a strong fish. He held on to the pole and let the fish tire itself. Then it came crashing out of the water! It was a smallmouth bass! It shook its head and tried to throw the hook. Mark gasped as it fell back in and made one last valiant run. Soon it came floating in on its back and admitted defeat.

Mark hand lined the spent bass in until he could grip its lower jaw with his thumb. He lifted the beautiful bass up and feasted his eyes on it. Its mottled brown and green sides contrasted with its white belly and angry red eyes. Mark was very pleased. After admiring it briefly, he raised it above his head and offered thanks for the gift. He never treated fish or game he caught and killed lightly. Like the Native American of old, he gave thanks. His dad had also taught him to respect the wild creatures. Fish and game were to be killed humanely, gutted, washed and given thanks for. Mark had once trapped two fat ground hogs when he was young. He skinned, gutted, washed and proudly presented them to his mom. She made them into a stew that made a tasty meal. It was his baptism as a hunter -gatherer.

He walked down the shore until he found a flat rock near the water where he killed and filleted it. After washing the fillets, he placed them in the zip lock bag that had recently held snacks. He made an offering to the scavengers. It was a gift of the fish's offal or remains that he placed on a boulder near shore. He glanced up as a sudden blast of wind struck from the east. The lake surface went from calm to being disturbed by little wind squalls. It could be a harbinger of a weather change. He trusted his instincts and made tracks towards camp.

Once there, he built the fire up and put water on to heat. The bass fillets were rolled in cornmeal, flour and coarse black pepper. With an eye on the sky, he tended his supper. A number of wispy "mare's tails" scudded across the lake. These clouds were subtle signals of change in upper wind patterns. A storm tensed nearby. Mark sensed something was amiss. The wind change from the east was another clue that the idyllic climate was soon to be a fond memory.

Mark hurried to prepare supper. He put the skillet on, poured in vegetable oil, and sliced up a large potato that he seasoned with salt, pepper and paprika. He placed the fillets in a sheet of heavy-duty aluminum foil, poured in oil and folded the foil over in a crimp at the edges. The fillets started to sizzle. He kept turning the sliced taters as they browned. The U.S. Army canteen cup's water was at a full boil. He let it boil for a minute to kill any bacteria or Guardia cysts that could cause real intestinal trouble if not killed first. Even perfectly clean appearing water can contain these microscopic critters or viruses. Better safe than suffering the "near death." He grabbed the foil packet and flipped it over to crisp the other side of the bass fillets.

Mark checked his watch and keyed the transmitter: "Calling base, this is red flag one. I am checking in."

After a short burst of static, a clear voice said, "Good evening, Mark. How is everything? Over."

Mark recognized Ray Bond's voice and answered, "A-OK, sir, thanks. Camp is made and a fine smallie is sizzling in the pan. Over."

"Good boy," Bond replied. "Just a heads up on a storm system that's brewing. I'm sure you noticed the signs such as mare's tails and a wind switch to the east. Over."

"I did notice," Mark said. "I must finish supper and prepare my camp. Until six a.m., this is red flag one-out."

"Goodnight and good luck, Mark. Base out."

Mark wanted to continue the nice conversation, but he had remembered the briefing about keeping radio transmissions short, both to conserve the batteries and so other finalists had a clear frequency channel to do their check-ins. There would be ample time to relate experiences with the other finalists and staff when they were all brought back together at base camp for debriefing and a rest before going home.

He probed the fried potatoes with a fork. They needed another 10 minutes to brown and crisp. The smallmouth fillets were golden brown and done. He moved the fry pan away from direct heat. A sudden splatter on the grille startled him. It was only the water boiling over. The wintergreen leaves went in the pan that was moved aside to steep. The leaves quickly turned a bright green and emitted an intoxicating vapor. After a few minutes, he removed the leaves and added some sugar to the tea. The fried taters were seasoned and slid onto his plate. The fillets were a succulent entrée. Mark settled back to enjoy the feast.

The first bite of the fillet was wonderful. It had a crispy outside with white, flaky meat inside. He alternated mouthfuls of fish and fried taters washed down with sips of hot wintergreen tea. It was incomparable. A few pesky mosquitoes buzzed noisily around his ears. The cool night would help disperse them. The fire radiated enough heat to make him back away. The breeze had died and his camp grew strangely quiet. He sipped his tea and enjoyed the day's end. The rapidly setting sun bathed the eastern shoreline with a brilliant glow.

Mr. Bond had told the class about the special time before sunset: "It is the time of day that photographers refer to as 'the golden hour.' During this last hour before dusk, the light effects are dramatic. It can mean the difference between an average photo and a great one."

With a full tummy, Mark turned his attention to the encroaching dusk. The sun had already set and long shadows reached across the lake. Objects grew more indistinct at twilight time. Mark got out his journal and wrote his name next to the date and then, Final Practical Test, course: Wilderness Survival & Lore, call sign: Red flag 1.

Mark wrote in his journal about his first day from drop off that morning to the present. This was a course requirement and for the benefit of the finalist. It was too easy to forget key items and chronology of events if the journal wasn't kept current. Their journal writing would also be used to help determine their final score for the test. Mr. Bond told them it was important to note their real emotions, problems and solutions, so it could be reconciled with individual interviews.

Darkness fell on his camp. The warm fire comforted him and lit up his shelter as he reflected on his busy day. Everything had gone well with perfect weather as a bonus. He had experienced a cold, wet campsite setup during a steady rain on one of the class' field trips. So far, everything had gone smoothly. Camping in the wild required vigilance. The perfect conditions could vanish in a heartbeat. Mother nature could be fickle. She often exacted a painful payment from those who lacked prudence.

Barely visible by the fire's light on the near shore was a "v" shaped animal swimming by. He saw the stocky, wedge-shaped head that identified it as a beaver. This large rodent has two strong sets of opposing chisel-like front teeth. It has a stocky, well-furred body, propelled by strong, short legs with heavily webbed toes. His teeth never stop growing. This enables him to cut down large trees without wearing his teeth down. He chews the trunks into pieces and drags the smaller tops to the water. Beaver feed exclusively on the bark of aspen. They store green branches on the lake bottom as winter food. Ever wary of large predators they confine most of their activities to darkness. Man is their most dangerous predator. Beaver were sought and taken with traps, guns and even were killed in winter by Indians who traded their pelts for rum and goods in the fur trade era of the 1600s-1800s in North America. Like the bison and the wolf, the beaver was decimated but slowly recovered. Despite man's desire for wearing beaver hats in Europe, the resilient rodent made an amazing comeback.

Mark accidentally hit his canteen cup against the iron grate. It rang like a bell! The beaver dove under after slapping its flat tail on the water with a loud "whack" that made Mark jump. He chuckled as the beaver re-surfaced and swam out of sight.

He always appreciated wildlife and enjoyed their antics and natural abilities, as well as their beautiful, unique coloration. He considered them to be his "brothers" and often found himself speaking softly to them. They were superbly equipped to not only survive but thrive.

However, he wasn't above some anger if a chipmunk or red squirrel stole his food. He also was no "bleeding heart" when it came to hunting or fishing. He was taught from a young lad to set rabbit snares and hunt grouse, ducks, and deer as part of his life.

Mr. Bond taught them how Native American tribes once thanked their "Great Spirit" when they killed fish or game for food. They thanked the fish or animal spirit for giving its life to sustain his. Mark gave thanks in a similar way when he took a wild fish, fowl or beast. Leaving the unused carcass as an offering to other creatures to feed on obeyed a primal law.

In the Bible, Mark had read in the Book of Genesis that in the beginning of this world, God killed the first animal and gave the hide to Adam to cover his nakedness. Nothing was said about the animal's carcass, but Mark knew it had been given to scavengers to eat. He figured if it was good enough for the Creator, then it was good enough for him, as long as it was done of need, not greed.

Mark also had a problem with some major religions. He grew up to attending a large church denomination that had a lot of elaborate ceremony and vestments for the clergy. There were opulent cathedrals and landholdings worldwide. Church laws controlled the members' lives and required constant cash contributions. Mark tried to equate the Bible's teachings on being content with basic needs and the warnings about the trappings of amassing riches and seeking power and position. He decided these church laws were wrong and rejected those teachings. By reading the Bible himself, he made more sense of life and paid homage to the Creator as best as he could.

He let the fire die and with his headlamp on, he lit a candle. There was something comforting about a candle burning in the dark. He shut his headlamp off, slapped his right hip and felt the reassuring shape of his fillet knife and sheath. It gave him a feeling of security and was very sharp and reliable. Few tools were as dear to him as a sharp knife and a fire starter.

A long, lone cry from the lake raised his neck hairs. However, as he listened he realized it was only a loon calling to its mate. Mark secretly wanted a canoe to explore the lake, fish and search for loon nests, but that would have to wait. This practical test put its emphasis on camp skills and keeping finalists more confined to a certain area. That ensured they would have ample time to be creative with their camp and cooking. Canoes encouraged more exploring with the inherent problems of being wind bound or capsizing. Mark understood the reasoning. Opportunity would knock soon. He looked forward to that special trip when canoes were the main way of travel, such as a BWCA trip. In a solo canoe with a beaver tail paddle, he could enjoy the ultimate in simple, unadulterated freedom. Mark was feeling the rigors of the long day. He lit his headlamp, washed his dishes and put them on his table to dry. He blew out the candle, switched the headlamp off and was asleep when his head hit the pillow.

Chapter Four

Dawn on Day Two

Mark awoke groggy after having slept like the dead all night. He had to clear his head and finish making his site more secure. Robins were singing before dawn and a woodpecker was hammering a dead tree trunk. It made a pleasant hollow sound as if someone was hitting a hollow tree with a stick. Another staccato sound came to his ears. It was similar to a motor that had a put-put sound that increased in speed until it reached a crescendo and stopped. It was only a cock ruffed grouse announcing its territory to potential mates and other male (cock) grouse. He remembered Mr. Bond had told his class about a true story that was told to him by an outfitter. "Some 'tenderfoot' wilderness visitors had complained to him that they had their trip spoiled by someone starting up a motor and turning it off, day and night!" He laughed when he saw they were upset that the "motor" noise ruined their wild experience. He told them it was only a cock grouse drumming and watched their faces redden with embarrassment!

Mark started a fire by lighting a handful of his stockpile of birch bark and dry tinder. Then added larger branches until it burned hot. He filled the large cook pot with lake water to boil. While he waited, he gathered more beaver chew sticks and other branches and wove them into his shelter walls along with extra slabs of birch bark. He hoped that would keep the rain and wind out. He dashed to the fire pit to move the pot which was boiling over. He found a packet of rich hot chocolate mix, poured it in his mug, and added some of the hot water from the pot. It was thick, creamy and rich. He gulped it too fast and felt it burn right down to his stomach. He enjoyed the warmth of the mug and cupped both hands around it, as he turned his attention to the lake and the morning sky. Other than a few ducks quacking and flying over in a tight group, it was quiet. Mark scanned the horizon and could make out a band of dark clouds massing and moving his way from the southeast.

It was check-in time, 6 a.m., as he turned the radio on. "Red flag 1 calling base-over." A familiar voice answered, "Good morning, Mark, hope you slept well. Over."

"Yes, I did," Mark replied. "What's your take on the cloud band in the southeast? Over."

Mr. Bond replied, "It looks like a corker, Mark and we're in its path, so prepare for a storm. There are reports of high winds, thunder, lightning and heavy rain, over."

Mark said, "I copy that and will keep my poncho and extra firewood handy. Thanks for the warning and watch y'er topknot, Red flag 1- out."

"This is a test within a test. Bonne chance, Mark, signing off until six p.m. Base out"

Mark hurried to build a good supply of firewood. He dragged lengths of logs to camp and dropped it at his wood cutting area. Since cutting wood on the ground was too difficult, he decided to make a quick sawbuck. Taking some stout log butts, he lashed two together in a large X, with the X at a good cutting height. He repeated this with two more logs and lashed logs to each side at the base. He then lashed two shorter, smaller pieces just above the upper edge of the X and it was done. He used his folding saw to cut a good supply of firewood and stacked them under the tarp, and put some bark slabs on top. He also determined to keep birch bark and tinder beside the fire grate whenever he was away from camp or before going to sleep. It would assure a quick fire if protected.

Mark checked the sky and found the storm was shifting to the northeast. It should spare him a direct hit and instead come in at an angle from his left. It seemed to be stalled or moving slowly, so he decided to do some exploring down the shoreline to the right. He would keep an eye on the situation and stay ready to return in a hurry. He had his rain poncho tied around his waist as he made his way down the shore. There was a tiny island with some stunted pines and shrubs that would be a perfect loon nesting spot.

As he neared the end of the lake before it began curving away, he noticed it was much shallower in the bay with bulrushes and a sand bottom. It would be a great spawning area for bass, bluegills and pike. He could see some nice bass in the shade of logs. A large pike cruised by. It followed a school of shiner minnows that moved in a tight mass. Their silver sides flashed, mesmerizing the pike. This "water wolf" or fresh water shark had earned a nasty reputation because of its aggressive behavior. Mark made a mental note to try fishing here. He'd been so engrossed in the spot that he forgot all about the storm. A low rumble brought him back to reality. The storm front was moving in. He needed to get back to his camp! As he hurried back, he untied his poncho. He put it on and glanced up at the lake. A large gray, rolled cloud with a dark purple sky behind it advanced towards him. Thunder grew louder as the front approached. Jagged lightning bolts danced from the cloud. He fought the urge to break into a run. Ray Bond emphasized that this was when people got injured. If he kept his head and made good time at a fast walk, he should beat the frontal windblast.

    He had done his best to make a sturdy shelter. He hoped the wind direction held so he wouldn't receive a direct hit from the violent storm. He thought of the dry tinder covered with bark waiting in the campfire pit and the warmth it promised. Just as he entered the shelter and turned to face the storm, the windblast hit. It shook large trees as though they were shrubs. He heard numerous snaps and loud cracks as some limbs crashed nearby. Some trees broke off with huge ripping sounds. He heard the dull thuds as they came to ground. It was raining hard. Green leaves littered the ground and blew out into the lake. He stood inside his camp safe and sound but worried. Things looked very grim, but he could do no more.

    The lightning lit up the sky. The thunder exploded furiously! It nearly knocked him to the ground with its power. Again came the blinding lightning that bathed everything in a stark, white glow that was followed immediately by the ground-shaking, deafening thunder. Mark didn't scare easy, but it was almost too intense. Fear entered him.

    He calmed himself by talking to the storm. He shouted, "You're mighty and I fear your power, but you will allow me to live!" He stood grasping the shelter's front poles with his head lowered and awaited his fate. After a while the wind abated somewhat. He raised his arms up as the rain fell straight down and then became intermittent. The little lake had been a maelstrom during the storm, but it was settling down again. Mark was grateful the storm had struck only a glancing blow. His camp suffered no real damage except for a few branches which were scattered over the area. It had lasted about an hour. He could hear the rumbling fade away as the storm moved on. It was just 11 a.m. The sky was getting brighter and the rain was turning into a mist. He heard the thunder in the distance as the storm moved on.

    Mark had taken precautions before he took his walk by the lake. He had put all his pots out to catch water and now had clean rainwater to drink. He refilled his canteen first, then put a potful of water on the grill. Taking out his waterproof matches, he tried lighting the tinder after removing the bark slab. He was damp and chilled to the bone. If he failed, his only option would be to crawl into his sleeping bag. That was a last resort and not what he cared to settle for.

He struck a match and carefully lit the birch bark in the center. It lit but sputtered and started to die! He groaned and shivered. Suddenly there appeared a puff of black smoke! A tongue of flame began to lick at the dry cedar twigs. He smiled as the flames ignited the cedar firewood on top. He held his red, cold hands toward the wondrous heat. Soon the whole fire grate was steaming as the fire evaporated the rain. Mark's pants were steaming also. He removed the wet poncho and hung it from the shelter front's forks. Nature was an enigma. It could be idyllic one moment and terrifying the next. Mark liked that quality. It was its own master, and no power of man could change or command it otherwise. Mr. Bond taught them how, with all of modern man's knowledge and power, space launches were still scrubbed due to uncooperative weather. All was right with his world once more. Mark held his arms skyward in thanks.

    The pot was boiling. He made some hot chocolate and snacked on some dried fruit and nuts. The sun was actually starting to send beams through breaks in the clouds. The trees were unburdening their branches and the dripping was like rain.

    Mark looked over the lake and was astounded to see a brilliant rainbow arching from one side to the other. It was a sight for sore eyes and glowed with all the colors of the spectrum. Mark thought of the passage in the Bible after the great flood. The Ark, along with Noah and his family and two of every living thing, were spared destruction. The Creator said he would put a bow in the sky to remind man that never again would the whole earth be flooded. Mark stood and watched the 'bow' as it grew less intense and then began to fade. Suddenly, a bright shaft of sunlight descended, and the wet rock ledge glowed. He thought of the nice smallie he caught off there yesterday and how good it tasted for supper.

    He found his fish pole that had been blown away several feet and was lying under some litter. It was in good shape. He searched the shoreline for another leech, but found none. He overturned a large rock and found a half dozen worms and two fat white grubs. Mark quickly impaled one of the grubs on the hook, tossed it over the rock ledge and watched it sink into the depths. He put the worms in his shirt pocket with some soil. He soon had a fat perch dancing in the air as he swung it ashore. Its colors were striking, with its golden sides, black vertical bars, bright orange fins and contrasting white belly. He placed it in the shade of a hollow in the ledge to keep it from flipping back into the lake. He baited his hook with worms and tossed it back in. As he turned around, another fish had been hooked. With his last grub, he caught a fifth perch. All were 10-to-12-inches long. It was plenty for a meal. He stowed his pole in the rock cleft and got a pot from camp. He placed the fish in it and proceeded to the filleting rock. Before drawing his fillet knife, Mark raised the fish in thanks. He was grateful they were going to feed his hunger. After he filleted the perch, he rinsed out the pot and put the fillets back in. The fish offal was taken to its normal place down the shore. He took the fresh fillets to camp. He could almost taste the sweet meat now. It was hours until mealtime, so he covered them to stay cool and safe from flies and other critters.

Since it was early and still a bit chilly, Mark decided to try the sweat lodge. He had previously tested some rocks and now put them into the fire pit. While they were heating, he checked on the sweat lodge's condition. It had blown over but was undamaged. He set it upright, re-braced the frame and it was ready. After re-digging the pit he returned to camp. When a burst of steam gushed upward, he dug the rocks out of the pit and dropped them in a large pot, then grabbed a pot of water and took both pots to the lodge. Mark then stripped off his clothes, entered the lodge, sat on the ground and splashed some water on the stones. He quickly secured the bark slab over the opening as a large cloud of steam gushed out and filled the lodge. He could feel the moist heat start to permeate his skin. His whole body sweated. He splashed more water to intensify the heat. His lungs worked hard to deal with the steam, but he felt his body relax and his stress floated away. Mr. Bond taught them that the Native American tribes used the sweat lodge to purify the body for various rituals. The sweating caused body toxins and unclean spirits to be eliminated through the skin's pores. He said it was very important to the tribes and was an integral part of their culture. It was also dear to Scandinavians, according to Mr. Bond. He said, "Immigrants came to our country and brought their saunas with them. In the local area some of their descendants have saunas in their homes. The towns of Negaunee, Ishpeming and Marquette are bastions of the sauna."

After dozing off for a while, Mark awoke and climbed out through the entry. He was drowsy and weak, but he felt cleansed and refreshed. He replaced the bark entry cover after removing the pot of rocks and his clothes. The air felt cool on his moist, hot skin. It was time to vacate the premises. He felt a bit giddy and let out a little "whoop." He sped toward the shore and dove into the lake. After the initial shock he took a short swim and cavorted. It was a celebration. Finally, he climbed out, feeling refreshed and chilly. He retrieved his clothes and the pan of rocks from the sweat lodge and hurried to camp. Once there he put more logs on, toweled off and let the fire warm and dry him as he dressed.

He glanced at the watch. It was nearly 5 p.m. – time to begin preparing his supper before the final check-in. He needed a new meal twist tonight. He pondered on it and then he had it! Cajun fried perch and Indian fry bread with coffee and a chocolate almond bar for dessert! Yes, it would be a celebration meal. Besides, it would be a nice spicy menu addition for his day's journal entry.

After the wild storm had cleared, it became a grand day. But he knew it might be less cheery for some of the other finalists. He survived by being prepared and very lucky. Nature doesn't plan its actions on a personal basis. She doles out punishment or favor randomly.

Now it was time to cook. The fry pan was warming with oil in it as he prepared the fry bread. He did it just as his mom had taught him. In a bowl, he placed one cup of flour, 3/4 T baking powder, 1/4 tsp salt, 1/2 T dry milk, 1/4 T butter and 1/2 cup of water. Mixing the ingredients created a dough that was kneaded until it was soft and easily shaped. The dough was then made into a flat pancake and placed in the waiting fry pan. He added more fuel so the fire would be hotter. While it was heating, he turned his attention to the fillets. Mark tossed them in a mix of cayenne pepper, black pepper, and cornmeal. He could hear the fry bread sizzling in the fry pan. He lifted one edge slightly and was pleased to see the bread browning nicely. It was also rising, thanks to the baking powder. The inch of oil was bubbling. When the bread was golden, he flipped it carefully. In a few minutes, it was done. He lifted it out of the oil, wrapped the bread in a paper towel and set it on the side to stay warm. He poured more oil in the fry pan and dropped in the fillets. When they started to sizzle, Mark filled the coffee pot with lake water, measured coffee into its basket and set it on to heat.

In five minutes the fillets were brown on the bottom. Mark took the fry pan off the grille and placed it on the edge of the fire. He tilted the fry pan at a steep angle to the hot fire so it would broil the fillets. He placed a log under it to hold it in place and added more wood for a hotter fire. Soon he heard a slight "plop" and knew the coffee was starting to perk. He moved it aside so it could finish without boiling over. He never grew tired of the perk noise and watching the hot coffee turn brown in the clear glass dome. It would have to perk for about five minutes. It was time enough for the fillets to broil.

Soon the celebration supper was ready to be served. Mark placed his enamelware steel plate on the table and put the fry bread on it. He tore it in half and spread some butter on its golden top. The fillets were nicely browned. He slid the sizzling beauties onto his plate. Last, he poured some of the perked coffee and inhaled the rich aroma. The fry bread was tasty with puffy air pockets in the crust. He alternated bites of fry bread and the fillet, which was spicy hot, crispy and flavorful. Every few bites were followed by a sip of hot coffee. When he finished his celebration supper, he put more lake water on in the big pot to heat for washing dishes. Then he sat back to soak up the fire's heat and enjoyed the chocolate almond bar dessert. It was a fitting way to finish off the feast.

It was time for the evening check-in. He hoped to find out how the other finalists fared. "Base, this is Red Flag 1, checking in. Over."

"Good afternoon, Mark. What is your situation since the storm? Are you okay and what damage did your camp sustain? Over"

Mark reported, "I'm fine. My camp was spared a direct hit. Lots of thunder and lighting, broken branches, leaf litter, and a few trees down. How are the other finalists? Over."

"The news isn't good, Mark," Mr. Bond reported. "Marla slipped and fell hard hurrying back to her camp while racing the storm. She suffered a severe ankle sprain and had to hobble and drag herself to camp. Drenched and near hypothermia, she wisely crawled into her sleeping bag. Fortunately she took her radio with her and called base for assistance. A canoe with two leaders left base and were at her camp in half an hour. They carried Marla still zipped into her sleeping bag to their canoe and left for base. Her gear was picked up later this morning. She was given dry clothing and fed hot soup and drinks near the fire pit last night. She was given pain pills and slept well. She's been evacuated this morning and will be treated at the hospital in Iron Mountain. It was tough luck, but she is safe and will have quite a tale to tell.

"I'm sorry to report there was another casualty. Your friend P.J. met with a mishap. A lightning strike split a large pine near his camp. One half fell on his shelter, knocking him unconscious and pinning him to the ground. When he came to, he was chilled, wet and couldn't reach his radio to check in that evening. When he missed his check in, two leaders were dispatched. They found him conscious, suffering hypothermia and soaked. The leaders cut him free from the tree branches, removed his wet clothes and got him into his dry sleeping bag. They carried him to the canoe, gave him a mug of hot chocolate and delivered him to base camp. His condition was much improved after being given hot food and drink near the fire. We treated his head wound and disinfected his cuts. It was decided to keep him in camp until morning. He slept well after taking some pain pills. The camp nurse even repaired his bent eyeglass frames! Two leaders left with P.J. this morning for transport to the hospital. Mike and Bob checked in and are fine. They were told about P.J. and Marla. Good luck, Mark. Base out."

The bad news about P.J. bothered Mark. He and P.J. were best friends. It hurt Mark to know he was eliminated and injured. At least he was on the mend. He would hear P.J's sad saga when the solo test ended.

There was one more day left. If the weather held, he planned to take a field trip and explore his area. Right now it was time to write his journal. He recorded all the details of the day. It was complete with his reactions, thoughts, cooking, fishing and the glorious sweat lodge!

The sky was cloudy, so he couldn't view the stars and constellations. But the loons were calling, frogs were singing and the ruffed grouse worked relentlessly on his drumming log. As he wrote, Mark re-lived the day. He still marveled at how stark terror reigned during the storm, but had quickly become calm; now he could enjoy a celebration supper. It had been quite an adventure. Darkness had fallen, along with his heavy eyelids. He gratefully crawled into his sleeping bag. Consciousness went out with his headlamp.

Chapter Five

Dawn of Day Three

Mark lay in his bag, listening to the early morning sounds of the false dawn. The booming of the ruffed grouse was seconded by a robin's song. An unseen flight of ducks rocketed by with their wings roaring overhead. The first shafts of sunlight began to illuminate the western shore's treetops. The sleeping bag was cozy and tempted him to snooze. But not today. It was his final day solo: time to explore his domain as a hunter-gatherer. A nice warm fire was first on his list. The dry tinder and birch bark awaited ignition. He unzipped the bag, assembled the fire tinder and struck a match. Flames devoured the bark and tinder and more wood was added. Mark walked to the calm lake and filled the coffee pot and cook pot with water. Before returning to camp, he paused and stood observing the placid lake. Sunrise was full blown. The sun was dazzling and promised a golden day. A mature eagle's white head glowed in the sunlight. It was perched high in a pine while scanning the lake. A beaver swam near the other shore. He was heading back to his lodge after a night's cutting and was dragging some of his succulent feed behind. Mark knew he'd made the right decision to rise early. His campfire beckoned.

He turned away reluctantly and carried the pots back. He added coffee to the perk pot and placed both pots on to boil. While waiting for the java to perk, he loaded his daypack with essentials. He'd take a pot for picking blueberries, snacks, journal, canteen and two plastic bags. These were in case he found some tender fiddlehead fern shoots or morel mushrooms. Pasta was the main course for supper, and wild edibles would be a welcome addition.

There was one more night solo, before it would change when the leaders arrived in the morning. After the interviews and camp inspections, he would be reunited with everyone at base camp. Time to eat and drink java. He was burning precious daylight! The coffee was perked. Pouring a cup, he took a sip of the rich brew. He cooked up some oatmeal with some nuts and dried fruit and a large spoon of brown sugar. After draining the small pot of coffee, he washed his bowl and hung his food pack from a tree limb. Since he might be gone for most of the day, he doused the fire.

After making his morning check-in at base camp and finding everything was normal, he grabbed his hat. Hoisting his pack, he took a last look around and headed down the shoreline. The day was picture perfect. There was a clear blue sky with a few fluffy cumulus clouds and sunshine warming his back. A mated pair of loons was fishing. They swam along with their heads submerged, hunting the depths. Upon spotting prey they dove and each surfaced with a fish which they swallowed head first. Their beautiful backs were coal black with white diamonds. They popped to the surface like corks, beaded with water. A pair of crows was dining on the fish offal he left yesterday. Mark spoke softly to the loons and crows, greeting them as his brothers. The loons dove back under while the crows tilted their heads at him and then turned back to their meal.

Mark remembered another remark Ray Bond had made about nature during class:

"Nothing is wasted in nature's economy. Ma Nature is totally self-sufficient. She sustains all life and with death, recycles the remains in a never-ending cycle. Nature does not need man, but man would not last a minute without nature. The very air he breathes is supplied by photosynthesis in every green leaf, blade of grass and algae."

As Mark ambled happily along, he thought how basic his needs were and how little was required to live there compared with his home life. He carried what he needed on his back and was free to live a lifestyle very close to the early voyageurs and native tribes. He felt free.

His eyes wandered over the terrain and back to the sun-dappled lake. A light breeze whispered through the tops of the large pines. It was a good place for a rest. A large boulder became a simple throne, near the shore. A painted turtle was sunning on a half-submerged log near shore. With one swift movement it disappeared into the lake with a splash.

Mark dropped his shoulder and slid off the pack. He took out some jerky and sunflower seeds and had a long drink of cool, sweet water from his canteen. After finding a convenient log, he sat with his back leaning against it. The sun warmed his back as he let his gaze stray over the water and shore. It was a good time to write in his journal. He pulled his pack onto his lap as a rest for his journal. He made detailed notes about his activities and thoughts to that point. The day was warming rapidly. Little clouds of insects drifted off the lake like puffs of smoke. The moon was full and appeared as a translucent disc, barely visible against the bright, clear sky.

Mr. Bond told them the moon was always present in the sky, day and night. It seemed to disappear due to clouds and haze. With luck, it might be displayed in its true glory that night. It reflected the sun's rays and bathed the Earth with a pure white light. The distant stars and special groups of stars, called constellations, with zodiac-inspired names, were a never-ending wonder. The Creator's handiwork was evident throughout his creation from earth to the stars.

A chickadee perched in a nearby tree and sang its pleasant song. He flipped the bird a little chunk of a nut. The chickadee quickly pounced on it. It deftly held it between its tiny feet and ate. It was hard for Mark not to spoil the pretty little bird. It displayed a winsome trust. The little guy would appear anywhere in the woods. He is a friend to whoever he encounters. Despite its size, it was hardy enough to take on the northern winter. They were regulars at his family's bird feeder along with the nuthatches and finches. They were all "little miracles," according to Ray Bond. Mark agreed. It would be a cheerless land without them.

Mark was relaxed and enjoying the stop, but he needed to explore more new country. The mixed sun and shade in some low clearings might hold some real treasure. He shouldered the pack and canteen and headed toward the clearings. They might be hiding some blueberries that should be ripe. He passed wild red raspberry bushes and blackberry canes, which were also delicious, but were programmed to ripen later in the summer.

Ahead in a clearing grew the sought-after prize. He squatted down, lowered the pack, and dug out the pot. He began picking the fat, sweet blueberries, with huckleberries mixed in. They varied from hard green to pink to a fully ripe purple. The Creator planned that fruits ripened at different times, offering food for a longer period, rather than all at once. Those plants growing in partial shade were slower to ripen and bore fruit when the ones in full sun were dried up. Some blueberries grew in clusters of ripe berries. With a gentle pull they would tumble as a group into the pot. He kept picking until the pot overflowed and filled half a plastic bag. This didn't count what had served as pay for the picker. It was a special treat. He placed the pot and the bag with blueberries carefully into his daypack. It was good harvest that would pay sweet dividends back at camp.

As he turned to gaze at the still visible lake, he almost stumbled on a red flag with a #1 in white. It was the north boundary flag. Maybe the leaders put it right there so it would mark the blueberry patch, as well as a boundary!

He continued down the shore and could see the end of the lake. There was a big pile of sticks and mud a ways out in the lake. It was a beaver lodge! It was like a tiny island bristling with pointed sticks. Mark remembered one day in class when Mr. Bond showed a movie that followed a beaver family for a year. It included underwater photography under the pond ice and inside the lodge.

Mark remembered what Mr. Bond had said after the movie:

"In winter the beaver can exit the lodge and pull succulent green sticks from a food pile they have stored on the bottom. While the lake is ice covered they must bring their cached branches up into the lodge to strip and eat the bark and have air to breathe. Living in a lake, these beaver are spared having to build a dam. Some beaver live on rivers and are called 'bank beaver'. They burrow into the bank and build a lodge of sticks and mud above it. Beaver mate for life and have their babies, called kits or 'mic-mics' by Native Americans. The young beaver stay with the parents for a year and then are forced out to start their own lives either in the same body of water or by traveling by land and water to a new area to live."

As Mark continued toward the end of the lake, it became marshy and sprouted a fine stand of cedar. A large area of sphagnum moss grew below their branches. This native moss is greenish brown with fast-growing roots that were thick and soft like a plush carpet. Mark knew some of his neighbors in Iron Mountain would harvest long pieces of the moss, dry on racks and sell to greenhouses in the area for plant bedding.

Mark couldn't resist lying down in the plush moss. He closed his eyes and inhaled the fragrant mix of moss and cedar. He lay quiet, enjoying being pampered, and drank in the sounds of the lake and forest. Unfortunately, his back and legs were becoming soaked. He reluctantly raised himself out of the cushy, damp bed. As soon as he stood he watched the moss begin to return to its normal shape.

Mark continued to the narrowed end of the lake and into the woods a little ways beyond the curve, then saw what he wanted in a little clearing: it was the third red flag, setting the west boundary. He wouldn't find the last one marking the south boundary since there wouldn't be enough time today. It was time to turn toward camp. It was already mid-afternoon and there were things to do.

He made one detour to pick some young, tender fiddle head sprouts and even found a small group of morel mushrooms that he didn't see right away and almost stepped on. He placed his valuable cargo of wild foods into the plastic bags and packed them into his daypack. The morels would be sautéed in butter. The tender fiddleheads would be boiled briefly and would make a tasty side dish with the pasta. Morels imitate meat in being chewy and flavorful. He was also conjuring up a recipe for blueberry cobbler as a special desert if he had the right ingredients. It had been a fun and rewarding hike but he headed back to camp. In a short time, camp came into view.

It was good to be back at camp and to find everything as he left it, intact and peaceful. It continued to be warm and sunny as if to make up for the storm. He lit the waiting tinder and soon a fire was heating the grill. Just in case he felt the need, he placed the sauna rocks on the edge of the fire pit. He also took the large pot and the coffee pot to the lake, filled them and put them on to heat. He added coffee to the perk basket and it was ready. Mark learned to like coffee at home where his parents often drank it. He let his food pack down and took out the box of pasta with tomato sauce. He mixed the sauce and seasonings with some olive oil and let it simmer on the outside edge of the grille.

He poured olive oil in the fry pan and sautéed the morels until they were dark brown. Then he added them to the simmering tomato sauce. A packet of grated Parmesan cheese was saved until the pasta and sauce were combined. It would be sprinkled over the pasta plate. He placed more wood on the fire's embers. Mr. Bond and Mark's mom both taught him how to bake. It could be tricky, but with practice, it was a gift that produced mouth-watering results.

Now that the main course was all set, he could work on the desert. Baked items, especially with wild berries, are a treat when camping. Mark checked his supplies and found that he could make the cobbler. He put 2 cups of blueberries, 1/4 cup of sugar and 1/2 T of cornstarch into a small pot and stirred until it boiled for a minute and then took it off the heat. Next was the biscuit topping. He added 1/2 cup flour, 1/2 T sugar 3.4 tsp. baking powder, dash of salt, 1 and 1/2 T butter and 1/4 cup of milk (dried milk and water). The ingredients were mixed until the dough formed a ball. He kneaded it, pressing it into a thin sheet, and covered the hot blueberry mixture. The cobbler pan was set down near the base of the fire and tilted towards the fire with a rock holding it. It would take a while for the biscuit crust to brown, so he returned to the pasta preparation. The pasta sauce simmered nicely.

The water started to boil. First, the fiddleheads were dropped in for only a few minutes. He took them out and wrapped them with some butter in foil. He then put the noodles in the boiling water with a dash of salt. They would need to boil for 10 minutes so they were soft but not mushy. The sauce was also ready, but the cobbler needed more time. It could bake while he enjoyed the main course. The noodles done, he drained off the water, added the sauce and morels and let it rest. It was finally time to eat.

He placed his plate on the table. He filled it with the pasta and morel sauce, andthen sprinkled the Parmesan cheese over it. The bright green fiddleheads made the plate a thing of beauty. He twirled his fork in the pasta and sauce. It tasted rich and spicy. The morels were great meat substitutes. The fiddleheads were slightly crunchy and tasted somewhat like green beans. His wild edible foraging changed the meal from average to gourmet!

Mark used a trick to help brown the cobbler topping by spreading butter over it. He resumed eating the pasta, savoring the symphony of flavors. His mom was an excellent cook and taught him not to waste food. Mark mused that with his Italian and English heritage, he grew up eating pasta and pasties, a meat pie.

With the pasta eaten, the plate went on the table for washing. The coffee began to perk. Desert, A.K.A. cobbler, was ready. The butter had done the trick. The nicely browned crust had sweet purple juice bubbling around the edge. He moved the pan to the table to cool. When the coffee finished, he poured a steaming mug of what some referred to as "java" or "Joe." With his mug cupped in his hands, he enjoyed its warmth and watched the lake. It was time to sample a spoonful of the cobbler! He blew on it until it stopped steaming, then inhaled it and closed his eyes. It was going to be tough to describe this in his journal. It was wonderful. What a day it had been, with a meal to match. The neat part was that he still had two cups of blueberries saved for a surprise breakfast. It was journal writing time. Alternating sips of java and blueberry cobbler, he wrote it joyfully.

He finished the day's log of events with the pasta supper as the final entry. He checked the time. It was almost 6 p.m.! Time for the last check-in of the test period. Tomorrow morning the leader evaluation team would arrive. It was a little scary but he was ready.

He hit the "on" button and checked in at base camp. Mark was greeted and told that all was well with the other finalists. He answered that his condition was good, also. The weather report was for a clear sky and no precipitation that night. Tomorrow afternoon could hold some drizzle, but nothing heavy.

Mr. Bond reminded Mark that the leader team would arrive by 8 a.m. to evaluate his camp. He also told Mark that no radio check was necessary in the morning, but not to hesitate to call in case of trouble. His journal would be collected. The leaders would help him break camp and pack it into the canoe. Mark signed off happy. It was almost over, but left him with a bittersweet feeling. He had survived, even prospered, and would enjoy the reunion with Ray Bond and his friends. However, he would miss the beauty, isolation and wonder of his camp.

He poured more perk coffee and finished the cobbler as he enjoyed the fire. He washed the dishes and took a walk to look for any problems with his camp. He cleared away some fallen branches and checked to see that nothing was damaged. The fishing pole was rolled up neatly and leaned against the shelter. Supper dishes and pots were washed.

A last warm sauna was tempting. The rocks had heated in the fire pit. It was now or never. There wouldn't be time tomorrow. He found a change of clothes, put the hot rocks in the large pot and left for the sweat lodge. Dumping the rocks inside, Mark returned with a pot of lake water. After stripping off his clothes, he entered the lodge, sat down, and splashed water on the rocks. A welcome cloud of steam filled the lodge. Muscles relaxed and his head drooped in the steam. As he inhaled the warm moist air deep in his lungs, beads of moisture formed. His skin's pores ejected sweat and toxins and dripped constantly to the floor.

Leaning back with his eyes closed, he heard a loon's long, quavering tremolo. It started low then rose to a high-pitched scream that repeated many times. It was as close to a jungle cry as possible. During the quiet moments came the rhythmic thuds of the ruffed grouse's drumming. The soft, eerie hooting of an owl completed nature's serenade. Mark cherished the impromptu concert. Admission was free and the entertainment, priceless.

There was another disturbing high-pitched sound. This one was more onerous. Legions of blood sucking creatures, tiny winged vampires, hovered just outside. Mark had lost track of time while luxuriating in the lodge's comfort and cleansing. It was time to vacate the tipi sauna and try a quick dip while outrunning the voracious cloud of mosquitoes. Until he reached camp and the fire, he'd be at their mercy. Thankful only the females sucked blood, he steeled himself for the task. It was cooling down inside the sweat lodge, anyway.

Quickly pushing the door flap aside, he grabbed his clothes and sprinted. It was still light enough to avoid obstacles, but he could feel his flesh being pierced. He gladly dove into the cool lake and thrashed about, rinsing off grime and insects. Climbing out in the chill made goose bumps spread across his body. Grabbing his clothes, he quickly reached the camp, toweling off before the glowing embers. After dressing in clean togs, he added wood to the fire and scratched at the itchy new bumps, courtesy of Mrs. Mosquito. There was still some coffee left, so he put it on to heat and set his mug on the edge. He retrieved his headlamp and a candle that he set aside for later. The coffee poured hot and strong into his mug. He sipped the brew while being entranced by the fire.

It was twilight time. The sun had hidden and the wind calmed. Mark hoped that later on the full moon would grace his camp. Times like this were unique anywhere, but magnified in wilderness. No artificial sounds or bright lights intruded. His senses had become more aware, acute to the sounds and natural rhythms. He was at peace.

Mark broke out the last big chunk of chocolate almond bar. It was a special treat with his coffee. He was a mountain man, a voyageur and hermit, all rolled into one.

Mr. Bond once said to the class: "Most people feared the wilderness and thought it should be tamed and conformed to feed their voracious appetites. Man tends to suck the goodness out of the land by over cutting its timber, ravaging its wildlife, damming rivers and poisoning the air. It was a blessing that man could still experience untamed wildness."

Thoreau once said, "The salvation of mankind is in wildness." Mark also remembered a quote by Ben Franklin who said, "My church is in my head." In other words, he needed no ornate, manmade building to seek spiritual closeness. It resonated with Mark's take on things. Being intimate with nature inspired his spirit more than any cold cathedral. There is a French phrase, joie de vivre, or the joy of life, which fit his time in this sacred place.

An owl hooted from the woods. Its soft call chimed in with the ruffed grouse's drumming. Its cupped wings compressed the air, which produced the booming sound without actually touching the log.

Then a light flashed through the lofty pines in the East. A full moon rose! It scattered its silvery beam like a path down the lake, shimmering, beckoning. It was a good omen when its full phase coincided with a camp out and a clear night sky. He could even see some mountains and craters, especially on the moon's edges. He wished for a pair of binoculars to appreciate more of the detail. It was desolate, lifeless and cold, but glorious nonetheless.

Mark recalled vividly that he was only 6 years old when he watched the first manned landing on the moon. Aside from the technological coup, it was still a cratered, lifeless desert. Mark never understood the huge amount of money spent on probes to uninhabitable planets, while we abuse our Earth, which has no equal! Man tends to foul his nest and seek others.

Mark took his coffee and stepped out away from the firelight where he had a clear view of the sky. He could recognize a couple of the major constellations in the northern sky, like the Great Bear, Ursa Major, better known as the Big Dipper. Its curved handle of stars led to a dipper made of four stars. By extending a line connecting the two stars at the dipper's end, one could find the North Star, Polaris, the only star that never changes its position. It was, therefore, a primary guide to man from time's beginning. In the south, he found the line of three closely aligned stars forming the belt of Orion, the hunter. He located two bright stars spread out above and below which marked Orion's hands and feet. He hoped to learn more about the constellations.

Most of the star groups changed with the seasons and an observer's position on the Earth. They were a constant, set in place and infinitely more reliable than anything man has done. In fact, the Bible relates how oriental wise men, kings, two thousand years ago followed a special star that led them to a small town named Bethlehem. There they offered gifts to a young child named Jesus, Messiah.

It was growing late and the rigors of the day were taking their toll on Mark. He needed a good night's sleep to be rested and alert when the leader evaluation team arrived in the morning. The fire still had a nice bed of coals. He warmed himself once more before turning on his headlamp and crawling into his mummy sleeping bag. He had lit the candle so he could complete his journal entry. As he finished the commentary for the day, he put the pencil inside its plastic bag with the journal, blew out the candle and fell asleep.

It was still dark when a loon's call broke the silence. Mark awoke and sat up in his bag, groggy, but rested. He was eager for the final morning to start. Dressing quickly, he put on his headlamp and moved to the fire pit. Grabbing a double handful of tinder, he laid some cedar twigs over it and lit a match. As it caught fire he added larger branches.

A welcome glow and heat warmed and lit up the shelter. Mark took the coffee pot and large cook pot to the lake and filled them. As he worked, he gazed into the slumbering lake. He slowly pivoted his head lamp, illuminating the shallow shoreline. He watched a crayfish scoot backward in alarm as the headlamp beam struck it.

Mark looked to the east where a dull pink glow grew on the horizon. Soon the faithful sun would send the greatest gift of all to the Earth. It was the basis for life. Without its energy, even for a day, there would only be cold, darkness and death.

As he returned to camp he turned off the headlamp. The fire's blaze was enough. He added coffee to the perk pot and placed both pots on to heat. He sat near the fire and extended his hands towards the welcome heat.

The false dawn produced some dim light. He took the food bag down and gathered items needed for breakfast: flour, baking powder, oil, butter, blueberries, egg substitute and syrup. He mixed all the ingredients, except the syrup and some blueberries that would be the topping for the pancakes. The coffee was percolating, so he moved it to the side to finish without boiling over. He dug out two more plates and cups and stacked them on the warm side. Dawn was finally breaking. He would wait until they arrived before starting breakfast.

It was 7:30 a.m. Mark decided to hike down the trail and meet the leader team. He took one more look around. He found his camp in order and proceeded. A high-pitched humming came from above. Though nothing was visible, he knew it was clouds of insects singing to the morning sunrise. The eastern sky was light blue, tinged with flecks of gold and coral, without a cloud in sight. It promised to be another fine day. The sun's rays began to burn off the morning dew, which sparkled like diamonds on blades of grass and spider webs.

Ahead in the trail and along both sides in sandy soil was a carpet of wild strawberries. Their tiny white blossoms brightened the path. Mark was reminded of the passage in the Bible where Christ said, "Consider the lilies of the field, they do not spin, nor do they weave; yet even Solomon in all his glory was not arrayed like one of these." That was a profound statement and Mark had to agree that native flowers' beauty put man's best efforts to shame.

As he rounded a curve he could hear waves lapping the shore. Descending the hill he found himself at the lake. It was placid with only a slight ruffling of its gin-clear water.

An osprey wheeled above the lake. Its mottled white and black underside and ability to hover while uttering a sharp cry identified it as a superior raptor. Ospreys are excellent fishermen and seldom miss their prey. As Mark admired the scene, the osprey hovered then dove. Streamlining its body into a weapon, it hurtled toward the lake surface at blinding speed. It struck the water, and then rose slowly as it labored upward with a fish gripped in its talons. Mark had heard that eagles would wait for the osprey to make a kill and then harass the osprey until it dropped the fish. Mark had not yet witnessed such thievery.

He noticed a flash that reflected out on the lake. Shading his eyes helped him to spot a tandem canoe approaching with two paddlers. He waited until he could distinguish their features, then waved his arms overhead in greeting. Both paddles flashed upward in the sun, returning his signal. Mark was excited but anxious. He felt he had done his best, but these leaders would scrutinize his camp for any flaws. As their canoe cruised toward him, the bow man rested. The leader in the stern braked with his paddle, and the canoe glided smoothly to shore.

The leaders shook his hand and introduced themselves as Craig and John, friends of Ray Bond. They were seasoned canoe campers who had been to the BWCAW. While they waited for the final judging, they had enjoyed fishing and exploring, as well as visiting. Mark invited them for breakfast, and they eagerly accepted. He had them sit and poured them coffee and started the pancakes. When the fry pan was hot, he poured the first pancake. Its surface was bumpy with the fresh blueberries.

As Mark waited for the telltale bubbles on top that signaled time to flip, Craig spoke: "Mark, this is an unexpected surprise. We left base camp too early for breakfast and now I'm famished!"

Mark nodded and flipped the cake, exposing a golden brown side.

"I'm happy to be of service," Mark said. "You are my first visitors in three days, so you're due the red carpet treatment."

Mark soon had several nice steaming hotcakes on their plates, which he topped off with more blueberries, butter and syrup. He poured the last hotcake for himself. Mark drooled as he watched the purple blueberry juice ooze out of the cake. Both Craig and John were enjoying their meal as evidenced by their lip-smacking sounds and comments. Mark topped off their cups. Mark sampled his hotcake. It was exceptional, with fine blueberry flavor.

He beamed and said, "Not bad for camp hotcakes, huh? I was lucky to find a nice patch of blueberries yesterday."

"Mark, this service goes above and beyond duty!" Craig exclaimed. "The hotcakes are delicious by themselves, but the blueberries' flavor makes them extra special! If the rest of your camp matches your cooking skills, you're going to be tough to beat."

After breakfast, Mark washed dishes and began packing up the cooking gear. Craig and John began their evaluations of his shelter. One held a legal pad on a clipboard and took notes about construction materials, strength, and general design. After they had completed their inspection of his shelter, Mark began packing his other camp gear into his pack. Both leaders continued on to check the rest of the camp, including the sweat lodge.

When they finished, John left to circle the lake and pick up all the flags. Craig stayed to help Mark dismantle the shelter, sweat lodge and furniture. This was in keeping with the no-trace ethic necessary in a wilderness setting. While Craig helped Mark pack, he asked Mark many questions and stopped often to take notes. He peppered him with several inquiries about his construction and use of the sweat lodge. It was the first time Craig had seen a tipi style sweat lodge, and he was very interested. This was normal procedure and required an interview to corroborate information from his journal and their site inspection.

By the time John returned from his hike, he came bearing the four red flags. All Mark's gear had been loaded in the center of the big tandem Old Towne Royalex canoe. The shelter and all furniture was dismantled and scattered in the surrounding forest. With Craig in the bow and Mark atop his gear in the center, John pushed off and they headed for base camp. Mark noted that there was little freeboard left. He was glad the lake was fairly calm and the trip short.

As Craig paddled, he said, "Two other teams are out evaluating and packing up Bob and Mike. The campsites belonging to Marla and P.J. have already been dismantled and their gear removed to base camp."

Mark rode proudly. It was novel to sit snugly, enjoy the ride, and chat with someone other than forest creatures. He was looking forward to a special supper tonight at base camp. Craig said it would be quite different from his camp meals for the past three days. He also learned that a special Whelen lean-to was ready for the three finalists to spend the night in. Mark looked forward to sharing camping experiences and thoughts with Mike and Bob.

As their canoe neared camp, he could see friends and staff waving. Another heavily laden canoe was just arriving. As their canoe slid into the shallows and stopped, Mark and his two leaders stepped out and shook hands. He took many good-hearted slaps to his back. The camaraderie and excitement was nice. In just a few minutes all his gear had been stowed inside the special Whelen lean-to. Mark recalled Mr. Bond telling the class about Colonel Townsend Whelen. He was a devout minimalist who preferred living intimately with nature. He liked camping without a tent at all, but wanted a simple, practical shelter for inclement weather.

His fellow finalists, Bob Forge and Mike Hohl, looked happy, fit and tanned. As they embraced in a group hug, they let out a loud "whoop" in unison. Mark was glad it was finished. Whatever the outcome, he was proud to be a part of this elite crew. The three chatted about their triumphs and trials during their solo camps until the loud ringing of the dinner bell interrupted them. They quickly joined the others streaming toward the central fire pit. A half circle of primitive log benches faced a large fire pit. The whole area was protected by a huge nylon rain tarp which was guy roped to the surrounding pine trees.

Mr. Bond waited for everyone to be seated and quiet down. He stood on an elevated platform and raised his hands above his head with palms out. A hush came over the large group as he began to speak:

"We are gathered here to give everyone a great meal, but our primary reason is to pay tribute to the three remaining solo camp finalists: Mark Fisher, Bob Forge and Mike Hoh."

An impromptu cheer rose out of the group and with Ray Bond's urging, the three stood for a round of applause.

Ray Bond stood again after the finalists were seated and it became quiet. He continued, "After lunch we'll hear a few comments from each of these three intrepid guys and then everyone can relax, canoe, fish, or nap until supper. But first grab yourselves a plate and dish up a fine, all-American lunch. Bon appétit!"

Mark could feel his olfactory sense come to attention as he neared the stack of large wood-grilled cheeseburgers, brats and kielbasa. There were large wooden bowls of potato chips, potato salad and all the condiments. At the end of the food line, a large cast iron kettle sat full of bubbling hot, baked beans. As Mark took a fresh cut bun and loaded a fat cheeseburger, he noticed a small table that stood separate. It had a sign that read "DESSERT" and held an enormous stainless steel bowl.

As he passed by it, his plate groaning with food, he peeked inside and was big-eyed. It was filled with ice and whole pints of three flavors of ice cream! Such fare was very special after eating regular camp food for a while.

During lunch, Mark wolfed the tasty food and plugged into the camp news provided by leaders at their bench. He learned that P.J. had wanted to stay until the test was over, but with his head injury in mind, Ray Bond convinced him to get it checked at the clinic in Iron Mountain. P.J. had left a note for Mark. It stated that he was disappointed, but wished Mark success. The note included an invitation for Mark to stop by P.J.'s home on Moon Lake to visit on his return. Marla had been released by her doctor and was resting at home. She would be laid up for quite a while with a bad ankle sprain and some torn ligaments.

Mark managed to eat the last of a bowl of strawberry ice cream before he said, "basta," Italian for enough. He sat for a while and let the meal settle while he listened to other conversations. He hadn't heard so much talking for a while. He could tell Bob and Mike felt the same. They were smiling and nodding and would roll their eyes or wink at each other often.

Then Ray Bond was standing up front again, tapping his tin cup with a spoon: "Ladies and gentlemen (there were two women leaders), I do hope you enjoyed your lunch." Applause and groans greeted his comment. "Now we will hear a few words from the three guys who are the reason we're all here. Let's begin with Mike, then Bob and last, but not least, Mark."

Mike stood and said that the lunch was a welcome treat, since he wasn't a great cook and didn't catch any fish. He enjoyed the solo test but was ready for company. He spoke:

"Three days of noodles and rice primed me for this feast! It was a fair test with mostly good weather in beautiful country. Thank you all for your planning and hard work. It was an honor to compete."

Bob related similar feelings. He said, "I enjoyed the test challenge and was a bit sad to pack up. I regretted not having a canoe to use but understood the reason".

Mark was last and reluctantly stood since he was shy standing in front of a group. He steeled himself and tried to be at ease. He took a deep breath and spoke:

"This test, to echo Bob and Mike's comments, was well organized and the wilderness setting superb. All our class work and practical field experience under Mr. Bond's watchful eye prepared us well. It was one of the grandest times of my life. I truly felt at home here. My only regret is that two of our finalist friends had injuries and were unable to complete the test."

Ray Bond stood and spoke. "Thanks for your comments, your hard work and your ingenuity. You adapted to whatever situations were thrown at you. While most of you are enjoying a well-deserved leisure afternoon, I and a few other leaders will thoroughly read and discuss your journals and combine the info with the onsite inspections and interviews. We will try our utmost to choose the best two finalists and will announce our decision after supper tonight. We will also include P.J. and Marla's unfinished notes and camp construction. Speaking of supper, you don't want to miss it! It will be broiled steak, fresh salad and baked potato with the fixings. Until then most of you are free to do as much or little as you desire. See you for supper."

Mark decided to take a solo paddle in a waiting Wenonah solo canoe with a sliding tractor seat and a beautiful laminated beaver tail paddle. He knew the importance of keeping his profile low when climbing into or out of the canoe, since most canoe tipping happens when people enter or leave a canoe. Mark grabbed the gunnels on both sides and with his body bent low, he sat quickly. He shoved off by digging the paddle into the sandy shore while leaning forward. He relaxed and adjusted the sliding seat by slightly raising his butt so he could slide the seat into position. He held the paddle across the gunnels and tested the stability by rocking his hips and upper body. He drew on the paddle and felt the rush of being able to pilot such a craft. It was a feeling as old as man. Some form of canoe had always been used: dugouts, Indian birch bark, wood laminate, fiberglass, aluminum, and today's newer and lighter materials.

Mark's canoe was a fiberglass composite which weighed 58 lbs. and was fifteen and a half feet long. He had tried doing a "J" stroke, but abandoned it after veering to his left. He would need much more practice. Instead, he paddled three times on a side, then switched. He increased the tempo until the canoe gave a leap forward with each thrust and fairly skimmed the lake surface. Mark laid the paddle across the gunnels and smiled as the canoe glided smoothly onward. It was a rush to feel the speed and freedom while drifting slowly and basking in the warm sunshine. Mark slowly continued paddling around the lake and enjoying the beauty while he practiced the J-stroke.

There were so many fine lakes in this area. He remembered the sign on a side road near Sylvania. It was called Thousand Lakes Road. Some courageous men had the foresight to set this land aside as a wilderness preserve, safe from private developers. It was made available to all who needed a safe haven from a noisy, machine dominated society. There were no requirements except a spirit of adventure and strength to carry your basic needs. This refuge was not only for man's recreation and rest, but also an island of refuge for the wild beasts, birds and fish. Here they could live free without man's meddling, except as a visitor.

As Mark propelled the canoe, he lost track of time. Delicious aromas began wafting by. He inhaled aromas of grilled steak and potatoes, grilling slowly. He could almost hear their juices dripping onto red-hot hardwood coals. Mouth-watering fare awaited! He covered the last fifty yards of open water at ramming speed. He quickly tied the canoe to a tree and flipped it over. He placed the paddle underneath. With a last pat on the canoe's hull, he hurried to the dining area. All was ready. Tables were set and groaning with large bowls of fresh salad with dressing, platters of thick beefsteak and mountains of hot, baked potatoes. It was simply wonderful.

Just as he neared the tables and took a seat, the dinner bell rang. Everyone took a seat and began passing food and loading their plates. Mark hadn't seen such a thick, broiled steak for a long time. As he took tasty bites of steak, salad and baked potato, he felt pampered. He hadn't expected such hearty fare at base camp. His respect soared for Ray Bond and his crew.

As everyone finished feasting and visiting, they tossed their heavy paper plates into the waiting fire. Then Ray Bond stood on a raised wood platform and called for quiet. He was ready to make the long-awaited announcement. Everyone was seated and a hush fell over the audience.

Chapter Six

And the Winners Are…

"After careful study of the finalists' journals, camps and abilities, we have made our final decision," Ray announced. "The two winning candidates are Bob and Mark. Would they please come forward to accept their trophies?"

Mark and Bob whooped and exchanged high fives, then hung their heads, feeling guilty. They turned to Mike, who was trying to smile but having some trouble. In their excitement, they forgot about Mike. It was not fair. Mark nodded at Bob and they turned toward Mike.

They reached down, lifted Mike upright and walked arm-in-arm with him to the platform, accompanied by loud applause and cheers. All three finalists had tears of joy streaming. As they approached, Ray Bond raised the trophies and a new round of applause erupted from the crowd. As the three finalists and Ray held a group hug, the audience rose to their feet and cheered. Mark and Bob accepted their trophies and raised them overhead. Their other arms were around Mike's shoulders. As they stood waving their hand-carved trophies in front of the standing crowd, Ray excused himself and returned with something held behind his back. He held up a hand and once again it was quiet.

Ray spoke: "We understand your concern for Mike, but we have to abide by the rules of the competition. There are but two top finalists. However, we did have a special award made for third place. It is an exact duplicate of your awards and is inscribed 'Third Place in the Sylvania Solo Test'. Trophies for P.J. and Marla will be inscribed and given to them. Would you guys bring your trophies to my house, and I'll see to it that your names and the dates are burned into each one? Congratulations, Mike."

With that said, he handed Mike his trophy. Mike smiled broadly, and once again all raised their trophies skyward.

"We should have known you wouldn't forget, since nothing else has been left to chance," said Mark.

Bob said, "I'd like to thank everyone for a fair, well-planned and executed solo survival camp. I'll cherish this beautiful trophy and this time for the rest of my life."

Mike spoke next, "I echo Bob's appreciation of all the preparation and hard work by Mr. Bond and his crew. I plan to set up a wilderness trip with my dad yet this summer, to Canada's Quetico Park."

Mr. Bond said, "Congratulations to our three intrepid finalists. I'll only add that the Boundary Waters trip will take place in early July and will last about a week. Now I'm sure these three guys have a lot to discuss tonight. We all should turn in at a reasonable hour, since we'll be packing and breaking camp early tomorrow morning. Goodnight and my thanks to you all for helpful advice, humor and perseverance that combined to make a successful camp."

Mark, Bob and Mike carried their trophies proudly toward their Whelen lean-to camp and started a fire with the kindling and firewood already prepared. Three comfortable folding chairs awaited them near the fire pit. The trio gladly sat down and relaxed.

Mike sat in the middle chair and reached his hands out to Bob and Mark. He clasped their hands and said, "I'm much obliged for your support. I knew you two would be my toughest competition, even if Marla and P.J. hadn't been injured. Now I want to know which one of you made an Indian sweat lodge! I overheard Craig talking about it today but didn't catch which of you made it."

"Not me," replied Bob, "I made an animal trap and actually caught a squirrel, but nothing that ambitious!"

"I confess, c'est moi," said Mark, grinning. "I had wanted to make one and decided this was the perfect time. Besides the edge it gave me in points, it actually worked well and was a real comfort."

Mike shook his head and said, "Well, between outdoing me on camp furniture, meal preparation and fishing, I understand why I was outclassed! The storm hit me head on and wrecked my shelter. I spent the better part of that day rebuilding it and drying out my gear. I used the third day to rest and soak up some sun and never explored my boundaries."

"That was a tough break, Mike, but at least you weren't injured and you didn't give up," replied Bob. "I took a pretty decent hit from the storm, but only had some limbs land on my shelter with no serious damage. I caught a small mouth bass and several bluegills that were a tasty change from jerky and gorp. I also explored along the river that fed my lake and saw a fair amount of wildlife, mainly waterfowl, deer, loons and an eagle. I'm not exactly a gourmet cook, so other than the pan-fried fish, my meals weren't anything special. I had brought along enough jerky, salted nuts and dried fruit for ample snacks."

Mark listened to Mike and Bob's camp stories. He poked the fire and added another chunk of dry hardwood. He could still see his neat camp and lake with all the natural beauty. There was a longing to be back there. His friends' eyes tracked him as they waited for his camp comments.

Mark smiled at their inquiring faces and simply said, "Well, guys, I ate well. I experimented some and found time to explore. There were beaver, loons, eagles, owls and grouse. I enjoyed the solitude and the unbelievable natural beauty of my area. My camp lake was crystal clear with good fishing. I found wild berries and mushrooms that added spice to my meals. It was nice to have enough time to wander slowly and to try new things. I, was lucky to have avoided a direct hit by the storm and was not far away from camp when it hit. I, too, found myself wishing for a canoe, but realized the risks involved. Canoe campers have been wind bound for days. Others capsized due to weather or their errors and lost gear. Mr. Bond had told us about the dangers of lightning strikes and downed trees, crushed tents and even death by lightning strikes that traveled along tree roots into camps."

The three tired but happy friends chatted about their various experiences, good and bad. They vocalized the joys and fears they felt deep inside. It was a special time of sharing with fellow survival campers. Mark found himself losing his concentration and everyone began yawning which signaled the end of their chat. He suggested they turn in for much needed rest and continue the conversation on the way home tomorrow. Bob and Mike agreed and all said their "good nights." They quickly slid into their bags and were out like snuffed candles.

Sometime during the night Mark awoke to a light tapping noise on the lean-to. He listened, then relaxed. He had identified the cause. Rain was falling gently and running in rivulets off the shelter front. He moved his sleeping bag closer to the center to avoid getting wet. The camp was quiet except for the rain and some soft snoring. He was warm, safe and enjoying being with friends which tempered his inner desire for solitude.

Both were good feelings, but his kinship with nature and its wonders was a dull ache in the center of his being. It was a complicated situation. Some might call him anti-social. It was a driving force that would not relent. He did like some people besides his family. It would be good to see them soon. There were many details to work out like a summer job, planning for his Boundary Waters trip and visiting P.J. His heart swelled with anticipation of the BWCA trip. He had trouble understanding those who spent their short lives on this planet, happy as clams in a largely artificial environment. They could be very satisfied with living cheek and jowl with people, bombarded by machine noise and breathing contaminated air. They busily pursue the gods of money and power. Most people have only a vague idea of the glorious rewards and healing available in what was left of the original Garden of Eden.

As Sigurd Olson wrote in the book, *Spirit of the North*, "Wilderness to the people of America is a spiritual necessity, an antidote to the high pressure of modern life, a means of regaining serenity and equilibrium." Mark wondered how many diseases both mental and physical that afflict our society had their roots in the fast-paced artificial world they call "the good life."

Mark could feel the weariness overtaking his thoughts. He rolled on his side and let sleep rule. His last lucid thought was of the packing to be done in the early dawn. A loon called somewhere in the night.

It seemed only minutes since he fell asleep when there was a loud clanging reverberating through the base camp. As he hurried to splash water in his face and brush his teeth, he saw Bob and Mike stretching and yawning. The whole camp was moving as tents and shelters were collapsed and packed into the waiting canoes. All the remaining food and non-burnable items were gathered and packed into the canoes. One large pack was left to contain any forgotten gear left lying about. There was fresh, piping hot coffee and donuts for a quick breakfast. The donuts had been brought back after delivering P.J. to the Iron Mountain Hospital. After breakfast, the paper doughnut cartons and coffee mugs were tossed into the fire pit, reduced to ash, and then doused thoroughly with lake water.

Mark accepted Ray Bond's offer to stow his packs in the Wenonah solo canoe for the trip back. Canoes left as they were loaded. It created a little flotilla of heavily laden canoes. Mark found it reminiscent of how a brigade of voyageur canoes might have looked 150 years ago.

Two leaders remained behind to make a perimeter check. They gathered the inevitable small bits of trash and gear and placed it into sacks. Whatever damage was done to the camp area, such as crushed plants or broken limbs, would heal in time.

Chapter Seven

Going Home

Mark watched the staggered line of mainly tandem canoes knife through the calm lake. After two short portages, they crossed the final lake and could make out the Sylvania Wilderness headquarters on a hill above the canoe take out. After the entire group had arrived, Mr. Bond and some leaders took a final headcount. They thanked the Sylvania Wilderness staff and packed the gear into either a school bus or personal vehicles. Most of the leaders boarded the bus with Mark, Mike and Bob for the trip back to Iron Mountain and Quinnesec Junior High School.

Mark would be dropped off near his home that was just West of Iron Mountain on U.S. Highway 2. The bus ride home was spirited and noisy but fun. Mark was given many pats on the back as he made his way to the front and was dropped off across U.S. 2. He waited for traffic to clear, then hoisted his bag and walked across the road to the white stucco house he had been born in.

His mom was standing in the doorway waving and smiling. Her hair was tucked under a flower print kerchief that was tied behind her head. He gave her a hug and caught a whiff of a mixture of aromas: fruit, supper and the wonderful scent of her hair. She was always busy with the fruit stand, field crops, the twins and being a homemaker. She also worked some nights at restaurants. His dad worked as a painter during the week and helped run the fruit stand on summer weekends. Mark helped his mom close the fruit stand by dropping the heavy hinged panels and hooking them closed until morning. His dad had built the stand so it was sturdy and simple. It was about forty yards from his home and had a semicircle of gravel driveway that made it convenient for customers to return to the highway.

When Mark's dad arrived and washed up, the family sat down to a fine meat and potato supper. When Mark broke the news about winning the survival solo test, there were little whoops of joy. He regaled them with stories of the camp out and answered their urgent questions. After supper, the twins were excused to play while Mark sat at the table with his parents, relaxed and happy.

His dad asked, "So, Mark, what are your plans for making some money before you go to the Boundary Waters? You only have about six weeks before the trip. Any prospects?"

Mark was just about to reply that he had none, when he recalled something Ray Bond had said to him about a possible job with a Boundary Waters outfitter in Ely, MN. In a flash, he replied, "Yes, I do have a possible job in northern Minnesota. Excuse me while I call Mr. Bond and get the details."

Mark left the table as his mom cleared the dishes. He dialed Ray Bond's number.

"Hello, Ray speaking."

"Hi, this is Mark Fisher. I hope you have a few minutes to answer some questions about the Minnesota outfitter job. Is it still available?"

"Mark, thanks for calling so promptly," Ray replied. "Yes, it is alive and well! A phone message was waiting when I got home. The outfitter is a friend who I've shared many a campfire with. He said my recommendation is good enough for him. It sounds like he can definitely use you and Bob for a special guiding contract in the Boundary Waters and soon! He knows you guys are young, but capable. He needs your savvy and strength to assist his own seasoned guide with a contract to lead a small group of people with disabilities. Your job will be to help portage some of their gear, take orders from the guide and use your camping and people skills to help make it a rewarding trip.

"Duties will run the gamut from cooking, rigging fishing poles and to just being a listening ear. The client group was chosen from applicants across the country. The clients are of both sexes and various ages with little actual wilderness experience. A philanthropist who knows that there is nothing like roughing it in the wilderness to challenge one physically and spiritually is paying for the guiding contract. This wealthy benefactor will pick up the tab, including guide wages for you and Bob. You both get free room and board! In addition, there may be a bonus, contingent on reports made by returning guides and clients. This might be a prelude to future opportunities. If you apply yourselves, it could pay very good dividends. I know you two guys will give it your best effort. I'm counting on you!"

Mark was ecstatic and thanked Ray Bond profusely, then begged to hang up to prepare and inform Bob and his parents. First, he told his mom and dad. When they heard the news, there was a jubilant response followed by a hug and a handshake. The free room and board offer they thought very generous besides the wages. He then dialed Bob.

"Hi, Bob, how are you doing?" Mark inquired.

"OK, Mark, it's been a little wild here, but I'm settling in and am trying to start looking for gainful employment!" Bob replied.

"Hold onto your hat!" interjected Mark. "I think I have an offer that you can't refuse! Remember my comment about the possibility of temporary work with an outfitter friend of Ray Bond? Well, I just talked with Ray and he offered us what seems like a dream job! Could you stand to be paid to work in the BWCA this summer out of Ely, Minnesota?"

"You've got to be kidding, Mark!" Bob exclaimed. "We get to work in the Boundary Waters and actually be paid? What a great deal! How do we get up to Ely?"

"We'll be working as assistant guides with free room and board and maybe even a bonus if we're proficient," Mark replied. "Notice the date we need to start work is June 25, which means leaving here on a Greyhound Bus on the twenty-second. We need some time to be briefed and gear up before the clients arrive."

"Fantastic! I'll inform my parents tonight and get their OK," replied Bob. "Consider yourself invited over tonight, and we'll plan the details. Bring a pad of paper to take notes so we can make our itinerary. We need to take care so we don't blow such a sweet offer. I still can't believe we are going to work in the BWCA! It might get late tonight, Mark, so bring your overnight bag."

Mark laughed and replied, "I'll be right over! I'll also bring some of my mom's fresh, homemade donuts if you'll provide the coffee."

Mark asked his parents about staying over at Bob's to plan logistics for the guide job. They said it was OK, so he grabbed his overnight bag, thanked his mom for the fresh donuts and strapped everything on his bike. Mark headed east on highway U.S. 2 and arrived at Bob's home on Iron Mountain's North side in ten minutes. His bike had good lights, and the cool wind felt invigorating. He pulled his bike around the back of Bob's home, unstrapped his gear and donuts, and knocked. Bob's parents were still eating supper as Bob escorted him into the dining room. Mark said a quick "Hi." They waved and said, "Congratulations!"

Bob hurried him down the stairs to the basement. A fresh pot of coffee awaited on the table. Alongside it were two jumbo stoneware mugs and a pile of Minnesota maps, including some Boundary Waters Canoe Area Wilderness (BWCAW) maps, Greyhound Bus schedules, etc.

Mark threw up his arms in surprise while shouting, "Wow, you outdid yourself with this spread, Bob. I did remember to bring a sack of fresh donuts, and there's a note pad in my bag."

Bob nodded his thanks while pouring hot, Colombian java into the large mugs. He dumped the donuts into a bowl sitting on a table. It stood between two padded leather chairs facing each other. The big console stereo was tuned to WLS, a Chicago radio station, which played a steady stream of their favorite 60's tunes, emceed by the legendary Dick Biondi.

Mark paused and listened. Andy Williams was crooning *Moon River*, a song Mark found haunting and a favorite. Since he was temporarily alone, he moved closer, cranked the volume up and closed his eyes. The next tune was also high on his hit parade, *The House of the Rising Sun* by the Animals. Then it was one from Elvis' album of spiritual hymns, *Crying in the Chapel*, followed by the Beatles' *I Want to Hold Your Hand*. Bob walked back in the middle of the early Beatles hit. Mark sensed Bob's approach and turned the volume down.

Bob gestured him toward the chair, bowing and sweeping his arm in exaggerated politeness, saying, "Please be seated, my friend and sherpa. I'm using that term since it sounds like we will be, among other things, pack mules, or beasts of burden!"

Mark belly laughed at his antics, but he knew there was more fact than fiction in the sherpa comparison. He cleared his throat and said, in a dignified way, "We will be like the French-Canadian-Indian voyageurs, hommes du nord, men of the North! Now, monsieur, to business. First, we need to make reservations and purchase tickets to board the Greyhound bus to Ely. Mark this down on the note pad. Today is June eighteenth. We should leave here by the twenty-second, which will get us into Ely that same day. I have the fact sheet from the outfitter that lists the contact phone numbers once we arrive. We will be picked up and taken to the outfitter bunkhouse. We'll help assemble and pack equipment for the trip while awaiting the clients' arrival."

Mark picked up the bus schedule. "I found a Greyhound Bus that travels to Ely," he said. "It departs Iron Mountain at six a.m., June twenty-second. It makes stops at several towns on the way, with a longer stop in downtown Duluth. Arrival in Ely is scheduled for between three p.m. and four p.m. that afternoon. The outfitter will supply our food and other needs, so all we need is personal clothes and gear. Mr. Bond will pick up our packs and the remaining gear we'll need for the bonus trip. We need to have everything ready at our homes. Ray will notify our parents and our Ely outfitter shortly before he and his wife leave for the bonus trip in early July."

Bob agreed it was a good plan. He poured more coffee and said, "We could do a lot worse. I didn't have a solid lead on a summer job, especially with a late start, so this is cool! We shouldn't count on any bonus from this mysterious philanthropist, but if we really shine, we may qualify."

"You hit the nail on the head, Bob," Mark replied, "It's the stuff dreams are made of! How neat to be helping others enjoy that beautiful realm. Mr. Bond once mentioned booking trips in the Boundary Waters with an outfitter who became a close friend. I seem to recall it was called Border Lakes Outfitters. It might be a perfect match: being trained by Ray Bond, then apprenticing under a real BWCA guide. We're young, tough and will work hard for food and experience.

"We'll need to be prepared for all types of weather, bugs and emergencies. This includes nylon shorts that can serve as a swimsuit, tough water sandals, knee boots, rain gear and some sort of light, warm, jacket. Most of this will be provided, but I plan to use some of my own gear also."

"On that note, have some donuts," said Bob, as he topped off his coffee mug. "I'm sure we'll learn a lot from the guide. These donuts are great, Mark, please thank your mom. I've never taken a bus anywhere other than to school and have not seen Duluth or Ely. It is going to be quite the adventure just traveling there! Have you been to Duluth or Ely?"

"No," replied Mark, "but I have been as far as Ashland on Lake Superior and also at Saxon Harbor. My family and I took a long hike along the beach last summer. In fact, Saxon Harbor was once the beginning of a major trade route. It followed a portage trail and paddle that covered forty-five miles of rugged country through Mercer and ended at Lac du Flambeau. The fur traders, voyageurs and Indians piloted their birch bark canoes full of fur and trade goods through all of the territory, including the mighty Lake Superior which can be treacherous for even large ships.

"There is a place on Lake Superior called Grand Portage, which is a nine-mile portage through hills and swamps and was the halfway point between a canoe trade route thirty-five hundred miles in length. Brigades from Montreal met those from Fort Chipewyan at the far west end of Lake Athabasca. They rested, enjoyed the annual rendezvous, were re-provisioned and returned the fifteen-hundred miles to Montreal with the furs. The fur trade voyageurs returned to the wilderness with trade goods before winter freeze up. Can you imagine packing heavy bales of furs and trade goods and food over difficult terrain for nine miles?

"According to Sigurd Olson's autobiography, *Open Horizons*, the famous explorer Alexander McKenzie, wrote of the grand portage:

'I have known some of them (voyageurs) to set off with two packages of 90 pounds each and return with two others (another 180 lbs.) in the course of six hours, being a distance of 18 miles over swamp, hills and mountains.'

"Some voyageurs carried three, 90-pound bales at a time," Mark continued. "One named La Bonga was able to carry five, 90-pound bales! Portaging heavy loads was only part of their long, 10-14 hour days, which commenced at dawn and ended at dusk. They took occasional smoke breaks and meals of salt pork and dried corn or a pea stew. The voyageurs rarely complained and often sang working songs called chansons as they paddled. French was their primary language, but it often became a patois, a mix of English and Ojibway thrown in. Most voyageurs were young and strong French Canadians with the North West Company and Orkney voyageurs from islands north of Scotland who worked for the Hudson's Bay Company. Métis and Indians were also used as voyageurs. They were mostly short and stout non-swimmers. They often suffered injuries and ruptures from the hard life and sometimes drowned when the large birch bark canoes capsized in boiling rapids or hurricane winds."

"Man, the voyageurs were a special breed," said Bob. "You really did your homework in reading about their special service. I'll bet it was an honor to be chosen for work on the fur trade routes, despite the hardships."

"Correct you are, my sherpa!" Mark added. They were young and strong and proud to be part of a courageous band, while blazing trails through virgin wilderness.

"There was no guarantee they would return home after their contract expired, usually three years. They worked in remote areas where any medical aid was primitive, except when they approached one of the fur trade forts. Forts were established and run by the large fur trade companies, either French, English or American. There were several buildings, clerks, supplies, rum and better medical treatment. Most forts were located near Indian camps. French traders and English clerks often took Indian wives and even lived in their villages. Mixed breed children were called Métis. French traders traded rum for furs, something the British didn't like to do, but did so as the competition for beaver pelts escalated."

Bob suddenly raised his coffee mug overhead and exclaimed, "Here's to those valiant men, English, Scot, American voyageur and Indian, who spearheaded the routes we soon will follow! Their almost superhuman feats are an inspiration. I can't wait to sense a little of their calling. We'll have it made compared to their strenuous, long days. But there are still wonders and dangers awaiting us modern day voyageurs."

"Mais oui," quipped Mark, using his limited French, meaning, but yes. "I'm certain there are many hours of solitude, interrupted by moments of terror. And it should be so when one travels the wilderness. Relying on basic gear and guided by instinct and maps, allows us freedom to roam God's green Earth."

"Amen to that, Mark!" cheered Bob. "Thanks to those dedicated men like Sigurd Olson, Bill Magie and Bob Marshall, we do have a place called the BWCAW. Now let's get back to our immediate plan and continue planning for our departure!"

"Right, then will you call Greyhound Bus and reserve our student rate tickets for the trip to Ely?" Mark asked. "I'll pick up your trophy while I'm here and take both to Ray Bond's place for personalizing. At the same time I'll bring him up to date on our plans and check if we need to obtain work permits, since we're under 16. I have a few other things to discuss, like possibly attending high school in Ely, but that can wait until we all get together in July. I hope we have some free time to reconnoiter the Ely area between the guide job and our trip with Mr. Bond."

"Yes, I'll make the bus reservation," Bob said. "Thanks for handling all the guide job details with Ray Bond. Ely sounds like a cool place. Now why don't I unburden you of these donuts. It's getting late and we need rest. Take the bedroom on the left, Mark and I'll take these donuts upstairs and chat with my parents. I'll also turn off the music when I return. You're welcome to take a shower or read some of the Boundary Waters Journal Magazines on the table by the bed. The stories and pictures should assure you of sweet dreams tonight! I'll call you when breakfast is ready in the morning, goodnight."

"Night," answered Mark. He stood and stretched. Tired but excited, he walked to the bedroom and started flipping through the magazines. He was too tired to shower so he undressed and lay in bed, reading some tales of modern day trips to the Boundary Waters. He enjoyed the beautiful scenery in the pictures, the fish, pictographs and stories. Mark knew it was time to douse the lights and slumber when he jerked awake at the sound of the magazine hitting the floor.

His next conscious moment began when he smelled something heavenly wafting into his room. The marvelous fragrance of bacon, fried potatoes and sausage assaulted his nostrils. He hurried to the bathroom, showered, dressed and rushed upstairs to find Bob and his parents preparing a "hungry man's breakfast."

"Good morning, sleepy head!" teased Bob, "I was just about to call you! I wanted to allow you ample beauty sleep!"

"Hi, to all of you. This is quite the surprise," Mark quipped. "I expected coffee and donuts but this is extravagant! Thanks, Bob, for extra winks. Beauty is my shortfall."

Everyone sat down and enjoyed scrambled eggs, fried taters, salsa, sausage, bacon, coffee, juice and toast. It was a grand time. The solo finalists shared laughter and stories about the survival camp. Bob and Mark fielded numerous questions on the camp, as well as the guide job and the July prize trip. Mark departed with Bob's trophy strapped to his bike next to his overnight bag. He headed straight home. He found his mom in the fruit stand, sorting bruised or imperfect fruit and veggies. His dad was at work and the twins were playing in a pup tent under the big maple next to the fruit stand.

Mark recapped the previous evening and the big surprise breakfast at Bob's. His mom had everything under control, so he asked if he could leave to visit Ray Bond. She just laughed and waved him out. He phoned Mr. Bond.

"Hi, Ray Bond here," he answered.

"Mr. Bond, it's Mark. Would it be OK if I came over in a half hour to drop off our trophies and ask a few questions about the guide job?"

"Yes," replied Ray, "I'll be home all morning and would be glad to talk and hear your plans. Just knock and enter. We'll be expecting you."

Mark unloaded his overnight bag, then strapped his trophy next to Bob's and headed back towards town. It was still calm and quiet. Doves called mournfully as he leaned into the oversized sprocket on his bike. Ray Bond lived on the west end of Lake Antoine. It wasn't far from where the old icehouse once stood.

Fifty years earlier, every winter when the lake ice was at least 20 inches thick, men and teams of horses would cut and load ice on wagons and bring them into the large icehouse for summer. Some men would use large, special handsaws to cut ice chunks weighing thirty to forty pounds. Other men pulled the floating chunks out onto the ice using pike poles and ice tongs. Still others would slide the ice up a wood ramp where it would be stacked by men using tongs, until the rows were as high as they could reach. The wagon driver would urge the big draft horses across the ice and into the icehouse. Sometimes the wagon's steel runners would freeze into the ice. The teamster would try breaking it loose by urging the team of work horses left and then hard right. The massive Percheron horses strained and blew their breath out in white plumes, straining until the sledge broke free. Once inside, more men unloaded the ice chunks. After stacking a few rows, they would shovel sawdust several inches thick on top to assure each row was insulated. It acted to keep the ice chunks from freezing into one solid hunk. When the ice house was full, sawdust was scattered thickly throughout, and all was ready for the summer.

These were the days before refrigerators and freezers became available. Everyone relied on ice coolers to keep their perishable food in the heat of summer. Each day in the summer, a man drove a horse-drawn wagon into the icehouse to load up Lake Antoine ice. He would peddle it to businesses and residences in the local area. The "ice man" was a popular and welcome sight. He would carve off chunks to order, after first halting his team of powerful workhorses. He delivered the ice with a large pair of tongs, which he carried over his shoulder. On hot summer days, he was envied for his cool job. Mark's parents had described the iceman's horse-drawn wagon. Its white wood wheels had steel bands around the edge. The wagon itself was bright red, and rivulets of water melted onto the street as he made his rounds. When someone hailed him, he would rein in the giant Percheron horses and ask how many pounds of ice they wanted. He then expertly chopped off the right size ice chunk and carried it to the waiting icebox. Children would follow the iceman's wagon in hopes of catching a shard of ice that might fall as it lumbered along. On the hot days of a U.P. summer, it was a welcome treat and the price was right.

The old icehouse had stood for years after it was no longer needed. Refrigerators had become common household items. Mark knew where it once stood, but now it was replaced by a sprawling lake home with a green lawn down to the shore. It faded into oblivion, like the old horse drawn milk wagon and the downtown street gaslights. One of Mark's dad's favorite old tunes was a poignant song titled, *The Old Lamp Lighter.*

As Mark rode closer to his destination, his eyes climbed into the once iron ore rich hills to the north. That industry which lured his grandfather from Italy and his grandmother's family from Cornwall, England, to labor in the iron mines, was gone. Tailing piles and massive open pits flooded with water were witnesses to that era. Here in Upper Michigan, Wisconsin and northern Minnesota, immigrants from many ethnic groups once toiled and died, while long trains of ore cars and freighters carried the red ore to the steel mills of America and Europe.

Mark and his brother Pete explored the old mine pits behind their home. They fished in the clear, bottomless water pits for perch or trout which they saw swimming deep in the frigid depths. Mining companies had erected cyclone fences to keep out intruders, but the kids knew where to sneak in and take a refreshing dip on hot days. Their mothers were not aware of this. Kids tended to lump their swim holes together and treated mine pits as more like lake beaches.

Mark stopped pedaling as he realized his daydreaming had caused him to ride right past Ray Bond's home. He made a wide U-turn and was there in no time. Ray Bond's home was a modest brick ranch style that overlooked the southwest end of Lake Antoine. As he parked his old Columbia bike, he extracted the trophies and held them for a moment, admiring their beauty. They had been fashioned out of thick cross-sections of bird's eye maple. It had been cut so they were free standing. The unique, stippled grain was brought to a golden glow by a hand-rubbed tung oil finish. When they returned from the summer in the Boundary Waters, their names would be carved into the maple under the survival camp titles, place and date. He walked to the door and knocked. Mrs. Bond opened the door and welcomed him.

"Would you like some coffee, Mark?" she asked.

"Yes," Mark replied, "with cream in it, please."

As she left to prepare the coffee, Mark set the trophies on the dining room table and turned around to see Ray Bond enter the room. He was carrying two mugs of steaming hot coffee and offered one to Mark. He thanked Ray and took a careful sip. It was a rich brew. Ray bond smiled at Mark's wide-eyed appreciation of their "Mountain Man" coffee as he sat down and faced Mark.

"Good morning, Mark!" Ray said. "Thanks for bringing the trophies. I'll see that they're inscribed with your names, and they'll be here when you return this fall. Now, what's your itinerary and what questions can I answer for you?"

Mark took a seat and said, "Bob and I want you to know how much we appreciate everything you've done. There is no way to repay your kindness and the guide job opportunity. Our immediate plans are to secure tickets with Greyhound Bus to Ely. Bob volunteered to handle that. We should be set to depart in the early morning on June twenty-second. We wondered if we need any special work permits since we're under 16. We would also like to have more details about the guide job."

Ray answered, "The bus trip should be fun, especially since you'll get a good look at the big lake at Ashland, Superior and Duluth. If your bus driver can be persuaded to take the scenic route that parallels the highway to Two Harbors, you're in for a real treat. The bypass hugs Superior's north shore all the way and rejoins Highway 61 just outside Two Harbors. Concerning the guide job: I've already taken care of the work permits, and the outfitter said he'd have the forms ready for your signatures when you get settled there. There are no new details about the job. This fact sheet will do until you can sit down with the boss, my friend Walter, and discuss it. Just relax, enjoy the trip and do your best for the outfitter. I wouldn't have recommended you and Bob if I had any reservations about your ability or maturity. You two guys are mature beyond your years, and it has been a joy to watch you develop in and out of the classroom. Just don't get sick of hard work and camping out there, 'cause the July trip will come up quickly."

"Right," Mark replied, "so we're set. It's just a matter of last-minute packing. We'll leave the majority of our camping gear for you to haul when you leave for Ely. Neither of us has ever seen much of Lake Superior or the Arrowhead country. We should be glued to the windows and might even spot a moose crossing!"

Ray stuck out his hand, smiling and said, "Mark, I could chew the fat and talk about my friend who's still hooked up with this outfitter, but I know you're pressed for time. You guys need to spend some time with friends and family before going. May the wind always be at your back and the sun shining on your shoulder."

Mark grinned back, blushing, as he grabbed Ray Bond's hand. He felt Ray's charisma and strength. He knew the man could easily bring him to his knees if he wanted. A strong need to show more gratitude overwhelmed Mark. He impulsively hugged his mentor, hero and friend.

"Many thanks," Mark squeaked, then left. As he mounted his bike, he glanced toward the house and saw Ray Bond and his wife arm in arm, waving.

Mark's eyes teared up. He wiped it away and pedaled on. Life was good. He cherished Ray Bond's friendship and guidance. Where he was going and what he had to do was a real gift. It was a fine summer day with gulls crying as he circled the shore. The sun was warm, with a light breeze gently rippling the water. To prolong the ride home, he chose to take a scenic tour of Lake Antoine. It was a place Mark and his brother Pete visited often in their childhood. Pete had just graduated from Kingsford High School and was working at a Pure Oil Gas Station across U.S. 2 from their home. He worked long hours as a mechanic and pumped gas. His time off was largely spent with his steady girlfriend, Nancy. Mark saw little of him except when he hurried across the highway with a covered plate of their mom's supper. Most times, he and Pete would hike across country to Lake Antoine from their home. They passed through the old sawmill and took a logging road to the railroad tracks that ran along the northern shore, above the lake. They followed the tracks until they paralleled the lake, then walked with their fishing gear across the lake road and down to the shore.

Mark's Grandpa Pete used to have an old wood rowboat chained to a tree, near shore. Mark and his brother would fish out of it, rowing along the shore and drifting with the wind. It was an adventure that consumed most of the day and sometimes produced a stringer of perch, bass and bluegills, but always a pair of happy, tired boys. Their bag lunches of sandwiches and fruit soon disappeared and hastened their departure for home. Lunch was often timed to coincide with arriving at "Old Faceful," an artesian spring that flowed constantly. It bubbled invitingly from a galvanized pipe and splattered down the rocky cliff into Lake Antoine. There was a pull off from the encircling road. It was a popular spot to stop for a cool, clear drink or to fill water coolers from an attached downspout.

Mark and Pete could row the boat or walk along shore, gaze out over the clear water and even fish during lunch. Sadly, the artesian was just a memory, having been quietly eliminated due to contamination. As Mark approached the old artesian area, he missed its refreshing beauty. A cool drink of its crystal clear water was only a memory. Further down the road, he came to the area just past Gene's Pond, where they once began their journey back along the railroad and home. Their mom would always make a big fuss over their fish, which they proudly presented. She would make a fish fry, which included a big cast iron fry pan of American fries with onions and an oil and cider vinegar salad. Any wild game or fish was welcome in his home, since it was good eating and the price was right. Nothing was wasted. Any leftover scraps were fed to their beagles. Wild berries and mushrooms supplemented their garden veggies and tame berries. Much of the surplus was canned in glass jars and kept in the cellar for the long Michigan winter.

Mark remembered how he and Pete had picked and sold angleworms in summer. They placed a "worms for sale" sign by their driveway and offered them to customers for the princely sum of eight cents per dozen. Mark continued on to the intersection with U.S. 2, leaving the lake and good memories behind. He rode on the highway shoulder the short distance to his home. As he passed by the Michigan State Police Barracks, another memory surfaced. He recalled the time when he and Pete had foraged in a low-walled dump behind the barracks. There was always some treasure awaiting discovery, including broken furniture, trash and even confiscated stuff. One day they found a confiscated slot machine that had been smashed and thrown out back. Gambling in Michigan was strictly illegal. Mark and Pete considered it a great find and worthy of further examination for any overlooked booty. They returned early the next morning when all was quiet. They dragged the prize back into cover of the woods. They attacked the slot machine with vigor by employing a hammer and screwdriver to pry it open. It finally coughed up a few coins. As the little wheels with fruits and face cards turned, they extracted some treasure. Several coins which had jammed inside the mechanism were liberated into their pockets. The happy scavengers quietly returned the damaged machine to the barracks dump and returned home feeling pleased with their efforts and reward. It would be quickly spent on comics or candy or saved for a matinee at the Braumart Theatre. The PTA published a calendar of Saturday matinees. There were movies, cartoons, popcorn and wondrous candies, including sour lemon drops, black crows, licorice, chocolate bars and pop.

Mark arrived home in time for lunch. After lunch, he was recruited to pick the ever-bearing strawberries that did not really bear throughout the summer. They did bear twice: in June and August. His mom had already been picking that morning before the fruit stand opened. A layer of red berries were sitting in the bottom of the crate. Mark grabbed a quart basket made of thin strips of flexible, woven wood and started picking. He couldn't resist popping a few of the small, slightly flattened berries into his mouth. Their sweet-tart flavor was wonderful. As he filled each basket, he would place it into one of two crates found at each end of the rows. Mark toiled, bending over, crouching or kneeling as he worked. When one of the crates was filled, he took it up to the stand. His mom would check them for defects and then display them with the other produce. Mark hauled the crates in a red wagon, picking up an empty crate on his return trip to the berry patch. Nearing the strawberries, he paused to check the status of the rows of red raspberries, Lathams, which were just starting to set small hard, green berries. They would likely ripen while he was gone to the Boundary Waters. He enjoyed picking the raspberries because you can do it while standing. He had picked his fair share of berries and beans every year since he was seven.

The next morning he continued picking strawberries and finished by noon. He carried the last of the picked quarts and the crates inside the stand. It was time to help close the stand while his mom got supper ready in the house. Mark's sore back began to tighten up as he ate supper with his family. Everyone except the twins was tuckered. After a brief chat, Mark asked his mom to rub some liniment on his back before he headed up to bed.

The next thing Mark heard was the twins fighting over a toy, with background sounds of fry pans banging on the gas range. He smiled groggily and muttered, "welcome home," to himself. He dressed and went down to the bathroom to wash. His dad had already left for work. The twins were sitting at the table making trouble as he entered the kitchen.

"I don't want to hear another peep out of you two, or I'll send Mark to the back woods to cut a nice switch" his mom threatened. "I'll paddle your backsides good!"

The twins knew she wasn't bluffing and suddenly were quiet. Mark grinned inwardly. He remembered misbehaving as a youngster and being sent to cut a switch that would be applied to his butt. It was pure torture, cruel and inhumane. She wasn't one to let punishment wait until his dad got home. That was good, because depending on his mood, his dad could dole out an impressive spanking.

Mark picked at a steady pace all morning. He stopped only to haul crates or to take a swig of water from the glass jug in the shade. When he finally finished the last row scheduled for picking and carried the crates to the stand, he was tired and ready for a break.

"Mom, if you don't need me any more today, can I do some personal stuff?" he asked.

"Yes, you may," she said and gave him a hug. "Thanks Mark, for all your hard work. By the way, P.J. called this morning and asked if you could visit him today. You're to bring your fishing gear and toothbrush!"

Mark grinned and blurted, "That's vintage Pat and his crazy humor. He always has a plan and I owe him. I'll call him and firm up the meeting."

Mark hoped Pat wouldn't be upset about his camp accident that removed him from contention for the BWCA trip. Mark appreciated their lasting friendship. They had enjoyed a "Huck Finn" lifestyle on Moon Lake. Mark picked up the phone and dialed P.J.'s number. It was answered by one of Pat's younger sisters, who answered and then screamed, "Pat, phone call for you. It's Mark!"

There was a long pause, more hollering, and finally Pat answered. "Hey, congrats, old man! How's the top dog?"

"I'm fit as a fiddle and ready to fish, thanks," Mark replied. "Is the Thompson available?"

"Yeah, man, your cruiser is primed and waiting, but the Sea King is balky," Pat answered.

Mark knew all about the fickle outboard motor attached to the stern of the rowboat. It was an ancient 5-horse Sea King motor with the starter pulley cover removed. They would wrap a rope around the pulley and yank numerous times until it started or balked. Often they just gave up and rowed. Sometimes it would roar to life for a brief time, only to cough and die. They became very deft at switching the engine selector from "cold start" to "run." They nursed and coaxed the beast until it settled into a steady roar. It was never a sure thing.

Mark said, "I'll come over in an hour by bike and will bring some worms and a toothbrush. If I can invite myself for supper, I'll also provide a couple of quarts of fresh strawberries for dessert!"

Pat laughed, "It's a deal, old chap. My dad's the chef tonight and you know how well he does pasta with garlic bread and salad, so come hungry. We'll have some time to fish for a few hours before supper. I used our homemade minnow dip net to catch a nice bucket of lake shiners."

"OK," said Mark. "I'll pack my gear on my bike and leave soon."

It took longer to ride his bike up U.S. 2 a mile and around half the lake, but there was a half-blind bull to outrun and three-strand barbed wire fences to tackle if he walked across Farmer Schindlerlie's pasture. He wore shorts to stay cooler. Another reason was to avoid getting his pants cuffs caught in the bike's chain. The bike's chain guard had been removed because it rubbed on the chain. Mark already experienced a few scary and painful pant leg tangles. It was a tough choice: the bull or the bike. He carefully crossed the highway and turned onto Moon Lake Drive, a short distance down the gravel road. He wondered if the bane of bicyclists, A.K.A. Gretchen, would try to exact tribute as he entered her territory. Gretchen, called the "troll," was a collie mix who took her job seriously. Her attack zone was at the base of the steepest hill on the road. She challenged all comers, but her forte was bicycles. Cars were chased, of course, but didn't allow her access to ankles. She would intercept a hapless bike rider by charging out of her owner's driveway, and she was fast. Mark was familiar with her tactics and had found a way to prevent the dog from chewing his ankles, which were her fetish. As he dropped over the top of her hill, Mark pedaled furiously. Gaining speed that bordered on insanity, he hurtled down the gravel slope. Sure enough, just before he reached the bottom, out shot Gretchen. Her bared fangs sought a tender ankle to nibble. Mark quickly raised his legs out of harm's way and put his shoes on the handlebars. His bike's momentum carried him at full speed with the troll gradually falling behind. She gave up and returned to wait for easier prey. Mark smiled as he enjoyed the small victory. He still had to return in the morning, but sometimes he could quietly sneak by her while walking his bike up the hill. He pedaled leisurely to P.J.'s home.

Chapter Eight

P.J.

The house was a wood frame, split level with the lower half bermed at the front and sides. The kids' bedrooms and the rec room were also in the basement, along with the furnace, hot water heater, shower and a bathroom. It also contained an old full-size electric bowling machine that Pat's dad rescued from a local bar. Many a rainy day was spent shooting a heavy metal puck and enjoying the wild sounds and flashing colored lights as they scored a strike. Mark leaned his bike against the concrete portal that connected the garage to the house and unstrapped his gear. He set the gear down and proceeded to the kitchen door. Pat's mom, Jean, was standing in the window, framed by her window box begonias. A cigarette dangled from her mouth as she washed dishes. She was a tall, slim, pretty woman, with a quick smile and neat sense of humor.

Mark knocked on the kitchen door with the two quarts of strawberries in hand. Jean opened the door and smiled. She tossed her flowing hair back, took a drag and greeted Mark.

"Hi, Mark, congrats on winning the solo survival camp! We're glad you'll stay for supper and overnight. Pat's down by the lake loading his fishing gear into the boat. You two have a good time. Make sure you're back by seven or you'll miss Jerry's famous pasta extravaganza! Many thanks for these great-looking strawberries. They'll be dessert."

Mark laughed, "It's a deal, thanks. Maybe we'll catch some fish. See you in a few hours."

He waved and retrieved his fishing gear and the worms. As he rounded the corner of the house and headed downhill towards the shore, he saw Pat. He stood in the rear of the Thompson and cast into the lake. Mark stopped and watched him, while surveying the lake they loved so much. It was a magical place, offering untold adventures, good fishing and the perfect ground to forge a strong bond between the two of them. The sky was partly cloudy, with a westerly breeze. The boat was all loaded with tackle boxes, fish poles and a minnow bucket. Pat was fishing with his trusty bronze-finish Shakespeare closed-face reel. Mark remembered the day the new spinning reels arrived from the Herter's Sporting Goods Co. in Minnesota.

Once a year, Pat's dad made an order from the Herter catalog that was thick as a Milwaukee phone book and full of all manner of fishing and hunting supplies. It was filled with pictures, testimonials and glowing descriptions that mesmerized young boys. Mark was allowed to join in the order and spent many an hour poring over the catalog with Pat. They agonizing over the myriad of wants but finally settled on basics, like hooks, wire leaders, and monofilament line. Mark's reel was a Johnson Century that he paid for with winnings from a bingo outing with his mom at a local church.

Mark announced his presence: "Hi, Pat, how're they hitting?"

"Just a few strikes, but I missed whatever it was," replied Pat. "Let's get the boat out further and give it a try!"

Mark put his gear into the boat, shoved them off and began rowing while P.J. fiddled with the old outboard. It fired on the third pull which may have been a record. It roared to life then quit and defied a restart.

Unperturbed, they baited up and let the breeze do the work as they drift fished toward the bull's pasture. Pat put a big lake shiner on a Wolf River Rig, and Mark used a bucktail jig festooned with a gob of worms. Nothing happened until they drifted into the kettle near the marsh. They began swapping stories about personal events during the solo survival camp.

Pat recounted his trip, including his scary experience during the storm. He also had been away from camp before the storm hit. He remembered leaving his rain parka hanging in a tree and dashed out for it just as the front struck. The front hit him hard, charging head on off the lake. Before he could reach the parka, the wind blast struck him, throwing him off balance. Then, too late, he heard a loud crack above and was struck hard. When he came to hours later, he found he was pinned to the ground, soaked and cold. The rain had stopped, but a large oak limb pinned him down. He felt a warm liquid running down his face. His head had been gashed and was bleeding. Fortunately, his rain poncho had been attached to the tree limb that pinned him. With great effort he managed to pull the poncho free so that it covered most of his body. Though he was prevented from turning over or moving much, he was able to claw through branches and pull his handkerchief out of his back pocket. By bringing it up to his face, he managed to use his fingers on one hand and his front teeth to tie the handkerchief's tail ends into a double granny knot. He then gradually slid it over and down his forehead, making a simple bandage over the head wound. It put pressure on the wound by constricting the blood vessels and slowed the bleeding. The wound eventually stabilized as the blood coagulated. The parka helped ward off hypothermia, his greatest fear. He couldn't reach his radio and his head was pounding, but he remained conscious.

Being cold and helpless frightened him. It was one of the drawbacks to wilderness camping solo. He also knew that with body heat loss and the head trauma, he was a candidate for shock and hypothermia. He hoped to be rescued before the advent of the cold and darkness. His saving grace was the mandatory, twice daily check-in with base camp. When he didn't check in at his normal 5:30 p.m. time slot, the procedure called for an immediate response team to be sent out. He knew that the base camp could have their own problems to deal with, such and logs adrift on the lakes and branches and downed trees which could obstruct portages.

Less than an hour after he failed to check in at his appointed time, a two-leader crew walked into his camp, calling his name. Pat was very glad to see help arrive. While one leader began cutting away at the tree limbs, the other administered first aid to Pat. The leader removed the blood-soaked hanky, then cleaned and bandaged his head wound. When the limbs that pinned him had been cut and tossed aside, both leaders pulled him out and helped him to the large Royalex hull canoe. After aiding him in removing his soaked outer clothing, they settled him into his dry sleeping bag. One leader sat with him. He poured hot chicken broth into an insulated mug, which P.J. slurped gratefully. It helped thaw his insides and decreased his shivering. While he was being cared for, the other leader gathered P.J.'s backpack and food pack. Then P.J was seated in the canoe. The leaders assured P.J. they would return the next day to gather the remaining gear and to dismantle any structures. When they arrived at base camp, P.J. was seated in a chair next to a hot fire and given hot food and drinks and some pain medicine. After he warmed up, P.J. was in good spirits. He informed staff that he felt much better and wanted to remain at base camp until the solo camp was over. But the staff met that evening and decided that P.J. needed to seek medical treatment in Iron Mountain. Early the next morning, P.J. was taken to the Sylvania ranger station and sent by ambulance to the Iron Mountain Hospital.

"I had a hit!" Pat shouted, ending his story about his camp experience. His fish pole was bent and throbbing with the strength of a big fish, while his spin reel's drag sang a tortured song. The boat was being pulled by the force of the fish. The wind pushed them closer to logs and brush that could tangle Pat's line.

Mark dropped his pole and tended the oars. He tried to keep the boat free from the logs the fish could use to tangle and break the line. After ten minutes of give and take, they caught a flash of white as the underbelly of a large Esox rose to the surface, appearing beat. But big pike know all the tricks. The lunker pike quickly rolled on the slack line like a crocodile and went airborne. It snapped Pat's line with a report like a gunshot. The pike lay on the surface for a few seconds, then recovered and with a mighty thrust shot into the depths. The two buddies sat looking at the snapped line.

"Damn! What a fish!" Pat cried, as he fingered his frayed line that danced in the breeze.

"Sorry you lost him, Pat! What do you think it weighed?" exclaimed Mark.

Pat sighed, "That one was about fifteen pounds and forty inches long. At least I had the big fella on, and we will meet again."

Mark patted P.J. on the shoulder and said, "I'm an eyewitness in case anyone tries to accuse you of fabricating a fish story, Pat."

They continued fishing. They landed a few bass and some "hammer handle" pike and set them all free. Then Mark checked his watch and saw it was almost 7 p.m. It was time to quit and head in. Mark put his back into the oars, fighting the wind. Pat tried to start the outboard. But after a few yanks on the starter cord with no result, he gave up and massaged his arm. Mark pulled for all he was worth and began making progress.

"Hey," Pat cried, "I can smell the aromas on the wind – supper's ready! I can almost taste that tangy sauce of my dad's. He is the undisputed king of pasta."

"I'm at ramming speed," Mark grunted. "I am hoping there are blue cheese crumbles for the salad!"

As the Thompson went aground, they both jumped out and pulled the boat up on shore. Pat dumped the shiners into the stainless steel bin that was dug into the shore sand while Mark carried the fishing tackle up to the house. The worm bucket was put in a spot by the wall where it was cool and shaded. They hurried into the lower level of the house, washed up and headed upstairs.

It was a sight to behold. Their large dining room table was set with fine china. A large bowl of salad greens and garlic bread made with fresh, hot Italian bread from Schinderle's bakery were on the table. Pat's siblings were waiting in their seats expectantly. Just as they sat down, Pat's dad, Jerry, entered. He carried a massive platter of linguini, festooned with meatballs. It was even better than Mark remembered. He spooned blue cheese crumbles on his fresh salad and sampled his big plate of pasta and meatballs. He felt blessed to be with his surrogate family. Few could match Pat's dad for creating a gastronomic delight. All were diligent about putting the tasty dish away. Mark thought of his mom's comment after he finished the meal. She would say, "If you didn't get enough to eat, it's your own fault." That fit the pasta "extravaganza" perfectly.

There was much joking around about the solo survival camp, past memories, summer plans, questions about Mark and Bob's guide jobs and the trip later with Ray Bond and his wife.

Mark and Pat finally pushed their chairs away and retired downstairs to relax and talk. They sat in recliners that faced the lake and let the fine feast settle. Mark had raised a root beer toast to Pat's dad and mom for the feed and for being his second set of parents during supper. Pat and he had spent many good times together the last four years and were more like brothers than friends. They spoke of times past spent fishing or exploring and present and future things.

Pat still had some pain and light headaches, but the doctor said he was on the mend. He had suffered a mild concussion. The gash on his head had healed and was itchy.

Mark related what he knew about his guide job and brought P.J. up to date on their plans and tentative start dates for the guide job and the later BWCA trip.

Pat planned to help his parents open and run a new business, a pasty shop. It would be named Jean Kay's Pasty Shop. It would offer pasties made with Jean's secret recipe. The Cornish pasty was a food staple in the U.P. of Michigan. If anyone could make and sell pasties, they could. It was one of Mark's favorite foods. He had grown up enjoying them at home. A pasty is a meat, potato and onion mixture baked in an oval crust to a golden brown. The end result was a self-contained, nutritious lunch that fit easily into a deep coat pocket or lunch box. Pasties could be eaten cold or heated on a wood stove or even on a clean shovel in the mine while using a carbide lamp for heat. Mark grew up eating a lot of pasty and pasta.

Mark started as he realized he was nodding off and woke to find P.J.'s eyes closing. The rigors of the day were catching up with them. Their belly full of pasta was the last straw.

"Pat!" Mark barked, "I'm going to brush my teeth and get ready to lie back. We can talk until we fail to elicit conscious replies from each other."

When Mark returned from the bathroom, Pat was propped up on the bed and still awake. They lay back and talked about Pat's summer plans.

Chapter Nine

Preparing for the Trip to Ely

The next thing Mark knew, bright sunlight illuminated the room. He rolled out and stood still. P.J. was sound asleep and the household was quiet. He dressed quietly and left Pat a note, thanking him and his parents for their kindness. After splashing some water in his face, Mark tiptoed over to the door. He closed it gently and faced the lake. It was still calm. A lone fisherman rowed an ancient green wood boat, trolling Moon Lake's depths. It was the man he knew only as Old Man Mossa, an ageless bit of local color. Mark stood and surveyed the placid lake. He would miss its beauty for the summer. He hoped that he and P.J. would remain friends now that their paths were diverging.

    He gathered his fish pole and tackle box and strapped them on his bike. The worms would stay with Pat where they would be appreciated. He mounted his trusty bike and dismounted as he approached Gretchen's hill. He quietly walked the bike uphill and evaded the wily dog one more time. On the ride home Mark's head was whirling with plans for his upcoming adventure.

    Arriving home, he found his dad had already left for work and his mom was out in the strawberry patch. The twins were "helping" to pick and doing their best to eat up the profit. As he entered the patch, the sun was still low in the northeast sky, but he knew his mom had been out since sun-up. The twins ran to meet him with red-stained hands and faces. They smiled up at him, hugged Mark's legs and raced back to the patch.

His mom stood up while pressing her palms into the small of her back. She was stiff and sore from the work. She wore a red bandana as a kerchief. It kept her hair out of her eyes and also soaked up sweat on her forehead. She had always been hard working. Mark remembered his mom and brother Pete working during the winter at Hoffman's Mink Ranch. The job entailed shaving flesh and fat off frozen mink pelts. The pelts hung on wedge-shaped boards and smelled awful. Mark's job was to tend the wood stove to keep the drafty, smelly shop warm. John Hoffman roasted cigar chunks on top of the stove to help hide the strong smell. His dad sold balsam and spruce trees in their front yard before Christmas, as well as his mom's balsam and princess pine wreaths that were decorated with pinecones, artificial red berries and a big red bow.

Mark gave his mom a hug and pitched in to help her finish the berry picking for the day. He hauled the full berry crates up to the stand. Back at the house, the rich aroma of vegetable beef soup lured him toward the kitchen. The big soup kettle was simmering. He filled a small bowl and sipped the rich broth. He thought it might be a good time to call Bob.

He picked up the phone and dialed.

"Hello," Bob answered.

"Hi," it's Mark. "I just returned from an overnight at P.J.'s, then biked home and picked berries until my back is barking."

Bob laughed and said, "That's good training for the Ely job – lots of bending, stooping and carrying heavy loads!"

"Gee, thanks," answered Mark. "Now what's the status on our bus reservations, my fine sherpa. Are we a go on the twenty-second?"

"We are good to go," replied Bob. "Our chariot departs the M&J depot the morning of the twenty-second and arrives in Ely late that afternoon. We got a break on the fare since we're students under eighteen. We should plan to bring a little cooler with lunch, as there may not be much available at the few quick bus stops."

"I agree," chimed in Mark. "I'll have a small cooler with some goodies and some fruit from our stand. May I impose on your folks to pick me up with my gear and deliver us to the depot that morning?"

"Yes sir," Bob answered. "My folks already volunteered to chauffeur us. My mom is staking us to a hearty going-away breakfast at our place before we leave. So plan on being picked up an hour and a half before our bus departure."

"Roger," answered Mark. "I'll be busy catching up what work I can at home the next few days. Unless I hear different, I'll be waiting for a pickup and a feeding early on the twemty-second."

Before he knew it, Mark was saying his farewells to his family and packing his camping and personal gear into Bob's parents' van. After devouring the tasty breakfast of ham, scrambled eggs and American fries, Mark became lost in thought about the trip.

"Mark!" whooped Bob. "Let's get going! There's no time to dawdle."

"Yeah, I'm ready and, uh, thanks a lot, Mrs. Forge, for the fine food and the lift," answered Mark with his face flushed red.

Chapter Ten

Leaving on a Greyhound Bus

At the bus depot, it was a blur of tickets and baggage claims, hugs, tears and waving. They had lucked out and would be travelling in a big, beautiful Greyhound Scenicruiser with an upper deck that allowed a panoramic view. Mark and Bob dashed into the bus, handed their tickets over and raced to the upper deck. They secured the first seat on the right of the driver. It gave them a commanding view. They rode above and slightly behind the driver. It was a good omen. They placed their lunch coolers on the floor and surveyed the terrain from the "catbird" seats.

"We're moving!" Bob exclaimed.

The Greyhound's diesel engine cleared its throat and accelerated rapidly through town. Mark soon saw his home looming ahead. It was still early. His parents would be eating breakfast and getting ready for the workday. He waved as the bus passed his home. There was a dull ache in his stomach as he left his family and everything familiar. Mark was glad that he had a friend to temper the fear of the unknown.

The bus rolled west. It passed quickly from Michigan to Wisconsin and back again as it repeatedly crossed the Menominee River boundary into Wisconsin. They passed through Spread Eagle, then Florence and once again crossed the Menominee River before passing through Crystal Falls and Iron River, MI. Here also, like his hometown, were tall iron mine pits and mounds of tailings. The spoiled land was being reclaimed by shrubs and trees as nature healed the scars. The northern forest was at its peak, lush and with enough shades of green to make an Irishman cry. The scenery was almost like watching a movie! They both excitedly pointed out the sights.

After a five-minute stop in Ironwood, MI, the bus accelerated west on U.S. 2 and soon approached the short road to Saxon Harbor. It offered a small marina, campground and an expansive beach, which could be hiked for miles along the big lake. Lake Superior lay just beyond the tree line. Its blue waters blended with the clear blue sky.

"I read that Saxon Harbor was once part of a major fur trade route," Mark commented. "Bales of trade goods were portaged by voyageurs from their birch bark canoes at Saxon Harbor all the way to Lac du Flambeau and Minocqua. It was a grueling forty-five mile hike and paddle through marshes, rugged hills and waterways. After reaching the trading fort at Lac du Flambeau, they shouldered the ninety-pound bales of furs and began the long trek back to Saxon Harbor. The furs were loaded into their birch bark canoes and carried out into the fresh water sea. The Indians named it Gitchi-Gummi, Ojibway for 'big shining sea.' They believed it had supernatural powers and was home to Mishipeshu, a beach stalker that devoured children and unleashed the fury of Gitchi-Gummi."

In class, Mr. Bond explained how the Ojibway were once a proud, strong, nomadic tribe who would seek wild berries, fish, wild rice and game in season. The Ojibway felt that the Great Spirit, Gitchi-Manidoo, had given the land with its bountiful food, waterways and seasons for their use. Then the white Europeans arrived. They brought wonderful goods and changed the Ojibwa's' lives forever. Faced with superior numbers of men and firepower, the tribe became dependent on the trinkets and other trade goods, such as steel hatchets, knives, cook pots, and blankets. The use of rum as a trade item and disease brought from Europe completed their demise. He continued telling the sad history of white and American Native conflict—a history dependent on trapping beaver and obtaining their valuable pelts at any cost. In the end the beaver were decimated and the Indians lost their heritage.

"The U.S. Government in its benevolent wisdom chose to confine this once-proud, nomadic people to a tiny part of their territory, with treaties that were often broken," he explained. "Such is the legacy of any conquering force that uses 'manifest destiny' to take whatever is deemed necessary to appease its appetite. There was but one exception: the Seminole tribe melted into the Florida Everglades rather than surrender to the U.S. Army."

Bob hung his head for a moment, pondering that sad time. Mark put his hand on Bob's shoulder as they watched the "res" pass by.

Speed limit signs ahead, signaled the outskirts of Ashland. The bus driver downshifted and continued slowly as the bus passed under an old wooden viaduct where trains passed overhead. The bus turned left and then west again, paralleling the highway. A loud road noise came from the street. It was paved with cobblestones! It was an old design that used paving bricks to create durable but bumpy streets. The cobblestone street remained mainly as a novelty for tourists. Soon the bus made a quick stop.

It allowed time to drop off some packages and a rider, but the passengers had to stay on the bus. In minutes the bus accelerated onto the highway, heading west. The bus continued in a gradual descent toward the harbor.

"Look!" Bob shouted. "There's the 'big shining sea'."

"Yes sir," Mark agreed. "Look at the big elevated docks where rail cars can dump their loads into freighters' holds. I think that big plant with the huge mountain of coal next to it is their power plant."

Gitchi-Gummi sat on their right side, shining in the warm sunshine, while ducks and many Canada geese swam along its shore. A little park with picnic tables was visible where the highway curved around the end of the bay. Mark asked the driver why people were carrying jugs into a small shed.

"That, my boy, is an artesian well, some of the finest drinking water available, and it's free to all," answered the driver. "People that know about it sometimes fill large containers and use it for drinking and making coffee. It runs constantly out of a galvanized pipe, with the overflow returning to Lake Superior. There is another artesian near the town of Cornucopia where a wood gazebo houses a similar water pipe. The town uses water from the same source and has it tapped into their businesses and homes."

Bob and Mark looked longingly at the people lined up, waiting for water. They swore that someday they would be able to drive up and partake of this wonder.

"Sorry we can't stop and let everyone sample the artesian, but once we stopped, nobody would want to get right back on the bus. I'd be in trouble," said the driver, smiling.

Now the lake was out of sight, and they settled down for the haul to Superior where they would get their next glimpse of the big water. Ray Bond had mentioned that Duluth was one of the busiest ports in the Great Lakes. He explained that cargo ships arrive from all over the world, mainly to load with grain. Wheat, barley, flax and oats are trucked to the huge grain elevators from fields in the Midwest prairie states. At one time, freight trains hauled loads of grain and iron ore to Duluth and hauled the old growth pine, birch and maple lumber and logs out. Passenger trains once arrived from all directions up to five times a day.

Soon the bus slowed for the long ride through Superior where gas stations, restaurants, and motels dotted the way. A large marina full of every kind of boat appeared on their right.

As the bus dropped down a gradual hill and curved west, it slowed to make a tight right turn. Suddenly the driver downshifted and bus was climbing up a steep ramp. They were on the bridge that crosses over the Duluth Harbor!

"Look at that!" Mark exclaimed, "There's the concrete grain elevators, and they're loading grain into a freighter. Another freighter is leaving the port and heading out into the 'Big Shining Sea'."

"This is some view!" replied Bob, "The sun is so brilliant! It paints the bay and the hill above with a golden sheen. It looks like we're descending rapidly, so seize the moment!"

"I'm glad we're seeing it now and not during winter," Mark added. "It's a spectacular setting. I hope we can explore the town and harbor area sometime."

The bus depot loomed ahead on Duluth's main drag. It was marked by a large sign that featured a running Greyhound. It was a welcome sight, with a cafe, a generous seating area and clean bathrooms. They needed a break from the bus. It was grand to stretch their legs, use the men's room, grab a sandwich and enjoy some hot coffee. It took about a half hour to disgorge some riders and take on new ones and their luggage. Mark and Bob hurried back to their catbird seats. They hoped no one else would try to evict them. All was as they left it. They settled back as the bus pulled out and headed east on Highway 61. It moved slowly through Duluth's outskirts, then crossed the Lester River and increased speed.

Mark leaned down and touched the driver's shoulder to get his attention.

"Sir, would it be asking too much for us to take the scenic route to Two Harbors?" he asked. "I've heard the views of the lake are good and it only takes an extra five minutes."

The driver beamed and said, "I've been asked to take the scenic route by others, and we're running ahead of schedule so we'll do it."

"Mark, this is amazing," exclaimed Bob. "The big lake is so powerful. Look how its swells move so powerfully and how its waves crash on the rocks.

"It's crystal clear and no land intrudes in the distance. Nothing but water to the horizon. I can now understand why it was considered sacred by the Ojibway. There is so much to explore. Oh, I picked up a free map of this area at the Duluth Depot. Now we can follow our progress to Ely and on our return trip."

"D'accord," Mark replied. "It will come in handy! Good thinking, my honorable sherpa. Look at how massive and mysterious this Gitchi-Gummi is! It even boasts its own National Park, called Isle Royale."

The waters of Gitchi-Gummi shone like brass, reflecting the morning sun as seagulls coasted in lazy spirals, catching the offshore breeze.

Though Lake Superior was almost idyllic this day, the lake has many moods. It can become deadly violent. Fur traders, voyageurs and Indians who plied her waters always left tobacco gifts and prayed before attempting a voyage. The spirits of the sacred lake could grow angry and swamp even forty-foot-long "Montreal canoes," claiming cargo and men if all the rituals were not observed and sometimes even if they were.

Three basic types of canoes were used in the fur trade, depending on the size of the rivers and lakes and the type of cargo. The Montreal canoes were birch bark behemoths, four- to six-feet wide, with a crew of 10 to 14 men, carrying five tons of trade goods and furs. The 36- to 40-foot canoes themselves weighed six-hundred pounds and were portaged by six men. The birch bark was often taken from one large birch tree and was stitched together with wattape, the Ojibway word for roots, usually spruce. All seams in the birch bark were resealed and any damage repaired daily by smearing pine pitch, heated with a torch.

The North Canoe, or "canot du Nord," was 25 feet long. It carried 3,000 pounds of cargo, besides the crew, and was used on the smaller lakes and streams found in most of the Boundary Waters. Between these two larger canoes was the batard, or "bastard ," which was used to haul the bourgeois and smaller loads. A "half canoe," it was 20 feet long and was used occasionally for light loads and to carry important dignitaries and passengers over rougher terrain with many rapids.

Indian canoes, 10 to 15 feet, were termed "light canoes" and were used to carry light loads or passengers and personal gear. They were not unlike today's tripping canoes. Voyageur canoes of all types were commonly painted with green and red paint, which gave them a gay look. The canoe's high bow and stern were often adorned with a painting of an animal or bird. Canoe paddles were also painted green and red. A voyageur canoe brigade of three or more canoes presented a colorful sight. Paddles flashed in the sun, driven relentlessly by voyageurs with their vivid waist sashes fluttering proudly. They paddled with a cadence of a stroke per second, singing chansons as they went.

The Greyhound Scenicruiser gradually left the shoreline and re-connected with Highway 61 just west of Two Harbors, MN. Soon the bus reached the turn onto Hwy. 2 that ran a northeast course and entered Superior National Forest. It eventually connected with Hwy. 1, which led to a long series of sharp curves and hills to Ely.

"This is moose country," quipped Mark. "It isn't unusual to spot one, especially in the lower, swampier areas."

"That would be a bonus!" said Bob. "I've seen a few deer and a grouse on the shoulder. But if not, I can wait until we are in the BWCAW."

Mark nodded in agreement. He recalled Mr. Bond's comments about BWCAW moose. He had said, "In the BWCAW, moose aren't hunted much beyond the edges and are able to live free and relatively safe from man. Their only predator to fear is the timber wolves that roam throughout the area."

As the bus slowly picked its way along the curvy road, Bob and Mark tired from the long bus ride. Both grew quiet and slipped peacefully into napville.

The bus's windshield wipers worked intermittently as a fine mist enveloped them. There were fewer tight curves and more signs of private property. Mark awoke as they passed the Birch Lake Forest Sservice Campground. He tapped Ace's shoulder to ask a question.

"Ace, are we getting close to Ely?"

"It's just up the road about ten miles," Ace replied. "It's a welcome change to have fewer sharp curves. The road improves as we draw closer to Ely."

As the bus neared Ely, Bob and Mark snacked on apples that Mark's mom had thoughtfully included. The bus climbed the hill into Ely's business district. It passed numerous outfitters and many cars and trucks hauling canoes. Stores and gas stations lined the long street. The driver turned left one block and drove onto a street that paralleled the main drag.

"We're here!" Mark shouted. "There's the bus stop just ahead at Britton's Cafe. I'll make the phone call to alert the outfitter we've arrived, if you'll collect our baggage."

"Roger," quipped Bob. "I'll grab our gear and maybe we can explore the town a little."

Mark nodded his assent and stepped down from the upper level. He paused to shake Ace's hand and to thank him for all his help. He descended the steps to the sidewalk and entered Britton's Cafe. It was an older place, clean and comfortable, with tantalizing aromas. Mark spied the pay phone near the register and after depositing a dime, dialed the outfitter's number.

"Hello, Border Waters Outfitters, June speaking."

"Hi, this is Mark Fisher with Bob Forge," Mark answered. "We just arrived in Ely and are at Britton's Cafe. Could you please have someone pick us up?"

"Yes," June replied. "But it may be an hour or so until he arrives. Why don't we meet you at the Chocolate Moose, a few blocks north of Britton's? There's a neat camping equipment store next door called Piragis Northwoods, where you can check out the latest equipment. After Piragis, you can indulge your sweet tooth at the Moose, which is next door! You're sure to enjoy your tour. We all look forward to meeting you. Your living quarters are ready, and supper will be served soon after your arrival."

"Thanks," Mark said. "We'll be there. Just have them page us."

As Mark hung up the phone, Bob laid their backpacks outside the café's door. He stepped out where Bob sat and wiped sweat off his brow.

"Hoist your pack and follow me," joked Mark. "We have time to see some sights, namely, Piragis and the Chocolate Moose, where we'll be picked up."

Bob looked up and shouldered his pack, and they ambled north. The town was old, with a massive multi-story brick library and post office. Lumbering, mining and outfitting were its origins and still held sway in this area. The massive log building that contained the Chocolate Moose had a hand-written menu board. Nearby on the adjoining Piragis wall was another handwritten list of used canoes and related gear. After spending almost an hour drooling over the abundant gear, they forced themselves to leave and walked into the Moose. Massive pine slab tables glistened with numerous coats of clear varnish. A young, pretty, college-age waitress provided menus and ice water. The main meal menu looked wonderful, but they knew supper was waiting for them, so they settled for fresh strawberry-rhubarb pie a-la-mode and mugs of hot, rich coffee. After quickly consuming the dessert, they sipped their coffee and took in the local color.

A group of noticeably clean guys and gals dressed to the teeth in fashionable duds sat at one table. They looked like an advertisement in a pricey Eddie Bauer catalog. They were having great fun and certainly were not going to break a sweat anytime soon. Mark had heard about such "town yuppies" who spent most of their days in or near town. They were always fresh faced, clean and smelled of herbs. There was no tattered clothing or muddy boots for this group. It was comparable to some girls who buy expensive bathing suits, but never go swimming.

The majority of patrons were bearded, dirty and sun burned. They wore stained, torn clothing. They wolfed their food as one can only do when he's been battling wind, waves and bugs for days or weeks. Mark knew the love of that tough but worthwhile life. How good it is to feel a hot shower and eat food you didn't have to cook yourself. It was well worth being tested daily by the power and the mystery of the wilderness. He looked forward to the challenge.

Mark spoke softly. "This little stroll and sightseeing trip was nice. I sure do like this fresh pie and coffee, and I can almost identify with one of these yuppies!"

"Not quite," joked Bob. "Your shabby duds tell the truth. You're just a wood rat."

Mark chuckled, "Well, I'll consider that a compliment. You know all I desire is to become an exceptional wood rat! Thank you. I can think of no higher praise, Monsieur Robert."

Just then, the restaurant door opened and in strode a dark, lithe man who peered about the room until his black eyes focused on them. He turned, cat-like, and crossed over to their table. As he drew close he extended his hand. They jumped up and shook hands with a voyageur incarnate.

"Welcome, mes amis," he said. "I be Pierre, head guide of Border Waters Outfitters. You must be our two new engagés–Mark and Bob."

Mark and Bob smiled and nodded while wincing at the man's vice-like grip. His was a strong and swarthy face. Mark knew he was in the presence of a French Canadian who could pass for a fur trade voyageur. Pierre's patois of speech and accent caused Mark's heart to hammer with joy. It would be a thrill to serve and learn from this homme du Nord.

Pierre motioned them to follow. They shouldered their packs and exited the Moose. Pierre stopped at an old '63 Dodge pickup with the Border Waters logo on the doors. After stowing their packs in back, Mark and Bob took their places beside Pierre. He fired up the slant-six engine and began climbing up the main drag of Ely. Mark mused about what Pierre had called them: engagés. It was a throwback term to the fur trade era. It was used to describe men who had signed a written contract with Hudson's Bay Company or North West Company as a voyageur for three years.

Pierre nursed the truck up the steep hill in second gear. He pointed out Zup's Grocery at the top of the hill, Whiteside Park on the flats, and the long row of outfitters and motels as they drove east. The highway narrowed and became the Fernberg Road, with lodge and outfitter signs at intervals. The truck took a sharp left turn where a pine slab sign sported the Border Waters logo. It was a pair of crossed red canoe paddles over a forest with a lake in its center.

After a short drive down a gravel road, the truck entered a wide turnaround with log buildings in a semi-circle. The buildings were striking in their solid, rustic appearance. A newer main lodge was flanked by older, rough log cabins and a longer log building that must be the bunkhouse. Pierre killed the engine and announced as he stepped out, "Alors, this be you hogan. Go settle in. Come back at souper bell."

Mark and Bob said, "Oui and merci," shouldered their packs and dropped them in the bunkhouse entry. They explored the building and peered into each of the six bunkrooms. They were spartan but practical. There were two double decker bunk beds in each, a clock, and a radio. The shower rooms and bathrooms were down the hall. Each room also had an efficiency kitchen with a propane range, sink and small refrigerator. An old stardust-pattern Melmac table with chrome legs and matching chairs with red seats and backs completed the kitchenette. They returned for their packs and chose a room on the end that had a nice view of the lake. Mark was tired and failed to pay any real attention to the large, old cabinet radio that stood in the back near the window.

"Well, my man, not bad digs!" said Bob. "Let's drop our packs and kick back until supper."

"It's perfect," Mark replied. "It has a nice old maple tree to shade it from the afternoon sun and a fine view. I'll see if I can find any good tunes on the old radio."

It was even darker in the back now, but Mark could just make out the display of knobs. He turned the volume knob to the right and with an audible click, the tuning dial lit up. As the vacuum tubes warmed, a low hum was followed by a crackle and static. Mark turned the tuning knob until he heard a familiar melody. It was Roy Orbison singing *Pretty Woman*. He nudged the volume higher and climbed into the upper bunk where he lay back and hummed along. The next hit was *Green, Green* by the New Christy Minstrels, then *Dream Lover* by Bobby Darin and *You Were On My Mind* by the Wee Five. A gradual loss of consciousness overtook the new engagés . The next sound they heard was the clanging of the dinner bell.

They both jerked awake at the sound that penetrated throughout the lodge grounds. Bob jumped up and headed for the bathroom while Mark turned the radio off. They both washed up and headed out the door. Since only paying guests ate in the lodge dining room, they were escorted to the kitchen by the desk clerk and shown where the staff ate.

Sue, the desk clerk, said, "Pick a table inside or out and your dinner will be brought to you. After dinner you will have a meeting with Pierre and Walter at seven-thirty."

"Thanks," answered Mark. "We'll be there. By the way, Sue, what's for supper tonight?"

"You're very lucky!" Sue answered. "It's our Friday night fish fry. It features fresh caught walleye with baked potatoes and garden salad! See ya later. Enjoy."

After Sue left, they chose a table in the shade and were soon drooling from the cooking aromas wafting out of the kitchen. It was a warm evening with fair skies. It felt good to be alive and a part of this place. The kitchen door banged open and a white-coated chef bearing a large tray bore down on them. Sue followed close behind. She carried a glass pitcher of ice water and two large glass mugs. The chef served their supper trays and greeted them:

"Gentlemen, welcome! I hope you enjoy your broiled walleye. I am called Dutch, and I am the head chef. Breakfast is at six-thirty, lunch at noon and supper at five p.m. Snacks are available in the kitchen, anytime. Bon appétit."

"Thanks, Dutch," responded Bob and Mark in unison. Their plates were metal and still sizzling under the large golden fillets that glistened with drizzled butter. They mashed and seasoned their baked potatoes and scooped a large dollop of sour cream on top.

Mark sank his teeth into the crisp, plump fillet. He could taste the subtle mix of herbs and spices that distinguished it from the ordinary. Bob caught Mark's grin and rolled his eyes. They were in hog heaven.

Bob swallowed a chunk of fish and smacked his lips. "It is going to be tough to leave this garden spot. It's into the bush we must go. However, we are growing boys and we need to feed!"

"Truer words were never spoken," Mark laughed. "But we'd soon weigh a ton if we stayed too long!"

After demolishing their supper, they leaned back, contented. The kitchen door banged and they looked up at Sue. She hovered nearby with a tray holding two steaming mugs of java and two jumbo oatmeal-raisin cookies! Mark and Bob quickly sat upright and thanked her warmly. She smiled, nodded, bowed and waved as she returned to the lodge. Their eyes followed her retreat as they sipped the robust coffee and nibbled the fresh, warm cookies. Mark recalled the untold thousands of these cookies his mom had made for his family.

That thought brought back more happy memories of his family. In the spring, the entire family picked wild mushrooms and leeks and traveled to nearby Lake Michigan when the spring smelt run was on in feeder streams. Mark remembered one spring night on No-See-Um Creek, a tiny tributary stream. It was dark when a wave washed a large mass of smelt into a deep hole. His dad dipped the long handled net into the circling school. He heaved on the net's long handle and the net came up full of smelt. Catching the small, writhing fish with their silver sides flashing was an ancient ritual. Each net-full was dumped into a galvanized washtub. His mom used sharp scissors to gut them. After a rinse the smelt went into another tub with crushed ice. Not one to waste the moment, she reserved a pan-full and dredged them in a flour and pepper batter. She then tossed them into a cast iron skillet containing hot oil and cooked them over a waiting wood fire grill. In a few minutes the fish were fried golden and curled up. Everyone held out their paper plates for a mound of the crispy morsels. They were very rich and flavorful. It was a pleasant memory for Mark. His family sat around the fire on lawn chairs. The firelight illuminated their greasy, happy faces. Mark smiled and closed his eyes, thinking those were the best times.

After finishing the oatmeal-raisin cookies and nursing their coffee refill, they were half-dazed from all the food and activity of the day. Mark glanced at his watch.

"It's seven-twenty!" he gasped, "allons-y, mon ami."

"Lead the way," shouted Bob. "We don't want to be late for our first meeting with the boss!"

They hurriedly put their dishes in the kitchen sink and headed directly to the fire pit. The meeting with Walter and Pierre went well. They were warmly greeted and given a quick overview of their work responsibilities before the BWCA trip and some facts about the various disabilities of the clients.

Walt made comments about each client's particular situation in a wilderness setting:

"First is Glenn, a Vietnam vet who lost his legs above the knee, due to walking over a land mine. He has two custom-made prosthetic legs and feet and is able to negotiate most terrain. He also uses two hiking staffs and has requested to carry his personal gear in a backpack. He doesn't regard himself as being severely handicapped and enjoys being physically challenged. Glenn has occasional flashbacks to the war and some latent anger about it. Glenn is in his thirties.

"Jack is a ten-year-old full-Ojibway boy who lost the use of his left arm due to a hunting accident. His arm was cut deeply when his knife slipped, severing tendons and nerves. Jack likes being outdoors and dreams of being in the wilderness. His grandfather, who lived the old nomadic lifestyle, taught him much of his people's lore. Jack is fun loving, quiet and intense. He is able to do more than most expect of him. He is an orphan and lives with his Ojibway grandparents.

"Ruby is twelve, African American and blind since birth. She comes from a big city and is willing to learn and anxious to 'see' the wilderness.

"Last in the group is Cora, a thirty-three-year old woman who teaches and has run several marathons, though totally deaf. She is tough, positive in her outlook, and looks forward to testing herself and to spending time 'just taking in the wild.'"

Walt, the "boss," was an imposing man with weathered features from a lifetime outdoors. He was a lumberjack in his younger days when the timber barons ruled the north. Loggers cut the majestic, old growth pine all the way up to the Canadian border. When the timber declined, Walt found that people wanted someone to guide them into what was to become the BWCA, Quetico area. He had been in the guide business for thirty years and now spends most of his time arranging client trips. He still makes the occasional trip into the wilderness he loves, but age has limited him physically. He is a long-time friend of Sig Olson, Ely's famous environmental giant. Sig spent much of his life guiding others and convincing people that the wild land to the north of Ely, that he knew and loved, should be saved for everyone. He went to battle against formidable lumber, mining and commercial lodge owners who wanted to divvy up the last wild places in northern Minnesota. Sig Olson and other brave, selfless men eventually prevailed. In 1964, the Federal Government designated over a million square acres of pristine wilderness, the BWCAW, for everyone to enjoy.

Walt stood again and spoke: "The philanthropist who is paying the freight for this trip is a medical doctor who has a love for this wild land. He is a veteran of many wilderness trips, long before the BWCAW was officially named. He still visits here, and we canoe and camp together but his age limits trips in difficulty and duration. He knows from personal and professional experience the power of wilderness to heal mind, body and spirit. He prefers to remain anonymous. Ray has joined us for canoe camping with the doctor over the years. The doctor wants to pay some of his debt owed to his beloved 'le beau pays'. This group of 'challenged' folks is part of his vision.

"Ray Bond has high praise for both of you boys' savvy, strength and maturity. As junior guides, you will receive half a regular guide's wages. There may be a performance bonus at the doctor's discretion upon completing the contract. This will be a five-day trip. Here's a map of the trip route with desirable campsites on Horse Lake. Keep these for reference later and to help visualize the important features as I preview the trip for you.

"On June twenty-fifth, we depart here and arrive at the Mudro Lake entry point number twenty-three at dawn. The staff, Pierre, Mark and Bob, will portage all camp gear and food from the Chainsaw Sisters' Saloon to the put-in on Mudro Creek. All gear and clients will be loaded into the three canoes and begin the trip down the creek into Mudro Lake. Paddling near the right shore the length of Mudro brings you to the portage to Sandpit Lake. This portage will be the toughest of the whole trip, due to its steep, rocky descent. Once on Sandpit Lake, continue on the right shoreline until reaching the next portage on the old rail bed to Tin Can Mike Lake. After crossing the lake, seek its northeast end and portage to your destination, Horse Lake. You will try to find a vacant campsite, just past the inlet of the Horse River. The two sites nearest the Horse River outflow are large enough and convenient for your use. This makes possible a day trip to Basswood Lake. Horse Lake has a good population of walleye, pike, largemouth, smallmouth bass and pan fish."

Walt finished the trip outline and told them that any details he didn't cover could be obtained from Pierre and the McKenzie maps he handed out to them. He dismissed them and told them to rest well. It would be a full day tomorrow preparing all the gear and packing it into the vans.

Bob and Mark bid their bosses good night and walked back to the bunkhouse talking softly, but excitedly.

"We're finally drawing close to D-day. I can't wait!" exclaimed Bob.

"It does sound like a good plan," Mark replied. "It's somewhat challenging, but doable. It'll be nice to hump gear, paddle hard, and be set up in our base camp by day's end. According to Pierre, this Horse Lake area was once a busy logging camp. Rafts of logs were floated to the south end of Horse Lake, cut to proper length and loaded onto a narrow gauge steam train. Evidence still remains of the logging era. Log boom chains are still attached to logs in some cases. One of the campsites on the extreme south end of Horse near the portage was the site of a logging camp. It has remnants that await discovery. A resort once stood on the north shore. We will also explore it on a day trip."

"That's cool," Bob replied. "This makes spending summer at home look tame. What else do you know about that railroad and logging camp at the south end?"

"The logging camp was run by the Hopkins and Swallow Railroad in the early 1900s," Mark answered. "The resort flew in rich guests fly in and provided guides and fishing trips on Horse Lake in motor boats."

As they neared the bunkhouse, the sun was setting and a heavy mist began to fall that convinced them to call it a day. It would be good to lie in their bunks and read or listen to some music until sleep took over for the night. Besides the gear selection and packing, the clients would be arriving later in the day.

"Mark, see if you can find more golden oldies on that radio," Bob asked.

Mark turned on the nearby table lamp so he could see better. He turned the volume knob, heard the click and listened for the low hum that signaled the vacuum tubes were warming. As he waited, he scrutinized the old radio's construction. It was of 1950s vintage and housed in a dark oak console about four feet high. A domed top contained a large multi-band tuner. Turning the tuner knob moved a six-inch arrow with red fletching that swung in an arc across all frequencies. Mark was enamored of its beauty and quality.

Its nameplate read ZENITH in bold, red letters emblazoned across the clear glass front. It was impressive, especially with the Z made to look like a lightning bolt. More a work of art than a radio, it was a wonder. Various frequency or wave bands were printed on the tuner face. One merely moved the selector to choose a band. The choices were: Police, Short wave, AM and FM.

Mark tried the police band first, but there was no traffic, only static. Next was the short wave band which produced some garbled transmissions, then a clear signal featuring a woman singing in Spanish. He moved the big tuner arrow slowly, stopping briefly to listen to a French conversation, then a BBC broadcast of world news. Mark enjoyed listening to the "Brit" accent.

"Hey," Bob barked. "Would you quit goofing around and find some solid tunes instead of that jabber?"

"Mais oui," Mark said and saluted. "I was just having some fun with all the wave bands. I'll select the FM band and look for some serious sounds."

Mark had noticed a radio antenna atop the bunkhouse roof. He checked behind the radio and found a wire connected to the antenna screw that snaked up the wall into the ceiling. This just might allow him to bring in stations far away in the U.S. He moved the tuner arrow directly to his favorite oldies station 970KC, WLS in Chicago. All at once, he hit a clear channel and heard a very familiar and welcome voice, Dick Biondi! Biondi was a maverick D.J. on WLS. He was often in trouble because of his on-air comments, but his fans loved him because he played the best music.

"Yahoo!" shouted Mark. "We are in high clover, my man."

Mark turned up the volume and adjusted the bass level just as the next platter began to spin on Biondi's magic turntable. Clear as a bell came Elvis' rich voice belting out *Heartbreak Hotel*. The large speakers, which filled the bottom of the console, had a sound like a Wurlitzer jukebox. As Elvis sang, the room vibrated and they both began gyrating in their version of American Bandstand.

"Can you believe this place," quipped Mark. "Here we are at the edge of the wilderness, and we're treated to the greatest songs ever made on one of the period's best radios!"

"It is special," agreed Bob. "Someone almost seems to have prepared this place with us in mind. I wonder if Ray Bond had his hand in this! I seem to recall him saying that he also enjoyed '60s music and that he had listened to some oldies when he stayed here! Knowing his connections to the good doctor, nothing would surprise me."

They relaxed on their bunks and read through some 1950s vintage outdoor magazines, such as Sports Afield and Outdoor Life. The old tunes kept pounding their lyrics into the room.

Mark's ear perked up at the soulful strains of Dion (and the Belmonts) singing *Runaround Sue*, Jerry Lee Lewis' *Great Balls of Fire*, Roy Orbison's *Crying* and *Ooby Dooby*, The Fendermen's *Muleskinner Blues*, Tommy James and the Shondells' *Crimson and Clover*, Del Shannon's *Runaway*, The Animals' *House of the Rising Sun*, and The Beatles' *Love Me Do*. The hits kept coming. The '60s hits were interspersed by zany dialogue that only Biondi could do. They paged through the old ads and enjoyed stepping back in time before the advent of spinning reels.

Mark even found an old Herter's Catalog that sold every type of outdoor hunting and fishing equipment from hooks and swivels to guns and outboard motors. It had mouth-watering descriptions and photos of anything a sportsman could dream of. Fond memories flooded into Mark's brain. Hours were spent with P.J. as they lingered over the smudged pages of the Herter's catalog. It was tough trying to whittle down their wants to match their finances. It was an annual ritual that was a part of their friendship at Moon Lake.

Mark and Bob hummed along to the never-ending tunes and pointed at interesting stories and ads until their eyes glazed over. Mark heard something whack the floor and realized he had nodded off and dropped his magazine. He staggered to the radio and said goodnight to Biondi. After switching off the radio, he made a final trip to the bathroom then slid between the sheets. In his last lucid moments, Mark thanked the Creator for all the blessings of the day and lapsed into the sleep of exhaustion. Bob had already succumbed to the rigors of the long day and was softly snoring. A loon sang a long, mournful song on the lake.

Suddenly, a loud clanging in the darkness brought them both bolt upright! It was the false dawn with promise of daylight coming. The sound was their early wake-up. It was 5:30 a.m. on the dot by Mark's watch. He hurried to the bathroom to brush his teeth and got dressed. Bob took his turn in the bathroom while Mark waited outside and watched a pair of loons fish in the foggy lake. They plunged their heads under before diving with a quickness and grace that belied their body size. Mark stood quietly under the big maple tree while he waited for Bob.

Chapter Eleven

Memories of Home and Family

His thoughts returned back home. His family would be at work in the fields, tending the fruit stand and monitoring the twins. He felt a little guilty not being there to help. They rarely took a vacation. They were tied to the fruit stand and paint "game" as his dad referred to his job. It demanded all their time to eke out enough income and to keep everyone supplied with the basics of shelter, food and clothing. Real vacations were rare and usually brief. It included local camping and fishing trips when the fruit stand was closed and there was no crop to harvest. Their first old black-and-white RCA television was a square metal box that offered three local channels. Mark and Pete never missed listening to episodes of nightly radio programs such as The Lone Ranger and Sergeant Preston.

The one amazing exception to seldom having a vacation happened when Mark was eight before the twins were born. His dad had been laid off for the winter. His parents packed up Grandpa's 1939 Ford coupe and hitched up an old green house trailer to it. Mark, his parents, brother Pete, grandpa and their Springer Spaniel began the long trek to Florida. The Ford had a floor shift and a Mercury V-8 engine, but struggled to climb hills. The warmer temperatures in the south pushed the Ford's radiator to its limit. Numerous stops were required to allow the steaming radiator to cool until his dad could add more water. These unscheduled rest stops allowed everyone to stretch their legs. His dad would try to nurse the overheated radiator to a decent pullover with some shade. His mom would set up a quick lunch for them while Pete and Mark walked Penny the dog, who spent most of the long ride south in the trailer. It took an hour to let the radiator cool before they hit the road again.

One near tragedy happened when Penny was thrown out of the trailer! Mark saw the trailer door swinging and had his dad stop the car.

He and Pete ran back down the ditch and found poor Penny dazed and skinned, but OK. After that, one of the boys rode with her and Grandpa Pete in the trailer. There was no air conditioning in the car or trailer. There was more room in the trailer, but it was illegal for them to ride there when they were travelling on the highway. They had to sit on the floor or lie on a bed and stay hidden.

Grandpa Pete was the only person in the family who had seen the ocean. He had emigrated to the U.S. on a ship from Italy as a young boy. He had a hard life. He worked in lumber camps, the iron mines and at the Ford Plant in nearby Kingsford, MI, where Ford produced the famous Woody station wagon. But Grandpa Pete was a talented self-taught oil painter who was well known for capturing the natural beauty of the local area on his easel. Skilled craftsmen, including Mark's grandpa, were employed to create beautiful wood panels for car and truck dashes and doors using timber from forestlands owned by Henry Ford.

The family spent most of the winter at trailer parks in Tampa and Naples. Mark and older brother Pete attended school where they were called "Yankees" by their Florida classmates. Mark and Pete retaliated by calling their classmates "crackers."

Mark and Pete beach combed, swam, and picked oranges and fallen coconuts. His parents earned money by picking citrus crops. Mark became adept at using a hammer and screwdriver to pry the husks off coconuts. One Sunday morning following a windy night, Mark and Pete gathered fallen coconuts and filled the Ford's trunk. The windfall harvest provided fun and food for weeks. Sometimes he and Pete would sneak into an orange grove and fill a paper sack of oranges. They would hide from traffic and run back to the "getaway" Ford. It made for an exciting and tasty time. Grampa Pete met them every day after school and gave them each a nickel to buy a fudgesicle. Mark once was walking in tall grass near the trailer court and heard a loud buzzing sound. It was a rattlesnake! He panicked, jumped over it and ran away safe but scared. Another day he was trying to cross the playground swing pipe, but lost his grip. He slid down a chain and tore his jeans. He inspected his inner thigh and saw torn skin and blood. Another hard lesson was learned. His mom applied some healing salve, and the wound healed quickly. He never told his mom how it really happened, but lied about falling on an axe that was driven into a chopping block by the woodpile.

Sometime in March they sold the house trailer. It was time to go home. Grandpa handed Mark and Pete a dollar each just as they were ready to leave in the Ford. Grandpa Pete flew back home. His wife, Mark's Grandma Georgina, had died young. Grandpa Pete raised five children and lost a young daughter to a fatal illness. He had small pensions from Ford Motor Co. and Social Security and owned his house. He and Mark became very close during his retirement years and were often found traveling to Escanaba, MI., or to the old camp near Sagola on Wells Grade. His grandpa would make them lunch and tell Mark countless stories about past hunts and old times. When Mark had his driver's license, his grandpa would let him drive his old Rambler to their destinations. He even took him into a bar on the way to Green Bay. It was filled with stuffed animals. His grandpa knew the bartender and bought Mark a beer. They were fast friends. Mark loved to drive, and his grandpa often slept as he drove.

The rest of the family took the Ford home to Iron Mountain. It was a long trip. They ran into snow and icy roads as they drove north. At least they had no trailer to tow, and there was more room for them and Penny in the back seat. They arrived home in the dark a week later to deep snow and a cold house. Mark never understood his dad's hurry to leave the nice warm "Sunshine State". One final surprise happened soon after returning home during the spring thaw. Before leaving Florida, Mark had dug up some bright-colored little clams at the beach. They were about the size of his fingernail and could dig out of sight in the beach sand in seconds. He had wrapped them in a hanky and hid them in the Ford's glove box. He had forgotten all about them until his mom's nose followed the stench to his cache. Mark was told to remove the very smelly mess and learned another hard, stinky lesson.

Chapter Twelve

Preparing for the Boundary Waters

"It's time for chow, my son!" Bob roared as he burst through the bunkhouse door. "If you don't want it they'll throw it to the hogs."

"Wait for me. I'm hungrier than a bear!" squawked Mark. "Let's get some vittles."

They raced to the lodge doors, locked in a dead heat. Breathlessly, they headed for the kitchen. They filled their trays with sausages, scrambled eggs, toast, oranges and hot mugs of coffee. There were chairs outside under the lodge's eave that offered a prime dining area. A card table sat between them and was perfect for their mugs of java. As they were enjoying their meal, the chef appeared and set down a steaming platter of golden American fries with onions.

"Bon appétit," the chef said. With a flourish, he swept back into the kitchen.

They split the fries and commenced to consume this "lumberjack" breakfast. Afterward, they leaned back in their chairs and let the fine fare percolate while they sipped a refill of coffee. It was time to earn their keep. They brought their dishes to the kitchen sink.

"Bonjour, mes amis!" Pierre greeted them. "Did you enjoy petit déjeuner?"

"Mais oui!" replied Mark. "It was très bon and we are ready for le travail."

"Excuse my patois of French and English, mes amis, but is my nature," Pierre said. "Glad you like breakfast, now allons-y, we begin day's travail."

Pierre motioned them to follow him towards what turned out to be the equipment shed. Bob and Mark had to hurry to keep up with his gait.

It was a large building that held more equipment in orderly array than they had ever seen in one place. It was a surplus WWII Quonset hut with a high, domed ceiling and sides covered by heavy corrugated steel panels bolted together. It had a concrete floor and was like being in a massive steel vault. Regular personnel doors were at each end; a wide garage door was at the side where the loading and maintenance took place. The side walls had a row of high windows for light. A narrow skylight ran the length of the building. It allowed ample working light on a sunny day. There were also several rows of fluorescent lights in case of dreary gray weather or for nighttime use. Pierre told them a large gas generator hidden in a sound-proofed shed supplied the property's electrical needs. No commercial electric service was available that far from Ely.

Various sizes and makes of canoes were stored on wooden racks closest to the large door. They were arranged on multiple levels and could be lowered and raised by clipping their bow and stern lines to cables. The overhead lift system rolled on a track and pivoted for positioning over any canoe. Canoes were then raised or lowered by using sets of pulleys and ropes to make it effortless. The types of craft varied from solo kayaks and canoes to tandem Royalex hulls that were tough and durable. Every category of equipment had its own special place which made finding various items a breeze. The well-though-out system demonstrated why Border Waters was a top outfitter. Mark felt privileged to be a part of it.

Pierre passed by carrying cartons of food. He was singing an old voyageur chanson! He wore a red beret that sat at a jaunty angle atop his head. He never seemed to complain and often sang while he worked. Mark looked up again, and Pierre was standing before them holding a list. He waited until their eyes met his and spoke.

"Here is gear we need assemble for client trip," Pierre explained. "All items must be in good shape. Sleeping bags need airing outside. Make repair as necessary, s'il vous plaît. Make piles of gear, double check later. Déjeuner at noon. Bonne chance, mes amis."

Bob let out a low whistle and said, "Waugh, this is some place, eh?"

"Yes, indeed," agreed Mark. "Let's get to work on this list and show them we can hustle. If there's anything that needs mending, set it aside. I found a heavy duty sewing kit with various sizes of needles, waxed cord and carpet thread."

Mark opened the overhead door to allow the morning sun and fresh breeze to speed the work. It promised to be a bluebird day. He and Bob had been taught how to mend canvas wall tent tears and to make many other repairs. They had worked with epoxy, fiberglass, and resin to repair canoe hulls, overseen by Ray Bond during class field trips. Bob tore into the tents. He checked their overall condition while searching for tears and stuck zippers and to make sure each set of tents was complete. Mark concentrated on sleeping bags, ground pads, life jackets and packs. All gear needing mending or missing parts was put in a separate pile.

For the party of seven they would take three tandem Royalex 18-foot canoes. They could carry a heavy payload, were stable and made to take rough abuse and ask for more. They were not as fast as fiberglass hull canoes and were heavy but bombproof. One of the smaller clients, probably Ruby, would need to sit in the center of one canoe with the gear. Pierre, Mark and Bob would take the stern position in each canoe to allow for optimum control.

They completed the list and were beginning to clean and make repairs when the lunch bell rang. Work stopped, and hunger propelled the two drooling engagés to the kitchen. It was a warm sunny day. A Weber grille was stuffed with juicy, broiled cheeseburgers. A Dutch oven was full of baked beans, and large bowls were filled with potato chips and sliced oranges and apples. A jug of ice tea and containers of milk rounded out the déjeuner. Walt came over while they ate to give them a heads up on the clients' schedule.

He waited until he had their attention before he spoke: "The clients should arrive sometime in the afternoon. They'll be tired from their long ride in the van. We'll give them a warm welcome and then show them to their sleeping quarters. They can explore the grounds and lodge or relax until supper. After supper, there will be a short meeting about tomorrow's trip. How do you like our equipment building and how goes the battle?"

Mark looked up, swallowed a bite of burger, and spoke: "It's like no other place! There is more gear than I've ever seen in one place, and it's so orderly. We're done with the trip list and will now make repairs as necessary."

"We also want to thank you and your staff," Bob added. "We can't believe the radio in our room! It brings in our favorite music on WLS!"

"Glad you like it here," replied Walt. "We appreciate your savvy about camp gear and your willingness to work hard until the job's done right. It seems that Ray knew best when he recommended you fellas! You two were fortunate to have Ray for a teacher about survival and camp lore. He is a fine man and a credit to his calling. I understand you guys will be joining Ray and his wife for a bonus trip in the BWCA in July."

"Yes sir!" answered Mark and Bob in unison. "We wondered if there might be some short-term work here before that trip begins."

"That has already been taken care of," Walt added. "We'll talk once you return from this trip. Tonight, after supper there will be a staff and client meeting to outline the trip and to answer any of the clients' questions. A staff briefing will follow the client meeting. If you finish repairing the camp gear before they arrive, take a break, have a swim, relax. Pierre will come to double check your assembled gear."

"Sounds like a good plan," Mark said over his shoulder. "Thanks for the heads up. Now it's back to work we go." He was happy to hear they were appreciated. He turned to Bob, who was just finishing his lunch.

"Are you going to be able to work after that humdinger of a lunch?" Mark asked.

Bob blushed and stammered, "S---shure boss, I mean, yes, boss man, I'll be OK"

They had a good laugh over Bob's comical reply and then dropped their plates in the kitchen sink. With bellies full and in good spirits, they hurried back to the equipment Quonset. Mark sat on a bench while he mended a torn seam on an old Duluth Pack.

"I've noticed Pierre can switch quickly between English and French and a patois of both," Mark observed. "Voyageurs also spoke with a patois in the fur trade days. It will be cool to learn of his ancestry and experiences. I'm sure he can tell us a lot about the fur trade, as well as his own life's story. No doubt he is a wealth of lore and experiences."

"Mais oui!" Bob agreed. "Even I might learn a few French terms. Between Pierre and you, I stand to sound like a French-Canadian voyageur at trip's end!"

By 2:30 that afternoon they had completed repairing and cleaning the camping equipment. They decided to leave the sleeping bags in the cleansing sunshine and light breeze to air out. Pierre would be by to check their work. Pierre would be head guide and chef in camp. He took charge of assembling all the camp food and menu planning. He was "The man."

Bob and Mark took a break and wandered down to the big dock. Some canoes and kayaks were pulled up on the sandy shore. A large pontoon boat with a 35 horsepower Johnson outboard was tethered to the dock. The boys chose a pair of plastic play kayaks that were made purely for fun. They had open cockpits and footrests, were short and could turn on a dime. The boys seated themselves and began maneuvers with the double-ended paddles. They raced around the cove just for fun. An impromptu race began around the swim raft and back to the dock. Bob plunged his paddle into the water, trying to stop before hitting the dock. They were both wet and laughing when they tied up the kayaks.

Just as they were climbing the hill back to the lodge, they heard a loud horn blow in the driveway. A large van had pulled in, and the clients were already piling out onto the gravel. There was much yawning, stretching and, most importantly, beaming.

First, they greeted the driver. He had thinning hair and was on the heavy side, but was jolly and glad to be out on terra firma. His name was Gus and he lived in Minneapolis. Next they met Cora, who couldn't hear their greetings until little Ruby pulled her around. Cora read Mark's lips and responded in a cheery but hoarse voice. It was a normal condition for deaf people since they can't hear their own voice. Ruby was quiet but sweet and held out her hand in their direction with a smile from ear to ear. Her other hand gripped Cora's tightly, indicating their already close friendship.

Jack, the young full blood Ojibway boy, walked towards them, and they shook hands. Mark was amazed at the strength of his good right hand. Jack's other arm hung uselessly at his side. He seemed happy as he smiled, with his jet black eyes shining.

The rest of the staff was now assembled and all had a pleasant social visit. Glenn, the Vietnam War vet, slid open the van's side door and easily swung his prosthetic legs down. After a little wobble, he gained control and headed toward the crowd. Mark watched him come and met him halfway. Glenn brushed his long brown hair out of his eyes and flashed a genuine smile. He extended a burly arm and again locked Mark and then Bob's hand like a vise. Often, when someone loses the use of a limb, their remaining limbs make up for the loss in strength.

After a short get together with the clients, Bob and Mark took them on a tour of the lodge and grounds. Then they dropped them off at the bunkhouse. Cora and Ruby were in one room; Glenn and Jack shared another. Mark and Bob returned to the clients' van and carried their overnight bags to their rooms. Mark reminded everyone about the planning meeting with the staff following supper. It was time to bid them "adieu" and return to meet Pierre.

As they approached the Quonset hut, Pierre met them. He said, "We pack gear now."

The Border Waters van was waiting. It had a trailer hitched behind that could carry four canoes. They helped Pierre lower and load three Old Town Royalex eighteen-foot canoes, along with extra paddles and life jackets. The Snugpak sleeping bags that had been aired out on the clothesline were stuffed into compression bags. Pierre said they were unequaled for their warmth. They compressed to the size of a loaf of bread. One large canvas Duluth Pack would hold all of the party's sleeping bags and ground pads. Clients, if able, would be expected to carry small packs containing their personal gear. Mark and Bob helped Pierre pack up the sleeping bags, ropes, repair kits for the gear, canoes, first aid kits, and tarps. The fishing poles were loaded into long plastic tubes that attached under the crossbars and were safe from breakage during the trip.

Pierre had already loaded the trip food and kitchen gear bags. He slid open the van door and said, "Alors, mes amis. You hand me gear, I pack."

"Oui," answered Mark and Bob in unison. They heaved the big Duluth packs into the van, and Pierre packed all expertly with little room to spare.

"C'est fini," chirped Pierre. "Good job, très bien, mes hommes! Is near time for souper, go clean up."

"D'accord," answered Mark. Turning to Bob, he said, "Allons-y, mon ami, to bunkhouse we go."

They reminded the clients to listen for the supper bell and headed for the showers and fresh duds. Mark was ready early. He found a place where he could sit on a stump and watch the clients pass on their way to the lodge. The late afternoon sky was a pale blue with wispy clouds that had fanned out like tails. "Mares' tails" signaled a weather change in the near future. It should be a clear night. Mark hoped the moon would be visible. The Ojibway had a special name for each month's moon. The full moon for June was called Strawberry or Rose Moon. Mark liked the practical, earthy way the Ojibway assigned names for each month's full moon.

The dinner bell rang. Mark heard the bunkhouse door slam as the clients began meandering toward the lodge. Jack was out in front with his bronze legs pumping while his jet-black hair streamed behind. He moved smoothly and fast. His left arm was the only thing not in synch. Behind Jack came Cora and Ruby. They walked hand in hand. They were happy and gave sight, hearing and friendship to each other. It was a mutual blessing that created a special bond. Mark waved at them. Cora saw him and waved back. She turned and spoke to Ruby who quickly gave a wild wave with both arms. Mark began to see that there was wisdom in these pairings of clients that bordered on genius. The good doctor had outdone himself. Mark stood in awe of the man.

Last in the entourage was Glenn. His artificial legs flashed in the slanting rays of the northern sun. He made good, steady progress across the uneven lawn and leaned forward to climb the rise up the hill. He had spent a couple years in rehab and more time in a wheelchair. He began walking on his artificial, state-of-the-art prosthetic legs and feet a year and a half ago. His upper body strength was incredible. Mark didn't expect any major problems with Glenn mastering the rigors of the canoe trip. He had requested to carry his own pack. He had grit. He had come a long way from nearly losing his life in the steaming jungles and rice paddies of Southeast Asia.

Mark met Bob bringing up the rear. They walked up to the lodge and joined the throng milling around the lounge area. There was a bit of a chill outside, so the windows had been shut and a cheery fire started in the large stone fireplace that was accessible from three sides. Two tables had been pulled together to form a "V." That allowed everyone to visit and to see the lectern and overhead screen.

Walt stood and greeted everyone: "Good evening and welcome to the main lodge. Please enter the buffet line, fill your plates and enjoy."

As he followed the group to join the buffet line, Mark noticed how attentive Cora was to Ruby's special needs. Cora whispered each food item to her. If Ruby nodded, Cora added it to her tray. Jack tackled the buffet with no concern about his useless left arm. He merely held his tray and slid it along as he gathered what he wanted. When the buffet line ended, he simply held the tray of food against his hip with his good arm and walked to his chair. Glenn had no trouble with the buffet. He only struggled a bit while getting himself seated.

Mark once again was amazed at the quality of the meal. There were platters of steaming roast turkey, dressing, gravy and mashed potatoes. There was also a separate salad bar.

"Man," whispered Bob, "if we can walk out of here after this feast tonight, they should hand out medals!"

"Mais oui," Mark agreed. "It's a dandy supper! The infusion of protein and carbs are just the ticket for the grueling day to come."

Later, after most of the staff and clients had finished, Walt stood with his glass raised. He tapped it smartly with his knife. It created a clear tone that brought total silence.

"If you're ready for dessert and coffee or tea, please stay seated," Walt announced. "It will be brought to you directly and your plates taken away at the same time. Right after dessert we'll have a meeting right here. I'll outline your Boundary Waters trip route and other pertinent information and will answer any questions you may have."

The chef's apple pie dessert was made from Cortland apples out of Bayfield, WI, where the proximity of Lake Superior and the higher elevation produce excellent apples. It was the perfect ending to a delicious "comfort" meal. The delicious pie was served with Columbian organic java.

Just as they were enjoying refills of the rich brew, Walt stood up and pulled a projection screen down. He placed an overlay transparency on the overhead projector. A huge map appeared on the screen. As he adjusted the focus, everyone moved their chairs for a good view. The room lights were doused, and their intended trip route lay before them.

Walt spoke, "You will begin here." He held a long wooden arrow as a pointer and jabbed it into the Mudro Creek entry. "You will start tomorrow morning from the parking lot at five a.m. We will take both vans. The trip to Mudro Lake and the Chainsaw Sisters parking lot will take about an hour. Once there, you will portage all the canoes and gear alongside Mudro Creek to the nearby canoe landing. From that point, you will be on your way with head guide Pierre and assistant guides Mark and Bob."

Walt moved the pointer from Mudro Creek across Mudro Lake to the far right shore.

"From the landing the portage trail climbs gradually to a hilltop before it drops down a steep slope," he explained. "It is festooned with exposed boulders and slick mud to the landing on Sandpit Lake. It will be your most difficult portage of the trip and seems longer than eighty-three rods. For your information, a rod is an old surveyor measurement that equals sixteen-and-a-half feet.

"Then you will reload the gear into the canoes and paddle the length of Sandpit Lake while staying close to the right shoreline. There are three reasons for this. If trouble strikes, the shore and safety is close. Second, the portage landing to Tin Can Mike Lake is best approached from that side. Last, this is best way to view wildlife. Please keep your body low when entering or departing the canoe. This keeps your center of gravity low and prevents a dunking. Always wear your life jacket when in the canoes, because accidents happen without notice. The water is still cold. Trying to swim in clothing and boots is difficult. Fifteen minutes in the frigid water can lead to hypothermia. Canoeists have survived swimming to shore, but were unable to start a fire and warm up their core temperature.

"Your landing at the end of the far northeast shore will be at what was once an old steam train railroad bed that was used to carry timber south to mill towns. It is a relatively flat one-hundred thirty-five-rod portage with a nice elevated boardwalk that carries you over a marsh to the large rock slab landing where you enter Tin Can Mike Lake. You will then paddle across Tin Can Mike Lake by heading north to the end of the bay. The portage trail makes a short uphill climb and levels off before it begins a gradual descent to end the eighty-five-rod portage at the south end of Horse Lake. This is your final destination lake. You must still paddle through the narrows and follow the right shore. As you enter the main part of the lake, look for a vacant campsite near the Horse River entry. Everything hinges on finding either one of two sites vacant, as it will be your base camp for the rest of the trip. With luck you should have the camp all set up by late tomorrow afternoon, with ample time after to do what you want. You may fish, explore, hike or just relax."

Walt stabbed at various points on the map and continued, "As you can see, there are numerous areas to explore on Horse Lake. This includes the remains of an old logging camp that operated on the southwest shore kettle in the early nineteen hundreds; a resort was once located on the opposite end of the lake. It was one of many resorts that were built in the Boundary Waters area before it was finally designated a National

Wilderness in 1964. If the commercial resort and logging interests had their way, that whole area would have belonged to the wealthy, with the attendant power boats, roads for four-wheelers, and sea planes; and the pristine lake shores would be lined with resorts and palatial homes.

"There are other potential day trip options. The nearby Horse River takes you to Basswood Lake that offers waterfalls and Indian pictographs. Another option would be to paddle across Horse Lake and take the Fourtown Lake portage to Tin Can Mike Lake that you passed through coming in. It has some nice size largemouth bass and pike in its waters. We also secured a primitive management area (PMA) permit for the area north of the old resort site. It will allow you to attempt to find evidence of a portage trail that once connected the resort to a small lake to the north. Just remember that there is no set schedule. Weather controls where and when you travel. You will not be expected to travel when inclement weather occurs. There may be a day when you may be "wind bound" and forced to seek temporary shelter or stay in camp.

"Where you're going, nature rules, and man has to bow to her will or take risks and suffer the consequences. Those who have tried to impose a rigid timetable and achieve a destination despite conditions, or run wild rapids instead of portaging, have lost all their gear, destroyed canoes, and sometimes paid for their folly with their very lives! Yes, people die in the Boundary Waters every year. It is often due to carelessness, impatience or contempt for nature. Some people are used to having total control and instant gratification.

"You should challenge yourselves, stretch your limits and listen to your guides. They have much experience and use common sense. Safety is paramount. A medical emergency can become a tragedy in such a remote area. Pierre will have a walkie-talkie in case of such an emergency or if there is a change of plans. Now are there any questions?"

Glenn's hand went up. He had an Alabama accent and drawled, "What kind of fish are there in these lakes and what bait or lures should we have?"

Walt replied, "Walleye, smallmouth and largemouth bass, pike, perch and some panfish. As for bait, you will carry in some night crawlers. Pierre sets a minnow net, but artificial lures work well. Mepps spinners, beetle spins, jigs, Rapala minnows and small spoons all work. A fly rod can be effective when using poppers, streamers or flies. You may have favorites of your own, or the guides can supply some. Since you don't have any solo canoes this trip, you'll need to fish two or three in a canoe or cast from shore.

"Chances are good that there will be at least a few rainy or blustery days during the stay at your camp. It's a good time to fish, read, sleep or sit around the campfire. Pierre always has hot coffee, tea and some surprise meals! There are enough fishing reels and rods available for all, as well as replacement rod tip guides and repair kits in case of breakage. Any other questions about fishing should be directed to your able guides once you are set up. Pierre knows Horse Lake and the connecting lakes, and Bob and Mark know fishing."

Cora, who was adept at lip reading, raised her hand and asked, "What about the toilet facilities at the campsite?"

Walt chuckled, then answered, "Well, Cora, that's a great question! The facility is basic as possible! There's a fiberglass pit toilet, or 'throne', at the end of a short trail at the rear of the site. It is situated to be fairly well hidden from view. However, the guides will erect a tarp that will better conceal it. A red flag on a stick should be raised above the tarp when occupied and lowered when you vacate. Something else to remember is to keep your flashlight handy, so you can safely find your way to and from the toilet at night. A roll of toilet paper will be placed inside a plastic bag. Please return the tissue to the bag to keep it dry and notify a guide when it's running short."

Cora asked another question, "What is the possibility of trouble with bears?"

"They are rarely a problem," Walt answered. "Usually a nuisance bear is due to a careless camper who leaves food out or takes snacks into their tent. Once a bear finds he can raid a pack or scare campers away from their food he becomes a problem. You should do whatever you can to protect your food supply. Bear have a superior sense of smell. They have been known to smell fragrant items like bacon for miles. It's important to keep a clean camp. All leftover food, including unwanted snacks, spoiled food and packaging must be burned completely. If you encounter a bear near camp, stand your ground, raise your arms and shout, and throw rocks. Do anything but run. Black bear have attacked people in rare instances in the wild, but consider yourself lucky to even see one at a distance. Your chances of being struck by lightning are far better."

When there were no more questions, Walt introduced the guides, in case anyone didn't catch their names earlier. Mark and Bob stood when their names were called, as did Pierre. When all the clients' questions had been answered, Walt dismissed them until 5 a.m. Walt asked the guides to remain for a short meeting.

He spoke to the guides. "I just have a few last-minute details, guys. The vans are packed, fueled and ready to go. I'll drive the outfitter van. Pierre will take the client van. Their driver, Gus, caught a Greyhound Bus back to the Minneapolis area and will return here to drive the clients home. Make a final check to be sure we haven't forgotten anything critical. Pierre has the list.

"Mark and Bob will be expected to haul the majority of the packs and canoes on the portages. Rest well and be prepared to do multiple trips. The clients may choose to carry a pack of their personal gear, but nothing is expected of them except to be careful and enjoy the time. Be alert to their needs and remember this trip will remain deeply ingrained in their memories, be it good or bad. Since they do have various disabilities and are new to wilderness living, you will need to be vigilant and put their needs before yours.

"Pierre has the radio in case of an emergency or schedule change for your departure. The clients' van will remain at the parking lot. I will have our van and their driver waiting at the Chainsaw Sisters Saloon parking lot at the scheduled date and time. Do the final gear check now, then get a good rest and we'll meet next early tomorrow."

Mark and Bob followed Pierre to the vans to make a final check. Nothing was amiss.

"C'est fini!" Pierre said, "See you tomorrow morning at five, mes amis."

"D' accord, Pierre!" Mark replied. "Sleep well, mon ami."

He and Bob made their way down the hill to the bunkhouse. The lake was like a reflecting pool. A lone beaver created a V-shaped wake on its surface while a lonesome loon called from a distance. The evening sky was gorgeous. Fluffy clouds were stacked against the horizon. All was tinged crimson against a pastel blue skyline.

The rookie guides stopped to admire the majestic sight and once again agreed that the best things in this world are free. They knew darkness would soon claim the natural beauty, and they needed some time to unwind. Soon after entering their room, they donned sweat pants and lay back on their bunks. It was exciting to be on the verge of their baptism in the boundary waters.

After chatting awhile about their day and the coming trip, Mark got up and wandered over to the old Zenith radio. His fingers turned the massive volume knob. After the initial humming faded, it was replaced by the strains of WLS, Chicago's golden oldies station. The beginning notes of one of the greatest duos, The Righteous Brothers' *Unchained Melody*, pulsed wonderfully through the big bass speakers. Both of them lay back to enjoy it with the lights out. Except for the soft glow from the lighted radio dial, darkness prevailed. The old hit songs flowed magically, along with zany commentary from Dick Biondi. The Tokens sang *The Lion Sleeps Tonight*, while Bob and Mark hummed along with the strange, primitive lyrics. It may have been their only hit song. "One hit wonders" were common in the '50s and '60s. There was more opportunity for an unknown singer to break into the pop charts, unlike the present where fewer "name" artists monopolized the music. Mark had followed some of the singers' success stories, such as how Elvis Presley cut his first record while employed as a truck driver. His meteoric success as "The King" forever changed rock and roll. Another unusual success was Rick Nelson. He had his start as a young boy on a TV sitcom, The Adventures of Ozzie and Harriet. This was his real family! Rick and brother Dave Nelson and their parents were a weekly series hit. Rick would always play his guitar and sing during the episodes. It was appropriate that the next song featured Rick Nelson's hit, *Poor Little fool*.

Next came a run of instrumentals: the poignant *Moon River, Stranger on the Shore, Greenfields, Cast Your Fate to the Wind, A Walk in the Black Forest, Pipeline, Telstar,* and *Apache*. Biondi switched suddenly to the British invasion groups and played hits by the Dave Clark Five, the Beatles, Herman's Hermits, the Kinks, Chad and Jeremy, Petula Clark, Dusty Springfield and more.

Enthralled by the music, time passed unnoticed until the hour was late. With their biological clocks winding down, both agreed to call it quits. It was time to take a quick shower and hit the bunks. Mark knew there wouldn't be time in the morning. It would be a long time until he could indulge in such luxury. Swimming or rolling a canoe over were the only options once the trip began. When he returned to the room, Bob was zoned out. Mark quietly silenced the radio and slipped under the sheets. He listened to the breeze whispering in the pines, and then heard nothing.

Chapter Thirteen

Into the Boundary Waters
The First Day

A loud, familiar noise woke them in the dark. It took a moment for their heads to clear and to realize the dinner bell was being used as a wakeup alarm! Covers were kicked off. Mark hit the light switch and they dressed quickly. Dress for the trip included light nylon pants, hooded sweatshirts, knee boots and camouflage "boonie" hats. Mark wore a pair of light wool socks in his boots. He found they insulated his feet when wet, unlike cotton socks which chill a person and take forever to dry.

After a trip to the bathroom, they left the bunkhouse and headed for the vans which were idling with the lights on and awaiting passengers. Mark climbed into the clients' van. Pierre was behind the wheel. Bob joined Walt in the outfitter van. Cora and Ruby looked sleepy, but were appropriately dressed and approaching his van. Mark jumped out and opened the van's side door for them.

"Good morning!" Mark called to them.

"Good morning!" the girls chimed as one.

Mark helped them enter the van, buckled Ruby in, and slid the door closed. He noticed Bob helping Glenn and Jack load their personal gear. Glenn was agile despite his disability. He climbed into the van and seated himself without help. He even gave a hand to Jack when he climbed in. It pleased Mark to see the cooperation between the clients.

Pierre motioned for Mark to return to his seat. Once in the van, Pierre presented Mark with a big travel mug of fresh, hot java and a roll studded with nuts. Mark brightened at the pastry and java! He made it all disappear quickly. As he dined, he noticed Ruby and Cora happily enjoying their rolls and drinks. Ruby's eyes were dead and staring into space, but a smile lit up her face.

Pierre spoke: "We follow Walt to Mudro Lake access. It take hour. Enjoy petit déjeuner; it be last food but jerky. At camp, after camp set up, I make déjeuner."

The remainder of the drive went well, with Pierre regaling the crew with stories of incidents, good and bad, on former trips. He referred to Ruby as a "petite jeune fille" which made her laugh. She and Cora came up with a name for Pierre, "canuck." It was a bit derogatory, but Pierre laughed and was pleased. He said it was better than being called either "pork eater" or "late to supper!" Mark asked what the term, "pork eater" meant in the days of the voyageur and the fur trade.

"It applied to short-term voyageur substitutes, who would rather eat pork and stay near home during winter than make the commitment of three years contract as engagés, who suffered winter in the wilderness," Pierre explained.

The van turned off the main road onto the Echo Trail, a gravel road which climbed some decent hills and snaked around curves. Deer stood near the road, their eyes reflecting the headlights, looking spooky. A few deer ran across in front of the van, causing Pierre to swerve and brake to avoid a collision. They turned right onto a narrower, rougher road where a large circular saw blade had "Chainsaw Sisters Saloon" painted on it and an arrow pointing the way. Cora asked how the saloon got its name, but first asked Ruby to be her ears, since she couldn't see to read Pierre's lips.

Pierre said, "There were two young women, sisters, who once worked as seasonal Forest Service employees. Their job was to keep roads and camper trails free of fallen trees and limbs, using axes and chainsaws. The piece of land at the Mudro access came available and they decided to buy. They put up a small bar and charged campers by the day to park their vehicles while in the BWCAW. They sell beer, pop, snacks and pizza to a captive audience. Saloon near, see it now? Parking lot near full at first light."

Mark asked, "With so many people already out in the wilderness, could we have trouble getting the campsite we want?"

"C'est vrais," Pierre responded, "It always risk, but it not holiday. Is worse time July through August. Mark and Bob find out when camp with Ray."

After finding two parking spots, the crew piled out and began unloading. Packs and canoes were portaged the short distance along Mudro Creek to the landing. There was a lot of groaning and laughter, but everyone pitched in. Since Bob, Mark and Pierre took the three canoes on their first trip, the packs could be put directly into them as they floated in shallow water. The guides made sure the packs were placed so the canoes would be balanced when underway.

Once everything was loaded into the three Old Town Royalex canoes, Pierre announced each person's position in the canoes. Pierre, Mark and Bob would sit in the stern of the three canoes. That position allows them the best control. Pierre's canoe had Cora in the bow and little Ruby riding amid-ships with the packs. Mark had Jack in the second, and Bob and Glenn manned the third canoe.

"Before we go there be some rules!" Pierre announced. "Never stand up in canoes. Stay low in crouch when get in or out. That is time when canoe trouble come. Watch for deadheads and boulders. Can damage canoes. If see trouble ahead, warn others, so can avoid. Clients will enter canoes now. Guides will shove canoes off. Bonne chance, mes amis, we go."

Pierre shoved his canoe off, hopped expertly into the stern and began paddling down the creek. Mark and Bob followed him, but had to jump out to push again when their canoes got stuck. They finally floated free and paddled on.

Soon they heard Cora cry out a warning: "Boulder on the left and another coming up on the right side!"

Jack and Glenn did the same for their partners. Other than a few glancing blows and trouble making the sharp creek bends, they safely entered Mudro Lake. All followed Pierre's lead along the right shore. Being near the shore was good in case of any trouble and to view the natural shoreline beauty and spot any passing wildlife.

The early morning calm made the lake look like glass. An overcast sky portended some rain later, but it was ideal for travel at the moment. Mark knew that as the sun rose and warmed the earth, the wind would pick up. Planning to paddle early or late in the day was wise. Traveling late in the day to make time can lead to being caught in the dark and unable to find a vacant campsite. It's better to find a campsite by mid-day.

Mudro was a smaller lake that was passed through quickly as a stepping-stone to distant lakes. Its one campsite saw little use. Most people were passing through toward Crooked Lake and beyond or heading home. Mark had seen some large swirls in the creek that was proof of big fish. It was certainly lightly fished. The same could be said for the next lake called Sandpit Lake. It also had only one campsite and was generally just a travel conduit. However, fatigue, bad weather or injury might force a night's stay. The steep, rock-strewn portage between Mudro and Sandpit was enough in itself to inspire an overnight. It was smart to be rested and fresh before tackling it in the cool of the morning.

It took about fifteen minutes to cross Mudro Lake. The portage to Tin Can Mike loomed at the end of a bay. Mark and Jack were in the last canoe. They waited a short distance from the small landing to allow the others room to dock. Pierre stepped out and guided his canoe to shore while avoiding the rocks. He steadied the canoe while Cora and Ruby climbed out. He then tied the bow rope to one side and began lifting packs out and placing them out of the way. When it was unloaded, he swung the Old Town canoe yoke onto his shoulders and disappeared up the trail. Cora carried her personal pack. Ruby had a small pack and held onto Cora's hand as they followed Pierre.

After Bob had landed and unloaded, Mark brought his canoe in. He jumped out and allowed Jack to get out and tie it to a tree root. Since this was a well-used route, they kept the center of the landing clear in case other groups came through. The long, rough portage began. Multiple trips were required of the staff.

Mark knew they were about to earn their pay the hard way. He and Bob wore wide brimmed "boonie" hats that protected from the harsh sun, wind and insects. The deerflies were relentless in the woods. Bob lifted his canoe and began carefully negotiating the steep, boulder-strewn trail. Mosquitoes extracted a toll in blood.

Cora and Ruby made their way with Ruby holding onto Cora's belt loop, while groping with her other hand. Glenn was making slow but sure progress and was actually helping Jack while carrying his pack.

Bob and Mark made numerous trips back and forth. They were glad for the cooler morning air, but still sweated profusely. They had stripped down to tee shirts and wore improvised sweatbands made from their hankies. Finally, they grunted the last load of gear down the hill they had christened "the lung burner."

They shook hands as they reached the bottom of the hill and were pleased to find their canoes were loaded and tied up. Pierre and the girls had already shoved off and were slowly making their way along the right shore of Sandpit Lake. A fitful breeze was stirring but it was still gentle. Mark was glad for his polarized sunglasses. The sky had cleared and the glare on the water caused eyestrain without protection.

As they paddled down the clear, narrow lake, the great numbers of tree trunks lying on the bottom impressed Mark. Thick woods, and a steep hill that rose at least a hundred yards up, bordered their side of the lake. Mark watched a turkey vulture ride the thermals, rocking sideways as it steadily circled while searching for telltale death throes.

Jack motioned that he wanted to try to catch Bob's canoe. Mark nodded, grinned and they paddled hard. Jack had a strong right arm. He found that if he used the fingers on his good arm and his teeth, he could lash the paddle shaft to his bad arm and paddle better. It was a stealthy approach. They soon gained on Bob's and Glenn's unsuspecting canoe.

They remained quiet until they caught Bob's canoe. Mark spoke as they silently drew alongside.

"En garde, engagés," Mark joked. "Jack suggested we challenge your lead, and, I must say, he is tough. He prefers being called by his nickname, Jacko, by the way."

"You said it," Glenn remarked. "If I ever have a son, I'd like him to be like Jacko."

"Our bodies will really be barking by morning," Bob groaned. "I'm very glad that was the worst portage we'll have."

"Mais oui!" exclaimed Mark. "It's as bad as they said. It makes you appreciate how important the waterways were for the Ojibway and voyageurs. It took us many tough trips and an hour's time to portage our gear a short distance. We've traveled many times further by paddling and in only a fraction of the time. Look! There's the portage to Tin Can Mike Lake."

Mark and Jacko slacked their pace to allow Bob and Glenn to make the landing. While they slowly paddled on, Mark recalled what Walt had said about the portage trail ahead. He remembered that it followed the old rail bed once used to haul logs out of Horse Lake. The Hopkins and Swallow Lumber Co. ran it. It used a steam locomotive on a narrow gauge track to take timber out via Range Lake that was now behind them to the south. As their canoe drew closer to the landing, Mark saw the sheer rock cliff that came within a few feet of the lake. It meant that part of the track had to be extended out into the lake with pilings and timbers to avoid hitting the cliff.

The cramped landing area dictated that Mark and Jacko would have to wait until the landing was less busy. Bob, Pierre and crew had already portaged their canoes and were on their second trip. They were making good time on the fairly straight and level trail.

"Mark," Jacko asked. "What did the steam engine burn for fuel? How did the train get turned around to haul the logs out?"

"I'm sure the train mainly burned coal for fuel," Mark answered. "But they probably started a fire with dead hardwood in the locomotive's firebox and switched to coal which burns hotter and longer than wood. You're correct about there not being room or means to turn the engine around. The simple solution was to run in forward and back out loaded, or vice-a-versa. Ideally it would be nice to be able to disconnect the engine and pivot it so the loaded cars could be pushed out. There would have been a small coal tender right behind the locomotive. They probably left a pile of coal at the camp for use there. It's possible they were able to rig a steam driven device to pull logs from the lake and snake them to where they were lifted and stacked on the flatcars. There were more questions than answers."

Mark and Jacko had landed and were making their first trip down the old rail grade. It was a cakewalk compared to the "lung burner" portage. They met Pierre and Bob returning for more gear. Pierre and Bob followed standard portage courtesy and gave them the right of way by standing off the trail.

"Is good trail, no?" Pierre called, as he passed by.

"Straight as a flèche" Mark responded.

"What is a flèche?" Jacko inquired.

"It means arrow in French," Mark replied. "We use a form of it in the word fletch, or fletching, which refers to the feathers which are attached to an arrow's shaft for stability."

Though this portage was twice as long as the last, all the gear was moved and loaded in half the time. There were some scattered cheers as the guides shoved off. Pierre's canoe quickly crossed the halfway point on tin Can Mike Lake. But one portage remained before they entered their destination, Horse Lake. The breeze had increased, but pushed them towards their goal.

Tin Can Mike had numerous interesting bays with high cliffs on the right side. There were two small, rocky islands on the southwest end and three campsites on the north end. A pair of loons was fishing about fifty yards away from Mark's canoe. One swam with its head underwater as it searched for a meal. It was Ruby's first time to "see" a loon. It was made possible via Cora's vivid description of this avian anomaly. It was not a duck, goose or a raptor, but flew through air and water.

As part of a research assignment for Ray Bond's course, Mark uncovered some cruel human past behavior. He read about how people thought it great sport in the late 1800s and early 1900s to shoot loons and let them rot. It echoed the white man's attempt to annihilate the native bison and timber wolves. These beasts which were sacred to the Native Americans were systematically slaughtered, poisoned and trapped. Passenger pigeons that once blackened the sky had become extinct due to over hunting. The pioneering European settlers repeated their abuse of wild beasts in the "Old Country". They took the Biblical imperative to heart and almost "subdued" the marvelous creations out of existence. So much for man's attempt at being the "caretakers" of the Earth and its creatures. Despite the murderous assault, a remnant survived. Native tribes, including the Ojibway, forsook their spiritual brotherhood with the forest creatures when tempted by the white Europeans' trade goods and liquor. Their ancient code of taking only enough to survive was replaced with indiscriminate slaughter of any animal that would please the traders. They became slaves to strangers from distant lands and surrendered their country and value system for a song. Their wise men failed to resist the evil that promised a better life as "the king's children" and instead stole their sacred lands and left them destitute both spiritually and physically when the beaver and buffalo were gone.

Ruby was enthralled with Cora's loon description and the variety of its calls. She tried to mimic the call while holding Cora's hand on her throat so Cora could feel the vibration. Bob and Mark burst into laughter! Ruby's version sounded like a cross between a weird yodel and a scream! But Cora smiled and gave her a big hug.

"Look, over on the left shore," interjected Jacko. He pointed out two yearling deer. They were well hidden by shoreline vegetation. Everyone agreed he had an eagle's eyesight. Jacko was proud to have spotted the deer that nobody else had noticed.

He had an inborn talent, honed by living under his grandfather's tutoring in the old ways. His people once dominated the whole area. They were nomadic warriors and lived in separate clans. They followed the game, fish, wild fruits and wild rice by season. The men hunted, fished and sometimes fought their bitter enemy, the Sioux. They were wise about the plants and animals and made effective use of them for food, healing and clothing. They were able to see all the forest and water creatures as part of a spiritual brotherhood. They killed what was needed for food, tools and clothing, wasting nothing. They hacked out their living from nature and were free men. They were subject only to their Great Spirit, Gitchi-Manitou, and owed no allegiance to any man. Their unique birch bark canoes were superior because of their light weight, cargo capacity and ease of repair. Canoes were used for gathering food, making war on enemies and to travel great distances. Other tribes made dugout canoes. Dugouts were much heavier and hard to maneuver, but were sturdy. They stood more abuse without needing repair, but were difficult to carry on portages. Life was full of compromise, then, as now.

Mark thought it was good that Jacko had his grandfather to teach him the old ways. Mark hoped to learn about the Ojibway way of life by picking Jacko's brain. He didn't expect to learn about life from everyone on the trip, but it happened anyway.

As the crew paddled through Tin Can Mike Lake they located the first campsite on the left. It was on a short, rocky point with a small bay on either side. As usual, the fire grate and log square were near the end of the point, while the tent sites were further up the steep rock path. It was vacant. Wild purple iris bloomed invitingly at the end of the point.

Right after the trio of canoes passed the campsite, Bob pointed to the right. Another campsite appeared just around a point. Soon they saw the last point on the left just before the portage. The fire pit was very exposed. Behind it stretched nothing but a narrow, rocky peninsula, for a long way. It wasn't a "four star" site but could be handy in a pinch.

Mark could see the lighter area ahead where many had trod. The heavy traffic had beaten the grass and soil off the portage landing. It exposed a light-colored area of sand, gravel and exposed roots. Once again, Mark back paddled and waited for Pierre and Bob to land and begin portaging. Mark noticed their first close encounter with fellow travelers was nigh as he jumped into the water and began unloading. It was a party of four men. The two in the lead were in their twenties, then a man in his forties and last in line was a man in his seventies. He took his time while carrying a smaller pack and paddles. It was a family group spanning three generations. The Boundary Waters draws all ages to its rugged beauty and wildness.

Mark greeted them in passing and made an inquiry of the old man: "Hello, old timer, where did your crew come from?"

"Hi," the old man said. "We just left Horse Lake, but we went as far as Basswood Lake to see the pictographs and fish and now are heading home. We spent five days fishing and away from phones and traffic, but my grandsons need to go back to work at their jobs. My son and I are looking forward to a hot shower and home-cooked food. We have wounds to nurse and heal before next year's trip!"

Everyone laughed at that. They waved as they shoved off. Just before they got underway, the old man mentioned they had just vacated the site nearest the entry to the Horse River, in case Mark's party was interested! Mark thanked him with a double arm wave and hoped they might be in luck. Mark and Jacko hurried to catch up with the rest of their party. Mark shouldered the canoe, while Jacko carried the life jackets and paddles over his good shoulder.

The fairly easy portage began with a little climb, then leveled off quickly and began a gradual descent with a steep finish near the landing on the southwest end of Horse Lake. There was a fallen tree trunk to step over, which Mark did without losing stride; Jacko clambered over it easily, using the paddle for balance. Everyone was waiting at the landing. It was time for a hard-earned snack and water break. Pierre called the rest break a pose, a fur trade term, when the voyageurs would smoke their clay pipes. A portage's distance was calculated by the number of poses taken, generally every half mile or less, depending on how difficult the terrain was.

"Pierre!" Mark said, breathlessly. "The party of four guys we just passed just left the campsite we want, next to the Horse River entry!"

"Très bien!" Pierre responded. "Now, dépêchez-vous! We need go capture site before others do."

Mark told the others to leave. He and Jacko still had a few more trips to make. They would catch up. Pierre handed Mark and Jacko some jerky strips and a water bottle before shoving off. Pierre and Bob paddled hard toward the narrows. The wind had strengthened but remained at their sterns. Mark figured that further down in the open lake there would be whitecap conditions. Two more trips completed their portage, and then they paddled along the right shore and into the narrows.

They came upon a few old logs leftover from the logging days that had been driven deep into the lake bottom. In winter, holes were chopped through the ice. Teams of wagons pulled by horses positioned logs to act as staging areas, where the logs could be attached to cables. Anchor points were also driven on shore. The group spotted a large steel ring that was still tightly embedded in the ledge below a rock dome at the narrows. Some of the anchor logs had been cut off, but depending on changes in water levels could lie just below the surface, invisible until an unlucky canoe struck it. The dark water in Horse Lake made these and submerged boulders a real hazard, especially when rough water camouflaged their presence.

As Mark and Jacko passed through the narrows and entered the main lake, they began to feel their stern raised up by rollers that propelled them faster. The rollers could cause trouble if the canoeists were caught off guard. If the rollers strike from behind, the canoe's stern is pushed upward; it can dump a paddler overboard or cause the loss of a paddle. The longer a canoe runs with the wind, the rollers continue to increase. Soon they begin to break over the gunnels and begin filling the canoe. Jacko was hit by some spray, but didn't panic and paddled on.

"Jacko," Mark shouted. "Look. Pierre is at the campsite up ahead and is waving his paddle high up! It's a good omen, right?"

"Yes," Jacko said. "It may sound foolish to you, but I know you study my people, the Ojibway, so I will tell you. Before we left the Mudro landing I made tobacco offering to the Great Spirit Gitchi-Manido and to Manidog, spirit of the trees and water, asking for safe passage."

"It could be you saved our necks and also gave us the campsite we wanted!" replied Mark. "I do honor the old Ojibway lifestyle and appreciate your return to its way. I want to learn more about the Ojibway and your skills and thoughts. The old ways are disappearing. Most Indians dress in white man's clothes, driving cars and living like a white man."

Mark and Jacko soon arrived at the rocky point where a sandy landing on the Horse River side beckoned, protected from the wind. The other two canoes had been pulled up the shore and were tied to trees. Everyone was hauling gear to various areas and setting up camp. Some of the clients had previously asked to buddy-up with another. Cora and Ruby shared one tent; Jacko and Glenn shared another.

Pierre had his own tent and it was a dandy! It was a hybrid tent, resembling a scaled-down Sioux tipi. Its covering was made of natural white canvas, with high tensile aluminum poles for support. There was even a smoke pole, which could position the top flap for the best fire draft. In a real Sioux tipi, the outer covering would have been made of buffalo hides, and the poles would have been made from "lodge-pole" pines. A fire pit would be located in the floor's center. It would be circled with stones, and the smoke would exit through the smoke flap hole at its top. Buffalo hides would be spread over the tipi floor for sitting or for sleeping. Cooking vessels, hunting gear and ceremonial pipes and garb would be stacked against the sides.

The entry flap on Pierre's tent had been ornately decorated with glass beads by Pierre's wife, who was a full blood Sioux. Pierre chose a site further back, where he had a better view of the morning sun. Its entry door faced the east to welcome the rising sun. The crowning touch was the decorative outer tipi walls which were adorned with colorful images of handprints and Indian Paint and Appaloosa ponies with frightening faces. Over the entry were French, Canadian and American flags on feathered lances. The tipi weighed about 25 pounds, twice as heavy as Mark's tent. Mark was determined to ask Pierre if he could purchase one like it or have some help to make his own. He sneaked a quick look inside and would have liked to remain for a while, but other matters required his attention.

Bob and Mark first helped the clients unload and find tent sites. If the clients needed help to erect their tents, they happily obliged. The outfitter tents were designated as three-man size, but were more suited to two, with ample room to store gear and spread out. It was especially handy when severe weather forced its occupants to spend long hours inside, waiting for fair weather. Their tents were made of light canvas and nylon with no-see-um netting, and awnings, supported by poles in front to provide extra rain protection.

Once the clients were settled, Bob and Mark hauled their own tents and gear to a reasonably level site with some shade and wind protection. Mark set up his light canvas Eureka Timberline, while Bob wrestled with an old Sears Roebuck canvas umbrella tent. It was a little heavier than Mark's, but was a quick set-up and offered more headroom.

The morning had been long and tiring, but they headed over to help Pierre set up the cook tent. It was actually a large canvas tarp with numerous grommets for tying lines to nearby trees. A pole was used to raise the tarp's center, thereby shedding debris and rain. The tent was located near and shielded the fire pit sitting logs, as well as some small fold-up stools.

After helping Pierre unpack the food and kitchenware, Mark and Bob found a nearby pine that had a stout limb about 12 feet up. By using a stone for a weight, they tied the pulley rope end to it and tossed it over the limb. Bob cheered when Mark made it over on the first try, without getting the line tangled. He grabbed the line and raised the pulley up just below the limb. Bob tied the other end of the pulley rope to a tree trunk. The rope that ran through the pulley was tied to the food pack. Mark pulled on the free end and using the pulley's help, hoisted the pack to chest level. This allowed access during the day, but kept the food safe from mice and squirrels. Before night or when leaving camp, the food sack would be raised high, out of reach of bears.

Their last task was to erect the toilet tarp. While Pierre prepared lunch, they carried the tarp and a red flag and followed the well-worn trail that led to the toilet in the back. It was fairly well hidden, as Walt had said. It was located on a level area with full-bodied spruce trees giving some privacy. The toilet was a squared-off, olive drab, fiberglass affair. It featured a flat rock to place your feet on, while sitting on the "throne" or "thunder box," as some referred to it. Forest Service Rangers, when traveling in the BWCAW, check the "headspace" available, to determine when to schedule a crew to dig a new hole.

Mark and Bob found some dead poles and made three tripods lashed at their tops for strength and to be self-standing. Two were placed at opposite ends of the side facing the camp and one at right angles, facing the water. The tarp was stretched and tied to the tripods and to poles laid across the tripods. It formed a totally private, three-sided enclosure. Last, they cut a pole about eight feet long and tied a red flag to its top. It would be raised during occupancy and lowered when vacant. Two rolls of toilet paper were sealed into a plastic bag and set near the toilet. Bob and Mark stepped back to admire their work before they strolled back towards camp. On arriving, they found that Pierre had lunch almost ready.

"Déjeuner be in fifteen, mes amis," Pierre announced. "Take time to look the site over, relax. I ring bell when ready. You both did tough job well today, merci."

Bob and Mark clicked their heels together and saluted Pierre, knowing how it tickled him. Pierre's rich laugh rewarded their effort. They resisted chortling and held their salutes, standing at attention until Pierre made a snappy return salute.

"You two take me back to World War II," Pierre stated. "I be about your age, serve as grunt in U.S. Army."

As Mark and Bob walked slowly towards the point to catch a better view of the lake, they saw several canoes with full loads of men and packs leaving the Horse River inlet. The canoers fought the blustery winds and headed for the narrows. A few canoes were crossing Horse, coming towards them from Fourtown Lake. A few intrepid, possibly foolhardy souls, hugged the near shore, fighting the chop. Some wilderness travelers will take risks and embark, come hell or high water. A wise traveler would not take such risks. Nature follows no rigid schedule. A prudent visitor must respect her. There are old canoeists and there are bold canoeists; but there are no old, bold canoeists. Mark appreciated the fact that man still failed at controlling weather or the four seasons. In the end he was only dust in the wind, despite all his skill and power.

He and Bob were happy to be set up with everyone safe and no rigid schedule to keep. A ringing sound intruded on their break. It was the high-pitched ringing of the little dinner bell. It was more subdued than the one at the lodge so it didn't disturb nearby wilderness campers.

They were famished and hurried back to the kitchen. Everyone was standing in line with their plates. They happily chatted and laughed as they waited for their lunch.

Lunch was simple and sufficient. It featured chicken noodle soup, crackers, cheddar cheese, Zup's summer sausage, and fruit cocktail for dessert. Beverage choices were lemonade and hot tea. Pierre had set up a battered but sturdy collapsible table that he had spread with a white linen tablecloth. It was a classy touch for the buffet lunch.

"Fill plates, you had tough day," Pierre offered. "If we run out of anything, there be more. Enjoy déjeuner."

Mark and Bob, as usual let the clients go first, and then threw themselves on the spread. After heaping their plates, they carried them and mugs of hot jasmine tea to the fire. It was nice to sit down and enjoy a meal with the hungry crew. Everyone was in good humor and well fed.

Their job required them to keep a good supply of campfire wood. It was their only source for cooking and heat and was the center of camp life, especially in the evenings. Their site was highly popular, and the wilderness ethic forbade gathering firewood on site. They would need to search the nearby shorelines. After helping Pierre clean up the kitchen area, they tossed the paper plates and cups into the fire. Pierre saved some broken saltines to bait the minnow trap.

Mark asked about setting up the trap. Pierre invited Mark and Bob to come along. They left with the minnow trap already baited with cracker crumbs and walked along the shoreline until Pierre found a good place. A huge log lay on the bottom with its top underwater and its lower trunk and branches exposed. It created a natural haven for minnows and fingerling game fish. Pierre first tied the long cord to the ring in the center of the net. He then tossed it carefully so it settled between submerged limbs in about three feet of water. The minnows and small fish enjoy safety from larger predators by hiding in tight cover, besides finding minute organisms to feed on.

"Maybe we be lucky, catch minnows today," Pierre commented. "It be handy for fishing in morning, at narrows. After fishing, we explore old logging camp. Maybe engagés check later today. If find minnows, can try fish tonight. It time you work on gear and tackle. When done, take canoe, cut plenty firewood. Can check if anyone want go along. Bonne chance."

Bob and Mark saluted with poker faces while standing rigidly at attention and waiting for their salute to be returned. They had Pierre chuckling and left with silly grins. They finished packing their personal gear and inspected their fishing tackle. Next, they left to visit the clients. The first ones were Cora and Ruby. They were just leaving for the sandy shoreline to sit and relax out of the wind, with hopes to wade and explore for treasures.

Glenn and Jacko were just finishing up with their tent and gear setup and were anxious to go with Bob and Mark to collect firewood. Bob loaded two canoes with collapsible saws, hatchets and canteens. There were also leather gloves for all, since anytime sharp cutting tools come into use, injuries follow. They shoved off with Bob and Mark in the stern of each canoe and proceeded to fish the edge of the bay near the Horse River entry. The trees were a mix of jack pine, poplar, hardwood, spruce, balsam and birch. Any species of tree would work, as long as it was dead and dry. Mark knew from his experience that some trees might look dead, but still have sections that were alive and not usable.

With their knee boots, long pants, gloves and hats, the four campers were dressed properly. There were countless ways to wound one's body while navigating through brush piles and over slick, moss-covered tree trunks and rocks. Another necessary ingredient was good insect repellent. The gnats, mosquitoes and no-see-ums could be savage. Later in summer, other blood-sucking insects, such as deerflies, black flies, and ticks add to the misery. Mark had known some campers who couldn't escape these relentless carnivores. They were even attacked out in the middle of the lake in a canoe. At peak fly season, campsites with good exposure to prevailing winds are precious.

The continuing wind kept the insect predation on their wood gathering to a minimum. In an hour's time the center of both canoes was filled with nice fire-size chunks. Glenn worked hard. Like a lumberjack, he trimmed branches off the trees, while Bob, Jacko and Mark cut up the logs and hauled them to the canoes. Mark thought that "Jacko" had a nice ring to it.

Mark was just returning for another load when he heard a loud metallic ring and the chopping went silent. He hurried over to check out Glenn and was relieved to find him laughing and pointing to his prosthetic leg. He had swung the hatchet to cut a pine branch, but a springy branch caused the hatchet blade to ricochet and strike his leg!

Glenn smiled and said, "For the first time since I lost my legs and started wearing these, I'm thankful! It doesn't excuse my carelessness, but that would have been a nasty gash in a regular flesh and blood leg."

"Amen," Mark agreed. "Look where the hatchet blade struck! Only a tiny nick in the prosthetic alloy. Now that's some tough metal!"

Everyone chuckled and sat down. It relieved the tension that, under different circumstances, would have involved a serious medical situation. If immediate first aid failed to stop the bleeding, the next step was an evacuation to the Ely Clinic. A valuable lesson was learned, with a happy ending.

Out of the blue, Jacko popped a question to Glenn. "Glenn," Jacko began, "How did you lose your legs in the war?"

Mark and Bob immediately stiffened at Jacko's audacious inquiry, but they were counting on the friendship between them to help mellow things. Glenn raised the hatchet and sank it into the log. When he paused for a few moments, Mark braced himself for the worst. But then a smile appeared on Glenn's sweaty face! He patted Jacko affectionately on the head. Glenn took a seat on a smooth log, sighed deeply and brought out his hanky to wipe sweat off his face. Jacko fetched a water bottle and offered Glenn a cool drink. Glenn wordlessly accepted and drained it.

After wiping his mouth and expelling a lungful of compressed air, he was ready to answer Jacko. "It was in 1967, while on an extended LURP, or in layman's terms, a long-range recon patrol, in South Vietnam. My unit had been chewed up during an attack by North Vietnamese regulars. We were beating a hasty retreat towards our appointed LZ, or landing zone. My foot caught a hidden trip wire. There was a tremendous explosion and I blacked out. The next thing I knew, I woke up on a hospital ship with tubes exiting my body. I owe my life to my buddies and to our excellent medic Jimbo.

"I was near suicidal the first few months after the incident. My independence was gone. I was dazed, drugged and felt helpless and useless. Then I began to heal and grew antagonistic to those around me and was no fun to be with. About six months later, Jimbo made a surprise visit! He found me sitting in a wheelchair in my bathrobe, staring out at the grounds from the second floor balcony. It was the only place I felt at peace. Loud noises, like a car backfiring, still made me cringe and cover up.

"Jimbo and I hugged and cried for a long time. Neither of us knew if the other had survived the war! He had smuggled in some good red wine in a little flask, which we shared discreetly. Jimbo had done his tour of duty in remarkably good shape. He suffered only one serious injury when he caught some shrapnel in his leg. Other than a slight limp, he looked good as new. He asked me what I planned to do after I was released. I told him I was scared to death to leave and preferred not to think of it. He looked me in the eye and spoke:

'Glenn, I didn't tie tourniquets on your thighs and call in a medivac chopper that probably saved your life so you could have a pity party! You are refusing to face reality! You have to suck it up and try to regain your bruised dignity! If you don't have the guts to lick this, perhaps you need to seek help from a higher power. Sometimes life is cruel, but you need to get on with living. Without a spiritual shoulder to lean on, it's a long, tough road. I'm speaking this in love, Glenn. I'll leave you this little Bible with tabs marking pertinent passages.'

"After Jimbo left," Glenn added, "I ignored the book for a while but couldn't shake his words. In desperation, I began to read the marked verses and his comments in the margins. Long story short, I am a new man with a spiritual facet. I am a new creation. It has worked a small miracle and is a daily wellspring of strength. I no longer consider myself handicapped and am finding I can do anything I really put my mind to. Do I still have pain and anger? Yes, but it only makes me more determined. I now do volunteer visits to maimed vets and cannot only sympathize, but empathize. When I walk unaided into their rooms, they are ready to talk. I enjoy living once again."

Jacko drank this all in but wasn't done with his quest. "Why did you choose to fight in Vietnam?" Jacko continued. "Why were the U.S. troops at war there?"

Glenn hesitated, closed his eyes and inhaled deeply. He sighed and looked into Jacko's night-black eyes. He patted Jacko's head and chose his words carefully. His eyes had welled up with tears. Jacko put his good arm around his neck and listened.

"I had no choice, Jacko," Glenn began. "I was drafted right after I graduated from college. The U.S. government determined that it must fight communism in the steaming jungles and rice paddies of a poor country in Southeast Asia. The powers that be in America were positive that should the North Vietnamese Communists take over, it would start a chain reaction. This 'Domino Theory' predicted communism would ruthlessly spread and involve all surrounding countries in Southeast Asia.

"It started, innocently enough with sending U.S. Army advisers, who were there ostensibly to assist the U.S.-backed South Vietnamese leadership of 'Nam', with no combat involvement. That began in 1960. By the time I was drafted in '67, The U.S. Army, Marines, Air Force and Navy were heavily involved. They concentrated all their considerable firepower, including using B-52 bombers to destroy enemy troops and defoliate the jungle that hid them with a toxic herbicide called 'Agent Orange'. Another nasty method used was the dropping of large canisters of Napalm by low-flying planes. It was an incendiary gel that exploded and splattered foliage, men and beasts with a sticky, intense fire that burned through skin and denuded large areas of jungle. In conjunction with this attack, three B-52s would fly in close formation and use saturation bombing from high altitudes.

"F-16 jets strafed suspected villages, and Huey helicopters used air to ground rockets and M-60 machine guns in support of U.S. and Army of the Republic of Vietnam (ARVN) troops. The richest, most powerful military machine in the world had complete air superiority. The U.S. eventually expanded the war into nearby Cambodia and Laos.

"Our armed forces used offshore battleships to shell positions, patrol boats on the rivers and even bombed Hanoi, the capitol of North Vietnam. Eventually, over five-hundred thousand U.S troops were sent there, fighting a determined, primitive, but resourceful North Vietnamese Army. Horrendous atrocities befell both combatants' armies and innocent civilians. It mirrored the past war in the U.S. when our army fought the Apache. Like the North Vietnamese regulars and Vietcong, the Apache used similar, 'guerilla' tactics. They made devastating strikes from ambush and then melted into the desert. The U.S. troops had superior numbers, firepower and supplies, but were frustrated.

"Like the Apache, who had far less firepower, but knew the country, the North Vietnamese launched guerila attacks and vanished. They used this simple strategy and zeal to fight a foreign enemy on their native soil. The end result of the Vietnam War was a massive waste of American young men. Over fifty-five thousand U.S. troops were killed, with thousands more maimed. There were tremendous North and South Vietnamese casualties: friend, foe and civilians. Billions of dollars were spent to wage a war that left a once beautiful country ravaged. The madness ended when anti-war protests finally forced the U.S. Congress to cut off funding for the war. Without cash support, the U.S. military evacuated Vietnam. That allowed the quick takeover by the North Vietnamese. Today the country is healing and may become a trade partner with the U.S. Shame on this country, addicted to making war."

The brief, powerful diatribe about the war left everyone silent. Glenn was visibly agitated. He began carrying the last of the firewood to the canoes. Jacko walked beside him, carrying a log in his good arm. When they dropped their wood into the canoe, he took Glenn's hand and stood, looking sadly up into Glenn's eyes. Glenn shuddered, and then fell to his knees and they hugged. Tears flowed. Wordlessly offering support, Mark and Bob joined their quiet embrace. Anger and pain was replaced with compassion and friendship. The embrace lasted for several minutes, until Jacko broke up the group with his comical statement: "If I don't step away, I'll wet down our firewood! I have to pee!"

Laughter rang out as everyone returned to smiles and wiped away tears. Jacko disappeared behind a tree. Mark, Bob and Glenn got the heavily laden canoes ready as if nothing had happened. But Mark knew that what had just transpired was anything but ordinary. It was a whole new experience to him, this unburdening of stress and raw emotional bonding. It was necessary: a primary part of emotional healing. The good doctor had used his wisdom and resources to foster individual healing in a wild, unspoiled setting, where the clamor and demands of "civilized" life couldn't interfere.

The four of them shoved the canoes off and fought the strong wind. It required caution even in the protected bay. Once they battled through the waves near shore and gained momentum, they headed for the camp. Closely hugging the shore, the laden canoes arrived safely at the landing. A seemingly routine chore had changed them into a close-knit group, but it would remain their secret. Men have an unwritten code that frowns on crying and group hugs, but sometimes traditional norms must be ignored.

As they slid the heavily laden canoes onto the bank, everyone hopped out and started unloading firewood. Once it was all unloaded, Mark and Bob persuaded Jacko and Glenn to take a rest in their tent. After thanking them and exchanging double handshakes, Mark and Bob carried the wood to the kitchen and stacked it under a tarp.

Mark stood back and gave a low whistle. "Bob, my man," Mark said. "That's a ton of wood! Should be enough to last at least three days. By the look of the dark sky to the north, we may be in for a storm. Quite often strong winds follow as the high pressure front pushes the storm clouds out."

"Mais oui!" Bob agreed. "We'll have the rain parkas and possibles bags handy, just in case, when we reach the tents. Mark, have you noticed the little beaded deerskin bag that hangs around Jacko's neck? I've seen him gripping it while his lips move as though he's talking or praying. Any ideas?"

"Most Indian tribes wore what were called medicine bags, around their necks," Mark explained. "They were closely guarded and contained sacred items which gave them protection and power. I'll try to bring it up, around the campfire."

Mark and Bob got a small fire going and set the big kettle full of water on to boil.

It would be a cooler, possibly rainy evening. There was nothing like hot drinks to chase away chills. A nice hot water bottle tossed inside a sleeping bag before bedtime can really warm the cockles.

As they walked toward the landing to better secure the canoes for the night, they saw Cora motioning for them to look up. It was an eagle soaring in tight ovals, riding on the strong winds. Cora was trying to explain the size and beauty of the raptor to Ruby. Ruby spread her arms and whirled in her impression of the eagle's flight. Her face was lit with joy as she did her eagle dance in the pine needles.

Cora almost fell down laughing at Ruby's antics. Ruby made herself dizzy and fell to the ground with her arms spread out, giggling. Mark applauded and had a gut feeling that despite some problems, the trip was showing promise. He and Bob left the girls behind after waving at Cora. They stopped near the shore and watched the weather front work its magic as it pushed thousands of white-capped waves to shore.

Mark and Bob returned to the kitchen area and found Pierre busy building up the fire. He approved of their firewood pile by saying, "très bien." He asked them to gather two more canvas buckets of clean lake water. After filling the buckets, they set them near the kitchen and covered them to keep dirt and insects out. The water was used for cooking and cleaning and for drinking after it was boiled. Pierre graciously gave them a couple hours off before supper duties after explaining that the dinner entrée would be a stew of dehydrated veggies and canned chicken with egg noodles.

"Mark," Pierre asked,"s'il vous plaît, bake nice Indian fry bread for stew?"

"Mais oui!" Mark replied. "Bob volunteers to make dessert!"

Before leaving, they sneaked some jerky, saluted Pierre and ambled toward their tents. They enjoyed the treats and washed down the tangy, salty snack with long drinks of cool water from their canteens.

Mark's tent had two big pines about four feet apart which gave Bob an idea. They each got their McKenzie maps out of their tents and sat on Mark's ground pad while leaning against the convenient tree trunks.

"Look at the elevations of those rock bluffs across the lake at the narrows and along most of the western shoreline," Mark said. "They top out at fourteen-hundred feet! Maybe we'll be able to climb them tomorrow during the visit to the old logging camp site."

"You betcha!" Bob agreed. "It would be a way to get a better view of this end of the lake."

As they pored over the map, they closely examined the lake bottom's depth lines in the narrows. Mark proposed a late evening fishing trip as a preview to tomorrow's group fish. It would depend on the lake's calming down near dusk. They made plans to check the minnow trap after supper. If they had luck catching fish, they could fillet them and combine them with tomorrow's catch. With the plan made, they sealed it by catching a snooze.

Their sleep was disturbed by a bell. Its muted ring was ignored at first, but it became insistent. They arose, yawned and groggily stumbled toward the kitchen. As their heads cleared with the stiff breeze, they decided to check on Cora's and Ruby's tent. It was a neat and tidy tent.

Mark paused and frowned as he considered how little protection it had if a storm ever came down the length of the lake from a northerly direction. He mentioned it to Bob, but they agreed it was probably OK for the moment. The girls had already left for the kitchen. They would move the girls' tent another day. Kitchen duty called. Their snap decision would come back to bite them.

Everyone was already gathered near the fire, where Pierre was stirring the big cast aluminum kettle full of stew. He beckoned for Bob and Mark to come.

"Mes amis," Pierre greeted them. "Taste stew. How you like?"

They both grabbed a spoon and dipped it into the bubbling stew. After giving it a moment to cool, they sipped some, letting its juices saturate their taste buds. Mark swallowed, then winked at Bob and started to gag.

"Mon dieu, help, it's so salty!" he gasped. He laughed at Pierre's shocked look.

"Sorry Pierre, Bob replied. "He was just kidding! It is très magnifique."

Bob and Mark grinned, turned to Pierre and both gave him thumbs up. Pierre beamed. Mark loved its robust flavor. The dried veggies tasted like fresh. The chicken was so flavorful that it must have come from a roasting hen. Mark suggested a little salt and pepper and it was perfect.

Pierre bowed and said, "Glad you like stew, even though heart stop when you pretend gag! Now, Mark, make fry bread, s'il vous plaît."

Mark nodded and went to work, still grinning. He first grabbed the large stainless steel skillet and placed it on the fire grate to warm, next to the simmering pot of stew. After slathering some cooking oil into the pan, he measured and mixed the fry bread ingredients. The only difference was making a much bigger batch than he would normally.

Jacko and Glenn took turns entertaining the others by giving them all the details of their earlier exploration of the Horse River inlet bay, including locating the portage landing at the river mouth. The Horse River ran north to the Basswood River and massive Basswood Lake.

Jacko mentioned that they saw a number of painted turtles sunning on exposed rocks and logs. True to his roots as a member of the Ojibway Clan of the Turtle, Jacko greeted them as brothers. As Jacko and Glenn began to be pulled by the current, they were confronted by boulders to navigate through. Their canoe went aground on an emergent, flat-topped boulder that fooled them. When Jacko got out to try to free the canoe, he promptly slipped off the boulder and floated away with the current! His life jacket kept him safe. Without his weight in the bow of the canoe, Glenn was able to back paddle and float free. He rescued Jacko, who was sitting on a big boulder out of the current. Both were laughing so hard that

Jacko almost swamped the canoe as he climbed in. The wind and sun had Jacko nearly dry by the time they returned to camp. It was the high point of their day!

The fry bread was raising and nicely browned. It was almost finished baking, so Mark wrapped it in a piece of tin foil and set it aside. Mark poured one more big fry bread batch into the hot, oiled pan. It guaranteed ample bread for the group and maybe even some leftovers. It made a fine breakfast pancake. When it was re-heated, spread with butter and sprinkled with cinnamon sugar, it was yummy. Bob was almost finished with the desert pudding. Supper was ready. Mark signaled Pierre.

Pierre beckoned to the hungry crew. They hurried to fill their plates with Pierre's stew and large slabs of warm, golden, fry bread, slathered with butter. Bob completed the three-course meal with a creamy butterscotch pudding. Drinks included a choice of hot coffee, tea or cider. The stew drew rave reviews from everyone, as did Mark's fry bread and Bob's desert.

With their bellies full, the happy campers joined in a toast. Cora and Ruby stood and cried, "Three cheers for Pierre and his able, très bon assistants, Mark and Bob!"

Pierre, Mark and Bob bowed low while doffing their hats with a flourish. That broke the group up. They convulsed with unbridled mirth. Fun was had by all. The campers soon meandered back to their tents, happy and content.

Mark and Bob helped Pierre clean up and burned the paper. They saved the leftover fry bread which was wrapped in waxed paper. Pierre placed it in the cooler, a canvas box wrapped in wet burlap. He thought the idea of Bob and Mark "test" fishing at the narrows was a "très bonne idée." He declined to go along with them, since he enjoyed his solitude at his tipi and could smoke his pipe.

His last request was that they check the clients' fishing tackle before leaving. He cautioned that a quick storm might be brewing, and he wanted to be sure the canoes and tents were secured. Their possible bags and headlamps were ready if needed.

Cora and Ruby were busy sorting their tangled fishing gear. One reel had its line tightly wrapped around the gear. Mark and Bob untangled the snarl, cut the line and re-tied it to a snap swivel. They also untangled the other pole's line and sharpened the hook. They leaned the two salvaged fish poles against a pine and checked out the other tackle. Ruby was excited about her first time fishing. Bob told them not to get their poles tangled again! He sounded gruff, but couldn't hide a grin. Bob winked at Cora, who chuckled and tickled Ruby. The girls stood rigidly at attention, holding salutes until they were returned. With a big grin and a wink, Mark invited the girls to go along but they declined.

"We'll wait until tomorrow, merci," Cora said. "We're excited about the time around the campfire tonight, and we don't want to be drowsy for it. Right, Ruby?"

Ruby nodded her head and waved in Bob and Mark's direction. They waved back, knowing only Cora could see them. Cora whispered in Ruby's ear and she waved wildly.

Bob and Mark headed down to check the minnow trap. They reached the trap, pulled it up and were well rewarded. It had caught at least a dozen nice shiners. On their way to the tents, they stopped by Glenn's and Jacko's tent, but they and their fishing gear were gone. Mark knew they couldn't be far since no canoes were out. They found the two friends fishing from shore on the protected shore. Bobbers floated with night crawlers impaled on hooks below. All was idyllic and quiet. The ardent anglers appeared to be asleep with their poles being mere props. Mark and Bob tiptoed quietly away.

With a whispered "adieu," they loaded up a canoe and shoved off. Mark had grabbed his headlamp in case they had to return to camp after dark. The canoe moved swiftly into a dying wind. They passed a small island on their left and soon were at the base of the high rock cliff. Below it was a deep drop off that continued along most of the east shore to the kettle.

Mark quit paddling and readied his Shakespeare model 2052 open-face reel for action. He selected a buck tail jig that was dyed red, green, white and black and tossed it close to the cliff's edge. He counted slowly, "One thousand one, one "thousand two..." as the jig dropped toward bottom. At the count of ten, the line went slack. Mark began using his wrist to lift the rod tip, causing the jig to jump, then settle, imitating a crayfish or a leech. He continued reeling and letting it drop to the bottom, then upward and slowly worked it back to the canoe.

Mark felt a slight hesitation, a "bump." He lowered his rod tip, and then jerked sharply upward. His rod bent and the tip dove down while Mark held on and let the fish take line against the drag. Suddenly, his line peeled away with the drag singing like a cicada. The fish went deep and sulked. Mark put as much pressure on the rod as he felt his six-pound test line could take. Gradually, he gained line, but with continued pressure, his line went slack!

"I may have lost him!" Mark cried. "Too much slack." Just then, a torpedo erupted into the air! It showered them both with water and snapped its toothy jaws, before diving back.

"Mon dieu," Mark shouted. "It must be a ten-pound pike and he's real angry!"

"Hello!" Bob yelped. "That's the biggest pike I've ever seen!"

Then the monster pike appeared on the opposite side. After giving them a baleful eye, it opened its maw full of razor-sharp teeth. With a savage shake, it threw water, spat out Mark's jig and disappeared. Mark was still for a moment, then slowly reeled in his line and inspected the end. He exhaled sharply through pursed lips.

"Pretty well chewed," Mark said, as he examined his jig and straightened hook.

"I'm sort of glad he got off. We would have been hard pressed to land him without a net."

"Not a problem," Bob replied. "My fillet knife would have cut him free in a jiffy. I just hope Ruby doesn't catch him for her first fish tomorrow!"

They continued to fish the shoreline until the end of the narrows. They caught a few more small walleye as the lake grew dead calm. They released the fish. The air was heavy as darkness began to fall.

"We should head back while we can still see where we're going," Mark advised. "I don't trust this dead calm quiet. There's something brewing. Allons-y, mon ami."

They reeled in their lines and put their backs into their paddling. The canoe fairly skimmed the surface while leaving a silvery wake. Soon they landed at camp where they quickly secured the canoe and turned it over. After stashing their fish rods and tackle, they put on their down vests to ward off the evening chill and walked toward the welcome glow of the fire pit.

Everyone was there, seated on logs and folding stools with their faces aglow in the reflected light of the cheery fire. Pierre saw them coming and motioned them to sit on two stools that awaited them. Greetings were exchanged. Glenn asked how the fishing had been.

"Mostly small walleye," Mark answered. "I had a big pike at the canoe, but he charged the canoe, breached on slack line and threw the hook. It pushed ten pounds. He's still out there, so be prepared tomorrow!"

They took their reserved seats after waving at the bevy of happy faces and held their cold hands out toward the fire's warmth. As he warmed himself, Mark surveyed the ruddy, expectant faces. He told them to be ready in case the eerily quiet night was an omen.

Pierre held up his hand for quiet and spoke: "There is rule for conversation around campfire. May speak freely, except complaint about other in group or staff. They be heard in private. Will deal fairly. Contact me or engagés. Like Native American tribes, speaker must hold candle lantern. It be metal with holes along sides. Has hole in top to illuminate speaker face. Long as person holds lantern, he has floor. Can ask short questions or comments, OK? It keep order." Pierre opened the back of the lantern and lit the candle inside, then closed it and held it out to the group.

"Who be first to speak?" Pierre asked.

Jacko raised his hand and the lantern was passed to him. He held it up and spoke: "What will tomorrow's field trip be?"

Pierre motioned for the lantern, which was returned to him. He held the lantern so it lit his face and began: "After we fish narrows, go to 'kettle.' We land at campsite by old log camp. If site vacant, we eat sack breakfast, and then explore area. After we done explore, there be free time, then eat lunch. May find log camp artifact. No keep. Is history. Must stay here. High bluffs nearby. Climb, fish, relax. Later, we return base camp."

Cora asked for the lantern. "What is the best bait or lures to use for fishing tomorrow?"

Mark asked for and took the lantern. He answered Cora. "Deer hair jigs seem to work, as well as Rapala minnows either cast or trolled. Jig and minnow or crawler fished tight line or with bobbers work well. There are times when walleye only want live bait. Pierre's minnow trap should supply each canoe with some lively shiners. They will be put in coffee cans with wire bails and should be kept cool and under the canoe seat in shade. Hook the shiners lightly, just below the dorsal fin so they stay lively. If you feel a fish hit your bait, lower your rod's tip, wait a few seconds, and then set the hook sharply. Don't reel when the reel drag is giving line: wait until drag noise stops. Let the rod put pressure on the fish. Pulling too hard, or 'horsing,' could cause the fish to break your line or tear the hook free. If you're fishing an artificial lure, set the hook immediately."

The lantern passed to various speakers. Some made serious and some humorous comments. It was straight from the heart talk, sometimes tearful, or funny. All was spoken in confidence and held in their hearts.

Jacko held the lantern for what was the last speech. He related how he had thrown a stone at a deadhead that stuck out of the water. It happened when he and Glenn were fishing from shore, earlier that day. He hadn't noticed that a large turtle was sunning on the back side. The rock hit the turtle, knocking it off. It surfaced, glared directly at Jacko, and then went under. Jacko's Ojibway clan animal was a turtle. He feared he had angered Manidog or one of the lesser water spirits. These spirits were thought to live everywhere in the forest and water. His tribe used to offer tobacco gifts regularly to appease them.

He had offered the last of his tobacco on the way in and was concerned that a mischievous spirit might cause them some trouble.

Pierre took the lantern and said, "I see bad deeds occur when in wilderness. Things are taken, canoe capsize for no reason. We make gift to spirit in morning, before go fishing. Try not disrespect land or creatures. Spirits make trouble, can sabotage careless wrongdoers."

As the candle in the lantern went out, Pierre dismissed the group to their tents for the night, with some final comments. "Things happen at night—wind, storm, animals come. Be prepared. Tomorrow, we fish – explore if weather allow. Sleep well, mes amis. Go in peace."

Headlamps and flashlights guided the tired campers back to their tents. They murmured quietly and bade each other muted "goodnights." The camp became still but for soft snores and a fresh whispering from the forest. A change in weather had begun. Loons cried a warning. The camp slumbered on, peacefully unaware that dark forces were at work.

Sometime later in the night, a wild wind whistled in from the far north. It hit without warning, raising whitecaps and causing the trees to bend and creak. The capricious freak front rolled down the lake toward the sleeping camp. Its full fury slammed into the camp! It snapped branches and shook loose a steady rain of pine branches, cones and needles. Most of the tents were somewhat protected, save one.

Blotting out the moon, the fury descended on the girls' tent. Ruby heard the wind shriek and felt the branches and debris hammer their tent. She was unable to see the cause and began crying and shaking Cora.

"Cora," she cried! "We're in trouble! The tent is going to blow down!"

Mark began to jerk and twitch in his slumber as his tent flapped. Small twigs and pinecones began to pelt the tent. He tried to ignore it. He was so groggy that he just rolled over. Suddenly the wind banged into his tent's side with a vengeance. He sat upright, shocked and fully awake. He listened while frantically dressing with his heart pounding. His first thought was of Cora and Ruby. He put his headlamp on and clipped his "panic" bag around his waist. As he unzipped his tent door, he felt the sting of wind driven debris. Did he hear a faint cry? It must be from the girls, he thought. His gut churned as he donned his rain parka and turned on his headlamp.

"Bob!" he shouted. He turned and bumped into Bob, who was dressed and ready. Mark cried over the wind, "We have to rescue the girls! It sounds like they're in trouble."

They raced blindly towards the cries. Their headlamps' beams were obscured by the windblown rain that fell in sheets. They stumbled over fallen tree branches while fighting to keep their footing. Finally, they saw a light ahead. It grew brighter and illuminated the girls' troubled tent as they approached. The girls were trapped in their tent that had collapsed on them. They had gamely stuck their flashlights through the tent door. Ruby was crying. Ignoring the wind driven sheets of water, Mark stabilized the windward side of the tent to keep it from further damage. He began clearing away tree branches with his free arm.

"Cora, Ruby!" Bob shouted. "Mark and I will get you out! Hang on!"

"Bob!" Mark cried. "I'll hold the tent steady while you help the girls out and lead them to my tent. Get them dried off and warmed up. I'll try to move their tent out of harm's way. Girls, put on your raincoats and boots and be ready to leave with Bob!"

While Mark held the tent, Bob cleared the branches before helping the girls exit the tent. With a loud, "bonne chance!" they were gone. Mark quickly sized up the tricky situation. His only option was to start pulling up the tent stakes and tie-out lines as he muscled the wet, heavy tent toward a protective stone ridge. Moving in a circle, he finally felt the tent and its contents break free. He manhandled it closer to the ridge by pulling it over the wet ground. Sweat stung his eyes as he gasped with the exertion. Adrenalin alone enabled him to reach the ridge. His muscles were about played out. With one last effort he hauled the tent around a stout spruce and safely behind the rock wall. The respite from the wind allowed him to catch his breath.

He rested momentarily before extending his arms upward in thanks for being delivered from the tempest. His labored breathing and hammering heart calmed. He shined his headlamp beam at the terrain next to the rock wall. He tried to drive in the tent stakes, but after a thin layer of soil, the ground was solid rock. Thinking quickly, he grabbed some heavy rock slabs to secure the tent's corners. He re-connected the tent support poles onto their mounting pins. The guy lines were secured to trees and large rocks. He cleared most of the offending branches and pinecones from around the tent entry. The tent stood on its own again, with only a bent support pole visible as outside damage.

Mark entered the tent and re-arranged the tangled pile of clothes and gear. He then checked the tent interior for any problems. As he spread the ground pads out, he found a tear in the floor fabric. There was a two-foot rip. He drew the edges together and dried it off. He pulled out the roll of military duct tape and sealed the tear with multiple strips. It made a good temporary patch. Ray Bond had insisted they include the versatile tape in their possibles bag. It had a myriad of uses and could repair many different problems.

Satisfied that the tent was stable and out of danger, he laid out the girls' sleeping bags and found them sound and only slightly damp. He knew that once they slid inside, their body warmth would dry the bags quickly. He zipped the door shut.

He headed back to his tent to see how everyone was doing. Upon arrival, he was pleased to see that Bob had used his small gas stove to heat water and also warm his tent. Cora and Ruby happily sipped their steaming mugs of hot chocolate while munching on graham crackers! They greeted Mark noisily and were attired in Mark's and Bob's clothing. Ruby wore Mark's down vest and a knit hat of Bob's. Cora was snuggled into Mark's Snugpak bag. She was sitting up and smiling broadly at him.

"Well," Mark said, "You girls sure look a lot more comfy than the last time I saw you! How are you doing?" He could see Cora was reading his lips as he spoke.

"We're warm and on a chocolate high!" Cora said, laughing.

"How bad is our tent?" Ruby asked, as she finished her hot chocolate.

"It's going to be fine," Mark answered. "I had to pull up its stakes and push and drag it to a more protected site. It's behind a rock wall where it is safe and is cleared off and self-standing. I apologize for not moving your tent earlier. I've learned a hard lesson. There's little damage except for a bent tent pole and a tear in the floor that I repaired. When you girls feel up to it, we will take you back. You are welcome to keep our clothing until tomorrow, except for my Snugpak! I think the rain has quit and the wind has begun to die! Once you girls get back into your bags, you can get some sleep. Right now I need to ward off some chill myself! Is there any more of that hot chocolate left?"

"You betcha!" Bob replied. "Let me scrounge an extra mug from my pack."

It was a bit crowded in Mark's tent, but it was cozy and such a delight to have everyone safe and in a festive spirit after a nasty ordeal. Bob had more chocolate heating on the stove, as well as a big package of grahams. Bob poured him a mug of creamy, hot chocolate and topped off everyone's mugs.

Mark asked Bob to check out Glenn's and Jacko's tent. Bob nodded and ducked out of the tent. Mark enjoyed his hot chocolate and visited with the two rescued "damsels," as they preferred to be called. Bob soon returned and gave his report.

"They were safe and quiet, with only sleep sounds evident, so I tiptoed away," Bob announced. "I also did a quick check on Pierre. Nothing seemed amiss, so I assumed he was safe and asleep."

After an hour of snacking and subdued laughing, it was high time for the unplanned tent party to end.

"Well, gallant fellas," Cora announced. "It's been a whale of a fun time and we really appreciate your rescuing us two damsels in distress. But it's late and we should return to our own tent! We need to get some rest. It will be a busy day tomorrow."

Mark and Bob nodded their agreement and began preparing to leave. They helped the girls out of the tent and then escorted them to their new tent site. The wind continued to decrease, and the moon once again shone on the lake. A loon's raucous call split the quiet with a long, quavering cry that was immediately answered. Mark could hardly believe how quickly stark terror had given way to a fun party. The rigors of the night had definitely tested them.

When the girls were settled in their new digs, they said warm "goodnights" and "thanks" while handing back the clothes they had borrowed. Mark stuck his head in for one last check. Both sleepy damsels smiled up at him, cozy and snuggled close together in their bags. He said, "Sweet dreams," and zipped their tent door shut.

Chapter Fourteen

Boundary Waters
The Second Day

Mark gave Bob's hand a shake as they walked back to their tents, tuckered but happy.

They parted, slipped into their tents and were soon asleep. The false dawn came way too soon for Mark, but there was work to do. He forced himself to vacate his toasty bag after resisting for a while. He listened to forest music that heralded a new day. To him, each dawn was a new creation. He raised his arms in thanks and said, "Praise Adonai," or praise the Lord. Robins sang loudly and crows raised a ruckus, while a morning fog enveloped the water. A formation of ducks rocketed by, invisible in the fog.

He stood outside his tent, stretching and rubbing his sore lower back as he witnessed more sounds of the new day. There was the familiar high-pitched hum of insects. A hollow tapping signaled a woodpecker probing for a meal. All was calm and still. The freak storm had abated.

The near crisis the night before flooded his mind. It had ended well. They had dodged a bullet and survived the first real challenge of the trip. He hoped Pierre would not find them negligent. The girls were unhurt after being relocated to safety and were in good spirits when he last saw them. That would have to be enough. He hoped their planned day trip was still on.

He surveyed the clumps of pine needles and branches strewn about. Soon, the life-giving, radiant energy of the great and constant sun would provide light and warmth. The lofty pines blocked a direct view, but as he looked across the lake, the high bluffs glowed golden. Mark remembered how the plains Indians always arranged their tipis so the door faced east. The first rays of sunshine lit a tipi's entry early each day. They would thank the Great Spirit for creating a new day. Mark had noticed Pierre's tipi was oriented that way, thanks to his full-blood Sioux wife's influence.

Mark found it hard to pull away from the spell that dawn had cast, but it was time to begin to prepare for the day. He walked towards Bob's tent to wake him. Bob had beaten him to the punch. He was already up and ready.

"Good morning, mon ami!" Mark joked. "I'm buying coffee if Pierre has it ready."

"I accept. Let's go get it!" Bob yawned.

They made their way toward the kitchen while stepping over pine branches. It cheered them up when they saw the fire was burning hot. Pierre brandished a big pot of fresh, steaming java.

He saluted them and offered a greeting: "Allons-y, mes amis! "I have très bon coffee for you."

"Merci," they answered. Both engagés clutched their mugs of hot strong brew. They took their precious cargo and sat near the cozy fire. Slabs of rock leaned against the sides of the grate to block drafts and concentrate the heat. Pierre asked what had happened during the night, since he had been exhausted and had slept through it all.

While Pierre busied himself making peanut butter and jelly breakfast sandwiches, they filled him in on the events of the storm. When they had finished sketching out the scenario, Pierre walked over to them. His black eyes shone, and he slapped both of them on their backs! They were stunned by his warm reception. It was a tremendous relief.

"Très bien!" Pierre gushed. "You earn keep last night – for sure! Alors! Girls come. Glenn and Jacko be behind." Pierre was smiling. He shook their hands while muttering French phrases that neither understood.

Then the girls arrived, breathless, giggling and wild! They smothered Bob and Mark with hugs and pecks on the cheek. Mark and Bob both blushed deep red while trying to keep their balance on the stools, but the girls were tenacious and overwhelming. In an instant they both fell off their stools with the girls in a big pile. Pierre was doubled over with mirth and doffed his red beret in delight. Soon, everyone recovered while laughter rang out. Once they were dusted off and back on their stools, they heard from Glenn and Jacko.

"I heard the wind and rain," Glenn said. "Jacko was sound asleep, and our tent was fine, so I went back to sleep. We met Cora and Ruby just now and heard about their plight."

"Too bad about what happened, but I'm happy Cora and Ruby are OK," Jacko said. "I angered Manidog by hitting the turtle. I am to blame."

"No worry, Jacko," Pierre responded. "I see this happen before, when spirit offended. I have tobacco twists like voyageur and Ojibway offer to spirits. After coffee, we take tobacco – make offering gift by the water. Make medicine with Gitchi-Manido and lesser spirits."

Mark had learned from Jacko that his great-grandfather's clan would offer tobacco gifts to the spirits before taking a journey and before hunting, fishing or gathering wild food. If they felt they had wronged a spirit, they would try to make medicine and be right with the spirit world. Even the voyageurs offered gifts to the spirits, especially before plying the waters of Gitchi-Gummi.

Mark and Bob began packing the three canoes with fishing tackle, life jackets and a few canvas tarps to sit on for eating and relaxing at the old logging site. While Pierre and Jacko were making medicine, Cora and Ruby finished up the breakfast sandwiches. They bagged them and put some in each canoe, along with two water bottles.

Pierre and a very happy Jacko came to the landing with Glenn. Each carried a bucket of shiner minnows. There were just enough so each canoe had a couple dozen.

"Look out, walleye!" Glenn joked. "We're going to offer them a meal they can't refuse."

Mark looked into their bucket and cried, "What a nice bunch of shiners! They're so fat and are silvery-green beauties!" He remembered catching many like them at Moon Lake.

"Bonne chance," Pierre called out. "Everyone, dépêchez-vous. We go!"

Everyone took their regular positions in the canoes and paddled on a course that hugged the left shore. The crew enjoyed a calm passage to the start of the narrows. Fog lay in patches on the lake and was thick in the bays. When the inevitable late morning breezes stirred, the fog would dissipate. Soon a gentle breeze blew the wispy groups of fog out of the bays. It was striking, almost animated. Sigurd Olson once described the phenomenon as "wild horses, charging out of the bays."

Mark and Jacko drifted near the rock ledge at the start of the narrows, with ten feet of dark water beneath them. Mark fished with a jig and minnow, while Jacko drifted a shiner with only a snap swivel for weight. Pierre and the girls drifted ahead of them. The girls chose night crawlers and minnows with bobbers. Pierre cast a #1 Mepps spinner, while Bob and Glenn trolled Rapala minnows and jigged shiners. A small flight of blue-winged teal whistled overhead, twisting expertly as they streaked by. They spiraled over the lake's surface, displaying their legendary speed and agility.

As Mark scanned the shoreline in the quiet of the morning, he spied an eagle perched atop a dead pine. The king of raptors surveyed his domain. His body remained motionless except for its great white head. The powerful yellow eyes enjoyed free rein.

While he mused about the eagle, there was a cry from Cora.

"Look!" she exclaimed. "Near the shore, what animals are swimming and diving?"

"Otter!" Pierre replied. "It is family fishing for breakfast. See how curious they are."

Mark concentrated on the group of cavorting beauties. Their prominent whiskers, short ears and pug faces proved they belonged to the weasel family. They surfaced, spitting and craning their necks. They briefly inspected the flotilla of canoes, and then submerged, leaving only a trail of bubbles. They seemed to play and enjoy life more than most creatures, yet were still able to catch their food effortlessly.

It was Mark's first encounter with this efficient, endearing predator. Ruby thought one would make a great pet until Pierre reminded her of their nasty teeth and stinky fish breath. She decided a ferret might be a better choice.

As they worked their way along the narrows, the sun warmed them and also encouraged a light breeze to stir. Mark managed to catch two keeper walleye, while Jacko caught a nice walleye and their first decent smallmouth. They found drifting while dragging shiners behind on a snap swivel and hook worked well. When a "bump" was felt through the rod tip, waiting two seconds before setting the hook assured success. Mark saw rods bending in the other canoes as the fishermen fought their challengers. Fish supper was a done deal!

After about an hour, the wind assumed its prevailing direction from the southwest. It signaled fair weather, though it could blow hard later and create tough paddling from the lake's east end. It might color an up-coming client trip to the old lodge site. Mark caught Bob's signal, a high overhead wave of his paddle, before turning to follow Pierre. He was already past the narrows and nearing the campsite atop the massive rock dome on the right shore. It meant that fishing was over. They would soon be going to check out the old logging camp ruins.

Mark and Jacko placed the stringer on the canoe's bottom under a wet burlap sack to keep their catch cool. The fish were lively and thumped loudly. Mark could see that the old logging camp's nearby campsite area was vacant. He watched as first Pierre's and then Bob's canoe landed and disgorged their cargo. Mark spotted the old dock pilings still sticking above the water at the shore. It was remnants of the early 1900s when a crew of lumberjacks wearing wool shirts and pants and hobnail boots used crosscut saws, axes and peaveys to cut, trim and load the massive pine logs. Rafts of logs were chained together and floated down the length of the lake. Brave men rode them.

Sigurd Olson once wrote of his experience canoeing on Basswood Lake. It is the boundary between Minnesota and Canada. He found the entire Minnesota side had been logged of its old growth pine right to the shoreline. He looked across the basswood lake boundary and found the Canadian side was untouched. It was a sight that sickened him. It fueled his determination to champion the creation of a northern Minnesota wilderness area, where the land and waters would forever be held in a sacred trust.

As they landed at the old logging site, it was evident that everyone had caught at least one fish. Even Ruby managed a fat walleye! After holding it up to feel its shape, she kissed it and was very proud! There was a grand total of six walleye, three smallmouths and one nice pike about 28 inches long. It was caught by a very proud Cora. She had Pierre take her picture with the big pike. Ruby held up its tail with her face aglow and splattered by pike slime.

"Mark, Bob, écoutez," Pierre spoke. "Take fish to other side—fillet, s'il vous plaît. Leave offal in woods – as gift to crows, eagles. There is large rubber pack in canoe for fillets. Cover to keep cool on canoe bottom." We go explore old logging camp."

"D'accord," Mark answered. "See you there. Allons-y, Bob. Make sure your fillet knife is razor sharp, 'cause you're elected to cut the 'y' bones out of the pike!"

They loaded all the fish and were across the kettle in ten minutes. They found flat boulders to fillet the fish. After rinsing the fillets in the lake, they placed them in the pack and tossed the fish offal at the forest edge. Mark turned their minnows loose, since they were fragile and would die with the warmer temperatures and small bucket. More would be available in Pierre's trap.

As they neared the logging site, they saw Jacko waving excitedly at them. He was anxious to lead them to see what had been found. After tying the canoe in the shade, they joined Jacko and asked what was up.

"We found the loggers' fuel pile for the locomotive!" Jacko bubbled. "It was all overgrown and looked like a knoll, but there's more! Come see."

Bob and Mark followed Jacko into the tall grass and alder-filled area. They passed old galvanized steel hoods and a large gear attached to a long pipe. Jacko led them to the group. They were gathered around Pierre. As they approached, Pierre grinned and held an object out to them. As they drew closer, there was no mistaking their find. It was a black, shiny chunk of coal that looked as pristine as the day it was formed, eons ago. This ancient rock, composed of plant matter and subjected to intense heat and pressure, was impervious to heat, cold, rain and snow and was a little powerhouse of stored energy. In the day, this was the fuel of choice to power the locomotives that crisscrossed North America. Only a few of these old, coal-burning steamers remained in operation. They have become merely tourist attractions of a bygone era of travel.

After everyone had examined the hunk of coal, Pierre returned it to its rightful place in the pile and arranged the grass and moss over it once again. If left undisturbed, it might last for generations, unless a forest fire claimed it. Coal was still in demand for producing steam that drives giant turbines, which produce much of America's electrical energy.

Pierre led the group in the direction of Tin Can Mike Lake. The rail bed had once run above the west shoreline and now formed the portage trail to Sandpit Lake. They found a relatively level grassy corridor that was overgrown with alder and spruce trees. The group followed it a ways, but it became too thick with trees to continue. Pierre concluded the rail bed had to follow the west shore of Tin Can Mike, above the high rocky shoreline. It ran between it and another set of bluffs and through the moist lowlands.

Pierre led the group back to the logging site. He continued north past the open meadow and the campsite and continued through the field of pines that were claiming it. An earlier camper had found an old kerosene lantern missing its globe and hung it from a small tree near the campsite. Mark thought this site a poor choice, but it was protected from the north winds and was definitely an easy setup and out of the heavy canoe traffic. There were no nearby trees high enough to raise a food sack out of a bear's reach. That could be a problem for a camper.

"We go, follow marsh where path leads," Pierre instructed. "It once road, travel from workplace, living quarters and kitchen. I once find sign of camp here, at garbage dump."

Jacko was off scouting to the left side and found a faint road, overgrown and hard to follow. Then he crouched down and picked something up and held it up while letting go with a sharp "whoop."

"Look," Jacko chirped. "This little bottle was partly covered, among other jars and cans!" He proudly showed it to the now assembled group. It was a small, flattened bottle with a short, round neck that had raised ridges running down its sides and a narrow, flat bottom. It could easily fit into a pocket but would also sit upright. Pierre identified the little "flask" as a "bitters bottle," which once contained an herbal drink commonly used for curing ailments. The rest of the group eagerly joined in searching the area. They lifted up their finds for Pierre to see what they discovered.

Pierre identified many of them, like old coffee tins which still had some visible colors, but most objects were rusted and full of holes. He had to guess what they were by their shape. Baking powder cans were always narrow and round; lard tins were wide, round and held about five pounds.

Pierre added that lard kept well without refrigeration and was the preferred cooking and baking oil. It was tasty and supplied necessary fats and nutritional needs. It was needed when frying lean wild meat or fish.

Cora was searching around some old twisted steel cables in a patch of wild raspberry vines when she found a treasure. She held up a bleached white wide blade that narrowed, like a short canoe paddle. It was an intriguing find.

"What is this?" Cora inquired. It was off white and chewed around the edges, with a raised spine running down one side and flat and concave on the other side of the blade. Mark examined it and guessed it was a shoulder blade from a large animal.

Pierre said, "C'est vrais. Is from moose! Camp work spring to fall. Fall cooler work. There be no bugs. Moose in rut. They no fear man when love for cows trump man fear. Bulls ornery. Sometimes fight – maybe injured or die. Loggers fish and hunt for food. Fish and wild game welcome change from beans. Moose kill be lifesaver. It keep well if hung high in shade. Jerky made by marinate, salt meat – then smoke. Bones be food for creatures to chew for minerals. This bone be from recent moose hunt. Maybe hunters camp here – debone meat so easier pack out."

The group wandered about the site and found more artifacts, as well as recent food, pop and beer cans left by lazy campers. Mark was angry that these slob campers ignore the rule that prohibits bottles and cans. Instead of crushing and packing them out, they add insult to injury by tossing their trash casually into the wilderness. He had even seen a can in their site's pit toilet, as well as other ignorant activity, such as slashed and chopped live trees. It made Mark wonder if the mighty but fragile wilderness would survive the thoughtless destruction.

After a while, Pierre led the girls back to the vacant campsite near the shore. He began to prepare lunch. Until lunch, Mark, Bob, Jacko and Glenn opted to climb and explore the bluffs that rose above the shoreline. The bluffs continued around the point into the main lake and ended at the narrow, swampy marsh that continued to the west.

The four explorers made it safely to the top of the bluffs and enjoyed a panoramic view of the kettle, their campsite point and the east shoreline of Horse Lake. Glenn had a problem when his prosthetic foot got tangled in some roots and he fell. He scraped some skin off his arm, but rubbed some of his saliva on it and stoically continued. Bob had been close by to steady him so he didn't fall any further. Mark enjoyed the many tiny, colorful warblers that flitted among the trees and shrubs while searching for food. They seemed to enjoy life as they danced like vivid butterflies during the brief northern summer. They escape before the snow comes back to the north and leave to bask in warmer climes.

Jacko suddenly ducked and almost fell down! He thought he was being attacked by a giant bee! Mark and Bob chuckled as they steadied Jacko and told him how a humming bird had buzzed his head. It was attracted by the bright orange fishing jig on his hat! Hummers are drawn to certain bright colors, like red, orange and blue, which they confuse with flower petals. Their long beaks and tongues allow them to gather nectar from large trumpet-shaped blossoms.

Glenn pointed to a pair of tandem canoes down in the narrows, heading south. A large hound sat in the middle of the lead canoe, among the packs. He was lying quietly, enjoying the ride. It was cool to see a dog in the Boundary Waters, especially one that was well trained and enjoying canoe travel.

Mark remembered a few of his family's dogs. Most had been beagles, which were kept in a large pen under the pines in back. They were mainly used to hunt snowshoe hares in fall and winter in the swamps bordering their old camp. They could be fun to play with, but would set up loud howling if they spotted a rabbit, deer or bear near their pen. It was Mark's and Pete's job to feed the beagles and to shovel their poop out of their pen when it stunk. Mark had once adopted a stray black-and-white dog he named Spot. He was a free spirit that Mark fed and cared for but never owned. He roamed the neighborhood, roads and woods at will. Spot was a great companion. When Mark made hikes to either Lake Antoine or in the back woods, Spot was always his sidekick. Mark hoped he would always be there.

Unfortunately, Spot tried crossing U.S. Highway 2 once too often. Mark found his crumpled body lying on the highway shoulder. He had nearly made it home. Mark loaded his old buddy's carcass into his red wagon and pulled him to the side yard. He dug a deep hole and after a tearful goodbye, buried him. His grave was next to their old cat, Betsy, a six-toed mouser extraordinaire. Spot had been a gift, coming out of nowhere and asking little but love. Mark missed his companionship, but knew that Spot felt no more pain and was once again a free spirit.

Mark was jolted back to the present by Glenn pulling on his arm.

"What's this?" Glenn asked. He was holding a hand full of dried scat pellets that were two inches long and almost as thick.

"Must be moose!" Mark replied. "They're certainly not deer, and there's only one other large herbivore living here. Moose are the largest of the deer family. They consume great amounts of vegetation, both on land and in the water, and can use their strong, long legs to climb and wade through deep snow.

"Well, we'd best be starting down the bluff to the campsite. It's lunchtime and I'm starving like a rat," Mark announced.

"Amen to that!" Bob agreed. "Let's take our time descending, though. No food is worth a nasty fall."

Climbing back down was uneventful. Mark considered their brief foray was a success. Nobody died! Soon all the "bluff walkers" alighted on terra firma with only minor scrapes and cuts. All wounds were treated with hydrogen peroxide and healing balm that Bob and Mark carried in small canvas shoulder bags. These "possibles" bags also contained a compass, waterproof matches and Mylar reflective survival blankets. Other items in the bag were a magnesium stick with a striker for starting a fire, waxed cord with heavy-duty needles, jerky and chocolate bars.

As they reached the open meadow, studded with young pines, they took a trail that passed the campsite toilet. Fortunately it was unoccupied. They entered the open meadow and found the girls and Pierre enjoying the warm sun. The girls sat together on the ground tarps while Pierre completed the lunch prep.

"Voila! Le campement du voyageurs," Mark announced.

"Bienvenue, hommes du nord!" Pierre answered. "Déjeuner almost ready, wash up in lake. We eat!"

Everyone jogged over to the water's edge and doused their faces and arms with cool water, using sand to scrub off stubborn grime. After quickly toweling off, they were in their places on the ground tarp. The early wake up and rigors of the day had sharpened their appetites. The peanut butter and jelly breakfast sandwiches were but a distant memory.

Pierre began passing platters of goodies around the seated "voyageurs." As he served lunch, he sang a voyageur "chanson d'amour," which charmed the group. Chansons were French songs that were sung during long days of paddling and portaging by the fur trade voyageurs. Many were about love for wives and girlfriends back home in Canada.

Pierre said there were literally hundreds of songs that helped temper the hard work. It was reminiscent of how the African slaves sang to lessen the pain of hard labor, while they labored on America's southern plantations before the Civil War. Union forces defeated the southern Confederates in 1865 abolishing slavery. At least the voyageurs were paid for their hard lives.

The plates of cold lunch delicacies included stacks of sliced Zup's summer sausage, cheddar cheese chunks, carrots, crackers, and an apple for dessert. Fresh fruit was a nice bonus and a fitting finish to a colorful, tasty lunch.

"Enjoy déjeuner, mes amis – mangeurs de lard," Pierre kidded. "There be pork in sausage, make all 'pork eaters'!" After déjeuner, we take le pose (rest) and allumez pipe, from sacs à feu."

"Mais oui, Pierre, donnez-moi du feu," Mark responded. Eating stopped momentarily, until Mark and Pierre laughed. Mark explained the

French phrasing. Pierre had said that they would take a rest and light up their pipes after lunch. Mark had asked Pierre to light his non-existent pipe! Everyone enjoyed a chuckle and continued eating their lard sausage. They joked about being voyageurs, "pork eaters," hommes du nord and filles du nord.

Mark marveled at Pierre's clever use of his patois to instill a sense of being in a historic voyageur setting. He felt a kinship, a stirring deep in his being. Pierre handed out the big, dark apples with a flourish. His red waist sash fluttered in the breeze. Pierre defined voyageur life for the lucky group of pork eaters.

After lunch everyone turned to relaxing or carefree strolling about. Bob and Mark cleaned up the lunch remains while saving leftovers for snacks. They bagged the paper items for starting the evening campfire at base camp. It was time to rest.

Mark lay back on a tarp with his possibles bag as a pillow. His boonie hat shaded his eyes. Bob, Jacko and Glenn chatted about the morning and admired the beauty and quiet of the day. Mark feigned sleep, letting the warm sun and breeze play over him as he rested. With his head slightly elevated, he could peek under his hat brim and watch others. Ruby and Cora sat at the landing, soaking their bare feet in the water. By turning his head slightly Mark could just see Pierre. He was seated on a log in the shade of a balsam.

Pierre had his white clay pipe lit, and he puffed contentedly. The smoke curled around his head as he meditated. Mark realized that though he and Pierre had very different backgrounds, they were alike in needing their own quiet time. Solitude didn't always mean being alone. It's possible to isolate yourself while among others. Pierre liked people but also craved solitude.

Mark was fascinated with Pierre's pipe. It was identical to those used in the fur trade era. It was a small but important link to his voyageur ancestors who cherished the poses. The pipes were a creature comfort in the midst of their long hard days. The white clay pipe had a round bowl with a narrow stem. It was identical to fur trade pipes Mark had seen preserved in museums. They were fragile, but precious, so the voyageurs carried several that were wrapped carefully. Extra moccasins were also held dear.

Mark closed his eyes, mulling these things over, and drifted off, contented and tired. He awoke with a jerk at the sound of a loon calling and raised himself to a sitting position. All was quiet as his eyes swept the area. Cora was reading something to Ruby. Glenn and Jacko were fishing from shore while Bob napped serenely.

Mark fixed Pierre in his gaze and saw he had fallen asleep. His head drooped to his chest. His clay pipe was lying on the ground. It reminded Mark of his grandfather. Mark had often found him fast asleep by the TV or in his garden. Grandpa's corncob pipe would fall to the ground or carpet and spill burnt tobacco. It was a wonder he never burned his house down with him in it. This practice finally caught up with his grandpa one day. He dropped his lit pipe on the floor of his old Nash Rambler station wagon and walked away. The carpeting smoldered and filled the interior with heat and acrid smoke. It never ignited into flames, but it discolored and warped the car's dash. He discovered it after the damage was done. He must have spent days cleaning the interior until it was serviceable. There remained a permanent scorched odor and warped, melted and discolored surfaces. The outer edges of the windshield and side windows remained smoky, but he drove the tough old car until he died at 84. He lost his battle with the damage to his lungs due to working in the local iron ore mines and his lifetime of smoking cigarettes and his beloved pipes.

Mark finally stood up and took a long drink of water, splashed some in his face and strolled towards the shore. He tiptoed past a still comatose Bob. He wandered on to check on the girls. He called to them as he approached.

"Hello, très jeune filles!" Mark said.

"Hi, très joli homme," Ruby exclaimed. She had heard Mark's advance and asked Cora who was coming. She grinned proudly at how quickly she caught on to the patois of French and English. Mark was caught by surprise. He blushed at being called a "very pretty man"!

Cora watched Ruby's face. She read Ruby's lips to catch her words, and then turned from her sitting position and smiled broadly.

"Hi, Mark!" Cora cooed. "I think Ruby has a crush on you! She has been waiting for a chance to try out her French on you."

Mark patted Ruby's head and she blushed a deeper brown. She bowed her head, but her face was beaming. He noted Cora's one hand was keeping her place in the book she had been reading.

"I hope you guys got some rest. You deserve it," Cora said. "Ruby and I have been enjoying this book, *Little House On The Prairie*, by Laura Ingalls Wilder. I brought it along since it is based on the author's life. She grew up in a pioneer family. This is a perfect setting and Ruby loves it."

"I remember it well," Mark replied. "It is a neat book. I recall having it read to me in grade school. We didn't have our own copies, so it was a special treat. There wasn't a peep out of the class. We sat enthralled with our hands folded on our desks. It was when I first realized I had been born two hundred years too late! The simple hard life in the country appealed to me. There was honesty, humor and love in her family story. Living close to nature without electricity or supermarkets, in a log cabin with wood for heat and cooking, was my dream. My family was poor, but had modern appliances such as a TV, oil heat and automobiles. The only place that was comparable was at our hunting camp where there was no electricity or indoor plumbing."

"Oh, Mark, I'm sorry you were born into the modern age, but look at you now!" Cora teased. "Seriously, the pioneer life was good. It made an impression on me also. I, too, read this book in grade school. I saw the value of respect for the creation and how wholesome it was to grow your own vegetables, keep livestock and live simply. I determined to try to live as close as possible to the old ways. My home is a log cabin. I use wood for heat and I cook on an old wood cook stove in my kitchen.

"I cheat by having a backup propane-fired heater, gas range, and indoor plumbing. I grow most of my own produce and raise chickens for meat and eggs. My house has skylights and insulated windows. There is a working windmill on my property. I preserve foods, ride public transportation or my bike and jog on a nearby hiking trail. It follows a river, through woods and meadows. It gives me peace. Please visit me sometime."

"My home is in a big city," Ruby interjected. "I like the story and having Cora here to read to me is great. I will ask my teacher if we can read it in class this year."

"That shines," Mark commented. "It should be a part of every grade school reading program. It's good to see how you two damsels have bonded. I was just thinking that if you girls don't live too far apart, maybe you could get together once you are back home! Cora's place sounds like a little bit of heaven on earth, and I know Ruby would love it."

"We've already exchanged addresses and phone numbers. Our homes are only about twenty-five miles apart!" Cora exclaimed. "I've already invited Ruby to visit and accompany me when I run next year's Grandma's Marathon. I live alone with my dog, cats, and chickens. I also promised to treat Ruby to the pre-race, all you can eat spaghetti feed in Canal Park, the night before. Ruby comes from a broken home and lives with her grandparents, who have financial and physical problems. My job is teaching deaf children for the Minnesota Department of Education, so we would have similar school vacations and summer vacation to get together. I do drive an old Subaru."

Ruby was snuggled up to Cora and holding her arm. She chattered excitedly about visiting Cora's "little house" and "seeing" her run the race by Lake Superior. Mark watched them as they talked about future meetings. He realized it was just one more piece of the amazing puzzle of the trip that fit perfectly. Be it fate or design, he didn't know. He felt the wilderness factor could have made the crucial difference. The mind, body and spirit connect in a special way when immersed in wilderness. Once again he pondered these things.

He gave them both hugs and bid them "adieu." He continued along the shore toward where Glenn and Jacko were fishing. A strong burst of wind buffeted him, ruffling the kettle as it passed by. There seemed to be a wind switch in the works. He quickened his pace. The idyllic visit and exploration of the old logging camp was due to end soon.

He approached the fishermen. They once again had succumbed to fatigue and fallen asleep. Their fishing rods were cradled in their hands with their bodies slumped together. Mark left them and checked the fish fillets in the canoe. He found the fillets cool and firm. It would be a welcome addition to their diet when they put it on that night's supper menu. Mark turned back toward the picnic area and found Pierre and Bob breaking camp. He helped them fold tarps and carry lunch items to the canoes.

"Time we go!" Pierre proclaimed. "Winds shift to southeast – blow hard."

"D'accord," Mark agreed. "I saw the wind ruffle the lake surface and felt its force on shore. Some thunderheads are building in the east."

Mark and Pierre carried the last of the gear to the canoes and packed it away. Cora and Ruby were already in Pierre's canoe. Its stern line was tied to the old piling. Bob held his canoe steady while Glenn packed their fishing gear and clambered in.

"Allons-y," Pierre cried, as he shoved off. Ruby waved.

Mark and Bob shoved their canoes off and fell in behind Pierre, hugging the left shoreline. The winds whistled in from conflicting directions and ricocheted away again.

As Pierre's canoe entered the narrows, Cora pointed at the end of the rock ledge, then continued paddling. When their canoes reached the place she had pointed to, they found out why. A massive iron ring as thick as a man's finger was drilled firmly into the rock ledge! It was an old logger's anchor, ready to belay a raft of pine logs. After a quick glance at the ring, they once again put their back into the paddles and were through the narrows with the wind picking up behind and forming whitecaps. At least camp was nearby. It was only a matter of holding the canoe steady and hugging the right shore. The life jackets were reassuring, as Mark dug his paddle in with vigor. Jacko switched sides and paddled gamely in the bow. Despite his useless left arm, he had an instinct for keeping the bow turned true to their goal.

The Old Towne Royalex canoe provided the strength and stability it was famous for. In tough conditions, speed comes in a poor second to safety. Its wide, flat bottom and tough hull took much abuse. They slowly but surely made progress and soon saw Pierre's and then Bob's canoe slip into safe harbor. Mark was glad, since his arms were burning from the exertion. His fingers were prickly from interrupted circulation caused by gripping the canoe paddle so tightly.

As he and Jacko cleared the point, they enjoyed the relative calm. They drove the canoe into the landing and jumped out, dragging the canoe up into the trees. They unloaded their gear, overturned the canoe and tied the painters, bow and stern lines to trees on both sides. They slid the paddles under the overturned canoe and carried the fishing tackle to their tents. After Mark was sure Glenn and Jacko were secure in their tent, he checked with Pierre who was organizing the kitchen.

"Mark!" hailed Pierre. "Start fire, s'il vous plaît. Will need keep warm if storm hits. I put on coffee pot and tea water."

"Mais oui!" Mark replied. He took out his tube of waterproof matches and struck one against the rock. Fire flashed as the wax coating caught. Mark applied it to the waiting, dry duff of small twigs and dry pine needles. It produced a thick cloud of white smoke that dissipated when flames ignited the dry, split pine. He followed these with a few larger chunks that would slow the fire, producing a steady, even heat. Once it burned down, some nice, hard pine knots would burn hot and long.

Mark placed a few more flat rock slabs against the bottom of the fire grate to further block the gusty winds. He positioned a stool and let the cozy, radiant heat permeate his bones. As he spread his arms toward the fire, he still could not understand how the tree stored energy in its fibers. It waited patiently until it was ignited to release its wonderful secret.

"Très bien, Mark," Pierre commented. "It good to have fire so hot so quick! Tonight's souper be fresh fish fillets. We bake in foil, butter, pepper, baked potatoes, buttered carrots. Desert be sugar-cinnamon dish."

"C'est un souper magnifique!" Mark exclaimed. "We can make hot tea and chocolate to finish it off!"

"I fix fish and taters," Pierre said. "Mark, s'il vous plaît, slice carrots – help Bob do desert."

"Mais oui," Mark replied. "I'll get the leftover bannock mixed with the sugar and cinnamon so it can bake while everyone is eating. The aroma of its baking will have them drooling. After we get the carrots and desert prepped, Bob and I plan to reconnoiter the backside of the camp. We'll climb the hill and check the area behind for any available wild fruit or berries."

Mark saluted Pierre, had it returned, and went to find Bob. He met him halfway to their tents. Bob eagerly led Mark toward Glenn's and Jacko's tent.

"Jacko wanted to try making fire with a bow drill," Bob said. "He wondered if we'd like to watch. I remember Ray Bond demonstrating it on one of our field trips, but we never tried it. It can be tricky and we do need to master the technique. Jacko, though young, seems to have the knack of his grandfather. In a real emergency without matches, it could make the difference between life and death."

They reached Jacko's and Glenn's tent and found them waiting with everything ready. Jacko showed them his bow drill. It was made out of a straight piece of dead cedar branch. It had a notch carved near the middle, with a deer ligament double wrapped and stretched taut. He fitted his drill into the notch carved in a smooth, half cedar log. He placed a rounded cap atop the drill which had a carved slot that fit the drill's upper end. Now he could lean his left shoulder to apply pressure on the cap. His right hand gripped the bow using a sideways sawing motion with the bow. Gathered around the base of the drill groove was a ball of dry moss, fine cedar bark and strips of birch bark. He leaned on the top of the drill and worked the bow while keeping an even pressure that allowed the drill to spin freely, causing the point to heat by friction.

At first, nothing seemed to change, so Mark tried to put his finger near the drill at the base. He let out a startled "yip" and sucked his finger tip to cool it off! Jacko smiled and kept the bow singing, as the slot began to darken. A tiny wisp of smoke appeared, but Jacko redoubled his effort. Drops of sweat beaded up on his brow from the exertion. More smoke poured upward. Jacko coughed, grinned and kept the bow drill moving steadily.

Mark could see a tiny spark fly into the nearby duff and begin to smoke. Suddenly Jacko put down the bow drill. He picked up the cedar drill log and carefully tapped the tiny ember into the nest of dry fluff. He gently folded the nest around the ember while blowing steadily into it. Soon white smoke billowed before it erupted in flame! Mark and Bob cheered! Glenn patted Jacko on the head and added a few twigs to the fire.

"Congratulations, Jacko!" Mark said. "We all learned something here today. Thanks to your skills, it should be possible for any of us to duplicate."

"My grandfather said this was the only way to make fire when he was young," Jacko said. "Striking flint came later, and he first saw stick matches when trading with the French. Stick matches were a mystery and were big medicine. Grandfather and I made this together. He said that if there was bad trouble and all matches were wet or lost, it might be only source of fire."

"He could be right," Bob agreed. "I'll bet there have been times when canoes have swamped and any lighters or matches were useless. I realize that this method won't work easily in wet weather. But even matches are useless without finding dry tinder to light. If you will douse the fire with lake water, Mark and I need to do some kitchen duty."

Glenn answered, "Roger, we'll see you at supper."

Mark and Bob waved at Jacko. He looked pleased with his fire demo. Glenn headed to fill a water bucket. They arrived at the kitchen and worked on the carrots and desert. Pierre was missing, so they left to find him. As they neared Pierre's tipi, they saw some wisps of smoke exiting the top. They stopped and tapped lightly on the canvas flap. Pierre invited them in and asked them to sit cross-legged, Indian fashion opposite him. The tipi entry required them to crouch to enter. Their eyes took a few seconds to adjust to the dimly lit interior as they found a place to sit cross-legged on the floor.

"Welcome to my home, mes amis" Pierre said. "I like sitting here having smoke. It re minds me of large tipi we have at home. I hope you like. We make together. My wife designed and decorated outside."

"Mais oui," Mark said. I like the high center and the way light enters from the top and channels air from the entry upward."

Mark watched Pierre sitting cross-legged on a blanket, holding his clay pipe which glowed warmly as he drew in its fragrant smoke and slowly exhaled. A small circle of stones in the center of the floor held a clay bowl. In the bowl smoldered a bundle of dried leaves. He smelled the fragrant, herbal essence and watched as Pierre leaned forward and used his hands to wave the smoke over his head. It was a ritual purification.

"Herb bundle be sage, "Pierre explained. "It used by plains tribes, cleanse mind body. Is reserved for special ceremonies. My wife, full blood Lakota Sioux. She get it from family, live on reservation in North Dakota. We visit them every year – stay in remote valley. No vehicles or modern conveniences allowed. Village mostly self-sufficient. Have own bison herd for meat, large gardens for vegetables. Tipis made same as old days. There be bison hide for walls also cover floor. Some bison sold for breeding or meat. Money used buy tools, food not grown."

"That's amazing!" Bob said. "I didn't know such places even existed today. Maybe you could speak more about it some night around the fire. We have to leave and go check out the land behind. We hope to find some wild fruit."

"D'accord!" Mark agreed. "We could very easily remain here until supper, but I respect your quiet time. We need to explore so, allons-y, we go."

"D'accord," Pierre replied. "We talk more later. Good to have engagés in tipi. See you souper – bonne chance."

Before they continued their foray, Mark grabbed a couple rolls of toilet paper and sealed them into plastic bags. They would leave them at the toilet enclosure. Bob grabbed two cook pots with handles in case they found any berries. Soon they arrived at the toilet area and dropped off the toilet paper. A steep hill confronted them. They climbed it by angling first right then left. The land behind it leveled off and was more of a high meadow with scattered clumps of trees and shrubs that gradually sloped toward the water on the Horse River side.

Mark noticed a small flock of birds making some racket and flying around a grove. It was worth checking out. They proceeded to the area of activity. As they neared the grove, Mark let out a "whoop!"

"Alors!" Mark cried, "sugar plums! They are also called June berries or service berries. This flock of robins led us to them. Robins and cedar waxwings love fruit."

"Yum," Bob said. "I'll bend a branch down, you pick." Mark plucked a handful of the deep purple to reddish berries and split them with Bob. As they chewed the berries, they smiled and continued picking. The pots began to fill, as did their stomachs.

"They're sweet but a little pithy. These would really be a treat baked with sugar in a cobbler!" Bob suggested.

"For sure," Mark replied. "They're just what the doctor ordered for a special dessert. It reminds me when I found some blueberries during the survival test. They made a mean cobbler."

"Say no more," exclaimed Bob.

In less than an hour their pots were nearly full to the brim. More berries would be available as they ripened. They would be a good food source for robins and other creatures. Mark had witnessed how bears climb up and break off tree limbs to feast on fruit.

The two engagés merrily toted their precious cargo back to camp. They were careful not to stumble and spill them. Soon they burst into the kitchen and proudly offered them to a stunned Pierre.

"C'est très magnifique!" Pierre cried. "We really knock client socks off at dessert time. I camp here before but no explore back there. We find raspberries everywhere in July. Plains Indians used when made pemmican. It made by pounding dried buffalo meat, fat and berries. Mix all together and tie inside bison hide. It be complete meal, keep well. It big food pour voyageur. Eat cold or cook in large kettle. Add water, dried corn, peas, flour, sugar, wild game, what find. It make thick stew called 'roobaboo'. Put tasty berries away from critters. It be our secret weapon at souper!"

Mark and Bob saluted and put a canvas bucket in the lake to soak, then washed and drained the berries. They placed the clean berries in a covered bowl and put them into the food sack. It was only a half hour before supper. Pierre asked Mark to make a pot of coffee. Mark thought it might be a good time to ask Pierre about making a tipi. Pierre was busy getting the potatoes washed and wrapped in foil. Mark scraped and cut the carrots into chunks, rinsed them and placed them in a pot of water. Pierre made seven tin foil packets. In each packet he placed fillets, butter, sliced onion and black pepper.

The coffee was perked and ready. Mark poured each of them a steaming mug while Pierre stoked his clay pipe and applied le feu. As he lit the tobacco, he drew the fragrant smoke in and expelled it in a white plume.

"Pierre," Mark began, "since we visited your Lakota Sioux tipi, I've been wondering if it would be possible to buy one or if could I learn how to make one?"

Pierre continued puffing while he considered Mark's request. Mark politely allowed him to think while he refreshed their coffee mugs. After a few more draws on his pipe, he turned to Mark.

"I honored tipi pleases you. When trip over, before Ray trip, come visit our home. I show big tipi. We parley, make medicine with wife, Clay Basket. We live in tipi pour warm season. Spend cold months in log home. It be same pattern wife's Sioux family use in North Dakota. She keep tipi pattern in head. It be good time. Teach you make tipi."

"That suits me right down to the ground," Mark replied.

By this time the whole group was assembled near the fire pit. Everyone sniffed the aromas coming from the fire grate. The dark clouds dispersed and the wind began to die as dusk drew nigh. Mark looked toward the main lake. Several groups of tandem canoers took advantage of the calm seas to make their move.

The carrots were done. Mark probed the baked potatoes with a fork and found them done. Pierre pronounced the fish ready. Mark and Bob set the table and began placing the covered pot of carrots and a wood bowl piled with hot bakers in the table's center. Pierre referred to them as "pommes de terre" or apples of the ground, which tickled the group.

There was a hush in the camp as Glenn raised his arms heavenward and bowed his head before saying grace. Each camper wore expectant looks as Pierre placed a tray full of the fish in steaming foil packets on the table. Butter was spread on the hot veggies and taters, then salt and pepper. All was quiet as the hungry crew attacked the bountiful buffet.

Mark excused himself to craft his secret dessert. He uncovered one bucket of June berries and mixed them with the bannock dough he had prepared earlier. After lathering butter and sugar over the top, he covered the pan and set it next to the fire's glowing coals to bake.

Mark wandered back to the table where the supper had been. The table was bare. Everyone sipped java, tea or chocolate, oblivious of the treat baking quietly. Jacko began sniffing and whispered into Ruby's ear. Her eyes popped and her hand covered her face.

Mark caught first Bob's eye, then Pierre's. He gave them a thumb's up sign and a wink. He checked on the dessert. As he pulled back the foil, he was greeted by purple berry juice bubbling up the sides. He inserted a butter knife underneath and found it nicely browned. All that remained was to pull the top foil sheet up. He placed the pan near the coals. The attached foil was propped up with two sticks to act as a reflector to brown the top.

Mark sneaked over to Pierre and whispered in his ear: "It will be ready in ten. Don't let anyone leave." Pierre grinned and nodded.

"Attention, mes amis," Pierre began. "There be special treat before we begin fireside chat. It be worth wait!"

Mark checked the pan and found the top nicely golden with berry juice bubbling out. He used a towel to lift the pan out and placed it on the table. The special cobbler stole the show and drew a chorus of praise. He cut the steaming June berry bannock into squares and shoveled them onto waiting plates. There was butter to slather on the golden crust and hot drink refills all around. Everyone patiently waited until all had been served, then forks flew into the savory dessert.

"Oh, Mark, after that wonderful meal, this is too much!" Cora blurted. "Where did you find the fresh berries and what kind are they? It is scrumptious!"

Mark smiled and said, "They're June berries. Bob and I found them in the hills out back." Mark finally had time to sample his buttered cobbler. He closed his eyes and let the sweet berry juices mingle with the buttered bannock. It passed inspection easily. He glanced around at the others and saw not a few who had butter and berry juice spattered on their faces. Ruby looked like she had washed her face with it! With the last crumb of desert swallowed and faces once again clean, the table was cleared and washed.

Pierre brought out the speaking lantern and lit the candle inside. The group grew quiet and waited. Pierre signaled he would speak first.

"Tomorrow, we rise early, like today," Pierre said. "We leave before wind pick up. Go north, paddle right shore to far end of lake. We explore where old resort stood. We have special TICK permit. It allow us to bushwhack old portage to No-See-Um Lake. May not find. We spend few hours there, then go to river inlet of Fourtown Lake. Any questions?

Cora raised her hand and asked, "If we run into strong winds heading south from the resort ruins, what can we do?"

"Good question," Pierre answered. "That happen before on lake. Can be trouble. There be island on way – protected shore. We land and wait out wind. French voyageur term be degrade or wind bound. It named Salvation Island. It big enough – fish, relax, eat lunch. There be large pines, boulder – protect from wind. Deep water off west end, good fishing."

Bob asked for the lantern, saying, "I have a question for Jacko. If this is too personal, please feel free to not answer. I've noticed you wear a small, decorated leather pouch that hangs from a leather thong around your neck. What is its purpose?"

Jacko took the lantern and answered, "It's my medicine bag. It was given to me by my grandfather when I was eight years old. My grandfather made it and placed sacred objects inside. It keeps me safe from evil spirits. It is big medicine. Sometimes I grip the bag in my good hand when I need to make a decision or am afraid. It helps me to be strong. It is not just a good luck charm: it connects me to the spirit world and to my Ojibway ancestors."

Mark took the speaker lantern. "Thank you for sharing that, Jacko. I find the old ways of the Ojibway fascinating. You are an inspiration to us all."

More discussion followed. Most were comments on the events of the day. The successful time spent fishing and exploring the logging camp ruins was a hit across the board. Now with full tummies and fatigued after a long day, they began to yawn. Pierre snuffed the speaking lantern and bade all a good night. Mark and Bob stayed on to help put the kitchen in order and ready it for the morning. When they finished, they were released by Pierre.

"Sleep well, mes amis," Pierre called after them while returning their departing salutes.

Mark clapped Bob on the back and voiced a weary "Good night" as they parted.

He then continued to his tent, where he stood listening to the night sounds. A light breeze whispered above as it can do only in the tops of pines. A faint hoot of an owl was eclipsed by the long, quavering chanson of a loon. It had been a full, fun day. He was asleep in seconds.

Chapter Fifteen

Boundary Waters
The Third Day

Early morning sounds woke Mark from a sound sleep. An eagle's "Ki-Ki-Chirr" cry split the pre-dawn stillness. A beaver swam around the point, heading to his lodge. He whacked the lake's placid surface with his wide, flat tail.

Mark basked in the cozy warmth of his sleeping bag and listened while his mind cleared. He thought about the day ahead and needful preparations before he fell asleep. A squirrel scolded as the first rays of the morning sun created a twilight effect. Mark reluctantly slid out of his cocoon and dressed. Kneeling on his ground pad, he unzipped the tent door. He crawled out and slowly stood erect while working the kinks out of his frame. Placing his boonie hat on at a jaunty angle, he checked for his fillet knife. He quietly walked past Bob's tent and continued on to the kitchen.

Pierre hovered over the fire, caressing its warmth. He watched the pot perk while stoking his clay pipe.

"Good morning, Pierre," Mark greeted him.

"Bonjour, Mark!" Pierre replied. "Coffee be strong and hot."

Pierre pulled up a stool which faced the fire for Mark and handed him a mug of rich, hot java. Mark thanked him and sipped the scalding brew carefully. Pierre drew smoke from his pipe and released it in a cloud. It circled his head briefly, and then dispersed. Mark was usually repelled by cigarette smoke, but the blend of tobacco Pierre used was deliciously fragrant. Mark closed his eyes and wondered if voyageurs' pipes were as aromatic. Pierre had told them how important the pose, or rest breaks, were for the French-Canadian voyageurs. They could only indulge in the luxury of smoking their pipes while enjoying a pose or at supper.

Bob appeared, disheveled, wiping sleep from his eyes. He mumbled "Mornin'" and waited for his java while staring into the roaring fire.

"Is good day to explore old resort ruins," Pierre announced. "Breeze still light and sky clear. I prepare take along petite déjeuner. S'il vous plaît, mes amis, gather minnows, load canoes."

"Mais oui," Mark and Bob chorused as one. They threw back the last slug of joe. With a quick salute, they grabbed bait buckets and left for the shoreline. A flock of teal feeding near shore spooked out of sight in seconds. Their blazing speed and small but powerful forms proved why they outwitted many duck hunters.

Mark found the trap's cord and pulled in another good catch of shiners. He opened the trap door and dumped equal amounts of the beauties into each bait can. After tossing the re-baited trap back, he and Bob hauled their booty to the landing.

Bob began loading gear into the canoes. Mark left to check how the clients were doing. All were up, dressed and hauling their gear toward the landing. Mark greeted the sleepy crew. He returned to his tent and secured his daypack and fishing gear. As he made his way he passed Jacko's and Glenn's tent. Jacko held up his good arm with his palm open.

"Wait up, Mark!" Jacko cried. "It's a good morning to travel, no?"

"Mais oui," Mark replied. "Maybe we'll catch some fat walleye today. We will try casting and trolling in the bay near the old resort ruins. Pierre suggested the island on the return trip as a good prospect."

"Allons-y, mes amis," Pierre called to them. "We go to place where only rich men once could enjoy. We go!"

The three canoes plied the lake, hugging the right shore. Everyone established a steady rhythm while keeping a watch for wildlife activity on shore and sea. Jacko had been first with a sighting of a mink with a black lustrous coat. It was hunting along the shore. Jacko cried out and pointed to it. The small, efficient member of the weasel family stopped. He sized up the intruders. Sensing no threat, the mink turned and quickly disappeared into a mass of roots.

Mark let his eyes pan over the lake and onto the upcoming island and bay at the far northern end. The sun's rays were striking the opposite shore. The lake surface ahead was dead calm. An eagle soared overhead. It glanced down at them then banked into the sunlight. Its pure white head and flared tail glowed. Mark raised his paddle high in a salute while mouthing "Brother eagle."

The lake's near shoreline rose a hundred feet above the lake and ran as a plateau, gradually descending to the lake's level at the kettle. Near the resort site, the shoreline became marshy lowland and swamp. Mark had checked the map and found one campsite on the western point of the island and another behind the island on the steep northeast shore.

As they began to round the backside of the island, they spotted the shoreline site. It was directly behind the island on the steep rocky cliff. It had a poor landing, but was better shielded from wind. The water on the back of the island grew shallow and was dotted with massive boulders that rose out of the dark water. Sounds of paddles doing battle with boulders and shouts of "Look out, boulder dead ahead" rang out ominously.

"Watch boulders, guard paddles!" Pierre shouted. "This area be shallow until we approach big island that guards narrow entrance to old resort. Once we round island, try fishing shallow bay. It has lily pads and reeds. Bass and pike prefer. If you not eat your sack breakfast, eat now."

Mark, Jacko, Bob and Glenn opted to try fishing. They cast floating Rapala minnows and spinners. Jacko nailed a hammer handle pike on his first cast and hauled it into the canoe festooned with weeds. Mark felt a fish hit his lure. He set the hook and laughed when a bronze rocket exploded shaking its head, then dove deep. Few fresh water fish fight as hard. The reel's drag screamed, severely testing his #6 test line. Finally, the golden smallmouth bass came alongside. But it was playing possum. Suddenly, the bass came to life. It exploded skyward, shook its head and fell back with a splash that soaked Jacko! Mark soon cradled the beautiful fish and admired its intricate color patterns. He raised it skyward in thanks and released it to live and grow.

"Nice bass, Mark!" Jacko said. "Do you furnish towels with your showers? Hey, look at that!" He pointed to a large dorsal fin undulating through weeds. As Jacko tried to touch it with his paddle, the big pike sensed the motion and exploded in a swirl of water and mud. They noticed that the other two canoes had already landed on shore and turned to do likewise.

The surrounding area was fairly open and sandy. Mark and Bob spread the ground tarps and anchored them with rocks at the corners. Some campers still hadn't eaten their breakfast sack goodies, so Pierre had everyone took a break. Pierre said a few words to them while they ate a late breakfast or relaxed in the warm sun on the beach.

"You sit where once only wealthy resort guests allowed," Pierre said. "Rich men flew here in floatplanes. They fish lake by motorboat. At main resort, eat meals, play cards. Fish all filleted by guides. Meals cooked by chef. When time up, all load in floatplane. Back in Ely in hour.

"This wilderness called 'Le beau pays,' by voyageur. It mean the beautiful country. It once up for grabs. U.S. Forest Service plan road deep in. Want road from Ely to Gunflint Trail, north of Grand Marais. They try to split wilderness in two! It in danger. It be tourist mecca – many roads, resorts, vehicles, motorboat access to once pristine land."

Ray Bond had commented on the near disaster during their Wilderness Survival and Lore class. Ray said, "It would be a far different place if nothing had been done to reverse the greedy assault. It was frighteningly close to succumbing to all the trappings: crowding, pollution and noise that 'development' brings. Though there are still areas such as Basswood Lake and other BWCA entry lakes that allow motorboat use and two motorized canoe shuttles, the majority of this domain is still wild and accessible only by portage and canoe."

"I can't imagine this place being bought and sold," Glenn said. "Imagine the lakes crowded with resorts and cabins and roads everywhere. I also studied the history of this miracle. There were a number of resorts like this one. The Federal Government even sent in agents that confiscated floatplanes and property after some resort owners declined to cease operations. After the feds enforced a buyout of each private resort, the buildings were dismantled and the land was once again free and wild."

Breakfast was over. The impromptu discussion had set the scene. After cleanup everyone was rested and ready to explore. The next vestige of the resort was found just to the right of the rest area.

Pierre pointed at a large rectangular area of depressed sod. He said, "This spot where main lodge was. Other smaller footprints be outbuildings." As the group continued to wander and search the area bordering the woods in the back, they found rusty steel cables, old pots and drums full of holes and dents. Some metal junk was purposely set up on a giant, flat-topped boulder.

Mark suddenly remembered the special TICK permit that allowed them to bushwhack. He drew out his area map and the U.S. Army lensatic compass that was a gift from Ray Bond. He began a search for any sign of a portage trail to the small lake named No-See -Um. Bob, Jacko and Glenn accompanied him as they made ready.

"Pierre," Mark asked. "May we make a search for any trace of a trail to the lake?"

"D 'accord," Pierre answered. "Be careful! If not find trail, come back quick. Bushwhack invite you be lost. We continue explore, wait for you. Must leave soon. We fight wind when return base camp."

The intrepid foursome all saluted Pierre and left. They searched for any sign of a trail leading north. A cleared, open area seemed to lead in that direction. They fanned out and hoped it led to the lake. It soon became impassable with trees and dense shrubs. They continued walking east, behind the old building footprints, and came to a marshy area that ran roughly north-south. Carefully following its edge for a ways, Mark checked his compass often. Further in, they couldn't see the lake or hear any wave action. He finally decided they were not going to find the lake. Mark attempted to re-trace their route. Taking a 180-degree back azimuth, they followed the compass on a south heading. Mark tried to stay on course, but trees and rough terrain made it tough. He felt a hint of panic as they stumbled along. He was hoping he had made a correct course.

"Look, there's that buck rub!" Jacko yelped. "We're on the right track, Mark."

"Good boy, Jacko!" Mark agreed. "I was having some doubts about our position."

Mark thought to himself how good it was to have Jacko along. His sharp eyes and woods savvy were special gifts. Soon they could feel the welcome wind and hear waves crashing on shore. Flashes of sunlight reflected off water and the beach came into view just before they broke through the woods. They stood on the very spot where they departed the old resort.

The crew was involved in packing the tarps and other gear into the canoes.

"Allons-y," Pierre called. "Good you back, we go soon."

"D' accord," Mark agreed. "We couldn't find any sign of a trail, but we gave it our best shot."

They quickly shoved off and paddled away from the calm bay. As they neared the narrow gap between the outer island and the west shore, the headwind awaited them. It delivered love whispers compared to what lay ahead behind the upcoming rocky points.

Mark and Jacko decided to try trolling floating Rapalas as they paddled at the rear of the flotilla. They crossed a long bay that pushed deep into the shoreline and tested at a uniform ten- to twelve-feet deep, according to Bob's reckoning.

The massive rocky point held back the force of the wind, which ruffled the water as it careened off it and continued unabated. Everyone stowed their tackle and pulled hats down tight, bracing for the shock. One by one, canoes rounded the point and were launched into the maelstrom. The crews fought to keep their canoes from being turned broadside. If that happened, they would risk swamping their canoe or worse. The bowmen strained as they battled to once again gain the quieter rocky shoreline beyond the point. The stern men kept their canoes stable and hugged the rocky shore. It required finesse to stay out just far enough to avoid a collision. Soon they entered a deep bay that was protected from the wind. Everyone stopped paddling and relaxed tired arms. The wind whistled through the massive shoreline pines. It was but a momentary rest while they quenched their thirst and chewed some jerky.

"We rest five minutes," Pierre instructed. "Strong wind wait around next point. Next bay has island, Salvation Island. It provide safe place. Will wait until wind die down. It may take hour or until dusk, not know. Relax, fish, read after lunch. Drop off on west end. Good fishing."

They approached the island, having weathered another pounding as they rounded the point. Once again they found rest in the lee of the wind and headed toward the island. It was a great relief to see Pierre's canoe swing easily onto the protected shore of the island. Everyone hopped out and happily hauled their canoes onto terra firma. Mark could see the wild lines of waves, white-capped rollers that pounded the opposite shore. It really was aptly named, this "Salvation Island."

Once all had landed, the tarps were stretched out on the grassy areas between rocks. The girls fell on them, basking in the warm sun, happy and safe. There was almost a giddy mood among the "castaways." They were overwhelmed with the beauty of the island. It was as welcome as an oasis in a desert. The island's central feature was a high rocky ridge that ran east to west that shielded them from the strong wind.

"This home for now," Pierre repeated. "We wait for wind die so can return camp. There be deep water with logs on west side – good fishing. I start gas stove, make hot coffee, tea or chocolate. Enjoy island. It sheltered others from wind and storms. Lunch be ready soon. Bell will ring."

The sun splashed its warm, life-giving rays over them like a blanket. It was a good omen. Mark turned his gaze to watch Jacko smiling broadly while holding his medicine bag. Jacko smiled at Mark and held up his good arm with his fingers formed in a 'V', a peace sign. Jacko and Glenn waved, quickly grabbed their fish poles and live bait, then vamoosed towards the west end. Cora and Ruby waved at them and curled up in a blanket. Cora read to Ruby while waiting for the promised hot drinks.

Pierre found a flat rock ledge that worked well as a stand for the gas stove. After pressurizing the Coleman stove's gas tank, he lit the burner, which flared up. He deftly turned the little handle that cleared the burner orifice. The burner settled into a comforting hiss, its flame electric blue with a red hot center.

Bob and Mark checked with Pierre, then saluted and left to reconnoiter the island. As they turned to go, Mark noticed Cora was once again reading aloud to Ruby from *Little House on the Prairie*.

As they climbed over the ridge of rock, the wind met them. It required effort to make progress. Waves slammed the shore. White foam was washed up on shore like soapsuds. They surveyed the scene, then quickly turned around and crossed back over the ridge. Once again they were sheltered from the savage wind.

Back over the high ridge and over the side, they were shielded from the wind's fury. They hunted for the two intrepid fishermen at the far end. As they neared the end, they approached a rock ledge. Peering over it, they spied their quarry. Glenn was in the process of landing a fat walleye.

"Nice fish!" Mark commented. "What are you using for bait?"

"Hi, and thanks!" Glenn answered. He proudly held the fish up with a look of pure joy on his face. "We've been using crawlers without a sinker, just a snap swivel and a shiner with a bobber. Jacko drew first blood with a nice walleye on a minnow right away!"

Jacko yelled "Hi," as he gleefully pulled in the stringer and hefted his prize.

Mark and Bob's eyes bulged at the sight of the 20-inch beauty. They saluted him and Glenn and promised to return. Off they sprinted, propelled by fish fever.

"These lads obviously need fresh blood to rescue them!" said Bob. "Let's hope we can take the pressure off the two obviously overworked fishermen!"

Bob and Mark hurried back to the canoes to get their tackle. They hoped the bite would continue until they could wet their lines. Without a word they saluted a grinning Pierre, and hotfooted it back. They climbed down on either side of the resident pros, baited up and cast out with high hopes. Jacko had a hit on a crawler and was having trouble bringing it in. Mark grabbed a forked stick from the shore and snagged the line, then pulled it in until he could grab the big walleye.

"It'll go twenty-four inches!" Bob cheered.

"Très bien," Mark agreed. "It's been a lucky stop here because of the wind; otherwise, we might have passed by this honey hole!"

Bob returned to his pole while Mark clipped "old marble eyes," the walleye, to the stringer. Jacko re-baited his hook and was fishing before Mark returned to his own pole. Just as Mark began to reel in his line to check the shiner, the bobber jerked and dove under. He opened his reel's bail and let the fish take about ten feet of line, then closed the bail. He whipped the rod tip up and was into a strong fish. He played the fish, letting the drag sing during the runs; then pumping and reeling in. Bob gave a cry and Mark turned his head to see Bob's rod bent and throbbing.

"It's a double!" Bob cried. "I was just starting to reel my crawler in when I felt a little bump. When I raised my rod tip, he was on."

Just as Bob spoke, his line began rising to the surface and a fine, chunky smallie rocketed skyward. It shook its head, trying to throw the hook, but Bob kept a tight line. Mark had neglected his own rod, but was quickly brought back to reality. His fish swam toward him, causing a slack line. The crafty fish was trying to throw the hook. Mark recovered line by reeling and pumping his rod to take up the slack. He sighed in relief as he found the fish was still attached. One last pull brought the fat walleye close enough to grab under the gill cover. He swept the fish that was as long as his arm skyward in thanks to the Creator. Mark held it proudly as it twisted and jerked. Bob already had his 20-inch smallie held high, as they celebrated the moment. They both clipped their trophies to a stringer and returned to fishing. A faint ringing reached their ears. It was the long-awaited lunch bell. Mark and Bob decided to roll up their poles and took off towards the waiting lunch. Jacko and Glenn secured their poles with rock slabs to hold them steady and soon followed their leaders. Pierre greeted them on arrival.

"Alors," Pierre sang out. "Mighty fishermen return. Did you catch us souper?"

"We did," Mark replied. "Jacko and Glenn caught the lion's share, but we managed to add a few fish to the stringer. All we need is another one, and there'll be a fine bunch of fillets for the group. Jacko and Glenn set their lines and will return to check for more after lunch."

"Très bien, hommes du nord," Pierre gushed. "It would be good to eat fish tonight. Mark, Bob, s'il vous plaît, take fish to near bay. Fillet after déjeuner, so ready if need leave soon. If wind dies, we go."

"Mais oui, Capitaine!" Mark joked. "We will check on the set lines right after lunch and do the task."

Lunch was more than welcome. Pierre had prepared a big pot of savory chicken noodle soup with crackers and more of Zup's summer sausage and cheddar cheese sandwiches. There were even sliced dill pickles, a rare treat this far away from home. Mark found a spot to sit with his back against a flat rock slab. With his lunch plate on his lap, he held a mug of hot coffee that warmed his hands. He sampled a big bite of the sandwich, followed by a spoonful of soup and a pickle slice.

The dill and garlic seasoning ignited thoughts of his mom's homemade pickles. In their home's dirt floor basement sat a massive stoneware crock that stood two feet high and 30 inches across. It was filled to the brim with a salt brine, garden cukes, fresh dill and garlic. The round wood lid was held in place by a rock that kept the pickles moist and dirt and critters out. Mark would often sneak a pickle to snack on. He often took it outside and made it part of his "frontier lunch," in the shelter of the big pines and hazelnut grove where he had his fort.

He could also taste the strong, frothy homemade root beer that he helped mix, bottle and stack on a shelf. The old bottle capper used to seal the cork-lined metal caps had a long handle on a swivel. He winced as he remembered tangling with the "torture machine" one day. He had been playing with the capper when it pinched his skin between his thumb and finger. He tried moving the lever up and down, but it still bit like an alligator. There were blood and tears. He finally realized he had to bite the bullet. As he pushed the lever to its upright position, his hand came free. He wrapped his hanky around his bloody hand. It was another lesson learned in the school of hard knocks.

Mark had chosen a spot apart from the others. He needed to have some solo time, to think and be still. Pierre was also sitting off by himself, having his customary smoke after eating his lunch. He wisely made their meals not only healthy but with special extras. It added to the general sense of contentment. Most of the group relaxed and chatted. Exceptions were Jacko and Glenn who gobbled their lunch and high-tailed it back to check their setlines. Mark couldn't help but compare their trip to a cruise ship where everyone is kept well fed and entertained. Difference was that here everyone pulled his weight.

Out in the windy lake was a pair of loons. They ignored the wild water by sticking their heads under water where all was serene. He envied them. If fishing was not good, they could move to where it was.

The blue sky allowed the sun full play on the water. It created a brilliant glare that would require sunglasses for their departure. They had been sheltered by Salvation Island, but hard reality awaited. They needed to be ready to "bug out," as Glenn put it. Mark sensed a slight drop in wind velocity and sought out Pierre. Pierre listened to his observation and nodded.

"D' accord, Mark," Pierre agreed. "It be less strong. We watch close. It maybe lull and allow us leave. Tell fishermen, fillet fish soon!"

"Mais oui, capitaine," Mark replied.

With a quick salute, he and Bob hurried to spread the good news to Glenn and Jacko. Pierre and the girls were packing up and starting to load the canoes as they departed. It was imperative they get the fish filleted. They launched a vacant canoe and followed the shore. Soon they approached the honey hole. Jacko was fighting another nice fat smallie.

Ray had told Mark and Bob that Sig Olson was responsible for introducing the smallmouth bass to the Boundary Waters. Olson and a buddy had planted some many years earlier, and the species had proliferated throughout the wilderness. Jacko hooked his finger under the gill of the bass and raised it triumphantly.

"Très bien," Bob shouted. "You are one slick fisherman, Jacko. You have the golden touch today!"

"This makes eight fish!" Jacko answered. "Glenn caught another on his set line when we arrived here after lunch."

"Good job! Untie the stringer, Jacko!" Mark cried. "We have to get the fish filleted. You guys should gather your tackle and make haste back to the canoes and help get ready."

Grabbing the stringer of fish, Bob and Mark scooted toward shore. In a couple of minutes they raised their paddles and slipped smoothly into a made-to-order beaver channel. They jumped out, laid their paddles on the grass and filleted the catch. The fish offal was left on shore for the scavengers. After rinsing the fillets, Bob stuffed them into a plastic bag and slid the bag under a wet burlap sack in the center of the canoe. That done, they hopped in and hurried back to the refuge area. The other canoes were packed and waiting. Pierre pushed off as they approached.

"Allons-y, mes amis!" Pierre cried.

Bob jumped out while Mark held the canoe steady. Then Bob traded places with Jacko and the trio shoved off, ready for action.

The line of canoes leaped ahead, powered by adrenaline and pent-up energy. The next rocky point loomed dead ahead. They could see rough water ahead but it looked less lethal. Pierre signaled to dig their paddles deep. They pushed hard as they hit the wind and turned the corner around the island. Soon they hugged the high rock cliff that led into another placid bay. Once again they could ease up and rest in the canoes.

After a short rest, they left the bay and worked their way up the shore towards the last point. It had a massive granite dome that knifed sharply into the water. There was a campsite on the back end of the dome. The high, open site offered a commanding view of the lake and sunrises.

As they paddled near the front of the dome, Mark heard men's voices hollering. Then came an unmistakable, deep roar! There were smaller animal cries, then a man screamed! Pierre had also heard the commotion and had landed where the dome met the lake. Bob and Mark also beached their canoes. Just as Bob and Mark were securing their canoe painters, the drama unfolded.

It was bedlam. An angry black bear was popping its jaws while chasing a man down the rock dome toward them. The poor man being chased was screaming. He had a tattered shirt and was bloody from his head to his waist! The man suddenly turned to face the enraged bear. He used a stick to whack the bear's nose. It made the bear hesitate. It stood on its hind feet and began pawing at the man. Suddenly another man came shouting and whaling on the bear with a paddle! As the bear turned toward the new threat, the injured man fell and rolled down into the water.

Bob and Mark both grabbed a paddle and ran towards the fracas, hollering and shaking their paddles overhead. Glenn and Jacko pulled the victim to where Pierre had landed.

The bear heard the new cries and dropped on all fours. She turned around and bounded up the dome. Bob stayed to help the second man, while Mark pressed on after the bear. As he reached the dome's top, Mark watched the mother bear disappear with two cubs in tow. Satisfied they were gone, Mark returned to the shore where Pierre and Bob were washing and bandaging the victim's wounds. Pierre knew that bear wounds from both teeth and claws were full of nasty bacteria and could become infected. Washing with antiseptic was critical, as was the urgent need to get the victim to a hospital.

"The bear ran off!" Mark shouted. "It was a mother bear with two cubs."

"C'est bonne!" Pierre replied. "This man named Paul be OK. His friend named Jerry. Cora and I clean, disinfect, bandage wounds. We need help to get to vehicle – clinic. Mark and Bob, go with men. Be strong. Help. Jerry want help gather, pack gear in their canoe. Take own canoe. Paul say he help paddle. No artery cut, only arms and head scratched. Try keep mind off wounds – bear attack. Offer jerky, water. Keep from go into shock. We be at camp. Bonne chance!"

Mark nodded, saluted and left with Bob and Jerry to help break down their camp and get it packed up. They kept an eye out for any bear. Jerry was dead quiet and moved about like someone possessed while making furtive glances into the woods. He was agitated and couldn't get their gear packed fast enough. In no time, they had it all carried down to the beach, where Bob packed it into both canoes. Pierre had left a sack of jerky and raisins and everyone gulped down a quick snack. After a swallow of water, they prepared to depart. Paul was looking better after a little rest and refreshment. The raisins would provide quick energy. The jerky was needed protein for strength and endurance. Each canoe had two canteens of water. Each man had several pieces of jerky in their pockets. That allowed them to have a handy, nourishing snack on the run. Bob took the stern of one canoe with Paul in the bow. In the second canoe, Mark was stern man, with Jerry in the bow.

With a last backward glance, they shoved off the dome and headed for the narrows. As they developed a rhythm, their canoes made good time. In a few minutes they were passing by the next campsite high on a dome of solid rock at the end of the narrows. They entered the calm kettle. Mark was curious about what caused the bear attack, but it could wait. The victims both seemed to be less agitated and more relaxed as they put distance between them and the attack. The portage to Tin Can Mike Lake loomed ahead. Mark knew if he were patient and offered them a listening ear, the tale would be told. First they needed to focus on paddling and portaging until their adrenalin-gorged blood dissipated. The physical work would furnish both through fatigue and escape.

With four to do the work of two they could single trip the portages. Paul put all his might into the work. Fortunately their food pack was light. Mark carried it and the canoe while Bob carried a smaller pack and the other canoe. Jerry and Paul carried the rest. They were at the shore of Tin Can Mike Lake in 15 minutes. The paddle across it went easy, with an azure blue sky and a light breeze rippling the water. A heron was fishing near the landing and uttered a startled cry. It sprang into the air with its long legs dangling.

Mark watched Paul paddle. He marveled at his attitude and strength. The bear attack must have rattled him. His cuts and bite wounds had to hurt, but the paddling seemed to energize him. The closer they drew to their vehicle provided a huge incentive. Jerry had escaped with only minor scratches and had stood his ground to fend off the enraged sow bear. He paddled strongly. The grave incident that tested the two men's courage fell behind them.

In 20 minutes, they were at the far end of Tin Can Mike and portaged on to Sandpit Lake. The elevated walkway offered a high road over the marshy area. They walked onto the good old railroad portage trail.

Paul and Jerry started to relax and began to relate the painful details of the incident. Mark and Bob listened intently. They needed to commit as much as possible to memory. All they could do was try to comfort the brave men. Mark patiently filed it away for later. He and Bob could compare notes later. Their progress continued like clockwork.

Once across short, narrow Sandpit Lake, they reached the "lung burner" hill that was the short but exhausting portage uphill to Mudro Lake. After a welcome drink of water and a short rest, they paddled quickly across Mudro Lake. They navigated through the field of exposed boulders at the Mudro Creek entrance, then up to the sandy landing. One last portage brought them to the Chainsaw Sisters parking lot. A jubilant Paul and Jerry hurried to start loading their gear into their Subaru wagon. Mark and Bob loaded their canoe on the roof rack and secured it. Mark was relieved that no other people were present. It made a difficult situation easier by avoiding well-meaning questions and attendant delays.

After giving them directions to the Ely Clinic, Mark obtained their promise to seek medical attention for Paul first. Next they needed to notify the Forest Service. Jerry and Paul were very emotional and happy. Mark and Bob exchanged hugs and handshakes with them before the two men hit the road to Ely. They stood waving as the red Subaru disappeared while dodging impressive potholes. All they had to do now was tackle their route in reverse.

"Well done, my man," Mark said, as he slapped Bob's shoulder.

"Mais oui," Bob replied. "Let's vamoose!"

They hurried back to their beached canoe while chewing on more jerky and gulping cool water. Back in the canoe they quickly crossed Mudro Lake. On the way back, they compared notes on information about the bear attack. Some details had been heard when they were separated. Now that Paul and Jerry were safe, their concern shifted to concern for the safety of the other campers in the Horse Lake area. Fortunately, only two other campsites were on that side of the lake. The Forest Service was sure to send a team to make an inquest. They might possibly put up warning signs or close the campsite where the incident happened.

There were extended silent periods during their return to camp. Their heads were reeling with the horror and the healings the day had brought. Though bear attacks are rare, they are frightening game changers. Mother bears will protect their cubs and fight to the death or until they are out of danger. An innocent comedy of errors and poor camper hygiene had led to the attack. What bothered both Mark and Bob was that it could be repeated. This was possible if the cubs had acquired a taste for human food. Wild animals normally shy from man and have an inherent fear of his scent. But familiarity with man invariably breeds contempt and a loss of normal fear. Once they associate free food with him, all bets are off.

"Last portage before we make our camp," Bob sighed.

"We might even salvage some leftover supper in the kitchen. I'm starved!" Mark joked.

As they crossed the Horse Lake kettle, they paddled hard toward the narrows. It had been a rewarding but fatiguing three hours. The camp landing was a welcome sight. The day's rigors were finally catching up with the two voyageurs. Mark felt like just eating supper and staggering into his tent to collapse. However, that wasn't in the cards tonight, and he knew it. The weary but happy duo trudged into the kitchen's inviting glow and enticing aromas.

"Welcome back, mes amis," Pierre greeted them. "Have a seat, brave hommes du nord."

Cora hugged Bob and Mark, while Ruby clutched their legs. Glenn and Jacko saluted them. Cora led them to their stools and to a table set for them. The entire group had decided to wait to eat until they returned!

As everyone shook their hands and patted their tired backs, they felt honored. They were a bit overwhelmed and shy, but basked in the warm welcome. Pierre removed the cover on the main course and set it down before them. The pan was filled with golden fillets from the catch earlier in the day. Parmesan cheese was melted and lightly browned atop the sizzling beauties. As the hungry group shoveled fillets onto their plates, Pierre presented the rest of the supper delights. He slid one big fry pan of fried potatoes and onions and another with hot, scratch biscuits onto the table.

Mark gave Bob a wink then shook his head and grinned at the feast before them. Glenn said grace. He included how thankful everyone was for Mark's and Bob's safe return, the rescue and good fishing. For a while there was little talk, as forks and knives ruled and appetites were satisfied.

Mark and Bob attacked the bountiful buffet with gusto. Steaming mugs of jasmine tea were set before them.

Mark stood, overcome with the warm reception and food. He spoke with head bowed. "Mes amis," he said. "You clearly have us at a disadvantage. Thank you from the bottom of our hearts. We are humbled. It's good to be home."

The group cheered them and tears flowed. The warm fellowship and feast was finished off with a big tapioca pudding. It was washed down by refills of jasmine tea. Pierre cleared away the plates and food pans with help from Cora and Glenn. Bob and Mark were not allowed to help. Not this night. As the used plates were thrown into the fire, the resulting blaze illuminated the cozy gathering. Dusk had fallen. As if to seal the spell, a loon launched its quavering call. The poignant cry pierced the still night and all fell silent. It was a vivid reminder that they were merely fortunate visitors in a wild place.

"Mes amis," Pierre said. "It was good but très difficile day. Now we back safe, need give thought how we proceed. I hold speaking lantern. It time for Bob and Mark speak details of bear attack heard from Paul and Jerry. After they give report, we keep discussion short. We sleep on it. Can decide more after much rest."

Mark accepted the lantern and paused, bowing his head before beginning. He wanted to be sure he had all the facts straight and in order. Jacko unconsciously gripped his medicine bag.

"As Paul and Jerry sat resting after setting up camp," Mark began, "they were having a gorp snack. Suddenly, a black bear and two cubs appeared nearby. As instructed by the Forest Service, they stood waving their arms overhead and hollered while moving slowly backward. In their excitement they dropped the bag of gorp. The cubs fell on it and began eating. Jerry and Paul began hurling rocks at the bears to frighten them off. One of Paul's rocks struck a cub, causing it to cry out. The mother bear growled at Paul. She made a bluff charge at him. He panicked and climbed up a pine tree. Jerry continued shouting at the mother bear and hit her with a rock. The bear began moving away, but one of the cubs spooked and began climbing the same tree Paul was in. It scurried past Paul on the opposite side of the trunk while crying pitifully. This placed Paul in a bad position. It was somewhat like being the meat between two pieces of bread. In a flash the mother bear was up the tree trying to rescue her cub. She pulled Paul kicking and screaming from his perch. She bit his leather boot and clawed his upper body. Fortunately, he was wearing sturdy hiking boots and a heavy denim jacket which gave him some protection.

"As Paul broke loose and ran toward the dome's descent to the water, the bear pursued and resumed its attack. Paul wisely covered his head with his arms. Jerry returned with a paddle and began whaling on the bear. This was when we arrived on the scene. Our charge and shouting caused the bear to turn away. I raced after her but found the cub had left the tree. I saw her and both cubs run into the woods. I will now hand the lantern to Bob."

Bob took the lantern as he stood, saying, "Mark summed up the incident well. There's not much I can add. However, I will recount some of my feelings about the situation and the trip back to the Mudro parking lot. Paul and Jerry were pretty well spooked and didn't start calming down until we put some miles between us and their old camp. Even with his wounds, Paul more than pulled his weight, and we covered the distance in jig time. They were very appreciative of our help. They were very emotional when they reached their vehicle in the Chainsaw Sister's parking lot.

"Their first priority was to seek medical attention at the Ely Clinic. Their next step was to make a beeline for the Ely Forest Service building to file a report of the incident. They promised to contact our outfitter once safe at home in Michigan. They stressed that they feel no ill will towards the mother bear. She had become too familiar with campers and was only trying to protect her cubs. They were somewhat concerned that our camp might be in some danger, but hoped it was only a freak incident."

Bob then handed the lantern to Jacko. Jacko stood and held the lantern and began to speak. "As I sat in the canoe, I was afraid as I watched the bear attacking the two men. I clutched my medicine bag and asked the Great Spirit, Gitchi-Manido, to turn the bear away and take her and her cubs deep into the wilderness where no man comes. There they will be safe and live as intended."

Cora took the lantern. "Jacko, we thank you for using your strong medicine to ask the spirits of the land and water to take them out of harm's way. Deep in the wilderness is where they belong. They will live in safety and never again seek food from men. You are proof that the old Ojibway values and respect for the Creation is part of a mystery we stand in awe of. Thank you for showing us a glimpse of the Ojibway Tribe's close ties with this beautiful land."

A cheer rose from the group in response and everyone saluted. Jacko bowed shyly, returning their salutes, while gripping his medicine bag.

Pierre held the lantern and spoke. "Today's events were tour de force. We proud of all. We play this by ear. Get good night sleep." Pierre snuffed the lantern candle, and headlamps guided the tuckered campers to their tents.

Mark was glad to say final "good nights" and slip into his tent. He must have drunk too much tea or was still riding the high from the wild day. He lay on his back, alert, listening to the wilderness talk, dog-tired. They had weathered a scary time, but all had worked out remarkably well. A slight breeze whispered through the pines, and waves soothingly lapped the shoreline. Mark's last lucid thought was that these natural sounds were better than taking sleeping pills to fall asleep.

Chapter Sixteen

Boundary Waters
The Fourth Day

A faint loon's lament made his eyes flutter. Mark's arm and leg muscles began twitching. His body was reacting to the strenuous day. A strange feeling made his body shudder. He was standing on a riverbank, watching a bearded man dressed in a soft buckskin shirt and pants with beaded moccasins on his feet! In his fatigue he knew it was a dream, his mind's fantasy, but he was powerless to resist. He was mesmerized by the amazing scene. He surrendered to the lifelike illusion and gazed at the scene unfolding below. Short dark men who wore red berets and sported colorful sashes about their waists manned a large birch bark canoe with a raven painted on its upturned bow and flashed red-bladed paddles! They sang a song as they labored. It was sung in French. He followed their progress, irresistibly drawn to the voyageur vision.

A dim light lit up his tent. It was the false dawn. Mark was stiff and groggy. He lay quiet for a while. He began playing the vivid dream back in his mind. It had seemed so real! His overactive mind had somehow allowed him a brief, exciting peek into the past. Maybe the dream would repeat. He fervently hoped it would. Even though it was an illusion, it was so vivid. He hummed the dream's chanson but it was futile.

He could smell rain in the breeze and glanced at his watch. It was sunrise but still remained dark and dreary. As he listened, a low rumble confirmed his diagnosis. A storm was coming. He unzipped the cozy bag and quickly dressed. He grabbed his hat, rain parka and possibles bag and pulled on his knee boots. He appreciated his warm down vest. A damp chill hit him on his way to Bob's tent. It was as if some resident evil slapped his face. A shiver coursed through him.

"Bonjour, mon ami," Mark said. "It looks like stormy weather. Will you check and secure the canoes? I'll head to the cook shack to help Pierre with breakfast. We may need to rig another tarp for greater protection. This could be a brutal storm. See you soon at the kitchen."

"Yes, boss man!" Bob replied groggily. "I'll do that and alert the other campers before joining you."

Mark hurried to the kitchen. He found Pierre was already busy rigging a new tarp that faced the southwest.

"Allons-y, Mark," Pierre greeted him. "Help get tarp up. It slip down, no good alone. Tie tarp fast. I hold in place."

"Mais oui," Mark answered. "I heard some rolling thunder in the distance. It comes closer!" Mark noticed Pierre was way ahead of him. He already had a big pot of coffee heating on the grille. Another pot of hot, multi-grain cereal bubbled away. Mark took over stirring the cereal. It was partly selfish because he loved the fragrant steam and stirring kept it from sticking to the pan bottom.

"This one be rough," Pierre commented. "Eastern sky blood red this morning. Dark clouds blot out sunrise. Lake dead calm. Birds no sing. Is bad omen, no?"

"Understood," Mark replied. "I asked Bob to secure the canoes and warn the others."

"Bien," Pierre said. "I see this other time, bring bad weather. Maybe thunder—lightning – heavy rain. Maybe last one – two day. Have plenty firewood, keep fire going. We need kitchen stay dry – warm. It help comfort group. Special meals planned, will raise spirits in camp."

A tremendous bolt of lightning split the dark morning sky, like a giant strobe light! It was followed closely by a ground-shaking crash of thunder. The storm front announced its arrival with a vicious wind blast that made the kitchen tarps snap like whips. Mark grabbed a tarp guy rope and held it down, using his body weight to help it take the strain. He winced as live and dead pine branches rained down on the camp. Loud cracks and sounds of limbs breaking were followed by dull thuds. It came from the shoreline trees that faced the savage windblast. In moments the windblast passed by. The wind continued but slackened. Large raindrops began to splatter the camp and then came down in torrents. Mark and Pierre grew very concerned about the fate of Bob and the rest. Mark thought quickly and blew three long blasts on his survival whistle. He heard Bob's faint whistle in reply. It was best to stay where they were and try the whistle again soon.

Mark snuggled his parka hood and pulled his boonie hat down tightly. A new round of lightning strikes and thunder brought heavy waves of rain. Suddenly, out of the downpour hurtled Bob with clients in tow. They had sprinted from their tents, propelled by fear and adrenalin. They had heard Mark's welcome whistle and hurried toward the sound's direction, through the murky maelstrom! All were big-eyed and dripping, but very happy to be at the safe, warm kitchen. All were chilled and gathered close to the roaring fire. They gratefully accepted warm, dry towels from Pierre. They stood drying off their faces and hair.

Suddenly Cora screamed, "I'm on fire!"

Pierre looked over at Cora and laughed. "You not on fire, Cora. It be steam from fire heat!"

Cora looked embarrassed and laughed with the group at her panic. She had never seen wet clothing steam before. Ruby was whimpering softly. Cora forgot about being on "fire" and fussed over her while she dried her face and hair. They were dry and safe. Pierre put his arms around Cora and Ruby. Suddenly, Glenn and Jacko burst into their midst! They had been down at the toilet and saw a tree get struck by a bolt of lightning. Jacko felt his neck hair stand up and led a startled Glenn to safety. They stood close to the fire and dried off with towels. Glenn was visibly shaken, but kept a tight grip around Jacko's shoulder.

Mark and Bob poured everyone hot coffee or hot chocolate. In minutes all was well. The rain settled into a steady downpour with diminished winds. Mark stirred the large bubbling pot of multi-grain cereal. The aroma of the combination of cereal, pecans, walnuts, prunes and maple syrup, worked its magic. Now that everyone was dry and warm, the wild storm was almost forgotten. Everyone sipped hot drinks and engaged in happy banter. The hot cereal was a heady, nutritious tonic.

"Bob," Mark whispered, "how did the tents take the storm's hammering?"

"They withstood the initial wind blast, but we bugged out shortly after it began, so it's hard to say what happened after that," Bob answered. "We could hear limbs cracking and hitting the ground as we ran here. It's possible there could be some trouble. We'll make a damage survey after breakfast."

Breakfast was a big hit as Mark figured it would be. It was what the old timers would call a "twenty-mile meal." It meant the meal would stay with you for a good distance. With the rain drumming steadily on the tarps and only occasional thunder, calm returned. The group began making future plans. Cora promised Ruby she would read to her from *Little House*. Jacko and Glenn were contemplating doing some fishing from shore. Mark saw it as a good omen. He hoped to work in a nap and also catch up on some neglected reading.

Since the clients were safe and in contented bliss, Bob and Mark pulled on their rain gear. They entered the steady downpour and headed out to check for storm damage. It was hard to leave the warmth of the kitchen, but duty called. Their last act on leaving was to pat Ruby's back. She was back to normal. Once again a happy smile lit her cherubic face.

Mark and Bob plodded slowly over the clutter of pine boughs and dead limbs. They were lost in their thoughts. Rivulets of rain sheeted off their hats as they walked with their heads bent forward. As they approached Glenn and Jacko's tent, they almost stumbled into it, due to the combination of fog and debris. A large pine limb lay over it, obscuring its outline. They each grabbed hold of one end of the limb, heaved it up and carried it away.

As the water-soaked weight was removed, they heard several metallic clicks. The tough aircraft aluminum tent poles had snapped the tent back into shape. With sighs of relief, they continued on. Their own tents had fared better. After removing a layer of small branches of pine needles and tightening guy ropes, they found that all was well. Feeling better after finding no damage, they continued on to the girls' tent. It was in similar shape. They put it right. After a good shake, it shed its load of water and looked good as new. Mark unzipped the door and checked the repair he had made to the floor. The repair was still holding. The inside of the tent was fine except for being damp. When camping in tents, everything gets soaked or damp after prolonged rain. As if to emphasize his thought, a heavier downpour ensued. He quickly zipped the door shut. The girls' tent had a handy feature that allowed air to vent out through mesh panels and exit under the rain fly. The two friends continued their tour.

"So far, so good!" Bob commented. "The tents took a beating but without real damage. Let's hope the canoes were as lucky."

"D'accord," Mark agreed. "So far we've dodged the bullet!"

As they approached the landing, the huge blanket of pine boughs and needles was cause for concern. However, once they put their backs to the task, it emerged unscathed! Bob called the canoes "bomb proof." The sturdy Old Town canoes once again lived up to their reputation. After checking the tie downs, they stood back and let the rain wash off the lighter stuff. All was well.

They turned their gaze toward the thumping sound of plastic canoe paddles hitting metal hulls. Two almost indestructible Grumman canoes passed by and carried a mountain of gear. The four hapless paddlers bent to their grim task. They could almost smell pizza and cheeseburgers waiting at the Chocolate Moose. Mark and Bob didn't envy their task. The torrential rain had soaked their gear and created slick portage trails. He cringed when he pictured their worst upcoming nightmare. The dreaded "lung burner," was waiting to test them.

They watched the two canoes disappear into the fog. Mark couldn't help wondering how Paul and Jerry were. After leaving the clinic and reporting the incident to the Forest Service, they may have stayed overnight in Ely or Duluth. It was a long drive back to lower Michigan. The Forest Service kept a current map of the Boundary Waters, with black pins designating reports of bear problems. Prospective visitors were advised if their intended route contained warnings. Bear problems, fire emergency and closed portages were a few of the conditions commonly noted.

Since bear attacks were rare, a Forest Service Ranger patrol would be launched to check out the scene. The rangers would post warnings if necessary. Rangers would come to Horse Lake to interview and warn campers. Their findings would be recorded in their incident reports and returned to their supervisors with their personal observations and summary. A plan of action would be assigned by the Forest Service. It could entail capture and relocation or even the killing of problem bear if it remained a threat to other campers.

After walking the shoreline a ways, Mark and Bob turned toward Cora's and Ruby's tent. As they drew near, they could hear Cora reading to Ruby. Mark called softly to them. Ruby answered happily. Cora greeted them and said that they were anxiously awaiting the special lunch.

As Mark and Bob approached the kitchen and began removing their rain parkas, Jacko and Glenn greeted them before quickly returning to their serious game of checkers. They were quite cozy near the fire as they nursed hot drinks and planned strategy.

Bob and Mark were glad to be back in the kitchen. They soon sat facing the fire with mugs of hot java in hand while conversing with Pierre.

Pierre began with a question: "So, mes amis, what be situation with tents, canoes?"

Mark answered, "All is well. Only some broken limbs and debris landed on them. We removed it and could find no visible damage."

"Bien," Pierre replied. "I worry. Merde weather hard on clients. We build esprit de corps (feelings of well-being) by preparing special meals. Déjeuner be big pot-chicken noodle soup. There also be my scratch sourdough biscuits – wife's wild strawberry jam. Crackers, cheese, Snicker bar for dessert. I need help make soup. I make list – ingredients, directions. Souper be tuna, cheese, noodle casserole, fresh-baked sourdough buns, and butter. Cinnamon rolls pour dessert."

"Magnifique!" Mark exclaimed. "Sounds like a sweet spread. You'll spoil them rotten!"

"That be plan – keep warm – full bellies," Pierre agreed. "Help forget miserable weather!"

"We are at your disposal," Bob offered. "It's good to have a plan."

They pitched in and began collecting ingredients for the soup. It felt good to make some real "comfort food." The relentless rain and dampness tended to produce apathy. The supper special would be just what the doctor ordered. Mark opened the bag of dehydrated chicken, spices and onion. He dumped it into a large kettle of water and set it on the grate to boil. He added a package of bouillon and a few tablespoons of olive oil. Once it came to a rolling boil, he added the bag of egg noodles. Mark loved egg noodles. He stirred the soup and let it come to a second boil. He then moved the kettle to the grate's edge and let it simmer while covered. Giving the soup ample time to simmer allows intense flavors to develop. Mark's mom sometimes let a homemade soup simmer all afternoon until supper.

Glenn and Jacko finally got tired of sitting and playing games. Jacko suggested they go check the minnow trap and try some fishing. Mark was content to remain in the kitchen area, sipping java and watching Pierre prepare the sourdough biscuits. He wasn't familiar with the word sourdough or the concept of nursing a lump of dough over an extended period. He had heard of old Alaskan miners or trappers referred to as sourdoughs, but had no real idea why.

Pierre welcomed Mark's questions. "My mother show me how make sourdough," Pierre explained. "She give me portion, her sourdough starter. She show me how add flour, water so yeast bacteria fill dough. Must keep moist, no freeze, no hot – kill bacteria. Need yeast bacteria need ferment. Give dough unique, sour flavor. I keep in deer hide sack, add little water – flour – keep bacteria happy. I take tablespoon starter, mix four cups of flour. Water make pliable dough – let work in covered bowl – warm place. When rise twice size, it ready – knead – make biscuits. Biscuits placed – flat pan, covered with towel. Let raise, bake. There be plenty for meal. Leftovers for snacks."

Mark watched the process carefully. He had plans to attempt his own in the future. He hoped tonight's supper might evoke excitement, second only to the morning storm's thunder and lightning show. Pierre had the sourdough mixed and raising. Mark had lifted the bowl's covering so he and Bob could sniff the heady aroma of the yeast working. With their lunch chores finished, they decided to stay put and sat down to a few games of checkers. Camp was a pleasant place to spend an hour. It was warm, dry and rife with enticing aromas.

"Bob, my son," Mark said. "We're close to the end of our firewood, so pray the rain quits. We should have enough to make it through today and tomorrow."

"D'accord," Bob answered. "I do hope this weather lifts. Otherwise it could be difficult unless we found a dead tree with dry heartwood. Another day of this stuff, and we'll have to hide any sharp objects away from the clients!"

Mark chuckled at that. "OK, it's your move. S'il vous plaît, crown my man and prepare for your demise!"

After playing a few spirited games that ended in a draw, they took a break, lifted the soup pot's lid and sneaked a few spoons full of the entrée.

"C'est magnifique!" Bob exclaimed.

Mark nodded in agreement as he savored the rich broth. He filled another and offered it to Pierre.

"C'est savoureux, tasty," Pierre replied. "Biscuits be formed, ready to bake. All be ready in forty. Maybe you check clients – alert pour déjeuner."

"Mais oui, capitaine," Mark said, as he made a snappy salute. "We're on our way."

Bob and Mark donned their rain gear and stepped into the waiting wetness. Their hoods streamed rivulets as they splashed their way to Jacko's and Glenn's tent. Subdued laughter was coming through the tent walls.

"Sounds like party time in there!" Bob announced. "What happened to your fishing plan?"

Glenn unzipped the tent door with a laugh. Jacko sat behind him, looking impish.

"Jacko told me an old Ojibway story about his grandfather," Glenn explained. "He was trying to spear a pike from a canoe. When he hit a big one with his spear, the pike pulled his grandfather into the water!"

"Glad to hear you're not letting the weather dampen your spirits!" Mark said. "Lunch will be served in about forty minutes. I wouldn't miss it if I could help it."

They moved on toward the girls' tent still chuckling about Jacko's story. Soon, they were standing next to a very quiet tent. Mark tapped the tent fabric. No response.

"Is there any life in there?" Mark asked.

There were a few groans, then more activity and giggles. The tent door was unzipped and a sleepy voice asked them, "What's up?" When the girls heard about the chicken soup and biscuits, they came alive.

"Oh, please wait!" Cora squeaked. "We fell asleep, but we'll get our rain gear on and go back with you."

Bob and Mark had to cover their mouths to stifle a guffaw. "Sorry we woke you, but it would be a sin to miss such fine vittles!" Bob apologized.

In no time the two maidens were dressed and ready. Together the foursome strolled through the light rain toward the kitchen. Bob was clowning. He held a pine branch over his and Mark's heads while they performed their "wood rat" version of Gene Kelly's "Singing in the Rain."

The lively ensemble noisily stumbled into the kitchen, giggling happily. Bob and Mark stood arm in arm and bowed in response to the girls' applause and laughter.

Pierre stood watching the amusing entrance with his arms folded and looking stern. Then he bent over forward and laughed in spite of himself.

He straightened up and said to them, "Now you here, bien, très jolie hommes et jeune filles, déjeuner ready. Take seat, s'il vous plaît! Mark, serve soup, s'il vous plaît. Bob go get Glenn and Jacko. I check biscuits."

Mark obliged Pierre with a smart salute. He lifted the soup kettle's handle with a hot pad, set it on the table and selected a white enamel ladle. Bob returned with Glenn and Jacko in tow. As Mark filled the waiting bowls, a delicious aroma tortured his senses. Pierre followed with hot, golden sourdough biscuits, two per plate. All eyes followed the food train while lips trembled. Everyone was seated and quiet as Glenn said grace. At the "Amen," they fell upon their déjeuner with little grunts of pleasure. They slathered the hot biscuits with butter, alternating a bite of biscuit with a spoon of chicken noodle soup. Mark offered refills of soup and the platter of remaining biscuits was passed around. A few remained on the platter for snacks. With a flourish, Pierre plopped a big Snicker bar down before each sated camper.

"Bon appétit, mes amis," Pierre announced.

Cora raised her mug in a toast, saying, "This is wonderful, merci beaucoup! If you don't mind, I'll save my dessert for later. There just isn't any room for it now."

Everyone raised their mugs in agreement with Cora. The weather remained dreary, so everyone hung around the fire. Some played checkers or chatted and drank more coffee or hot chocolate. Pierre's parting comment before he left for his tent was that they should show up hungry for supper in five hours. This was met with wide eyes! They had just been stuffed to the gills. Glenn said the only option might be to do as the Romans once did. When Jacko asked what that was by, Glenn replied, "They regurgitated their stomach contents and could continue to feast." That was not what everyone wanted to hear, but Jacko pretended to retch.

Pierre left for a quiet pose with his fragrant pipe. He was pleased with the good morale, esprit de corps, evident in the group. Supper would finish the day on a positive note, despite the weather. Entering his tipi was like going home. He thought fondly of his wife, Clay Basket, as he fanned the aromatic smoke over his head.

Bob and Mark cleaned up in the kitchen. Afterward they decided to supply the thunder box with a fresh roll of paper. They also checked the minnow trap. After emptying the few shiners, they put biscuit crumbs inside and threw the minnow trap back in. The afternoon passed slowly. Some campers were content to remain in the warm, roomy kitchen. Others retreated to their tents to read or rest. After checking out the campsite thoroughly, Mark and Bob retired to their tents and soon joined others in slumber land.

Mark jerked awake when strange voices announced they had company. He quickly pulled on his boots and parka. He stepped outside his tent, somewhat embarrassed at being caught asleep. At least he had some warning. He alerted Bob and was met halfway to the landing by two Forest Service rangers. Mark could see their Forest Service insignia on their jackets and hats. The tall, husky, male ranger greeted Mark.

"Hi, I'm Mike and my partner is Becca," the ranger said. "We're here to investigate the recent bear attack."

"Hello, and welcome!" Mark said. "I'm Mark. I'll take you to meet our guide, Pierre, at the camp kitchen. It is warm and dry and hot coffee awaits."

"That suits us!" Becca said. "We've been out in the rain all day, traveling and checking out the campsite where the bear attack occurred. We could kill for some good, hot java!"

Pierre greeted them warmly. Mark and Bob hung their raincoats and seated them near the hot fire. Pierre placed large mugs of hot coffee into their eager hands. Mark and Bob gratefully accepted their own steaming mugs. All was blissfully quiet as they all sipped their joe and soaked up the fire's radiant heat. Mark judged Mike to be in his thirties and Becca, somewhat shy and younger. Becca clearly deferred to Mike when asked questions related to the investigation. Mike was a seasoned ranger, with 15 years' experience, while Becca had served two years with the Forest Service.

"You welcome to pitch tents here." Pierre offered. "Later, be big souper. You come – s'il vous plaît."

The rangers exchanged glances then smiled and nodded. Mike answered, "We accept your kind offer of supper and lodging. After we are warm and have bummed more of your great joe, we'll collect your statements. Then we'll get our tents set up and maybe sneak a nap before supper."

Mike swallowed the last of his coffee and held it up for more, then drew a legal pad from a zippered, waterproof case. He read them a copy of the statements given by Jerry and Paul, the day of the attack. By this time the rest of the group had showed up and introductions were made. Becca handed out incident response forms to everyone. Mike summed up Jerry and Paul's statement.

"According to their statements, Paul and Jerry had been traveling in the Boundary Waters for seven days," Mike began. "They entered at

Mudro Lake, portaged to Fourtown Lake, Fairy Lake, Boot Lake, Bullet Lake and Moosecamp Lake, before looping back to Fourtown via a creek. They continued to Horse Lake the day before the incident."

Becca passed the statement around the group, allowing everyone a look. Each person wrote their own comments on separate Incident Report forms. After signing their reports, they were free to go.

Mike and Becca thanked everyone and left to set up their camp. Pierre had advised them of the supper bell that would ring to announce supper was ready.

Mark and Bob remained and helped Pierre prep for supper. The egg noodles were already heating, under the close watch of Pierre. He wanted them to be slightly undercooked, so they would remain firm when combined with the other ingredients. Mark mixed the flour, butter, cheese and dry milk together and heated it in a covered pot. When the cheese was melted and stirred, he added the tuna fish. Then he poured the mixture over the waiting egg noodles into a casserole pan. A foil cover was sealed over the top, and the casserole was put on the grate to bake. In a half hour, the pan bubbled nicely around the edges. Pierre removed the foil cover and placed the pan down near the hot coals. He tilted it to allow the foil to be a reflector. It would toast the top to a golden crispy delight. Mark put a bowl of homemade dill pickles on the table as an appetizer. The sourdough rolls had raised and were nearly finished baking. Mark had rolled the sugar and cinnamon into the desert, which had risen fat and glistening. He put them by the coals to bake. The sourdough buns were slid off to the side and covered to keep warm. The fragrance of the cinnamon and sourdough was mouthwatering. Paired with the robust cheesy tuna noodle casserole aroma, it sent out enticing signals.

Damp, sleepy campers were magically drawn to the source of the delightful entrée. The rain had subsided to a heavy mist, leaving some large puddles and soggy areas to traverse. But it was much brighter. That, when combined with the supper aromas, hastened their arrival in good spirits. Tossing their rain parkas over the waiting tarp ropes, Cora, Ruby, Glenn and Jacko washed up at the water bucket, which caught the tarp's overflow.

Mark turned toward the wash stand when a fracas erupted. Someone had been splashed and returned it to sender. It became a spirited battle! Everyone was squealing and laughing or wiping off with towels. They jockeyed for a look at their mugs in the polished metal "mirror," that hung from a cord. Cora primped herself and Ruby, and everyone rushed to the table. Just then Pierre placed the toasty, golden casserole onto the table. Bob rang the dinner bell because the two rangers hadn't showed.

"Mike and Becca must have nodded off after setting up their tents," Bob said.

"It no wonder," Pierre agreed. "Souper fix rangers up! We save souper if late."

Mark began taking orders for drinks. He brought out paper plates and set a stack beside the entrée. Bob served the covered wooden bowl of hot sourdough rolls. Mark filled water glasses and set the silverware. Mike and Becca suddenly rushed in. They splashed water on their faces, wiped it off and slid onto their stools. They looked happy and hungry.

"Sorry we're late!" Mike said. "We were wiped out and barely got our tents up before we conked out."

"You be in time!" Pierre replied. He smiled, as he removed the towel from the sourdough rolls. Mark uncovered the casserole. It steamed fragrantly. He set a big wooden spoon on top. Glenn gave thanks. Pierre scooped generous portions of the creamy, cheese-noodle-tuna casserole onto their plates. Mark served the sourdough buns with butter. As the crew of famished campers tucked into the meal, there was little talking. Some mouths were burned due to eating in haste. Little grunts of pleasure escaped as they alternated savory bites of the casserole with the decadent sourdough buns. Bob poured refills of hibiscus tea, joe, or hot chocolate.

"There plenty left for seconds!" Pierre announced. "Save room for special desert."

Bob, Mark, Glenn and Mike all shared the last of the casserole. Mark chased his final mouthful down with a swig of coffee then excused himself. He checked the cinnamon rolls. They were nicely browned with their tops oozing cinnamon and sugar syrup. He hoisted the pan from its lair and displayed the decadent delight, with a joyful, "voila"!

"Mark, you're killing me!" Mike groaned.

"Gotta' love these rainy day delights!" Glenn cheered.

Cora served a big roll to Ruby, freshly buttered. Ruby touched the gooey surface and sucked her finger. Her face lit up. With her eyes wide and mouth agape, she grabbed the sweet roll in both hands and attacked. The comical sight tickled the group, as they launched their own assault. It was another stroke of culinary genius.

Pierre raised his mug in salute to Mark and Bob. They impishly returned it while standing rigid at attention. They held their mugs high, while holding salutes with their right hands. Pierre lost his composure at this, spilling some of his coffee on Jacko, as he tried to return their salute. Jacko howled and fell over backwards! Mike and Becca joined the rest of the group, first in shock, then joined the raucous laughter. Jacko was reseated and subjected to a rough toweling by Pierre. Jacko was flushed, but happy. Pierre rewarded him with more dessert. It was the kind of thing that helped knit the group together. Ruby's face was covered with butter and cinnamon. Happy and on a sugar high, she finally allowed Cora to scrub her face with a damp towel. Everyone lounged and chatted contentedly near the cozy fire.

Mark and Bob cleared away the plates and fed them to the fire. Pierre lit the speaking lantern, as the last few hours of daylight ebbed. Pierre explained the speaking lantern's history and invited the rangers to participate.

Mike requested the lantern and rose to speak. "Becca and I want to thank you all for your hospitality, especially this bountiful buffet tonight! Since you are the only actual witnesses to yesterday's bear attack, besides Paul and Jerry, your comments and cooperation are very important. Your appearance at the bear attack in progress was crucial to defuse the situation. Your quick action, first aid and help to evacuate the victims were little short of amazing. It will be duly noted and combined with the victims' statements and our observations.

"We have already contacted Walt at Border Waters Outfitters and filled him in on the situation. We will report that both the victims and you feel that the bear was only acting to protect her cubs. We are going to recommend that the bear be monitored for any subsequent bad behavior. If she and her cubs steer clear of other campers and cause no further trouble, we will take no further action. There have been no other reports of bear problems in this area lately. Problems usually begin when a camper, sometimes a previous one, is careless with food preparation, or leaves food for 'the poor hungry bears.' Bears learn to associate food with camp leftovers that are thrown away. Bears may also find food lost on portage trails. Becca and I carefully checked Paul's and Jerry's camp across the lake. We did find some leftover food that had been dumped behind a log, probably left by a former camper. There were also a few aluminum cans in the toilet, which we managed to fish out. Some visitors are slobs. They trash a campsite with no thought about the consequences. At best it's an eyesore. At its worst it causes real trouble for the next group. Bear are opportunists and will quickly learn to scavenge campsites for food. They quickly lose their natural fear of man. The cubs may have located the leftover food from the former campers. They probably returned to check the site for more when they ran into Jerry and Paul."

Jacko motioned for the lantern and stood to speak. "During the bear attack, as Bob and Mark rushed to help drive off the bear, I gripped my medicine bag and prayed to Gitchi-Manitou and lesser spirits. I asked the spirits to lead the bears away into the deep woods where they not cause trouble and can live free and wild. My clan of the Ojibway tribe, the turtle, has spoken to land and water spirits for generations. Many shun the old ways and have been corrupted by strong drink. They have adopted the white man's ways. I am learning the old ways from my grandfather who still lives free and has not adopted the white man's way. The bear will not bother man. She will raise her cubs deep in the wild, far from harm. There are few wild places left where these, our brothers, can live as intended."

The lantern went back to Mike. "Well said, Jacko!" Mike replied. "It is good that you have intervened with the spirits as your ancestors did. Your comments were noted by Becca and will complete our report. If the bear obeys and departs the area, it will be good for all. It is a testament to your connection with the spirits of your ancestors. Our thanks go out to all of you for sharing your observations, the fine grub, campsite and conversation. Becca and I will pack up and leave early tomorrow, since we have to check all the sites on Horse Lake, as well as the other lakes, on our way back to Mudro Lake. Becca wants me to convey her thanks for a memorable visit. We arrived here wet, tired and hungry and are leaving in the opposite condition. Goodnight and fare thee well."

As Pierre accepted the speaking lantern, he signaled night's end by snuffing out its candle.

"Goodnight, mes amis, " Pierre said. "Sleep well. If rain quits by morning, we do day trip. Be ready explore, fish Tin Can Mike Lake. We go early."

The group left, bone weary but excited about escaping to an adventure. They would be free to explore and relax. The rain had diminished to an intermittent mist. Mark's mind still buzzed with the day's events. He undressed and relaxed on his sleeping bag. He savored the quiet coolness then pulled the bag over himself to ward off a chill. He was comfy and drowsed as his brain shut his tired body down. He stirred at the soft hooting of an owl then was lost in oblivion.

Chapter Seventeen

Boundary Waters
The Fifth Day

In the murky false dawn, the two Forest Service rangers quietly broke down their tents, loaded their gear and pushed their canoe off. They had a full day ahead of checking campsites for their general condition. It sometimes depressed them to find willful destruction of trees or fire grates. Some slob travelers would think nothing of packing in beer bottles or cans, but left the empties in the wilderness. Any destruction or trash was noted, and the trash was carried out if possible. If a toilet needed to be dug or a tree was down at a camp, another work crew would be alerted and dispatched. Simpler tasks were handled by the pair, depending on tools needed and their time frame. Special trail crews worked to keep the portage routes and landings clear of trees and debris along with help from volunteers. In spring there was much work to complete before the heavy traffic began. The winter snowstorms blocked portage trails with downed trees and limbs. In summer, severe storms sometimes put campers, portages and campsites in jeopardy. That was when the work was most arduous.

Dawn began with a brilliant sunrise that lit the heavens. Mark left his cozy cocoon and unzipped his tent door. The sky was partly cloudy with no sign of the storm that had lingered overhead for a long day. Mark zipped his vest up to combat the chill. A woodpecker hammered a dead tree and a loon's wild call echoed through the quiet morning. Just another day in paradise.

Mark stopped by Bob's tent and heard him stirring. He greeted him and waited for a lucid response. Once Bob was up and ready, they agreed to split up. Bob headed out to wake the clients and Mark went to the kitchen. A pot of java was heating over the fire when he arrived. The firewood would last the day before it would need replenishing. It was the fifth day of the trip and promised to be a stellar one, if the weather held. It was an easy portage and paddle to Tin Can Mike Lake. Once there, they had ample, unhurried time to explore, fish, and relax. An option was a nice stroll on the portage to Sandpit Lake, sans packs!

Mark met Pierre who had just returned from a visit to the food pack. The coffee began to percolate. They began to assemble peanut butter and jam breakfast sandwiches and dried fruit for breakfast. Pierre poured them both coffees. There would be ample time for a leisurely lunch at Tin Can Mike. Pierre placed lunch fixings into a waterproof sack. Their campground still held several small puddles and a few swampy areas. The thin soil and rock couldn't trap the moisture. Mark found it amazing that the lack of topsoil in the rocky wilderness grew such a wide variety of plants, shrubs and several species of trees, including some majestic old growth pines that pushed their 150-foot spires skyward. He had seen twisted, stunted pines growing out of a crack in a rock cliff. Somehow nature finds a way to survive seemingly impossible conditions.

The hungry group soon arrived and fell upon the breakfast. They washed the cold breakfast down with hot coffee and chocolate. Immediately after breakfast they gathered their gear and assembled at the landing. Mark and Bob checked that each canoe had maps, possibles bags and water jugs. The campers were eager beavers chomping at the bit to be on the water. At Pierre's command of "Allons-y, mes amis," they shoved off on their adventure. It felt great to be paddling down the lake. The lake was calm as glass. There was a general camaraderie as they passed through the narrows. The still morning was charged with excited chatter and pent up energy. The canoe country had been well watered and it fairly glowed. The lake sparkled in the bright morning sunshine. Mark sensed that the day seemed to hum. It was a vibrant living organism of flesh, fur, scale and feather: all tuned like a fine watch by the Creator. This was but a glimpse of how it must have been on the first morning in the Garden of Eden.

"It's a thing of glorious beauty!" Glenn exclaimed, as he spread his arms wide.

Mark's canoe drew up beside theirs at the portage. Mark nodded his agreement with Glenn. Jacko hopped out and grabbed the paddles. Mark grunted as he heaved the 85-pound canoe up onto his shoulders. After making a small adjustment under the yoke, he caught the bowline and started climbing. White-throated sparrows filled the woods with a symphony of their song. The call began with a high-pitched note that trailed off. Loons auditioned from their destination at Tin Can Mike. Traveling light with only small packs and fishing poles made it a quick and easy one-trip portage. Ten minutes later they descended to the sun-dappled, sandy landing. Tin Can Mike wasn't a large lake, but its steep rock cliffs and secluded bays begged to be explored and fished. One could nearly see the high rock shelf at the narrow lake's far end.

The party split up after entering the lake. Mark and Jacko headed along the west shore. Pierre and Bob steered their canoes along the eastern shore. With paddles raised high, they signaled a rendezvous for lunch at the portage to Sandpit Lake. High noon was the designated time. Pierre stood with his arms together over his head to make the sign for high noon.

Mark and Jacko waved to the departing canoes and slowed their pace. They were free to explore and fish at will. With several sunny hours to float, fish and explore, they were ecstatic. They first paddled alongside a long, narrow point. An exposed campsite fire grate almost seemed to float near the end of the point. Mark realized it was an illusion, a mirage. As they watched the mirage, they lost track of their position, and their canoe passed too close to the rocks that hid under the dark water. Suddenly their paddles struck rocks. They recovered without damage and back-paddled out into deeper water. They spotted a solid rock path that climbed steadily up along the point a long ways to where a tent site might be found. It wouldn't earn a four-star rating in anyone's book. Just past the point was a creek that disappeared into a grassy marsh. They decided to try to follow it as far as possible. They pushed, paddled and slid over submerged logs. They sometimes needed to shove off the narrow banks to make any progress.

After following its many turns, they came to an abrupt end. An imposing beaver dam blocked any further progress. Instead of trying to turn the canoe around, they decided to turn themselves around and paddled back to the main lake. It was easier going with the stream's current. Ahead loomed a high cliff that usually signals deep water below it. They drifted alongside and bumped jigs and crawlers along its bottom. The cliff gradually disappeared as they reached a pretty little bay that was bordered on the west by another rocky point. It sloped down to a small bay just to the right of another campsite, on a point. This campsite was also vacant. Mark positioned the canoe near the point's right side. They could cast into the middle of the fishy looking bay that was crisscrossed with sunken logs. Lily pads sported pure white blooms that floated serenely. It had the look of a perfect lair for a fat largemouth bass. Mark removed his jig, clipped on a long shank hook and impaled a fat crawler. Jacko cast to a tangle of logs and lily pads near the far shore. He used a slow retrieve that kept his Mepps spinner above the logs while its silver blade flashed brightly.

Mark cast his fragile bait gently, propelling it in a lazy arc to the center of the bay. It hit the surface with a slight splash and sank slowly. Five seconds after the ripples died, the line began moving. Mark had left the reel's bail open which allowed the fish to take line. Moments later he engaged the reel's bail. As the line tightened, he rocked back, gave the rod a hard jerk and set the hook. The fish stopped dead but didn't react at first. Then Mark felt it shake its head. The bass realized its mistake. It sped away, putting a bend in his rod while making the drag sing. The battle was joined. Mark braced his knees against the canoe hull and tried to stop the brute from tangling in a log. Jacko had reeled in when he saw Mark's pole bend and paddled the canoe into deeper water. The fish was thwarted from gaining the logs but dove deep. Mark knew that trick and kept the pressure on. His reel's drag sang as the strong fish reversed its direction and rushed toward the surface. Mark saw its new tactic unfold. Just before the sly largemouth bass split the surface, Mark gave it some slack. It launched its body into the air while shaking its massive head. Its crimson gills flashed as it tried to throw the hook. Without a tight line to pull against, its ploy failed. The angry bass fell back and sounded while Mark reeled in the slack. He tightened his drag to apply more pressure. The fish finally tired and allowed itself to be pulled toward the canoe. Jacko made a grab for it, but the bass made one last move to evade capture. As it surfaced close by, Mark placed his thumb inside the lower jaw. He gripped its massive jaw tightly and lifted it clear of the water. He pushed it high above his head, in thanks.

"That's a monster!" Jacko cried. "It must weigh five or six pounds!"

"Biggest bass I've ever caught!" Mark replied. He lowered the lunker gently to the bottom of the canoe and removed the hook. After admiring the trophy, he quickly lowered the fish into the water. By moving the spent bass back and forth, he forced oxygen rich water past its gills. With a shudder it began to move its fins, then gained strength and curved its strong tail. With a mighty lurch it tore free and exploded into the depths.

Mark trembled and said, "A bass that big in this cold north country could be ten or more years old. He's a real beauty that deserves his freedom. Fish grow slowly where the lakes are frozen over eight months a year."

Jacko smiled and quipped, "That fish was a whopper and almost my age. We're practically twins! Hey Mark! Maybe he has a big brother living in the bay on the other side of this point!"

"Let's give it a whirl!" Mark suggested. He turned the canoe around and handed Jacko his rod. He would be the guide while Jacko tried for the big bass' "brother." Jacko put a fresh crawler on the hook and waited until Mark paddled them around the point to the opposite bay.

"You get to try this one," Mark offered. "I'll be your guide and net man."

Mark steered the canoe into position, then glided to a stop. It was Jacko's turn.

"Jacko, cast over toward the middle as I did on the other side and open your reel's bail," Mark directed. "If a fish runs with it, give him slack then hit him hard."

Jacko checked his knot tied to the snap swivel and held up the impaled crawler for Mark's inspection. Mark nodded his approval as the crawler was skewered. Jacko lobbed his squirming rig high and watched it drop on target. Nothing happened after a few minutes. He reeled it in and cast toward a log that protruded out of the water. It had no sooner hit the surface when that spot boiled wildly and line peeled off his reel! Jacko quickly rammed his fish rod butt between his knees. He let the fish take up the slack, closed his reel's bail and pulled back hard. When the fish felt the hook's barb, it immediately went airborne. A big, feisty largemouth bass threw water everywhere. It violently shook its great head and flared its gill covers, exposing his vivid red gills. The powerful fish put Jacko's bad arm and his tackle to the test. Mark was tempted to offer assistance but resisted and let Jacko go solo. It was his time to fight his "twin": win, lose or draw.

"Man, he is a whopper!" Jacko grunted. His reel's drag screamed as he strained to hold the bent pole between his knees. Mark feared he might be pulled out of the canoe or lose his fish pole over board. But Jacko gamely braced his feet against the canoe hull and leaned backward. He stopped the bass's run. Undeterred, the smart bass pulled another ploy. It instantly reversed its direction and rocketed toward the canoe. Jacko reeled frantically as he desperately tried to regain the slack line. The lunker bass felt the slack line and knew how to make his escape. One powerful dive into a submerged treetop and he was free. Jacko sadly reeled in his limp line. He sat a while fingering the frayed line and shook his head. Mark held his breath and waited patiently.

"He was too big and smart for me!" Jacko wailed. He handed Mark's pole back.

Mark watched Jacko stare off into space. Jacko held his medicine bag while his lips moved.

"Don't let it get you down, Jacko," Mark replied. "He was bigger and smarter than mine! You gave him one heck of a fight, and he'll be here for someone else."

Jacko finally smiled then sighed, and picked up his paddle. Together they turned the canoe toward open water and paddled out. The late morning sun shone brightly. It was idyllic. A gentle breeze cooled them as they continued west along the shore. Mark noticed a canoe moving slowly along the opposite shore. The sunlight reflected off the thin monofilament as someone cast a lure. A sheer cliff behind the canoe dwarfed it.

Mark and Jacko decided to try trolling Rapala floating minnows as they paddled along, so they would at least look like they were fishing. They each had fought a great fish and were now content to rest and let the passing scenery fill their senses. The receding hills were a mix of pine, aspen and wild cherry trees, with many small warblers flitting about. The breeze felt great, blowing gently though their hair. It ruffled their shirts and was excitement enough for the moment. Mark had heard of lazy fishermen who didn't even tie on a lure so they could relax and enjoy the scenery. Fortunately, no fish disturbed their slow trolling while nature continued its enchanting program.

Soon, mild pangs of hunger began to interfere with their solitude. They had drifted near the far end of the lake. Jacko's keen eyes could see that one of their group's canoes was already at the landing. Three people moved about on the rock hump above the beached canoe. Mark took his small binoculars out of his daypack and adjusted the focus. Pierre was moving about while his red sash fluttered in the breeze. Cora and Ruby had climbed up on the big table rock. As Mark and Jack drew closer, they noticed cabbage weeds passing under the canoe. It signaled shallow water and perfect hunting grounds for pike. Jacko pointed ahead to a canoe. One occupant was fighting a fish. As they closed on the canoe, Jacko saw that it was Bob! His fish pole was bent almost double. Water sprayed him as he tried to boat a big pike. As they passed by, they watched Bob and Glenn both fighting to subdue the pike. The angry pike was thrashing about mightily in their canoe.

Suddenly, both Mark's and Jacko's poles began to throb! They had forgotten their lines were still in the water! Mark cried out, "Fish on!" and waved greetings to Bob and Glenn, as they passed and fought their own battles.

It was a two-ring circus with fish diving under their canoe. The wily pike teamed up and tried their best to tangle and break off. More than once the two pike nearly succeeded. Mark envisioned himself and Jacko swimming with the pike if things got any more out of control. Jacko's fish solved the problem by wrapping itself around a big clump of weeds and broke off. Jacko sadly reeled his slack line in. It was game over for him. Foiled by a big fish for the second time today, Jacko was not pleased.

Mark still had his quarry on and it was full of fight. After a short, violent tussle, the nice-sized pike swam obediently to the canoe. It pretended to be whipped, but Mark saw its evil eye and knew its true intentions. A pike likes to save its real fight until he's inside the canoe. Mark knew from experience fishing pike with P.J. on Moon Lake. He had witnessed what savage mayhem a large pike could wreak when he once took a big one aboard P.J.'s Thompson boat. It careened wildly about the boat, slashing clothes and flesh with its sharp teeth, treble hooks and brute force. The pike took full advantage and gleefully thrashed about with abandon. It tangled nets, scattered tackle and splattered slime everywhere. Sometimes pike could break a line and jump back into the lake. In a worst-case scenario, the angry pike and its captor could end up in the drink. Experienced pike fishermen learned to carry a small wood bat or billy club to whack the fish. A good hit on the head would stun or kill it.

Mark had listened to Ray Bond tell about fishing for halibut long ago in Alaska. Halibut are built like a giant flounder. They live in cold arctic depths over a 100 feet deep and can weigh hundreds of pounds. It is necessary to shoot a strong halibut before bringing him aboard to avert mayhem.

"Don't lose him, Mark!" Jacko cried. "He's a giant and we need him for our supper!"

Mark kept his Shakespeare Ugly stick rod high, tiring the pike until it floated on its back alongside. Mark grabbed it behind the head with one hand and with his other hand around its tail, lifted it overhead in thanks. He and Jacko admired the broad green back and markings, as it oozed slime. It was close to 30 inches long and ready to commit mayhem. As he held it securely on the bottom of the canoe, Jacko gave it a sound "coup de grâce" with the flat end of a hatchet. It shuddered, then lay still. Mark clipped it to the stringer and let it ride alongside. He rinsed off what slime he could from his hands. He used his needle nose pliers to remove the Rapala's extremely sharp treble hooks. It was time to head for shore to fillet the pike and eat lunch. As they slid the canoe onto the shore and jumped out, Mark held the pike high and started up the rock.

"Wow, Mark, great fish!" Cora cried.

Ruby waved wildly, not seeing but taking Cora's word for it. Pierre was busy setting up a cold lunch. Bob and Glenn were already filleting their pike. Mark hauled his fish up to the flat table rock that offered a place to fillet while he was standing. They compared the two pike and found they were "almost twins." As they carefully slid their fillet knives behind the dreaded "y" bones, they compared fish stories.

"Nice fish, Bob, they're about the same length, but yours is heavier," Mark said.

"Thanks," Bob replied. "He fought like a savage beast. Without Glenn's quick thinking, it might have been a disaster! He pulled off his prosthetic foot and whacked him. Glenn is claiming it to be a first. He might enter it in the Guinness Book of Records!"

Mark chuckled and said, "Remind me never to get on Glenn's bad side. He's like a bionic man. His whole body, biological or synthetic, is a deadly weapon!"

After washing the scales and slime off the rock, they rinsed their fillets in the lake as they traded fishing stories, present and past. Bob and

Glenn had also hooked a few largemouth bass. Their bass were smaller but feisty. They had caught them around the old pier posts across the lake.

Mark placed all the fillets into a plastic bag and put the bag under the wet burlap in the shaded canoe. Bob carried the fish offal down the portage trail and onto a rocky outcrop, well away from the portage trail. He hurried back to the landing and found lunch about to commence. Pierre had three large platters piled with good old Zup's summer sausage, cheddar cheese and the leftover sourdough buns. Desert was a choice of Hershey or Bit-o-Honey bars. Everything was quickly gobbled up. Cora announced they were all members of the "clean plate club!" After lunch they lolled around the little rock dome and basked in the warm sun. They were so happy to be dry, well fed and free to roam.

Mark suggested a leisurely hike to Sandpit Lake. Everyone but Pierre decided to go. They all grabbed daypacks and waved goodbye to Pierre. He waved and then lit his pipe.

It was so nice to hike along the old rail bed without heavy packs or canoes. Along the way they drank their fill from a little spring-fed rivulet that tumbled down a hill and onto the trail. It was clear, cold, and refreshing. Jacko pointed to the trail where original railroad ties were outlined, with spike heads visible. The sun shone through some large trees, spreading a dappled pattern over the portage. White-throated sparrows serenaded them as they hiked the easiest portage of the trip. At the other end of the trail, they ran into the sheer rock cliff on the left that descended into the water of Sandpit Lake.

Jacko spotted movement across Sandpit Lake on a rock escarpment. Mark focused his binoculars and found it was the lone campsite on the lake. Two young women and a dog occupied it. Once again Jacko's sharp vision made a discovery. Jacko and Glenn voted to continue following the old railroad bed a ways. There was ample time, so off they went. They crossed the creek and soon spied the short trail that led to the Range River.

The mosquitoes began to bite, so they turned around and returned to the landing on Sandpit Lake. Four women campers met them there. The women had just unloaded two large aluminum canoes. There was a mountain of packs and gear. They said they had just paddled in from Mudro Lake and suffered through the dreaded "lung burner" portage to Sandpit. The four women looked exhausted.

"Hey, girls!" Cora said. "Can we help carry some of your burden to Tin Can Mike?"

That changed everything. The four women travelers came alive and grinned and nodded their heads. Bob and Mark led the way with the two heavy canoes, as well as a couple of the smaller packs. Everyone else carried what they could. One trip completed the carry to Tin Can Mike. The women confessed that they were new to canoe tripping and portaging.

"Thanks for all your help!" Sondra, the leader, said. "We hope to get stronger and more fit as we continue deeper into the wilderness. My name is Sondra and my friends are Pam, Rita, and Teresa. We are all having various life struggles. We wanted to escape here where we can try to find peace and direction. Our first camp will be at Tin Can Mike. We hope to journey as far as Moosecamp Lake and return home in a week."

While they packed their gear into their canoes at the landing, Pierre greeted them and offered them some jerky. They gladly accepted and took a break on the rocks. They appreciated the rest break and chatted with Pierre and the crew. They took many long drinks of water. Eager to get set up at a campsite, the four women hugged everyone, waved goodbye and shoved off.

Mark and the crew stood and waved as they paddled out on Tin Can Mike. Mark remembered what the leader, Sondra, had said about their all being friends since childhood. He knew it would certainly test their mettle and lead their friendships and plans to a higher plane. Exposure to the beauty and demands of wilderness travel left no one neutral. Each one experiences his or her epiphany. Mark gazed proudly at his group. There was an aspect of a wilderness trek that needed to come unbidden from within. It was the bonding that comes from working, laughing, crying and celebrating life together. It meant helping others to persevere in their quest.

Pierre reminded the crew that they had only a few hours left to remain there. He stressed that with the dwindling food sack, there was a real need for more fillets for supper. Mark spoke with the guys and all were eager to go back out. It was their "civic duty," according to Glenn. Gold and black floating Rapalas were the lure of choice for Mark and Jacko. Bob and Glenn chose the silver and black version. They would need to catch at least two more decent-sized pike. That would guarantee everyone got a heaping plate of "poor man's lobster."

Jacko said, "This little bay seems to have pike to spare! Let's do Pierre proud."

"D'accord," Mark said. "I know how great the fillets will taste. I want to have seconds! Bonne chance, mes amis."

Pierre stood and returned the guys' salutes. Cora and Ruby waved from a comfortable grassy area high on the dome. The canoes split up, and the fishermen trolled their lures on short lines due to the shallow depth of the water and many weeds. They no sooner began when their quest was answered. They beached their canoes an hour later with a pike bonanza. Mark lifted their stringer with three nice pike. Jacko had redeemed himself by catching two of them. Bob and Glenn proudly produced a stringer of two big pike. It would be plenty.

Pierre did a little jig when he saw the heavy stringers of fat pike. He saluted them and voiced a loud "très bien," as the proud fishermen returned snappy salutes and hauled their catch to the filleting table. After the filleting, Jacko and Glenn carried the fish offal away while Bob and Mark rinsed the fillets and put them in the cool sack in Pierre's canoe.

"Allons-y, we go," Pierre ordered. "Time we head back. Still need get firewood and prepare supper. Need plan tomorrow – day trip. It be très bon trip. We go Basswood Lake!"

The last comment by Pierre charged the group. Everyone hastily packed their gear and hopped in the canoes, eager to get back to base camp. The sun was dropping lower in the northwest, but the air was warm. A southwesterly breeze kissed their backs.

As they approached the far end of Tin Can Mike Lake, Jacko sang out, "There they are!" He proudly pointed to the four women they had helped. Their camp was set up, and the four intrepid women waved back at them. They had taken the campsite on the northeast point.

An hour after departing, the group arrived at the camp. It had been an enjoyable day. As soon as they beached their canoe, Bob and Mark gathered the saws and an axe and left to cut more wood. In an hour they returned with enough to last the few days remaining in their trip. Any extra wood was a cheap insurance policy against further inclement weather. Any leftover wood would be left in a stack. It would be greatly appreciated by the next campers. After hauling all the firewood to the kitchen, they stacked and covered it with a tarp. That done, they retired to their tents to rest and to prepare for their last day trip. The late afternoon sun still beat down, but was only three fingers above the horizon. As dusk was nigh, the temperature began to fall and the breeze died. The lake soon becalmed, and picturesque cloud formations set the stage for a stunning sunset.

Supper would be their next task. Mark joined Bob at the kitchen where Pierre laid out the menu. Bob was assigned the desert, a pistachio pudding with real pistachio nut pieces. Mark peeled the last of the potatoes and put them in the big skillet with oil. He watched them sizzle and turned them as they browned. Pierre had a nice fire going and was busy preparing the fish fillets. Mark sliced the last of the onions and scattered them over the potatoes. He gave the taters a good shot of coarse black pepper and salt. Then he covered it and moved it off to rest. Pierre rolled the pike fillets in a seasoned batter and began dropping the sweet, succulent fillets into the hot oil in the fry pan. The fresh fillets sizzled and quickly turned a golden brown. He flipped them over and let them finish. When he pierced them with a fork, they were flaky white and exuded steam and a tantalizing aroma. He transferred the first batch to a platter to stay warm and began a new batch.

Mark lifted the cover and found the American fries nicely done with the onions nicely caramelized. Bob kept a close watch on the pudding that he stirred constantly to so it wouldn't burn. Supper was ready except for setting the table. As Mark made the last preparations, Pierre rang the bell. The tired chef trio took a break and sipped some rich java that perked them up. Pierre lit up his clay pipe, and they talked about the coming adventure.

Soon, the clients arrived. Most were dressed in shorts and sandals since the air was still warm. They settled into their usual places. The crew sported dark tanned faces, especially Jacko, who looked like an Ojibway warrior, and Ruby who glowed dark ebony. All noses were busily sniffing the heady cooking aromas. Pierre made a deep bow, his red beret and scarlet sash resplendent in the firelight.

He stood up straight and greeted them: "Bonsoir, mes amis! Souper be ready. Fresh caught pike, American Fries – special dessert. We pay homage to homes du nord, pour bonne fish. No food shortage tonight. It be très bon day. Enjoy souper!"

Glenn delivered the grace. Heaped platters of crisp golden pike fillets and fried taters were passed around the table. Mark poured coffee while Bob handled requests for hot tea or hot chocolate. Everyone dove hungrily into their heaping plates. Seconds were available to all.

"Fantastic grub, guys!" Cora exclaimed.

"Amen to that," Glenn added.

Now Bob slipped the covered pot of pudding onto the table, along with a heaping bowl of shelled pistachios. The rare sweet treat was gobbled in record time. Some mixed the nuts into their pudding while others preferred the pudding plain. All spoons were licked and bowls were scraped clean. This was proof the dessert was a resounding hit. It was another stroke of genius by Chef Pierre. When Mark asked how the meal rated, he received cries such as: "magnifique!" "smashing!" "gourmet!" and "decadent!"

Pierre stood and bowed to the group's appreciative applause. He then doffed his beret and bowed towards Bob and Mark.

After lighting the speaking lantern, Pierre said, "Mes amis, bonsoir! Tomorrow we embark on last, maybe best, day trip. We explore new très jolie wild area – Basswood Lake. It be boundary with Canada. There be beauty and danger. There be waterfalls, rapids. Some take chance, try run rapids, overturn canoe – die. We not tempt fate. We go at dawn – enter Horse River. We head north – Crooked Lake, take portage to Lower Basswood Falls. See ancient cliff paintings. It be tough – très magnifique day. Bonne chance! We do déjeuner, then return. Sleep well, come early pour java – pancakes—first light."

The gathering quickly broke up as they all walked toward their tents. The tired but happy group couldn't resist a brief detour to the shore. A brilliant sunset with red and coral streaks against an azure blue sky greeted them. It was a harbinger of good weather, if the old adage "Red sky at night, sailor's delight" held true.

Mark and Bob stayed with Pierre and cleaned up. There were just enough leftover sourdough buns for lunch sandwiches. They were spread with butter, filled with the last of the summer sausage and supplemented with dried fruit. The food pack was shrinking rapidly and would be a breeze to carry out. It was hard to believe that the trip was quickly drawing to a close.

After finishing their chores, Bob and Mark decided to walk to the shoreline and gaze at the last vestiges of the once fiery sunset. Its intensity was muted as it struggled to light the sky with glowing pastels. All color would soon succumb to the darkness. While the pseudo-voyageurs slept, the creatures of the forest and waters hunted prey. The lake was calm except for a V-shaped wake, as a beaver journeyed to his feeding area. Loons called to announce the coming night. Mark could hear the "splats" of a loon's webbed feet running on the surface while strong wings provided lift. Once airborne the loon lifted off. Its strong wings made a "whoosh" sound. In parting, it loosed its strange, tremolo call. A tight formation of ducks roared over at treetop level as the two friends turned and walked back toward their tents. No human noise broke the silence, except for soft snoring as they passed Glenn and Jacko's tent.

Mark bid Bob "bonsoir" and entered his tent. He prepared his gear for an early start and slipped into his bag. His mind raced ahead to the exciting day to come. None of them except Pierre had ever seen pictographs, ancient rock paintings, except in books. These mysterious paintings, done by creators unknown, had stood the test of time and elements. If all went according to plan, their last day trip would register off the wonder scale.

Chapter Eighteen

Boundary Waters
The Sixth Day

Darkness settled over the quiet camp. The warm bag felt good as Mark let his heavy eyelids close. An owl hooted softly, startling Mark into a semi-awake state. He was lulled back to sleep. His body tingled as his brain shut it down. His autonomic nervous system set his fingers twitching. His eyes moved under closed lids.

Mark found himself above a river bank, watching a large birch bark canoe. It was part of a north canoe manned by fur trade voyageurs! They wore red berets and bright sashes about their waist and dipped their red paddles at a fast pace, in harmony with a French chanson they sang. They spotted a tall man in buckskins on shore and all stopped paddling. The buckskin-clad figure raised his arm high with his palm turned out. His camp was pitched near a portage landing just downstream from a rapid. The trade canoe's guide waved his arms overhead and then commanded the three-canoe brigade to head for the buckskin-clad man's camp. The guide signaled for a parley. As the canoe drew near shore, its crew of swarthy, stocky, French-Canadian voyageurs hopped into the water. They held the canoe so they would not scrape the fragile hull. A passenger in the canoe with reddish hair and wearing a scotch-plaid beret waved at the man dressed in buckskin. The buckskin-clad man waved back, then climbed aboard the canoe and they paddled away.

Mark jerked his body, unsure where he was. He had dozed off for a while. He still saw clearly the vision of the voyageurs, with their bright-colored sashes and red berets. He lay still and listened, hoping it was not near morning. Then he heard the unmistakable sounds of a woodpecker drumming a tattoo on a dead tree. Looking through his tent door, he could see the faintest glimmer of light in the east. He realized he had slept and dreamed through the night! He wiped the sleep out of his eyes and unzipped the warm bag. After quickly dressing, he stepped out into the false dawn with much yawning and stretching. Closing his eyes, Mark inhaled a big lungful of the sweet morning air. He turned just as Bob approached. They managed a sleepy high five and made a beeline for the kitchen. Their great need for hot java and a cozy fire were crucial to their "survival".

"Allons-y, mes amis," Pierre greeted them. "No time to lose. Have coffee then wake group. I start pancakes." Mark and Bob complied by grabbing two mugs of hot java and saluted before they headed out to wake the troops. After making sure they received adequate responses from each tent, beyond semi-lucid grunts, they announced that hotcakes with syrup and hot drinks awaited at the kitchen.

The crew soon arrived, disheveled and groggy, but excited. After putting away several hot-buttered, syrup-drenched cakes and drinking hot coffee or chocolate, they trotted away. Everyone fetched their packs and congregated at the canoes. All was ready for the trip. Mark made sure both he and Pierre had a map, just in case one was lost in the fray.

With a final look back at the camp, Pierre signaled them to board canoes. Three canots du nord full of intrepid voyageurs shoved off, turned into the bay and followed the current that was the Horse River. The shallow bay was a minefield of large boulders. Some lay just below the water line, poised to surprise overzealous canoeists. Soon, a current tugged at the canoes. They traversed the narrow opening between exposed boulders and hidden ones. It made for a pulse-quickening passage. The current subsided into deep pools just before the rapids were heard. They all pulled over to the left side for the first portage. The portage ran alongside the narrow river as it cascaded through a rocky chute. Two hours later, they had passed Lower Basswood Falls and crossed the bay of Basswood Lake. A one-and-a-half mile paddle through the picturesque scenery brought the group to a region of steep, high cliffs.

"We proceed to bay's south end," Pierre explained. "Look pour big overhang."

As the flotilla reached the north end of the cliff, Jacko, in the lead canoe, once again proved his superior vision.

"I see a pictograph!" Jacko cried. He pointed above his head as the others closed in. Mark steadied the canoe while they studied the ancient painting. It appeared to be a fish in a net. Jacko identified it as a sturgeon, a beautiful but primitive bottom feeder that he had once helped to catch with his tribe. Next down the line was a pair of horned figures that might possibly be spirit beings. Cora pointed to some figures that were definitely moose. Then they saw a pair of strange looking birds that Pierre called pelicans. Further down the cliff was a pictograph of a canoe flying a medicine flag adorned with an elk, a heron and a bear. Another spirit being that depicted Manidog was found. The group carefully searched for more on the overhang. Besides the recognizable paintings, there were some abstract symbols. Two of the more intriguing ones were located below an orange lichen ring. A vertical crack in the cliff separated two paintings. On the left was a long, upright horned figure. It was similar to a humpbacked man with his arms crossed on his chest. On the right was a figure that Glenn thought represented another sturgeon in a net. Cora asked to have a second look at what she named the "eccentric moose." She was positive the moose was smoking a pipe!

As they carefully inspected the ancient art and discussed its merits and mysteries, valuable time passed. Pierre wanted to begin the return trip while the weather and daylight were optimal. He let the group linger as long as possible, but finally gave the command:

"Mes amis, allons-y, we start back, now! Make déjeuner, take pose at overlook Lower Basswood Falls."

Pierre's suggestion seemed premature to them. The ancient paintings were fascinating and the weather idyllic. But his judgment trumped theirs and they complied. They knew how easily time could slip away and how suddenly weather could change. Pierre merited their respect. They knew they were far from their cozy and safe campsite. Pierre led the way and set a voyageur pace that made their arms ache. In less than an hour they pulled into a picturesque grassy area that overlooked enchanting Lower Basswood Falls. Déjeuner was basic but welcome. It was a small feast composed of jerky, buttered sourdough buns, dried fruit and water. The group sat or lay in the comfortable sun-splashed grass. While dining, they took in the natural beauty of the splashing waterfall that sparkled and frolicked below. A gentle breeze whispered soothingly through the pines overhead. Jacko mentioned he had spotted an aluminum canoe that had wrapped around a big rock in one of the rapids they had portaged around. Everyone chatted and ate. Pierre gave out toothpicks so they could free the jerky strings that caught in their teeth. Pierre allowed an hour for the rest then called them back to their canoes.

"Allons-y, mes amis, we go!"

Without a complaint, the group got up and pushed off. They were sad to leave the little "Eden," but were ready to return to base camp. They dragged their lazy bodies up and piled into their canoes with one last glance back at the lovely garden spot. The return trip was uneventful except for the normal cuts, bruises and strains one encounters when traversing a jumble of rocks and roots. Upon reaching the last portage before entering the Bay of Horse Lake, they were grimy. Sweat, dirt and mud had splattered them liberally. It had been especially mucky where they had to line their canoes. It was tough pulling them against the swift river current that flowed over a foot of muck. They had to fight the current without the surge of adrenaline that propelled them earlier.

The tired and disgustingly filthy group finally reached the campsite's landing. The bedraggled voyageurs disembarked and clambered wearily ashore. All their energy was spent and all they desired was to collapse in their tents. Pierre watched the tired, grubby group as they left. He stood on the shore and smiled as he stoked and lit his pipe. Mark and Bob put away the lunch leftovers, but Pierre told them to leave the canoes and paddles alone. He knew just the cure for the crew's maladies. Pierre instructed Mark to have the entire group change into swimsuits and return to the canoes immediately. Pierre knew a perfect swimming beach that would not only clean them up, but also energize them and build a healthy appetite. Bob left to change and met Mark coming back. Mark was attired in swimsuit, water sandals and his ever-present boonie hat. He carried a sack of jerky that he had taken from the food sack. Each camper was handed a few sticks as they appeared. Minor grumbling vanished when the jerky was handed out. The group shoved off in the canoes. Excitement began to show in their faces. They craved a cool, purifying swim.

Pierre led the anxious, sweaty mob along the near shoreline, heading north. Wearing his red beret and with his scarlet sash fluttering, Pierre smoked his pipe as he paddled. Mark felt it was the closest he would probably ever get to a historic voyageur. After passing a campsite, they approached a large open point with majestic pines and an inviting beach. There were shaded areas lined with thick blankets of pine needles and sunny areas near the fine, white sand beach. The great majority of Boundary Waters shorelines feature boulders, rocks, rock shelves and domes. This beach was a rare gem. The tannin-stained water was in marked contrast to the white sand. The slope increased as one left the shore and hiked uphill, where massive boulders and rock cliffs stood guard.

After landing, everyone, including Pierre, waded in and washed away the day's accumulation of grime. Most of the group completely submerged, however briefly. Pierre had removed his sash and boots and was wet except for his head. He continued smoking his pipe while he escaped to a sunny spot where he could watch the follies. There was a furious but brief water fight. It started when Jacko splashed Cora because she wouldn't dive under. Soon the whole group was involved, with much hollering and squealing. Everyone was thoroughly drenched and much cleaner when it ended. Pierre had made another wise choice. Soon, the giddy group departed the lake and ran up the hill. A thick layer of pine needles provided them soft seating in the warm late afternoon sun. The shoreline faced southwest. The sinking sun had dropped to an angle, which concentrated its rays on the slope.

"Man!" Bob said. "This would have made a great campsite!"

Pierre withdrew his pipe and answered, "It be true pour one camper. Better it belong to all so can use pour free. We need return camp. It late. Food pack dry up. Souper be skinny. Must save flour, jam pour tomorrow petit déjeuner."

Everyone began to feel hunger pangs as Pierre spoke. They jumped back in their canoes in a flash, anxious to change and scavenge the food sack. A ten-minute paddle in wet suits brought them home. Following a quick change into dry clothes, they raced for the kitchen. They were refreshed and happy but starved. Mark got a fire started while Bob lowered the very light food pack. He separated the supper eatables from the next day's breakfast goods. He slowly piled supper fare on the table and sorted it into stacks. The hungry crew watched him. Their limited choices were: lots of hardtack, a large chunk of cheddar cheese, one full summer sausage, coffee and hot chocolate. It was meager but tasty fare. The famished crew ravenously consumed every last bit in less than an hour.

The hardtack was brought along because of its unrivaled keeping quality. It was nutritious, crispy and best of all, in good supply. It was meant to be an emergency food item and was a nice complement to the cheese and sausage. It filled the void nicely. Cora made some innovative use of it by dunking it into her hot chocolate. There were unlimited hot drinks. The rigors of the full day began to slow the crew down after supper. They chatted excitedly about their last "best" day trip and tomorrow's pack up and return home.

Pierre added a lump of sourdough starter to a flour, sugar and water slurry. The sourdough yeast would have the night to work its magic throughout the mix. He covered it and gave it to Bob set in the food sack. Bob raised the food sack for the last time. Pierre would add more flour or water in the morning to attain correct batter consistency. The sourdough yeast would not only impart great flavor, but the hotcakes would rise higher. Pierre set their leave time at 9 a.m. That would allow the group to have a leisurely trip out to meet their vans. The sky was still holding fair, but the east wind and some nagging dark clouds on the eastern horizon would bear watching. Pierre lit the lantern. The happy but tuckered group gathered around with rapt attention.

Pierre spoke: This be last evening in camp, mes amis. I hope you like. On behalf of all of guides, we say, 'merci,' pour your bonne travail. You teach us sense of humor. You be très tough campers. We say farewell. Tomorrow – Chainsaw Sisters Parking lot."

A hush hung over the table for a minute. Glenn raised his hand and held it palm out as a signal for the staff to wait. The clients formed an impromptu huddle. Bob, Mark and Pierre stood quietly by the fire and waited. Then the huddle broke up with peals of laughter. The four grinning campers lined up facing them. They saluted in unison and held it, until it was returned by all of the guides. Then with damp eyes and smiles, the four imps turned on their heels, joined hands and waved. The foursome chanted in unison as they departed:

"Bonsoir, très beaux hommes du nord, merci beaucoup!"

"Bonsoir, mes amis," Pierre replied. "You all voyageur. You be in notre coeurs. (You are in our hearts). Petit déjeuner be early. Sleep well."

Mark wiped tears from his eyes and turned to give hearty double handshakes to Bob and Pierre. It was a moving, bittersweet moment. Emotions ran high. Pierre snuffed the lantern candle and packed it away for the last time. He then lit his clay pipe. Bob and Mark quietly cleared the table and burned the plates.

While the fire roared Pierre spoke to them: "Clients hit nail on head. You be vraiment les hommes du Nord. You be mature, savvy smart – protect , laugh avec clients. I be honored have you here. Now you free. Rest. It be easier to go out."

Mark and Bob were still basking in the heady warmth of praise they had only hoped for. With big goofy grins they said, "Merci, bonsoir" in unison and held their salute until it was returned. They made a crisp military turn and faded into the sunset. They walked proudly, even jauntily, to their tents. At Bob's tent, Mark clapped Bob's shoulder goodnight and walked out by the shoreline. He stood there quietly. He was proud and happy but also near tears.

Mark relied on nature's symphony to calm his heart. Something big splashed in the darkness. It might have been a fish, a loon or a beaver. It was too dark to see without moonlight, so he headed for his tent. He stood quietly in the pitch-dark night. He hoped to prolong the day's magic. It was childish, but Mark resisted the urge to switch on his headlamp and enter his tent. It may have been minutes or an hour that he stood there. Like a big ear, he listened to the night talk. Mosquitoes hummed about and homed in on his body's warmth and the carbon dioxide he exhaled. The wilderness' tiniest vampire probed behind his ear. He swatted it and felt it gush blood. Large wings beat overhead and another bigger splash echoed through the camp. A moose must have fallen in the lake! Just as he bent down to unzip his tent, an ancient wild cry made his neck hairs stand up! Though he'd never heard it before, he knew it was a wolf howling! It started with a low deep bass sound that rose to a chilling, mournful pitch, then cycled back down again. It was probably a lone wolf who either had been driven out or was separated from its pack. There were no other wolf howls from his location or from elsewhere. It saddened Mark. A lone wolf leads a precarious existence. It was denied the protection and hunting prowess of a wolf pack. It may have been an older, alpha male that lost the battle to a younger challenger that became the new leader of his pack. Nature sometimes was a harsh mother.

All was quiet as Mark unzipped his tent, but he suddenly froze. The full moon had slid free of the clouds! It bathed the site with a brilliant light. His headlamp was unnecessary. He slid into his sleeping bag and lay on his back. The lifeless, silvery orb mesmerized him. It carried out its cosmic duty. It illuminated the Earth by becoming a great mirror that reflected the constant light of the sun. Mark knew the moon was lifeless. Its dust-covered surface was pockmarked with mountains and craters from meteorite hits. It had no atmosphere and little gravity, but that didn't matter. This small sphere exerts special powers over the earth. It actually affects the ocean tides, fish activity and men's minds. The root word luna, Latin for moon, influences language terms like lunatic, meaning someone who acts strangely. Solunar tables that calculate fish feeding periods according to sol (sun) and lunar positions are also a testament to the moon's power.

Mark hoped to hear the wolf howl again but did not. He lay still while his heart raced. He hoped that Jacko had heard it also. He would have judged it a good omen. It would be something special to hear a whole pack of wolves howl. Ray Bond once told his survival class that the best time to hear a pack of wolves howl was in the fall. That is when the new pups are old enough to be taken out on their first hunt. The pack's leader, the alpha male, and its mate start the howl. When the pups join in, their higher-pitched howls and yips are clearly heard.

Ray had stressed that wolf howls aren't to be confused with the higher pitched, staccato howls, yips and barks of a coyote pack. Coyotes are much more tolerant of man and seem to enjoy being where they can dine on man's stray pets and chickens.

With his first trip into the wilderness drawing to a close, Mark let his concentration shift. He thought ahead to the return to the outfitter resort. He hoped Walt had a few days' work for them. He also would need to ask for some time to visit Pierre and his wife before preparing for their trip with Ray Bond. Some mail would be waiting, since his mom was a faithful writer.

He had sent a postcard home before they left for the Boundary Waters' trip. It had a glossy picture of a heavily antlered bull moose. Its jet-black coat and foreboding look was majestic against the colorful fall foliage. It was a scene that Mark's Grandpa Pete would have liked to paint in oils. He had given his parents a brief, general itinerary. He named the lakes they would paddle and portage through and their base camp at Horse Lake. The card would thrill his dad who had never seen a real moose; the twins, Wendy and Frank, would be bug-eyed. This was his first real time away from home except for the week spent at Camp Sanford during his seventh and eighth grade years at Quinnesec Junior High.

His thoughts returned back home and to good times with family and with P.J. and their stomping grounds at Moon Lake. A twinge of homesickness jolted Mark. He wondered how the pasty shop was doing for P.J. and his family. Then he thought of the hard, tedious summer work he would have found near home. There were always lawn mowing, painting and other odd jobs, besides picking tame berries and other crops. Having put things in proper perspective, he counted his blessings. Here he stood in "Le beau pays," living his dream, with pay! There would be wages and a chance for a cash bonus at the good doctor's discretion. His generous decision to finance the entire trip expense blew Mark's mind. Mark knew he must be frugal with his earnings. He would soon be taking a trip with Ray and also planned a few days' visit at Pierre's home.

The rest of the summer would pass quickly with high school starting in September. He had once thought it would be neat to attend high school in Ely, but he learned that being a non-resident and paying room and board would be prohibitive. The best plan would be to attend Kingsford High School back home. He hoped to return to Ely and guide again. If he could only find work through the rest of July, he could catch a bus back home and work at the family fruit stand through August. He understood that, though his parents worked hard and were frugal, they didn't have enough excess income to lavish on all of his needs. They were good providers and his mom's cooking was tops, but money was tight. His mom had already told Mark that he would have to finance his college expense. He wouldn't have it any other way. He wanted to work it through and was content with receiving their love and a home.

His thoughts were rudely interrupted. A loud, frantic scratching was coming from the side of his tent! He came to full alert. He switched his headlamp on and shined it on the tent wall. His viewing angle exaggerated the size of the cheeky intruder. All he could see was a hairy humped creature that was rubbing its furry side against the tent! Was it trying to dig into or under it? He was very close to hollering "Bear!" Mark raised himself up on his elbow while holding onto his belt knife. Then he saw the real size of the critter and whacked the tent wall, smartly. The critter, probably a muskrat, scurried away as Mark allowed himself a chuckle. It had him going for a minute. It was an optical illusion or, as Pierre called it, "a tent mirage." Once again all was quiet. He recalled how much noise a couple of gray squirrels could make in dry leaves near his deer stand. He thought two bucks were having a fight behind him! He switched the light out and let his heavy eyelids slam shut. With a weak smile, he gave in to fatigue's relentless force and lost voluntary control of his body. He barely noticed a twitch in his right hand as his body's autonomic system took over the night shift. It would repair damaged tissue, muscle tears, bruises and cuts while he slept. Without direction, his brain's computer pulled a total maintenance program while he was blissfully unaware.

Mark was watching a large birch bark canoe with eight French-Canadian voyageurs. They were wearing leggings and moose hide moccasins. On their heads they wore red berets, and brightly-colored sashes were tied about their waists. Bent to their work, the stocky, swarthy voyageurs paddled at a fast cadence called by the bowman. Heavy bales of animal furs of beaver, otter, wolf, wolverine, weasel, fox and mink filled the spaces between the paddlers. Their canoe was about 26 feet long, a canot du nord, carrying three tons of cargo including the voyageurs. It traveled the wilderness canoe routes on its way to the fabled Grand Portage on Gitchi-Gummi. The buckskin-clad man joined them in singing a poignant French chanson. It told about the women they left behind and how far away home was.

The wondrous dream continued. There was only one problem. His presence was not a physical flesh and bone reality. It was as though he hovered above the scene. He saw and heard everything, but could not touch or interact. The buckskin-clad man he shadowed was older and taller than he was. Any sensations he seemed to feel were somehow transmitted to him. He accepted the strange situation and treasured his peek into the fascinating fur trade era. He was a voyeur of a voyageur brigade. These hard-working French Canadians were some of the first non-Indians to travel deep into the wild, uncharted wilderness. Soon the paddling ceased. The bowman had signaled it was time for a pose. The voyageur crew would take a short rest. They filled their clay pipes with tobacco, lit them and smoked contentedly. He listened to them speaking French about how good their big pemmican, grease and corn "roo-ba-boo" would be that night. His own mouth watered at the thought.

Suddenly a bell began ringing! Mark jerked hard and pushed his head into the side wall of his tent! It was Pierre ringing the dinner bell! He had been dreaming again and had slept right past the dawn. With a flurry of activity, he dressed and ran out of his tent in record time. He stopped briefly at Bob's tent, but Bob was already gone. He made a beeline for the kitchen. He arrived just ahead of the thundering herd. Bob was there and grinning like a Cheshire cat. He held out a steaming mug of java for him. Mark accepted it gratefully but warily. He was spooked by Bob's lingering grin.

"Thanks, my man!" Mark said. "Now, why all the grinning? Why didn't you wake me?"

"Well, to be honest," Bob answered, "I tried, but as I stood in front of your tent, I heard you singing in French, so I left you alone!"

"Oh, boy," Mark sighed. "I was having a dream where I was part of a voyageur brigade and joined in singing a chanson. The dinner bell woke me! Otherwise I'd be enjoying a pose and smoking my clay pipe, right now."

They both doubled over in a fit of laughter that took a while to subside. Mark finally recovered, wiped his eyes and took a deep breath. Just then the whole group rolled into the kitchen. Mark greeted them and turned to Pierre. He also wore a big grin and held his lit clay pipe out to Mark! Mark blushed and put his hand up, refusing the pipe. Mark was at their mercy. Then Pierre began softly singing a chanson in French. He ended it with a wink at Mark. The assembled clients applauded wildly. Mark joined them in applauding Pierre's impromptu chanson. He knew his secret was secure with Pierre and Bob. They could have made him look a fool, but chose to keep it their little secret. Besides, it prompted Pierre to sing a voyageur chanson that brought down the house! An embarrassing sequence of a distant dreamer had become a blessing!

The dream sequence had seemed so vivid, as it was with most dreams; he might never have remembered it had he not been awakened during it. Even more interesting was the fact that he had been heard singing a chanson in French. He had no such knowledge or talent. Maybe sometime the dream would revisit him. It was still so fresh in his mind that he could almost smell the wild odors of the fur bales and feel the sticky birch bark seams sealed with pine pitch.

Pierre set a big platter of sourdough hotcakes in front of them. Mark grabbed one and passed it on. He reached for the last of the butter and Pierre's wife's homemade jam. More cakes were sizzling in the big fry pan. Mark poured refills of java for the group while waiting for another hot cake. The yeast in Pierre's batter had multiplied mightily and fried up into a tangy, gourmet delight. After the last morsel was eaten and washed down, Pierre dismissed everyone to start packing their tents and gear.

Mark's and Bob's duty was to dismantle the kitchen and help Pierre pack it all away before tending to their own tents and gear. Their last function before departure would be to tear down the toilet enclosure and pack it up. Mark finished up at the kitchen. He burned the breakfast plates, folded up the table and tarps and carried it all to the landing. Pierre carefully packed everything into the canoe. Mark then tore down his tent and packed up his gear. He distributed the gear evenly to balance the load in the canoe. The weather looked good. There was a light breeze with full sun. Hopefully, it would remain stable. Mark went to help the clients pack. Jacko and Glenn had their tent packed and were nearly finished with their other gear. They strained to buckle the pack straps over the bulging load. Mark shouted encouraging words at them and headed for the girls' tent. As he approached, Cora turned toward him after being alerted by Ruby. She'd heard Mark's footsteps.

"Bonjour!" Cora greeted Mark. "Are you ready to leave this paradise?"

"Mais oui!" Mark answered. He met Cora's eyes and smiled as she wiped her sweaty brow. Her brunette hair was damp and curly. Ruby was having a problem making her clothing fit in her pack. She couldn't tell that some items were still lying on the ground. Mark helped retrieve them and together they packed and strapped it down securely. Ruby gave him a big hug around his neck in thanks. Mark picked her up and swung her in a circle. It made her squeal with delight before he set her on the ground. Cora came up, put her arm around Mark's waist and gave him a little peck on his cheek. Then they all grabbed a load and lugged it to the canoe. Bob was busy finishing up loading his canoe. It was tied in the shallows so it would float the load. Glenn and Jacko assisted and made sure their fishing rods were well protected. Pierre had already loaded his tipi. He arrived with another load and began packing it in the canoes.

"Allons-y!" Pierre greeted them. "After canoes loaded, Bob stay avec canoes. The rest police camp. Can leave no debris! Mark et moi dismantle toilet enclosure – meet back here."

While the crew policed the camp, Pierre and Mark took down the toilet tarp and carried it out. The sack of toilet paper could be handy on the trip out. All gear was packed in the waiting canoes. Just before they shoved off, Pierre and Jacko made a final offering of twist tobacco to the spirits. Pierre spoke solemn words in the Sioux tongue of his wife. Jacko spoke in his native Ojibway tongue. The rest of the group quietly observed the ceremony, then found their canoe positions and waited for Pierre's command: "Allons-y, mes amis! We go home!"

Everyone turned to have a last look at the campsite before shoving off. As Cora turned back, Mark noticed she was wiping away tears. Mark had to stifle some tears of his own, as his eyes welled up. Their campsite had been their sanctuary, a safe port. Its gourmet meals by chef Pierre, the kitchen with its toasty fire, and nature's wonders had guided their lives for a magical week. Cora was darkly tanned, to the degree that she and Ruby could almost be mistaken as mother and daughter. The two were such a perfect pair. It was good to know that their friendship would continue into the future. Ruby sat among the packs in the center, looking happy and strong. She had experienced nature's many moods. She knew its creatures, wild sounds and fear of storms in the night. She felt the wilderness' pulse despite being sightless. Cora had braided her hair and pinned a little curl of birch bark at its end. Jacko seemed stronger and more confident as he paddled. He used his injured left arm to cradle the paddle while paddling with his strong right arm. His medicine bag flapped over his shoulder. Glenn sported a dark tan with a little burn that made him look tough. That combined with a new confidence gained by a tough week in the wilderness and fine grub had been a good tonic. Mark wouldn't soon forget the day on Tin Can Mike when Glenn removed his prosthetic foot and used it to subdue a pike.

At the narrows, a pair of loons suddenly surfaced, streaming water. They eyeballed Pierre and Cora then slid under the surface and disappeared. Cora and Ruby thought it was their way of saying goodbye. Pierre wisely smiled and said, "Mais oui," as they entered the kettle. The breeze remained light and at their backs.

As Mark paddled, he shifted his gaze up above the high bluffs and into the pastel blue sky. An eagle soared above. The king of raptors glided effortlessly, utilizing the rising thermals, watching for prey. The brigade reached the portage landing to their favorite fishing lake. Now the sourdough pancakes kicked in extra energy for the grunt ahead.

The portaging of the heavy packs up the rock ledge went quickly. In 25 minutes they had all the gear at the landing on Tin Can Mike. They were in better shape, and the empty food pack helped get it done in two trips. The trio of canoes was packed and shoved off.

Once again they plied the familiar water of Tin Can Mike. Everyone took a cool drink before shoving off. As Mark and Jacko passed the second campsite on the west shore, Jacko pointed his paddle at the two bays they had fished. He wouldn't forget his battle with the big bass for a long time. The campsite was occupied but nobody was visible.

The campsite across the lake where the four women had camped was also taken. It was the weekend during prime time when campsites on popular routes tend to fill up fast. Mark knew that their campsite on Horse might already be taken. This route was one of the more popular and heavily used from June through Labor Day. After that the canoe traffic dropped noticeably. The portage from Tin Can Mike to Sandpit went smoothly. Once loaded, the trio of canoes enjoyed a quick passage down the length of Sandpit. The sky was overcast and Mark thought he smelled rain.

Then they landed and began to tackle the "lung burner" that started its upward ascent within a few steps of the landing. It was a deceptive beginning with a rocky but gradual climb. After a few yards of the tease, it showed its true colors and made a sharp upward turn, then rose at a severe angle up through a veritable minefield of exposed boulders and exposed roots. Heavy use had worn away all the covering of soil and grass, making for a staircase of unlimited trips, slips and savage crashes. Mark could tell that there had been some memorable accidents that left broken gear and dried blood on the rocks. Worst of all was descending the evil staircase. Woe to those who opted to hurry down its treacherous slope after or during a rain. It was an extreme fitness test that required three trips to lug the group's canoes and gear up its tricky face. The last trip was the hardest. Mark was finally standing on top. He caught his breath before loading the canoes on the Mudro Lake side. He wondered if it was like a woman having a baby. Once the delivery's over, she forgets the pain and is willing to try again. After everyone took long drinks and ate the last of the jerky, the group set off. It was time to take on the last obstacle.

The crossing of Mudro Lake was easy. Once past the sentinel boulders lurking at the mouth of the creek, they figured out how to ferry the canoes against the current and the tricky bends.

The clients had already decided they would ask their driver to take them to Ely. After arriving, they would first buy a hot shower from an outfitter. Last on their list was to order sandwiches and malts at the Chocolate Moose. They guaranteed the driver would cooperate if they insisted on buying his lunch!

After negotiating several turns, they spied the sandy shore ahead that was the landing. Cries of joy resounded as each canoe slid onto the wet sand. Their adrenaline pumped as everyone hoisted a pack or canoe and fairly jogged over the short, shady trail to the parking lot. They had made good time to reach the waiting vans before noon. Walt and Gus greeted each load-bearing camper and helped them pack their belongings in their van. A large cooler of ice water and a big bowl of fresh fruit sat on the outfitter van's tailgate. Bob and Mark placed the canoes on the trailer racks and strapped them down. Then they finished stuffing their gear into the outfitter van. Their work done, they grabbed a big paper cup of ice water and some fruit. With departure nigh, there was a last flurry of handshaking, hugging and tears before the group's van doors closed. The van began a slow exit with lots of waving and some blown kisses and was gone.

Mark, Bob, Pierre and Walt watched them leave, then double checked that all their gear was loaded and the canoes secured. Mark and Bob were sent to check for any lost gear or trash left on the portage trail and the landing. They both felt a little prick in their hearts. It had been a special time. Just before their van left, Mark had clasped forearms, Indian style, with Jacko. Jacko then dug something out of his pack and offered it to Mark. Mark unwrapped the soft deer hide and found Jacko's handmade fire bow drill inside! Mark was caught off guard and at a loss for words. As his eyes met Jacko's, he had a golden idea. He undid his belt, slid his Rapala fillet knife off with its leather scabbard, and presented it to Jacko. It was a good trade. He could see it in Jacko's wide eyes and big grin. They clasped arms again. Before Jacko hopped into the van, he whispered "until we meet again" and sat by the window. Both his and Glenn's fingers made a "V" on the window, the sign for peace. Mark returned the peace sign.

Walt took the driver's seat with Pierre riding shotgun. Bob and Mark rode amid the packs in back. They happily nibbled on the fresh fruit that satisfied a craving. Mark's love for fruit started from a young age thanks to his family's summer fruit and veggie stand. There was always a bowl of overripe or damaged items that his mom had salvaged. Very little went to waste in their household. That and an occasional treat of a cold bottle of Dad's root beer or a candy bar were his wages. The hour's ride over back roads, combined with the radio's tunes, lulled the two tuckered boys to sleep. Pierre looked back at his intrepid guides. The two were unconscious, but still gripped their apples. Pierre leaned close to Walt and whispered. They both had to cover their mouths to muffle their mirth. As the van pulled into the driveway, Walt parked the canoe trailer beside the large overhead door of the big Quonset hut. At the sound of the front doors closing, Bob and Mark jumped up and attempted to get their foggy bearings.

"Good afternoon, mes amis!" Pierre barked. "Go to kitchen – wash up, eat late déjeuner. Unload canoes – put gear away, after. If done before souper, you done for day – can rest."

Needing no further encouragement, Bob and Mark hopped out of the van and hurried to wash up. After scrubbing off the worst of the grime they followed their noses to the big stoves. They helped themselves to a bowl of chili and a toasted cheese sandwich. They took their tasty meal outside where they savored the spicy chili and the rich, yummy toasted cheese sandwich. After gorging on the fine fare, they washed it down with big glasses of real lemonade.

"It hit the jackpot," Bob quipped.

They rinsed their plates, walked to the Quonset and opened the big door to let the warm breeze inside. After unloading everything outside on the dry ground, they checked the tents and tarps for any tears or other damage. Any tents or packs that were damp were spread out to dry in the warm breeze. The sleeping bags were turned inside out and aired out in the sun. Cora and Ruby's tent was put aside until everything else had been put away, including the coils of rope.

Later, the sleeping bags were brought back from airing in the sun where the fresh breeze had sweetened them nicely. The bags and dry tents were stuffed into their sacks and stacked on a high shelf. Last on the list was to clean the ripped area on Cora and Ruby's tent and apply a tough military duct tape to both sides. The tape was specially made to be waterproof and would stretch with the fabric, but not peel off.

Their work done, they reported to Pierre who released them for the day. Gratefully, they lounged in the Adirondack chairs, content to watch the fluffy clouds scud by. It had been a good day, bittersweet and tiring, but without any nasty incidents. As they sat sipping more lemonade, it dawned on Mark: They had access to hot, running water! The lure of a hot shower was overpowering. Hauling their sweaty, tired bodies out of the comfy chairs, they trotted to their room. After gathering a change of clothes, they barefooted it to the showers. With soap, shampoo and scrubbing, the hot water transformed them. They became flushed and weak, sapped of their strength and totally relaxed. Now they knew why the clients had demanded a hot shower first, then food! They dressed in fresh underwear and shorts and went back to the chairs. They were clean and carefree. When the dinner bell rang, they rushed to the kitchen with stomachs growling, ready to feed. Their eyes fairly popped when Pierre ushered them to a big table. It was set with three platters. One held a huge, broiled Porterhouse steak smothered in mushrooms, another brimmed with salad and the third was full of baked potatoes. Sour cream, bacon bits and other seasonings sat waiting on a tray. It was enough to convert a vegan into a meat eater.

"Momma mia!" Mark exclaimed. "What a feast."

"Did you guys butcher a steer, or what?" Bob joked.

"Bon appétit!" Pierre and Walt answered in unison.

Walt motioned for them to take their seats and "commence feasting." Mark never ceased to be amazed at their generosity. He paused with eyes closed to express silent thanks for the abundant favors. He cut the baked tater and slathered it with sour cream, salt and pepper. The steak was thick, tender and done medium well. They shared different stories about the client trip as Walt listened intently. He shook his head, laughed and rolled his eyes. He seemed to enjoy hearing their recap of the campout – even minor details. When Mark decided to tell about his "voyageur dream" the last morning at camp, tears welled up in Walt's eyes! He excused himself from the table, laughing and wiping his eyes. When he returned, they had finished the feast and were starting on fresh wedges of pumpkin pie. Walt poured their mugs full of fresh, hot coffee. He then set the carafe down and produced a large manila envelope. He reached in and took out six smaller sealed envelopes. He gave two personalized ones to Mark and Bob. Mark noticed their names were written in script and the envelopes were sealed with red wax. The wax seals were embossed with the face of the good doctor's ring. It was how important correspondence was marked when sent by royalty in the day.

"These came a few days ago from the good doctor," Walt said. "He has been very interested in all news of the client trip. He was sent any reports that we received including the bear attack. We also sent copies of the Forest Service summary which included your statements, as well as those from the victims and the rangers. The good doctor asked me to convey his thanks to you both for a doing a difficult job so well. In one envelope is your regular pay. The other contains a bonus. He appreciates how well you men handled his group with love and for assisting the injured campers. I have spoken to Ray Bond at length concerning the bear attack and the rescue. He sends his regards and is very proud of you both. You'll find your mail in your room. Also, since you finished unloading, restocking, breaking camp, and paddling out to Mudro Landing, you deserve a break! Tomorrow is Sunday. You have no duties here. Pierre has some appointments in Ely tomorrow and would like you to accompany him. He'll fill you in on the details."

Mark raised his coffee mug and stood to make a toast. "Many thanks to the good doctor for trusting us and for his generosity," Mark said. "We also thank you, Walt, for trusting us and letting us prove our mettle. What can we say about Pierre other than he is un magnifique homme du nord! We learned a lot about guiding some special people in le beau pays. We developed close friendships within the group and will miss them and all the experiences, good and bad. But we are also glad to be back, and we're ready for some town life. It will be a nice change to hike in town, shop and sit in the sun like tourists!"

"I want to echo Mark's thanks for a chance to prove ourselves," Bob added. "With Pierre's wisdom and experience, we stretched our limits and learned some priceless lessons. Walt, could we write a note to thank the good doctor for all he's done? Also, is there any work we might do to earn our keep until we meet Ray Bond on Thursday?"

"Sure, you can write the doctor, Bob," Walt replied. "I know he'd enjoy hearing from you both. Just put your notes in an envelope marked 'Doctor,' and I'll forward it to him. To answer your other question: Yes, you are both welcome to accompany and assist Pierre when he travels to the Wenonah Canoe Factory in Winona, MN. You will be paid and will leave here Monday morning. You will stay overnight in Winona, then drive back Tuesday. You will help load several canoes, paddles and other gear. On Wednesday you can put the new canoes and other gear away and pack your personal gear for your upcoming trip. Ray plans to pick you up at first light Thursday morning."

"Perfect," Mark said. "We'll be ready to do the town in the morning. Thanks for spoiling us with this fabulous feast!"

As they dined on their pie and accepted refills of pure Columbian joe, they chatted amiably with Walt and Pierre. An hour slipped away as Pierre related stories about their trip that kept Walt entertained. Walt left to take a phone call and excused himself for the night. Pierre stayed a while longer, then rose and wished them "bonsoir." He set their departure time at 8 a.m.

With their pay envelopes gripped tightly and their bellies full, they staggered out the door and down the hill to the bunkhouse. They were on top of the world. As they opened the bunkhouse door, they each picked up a bundle of mail and fell into their bunks. It was nice to have a real mattress again and amenities such as hot and cold running water and electric lights. They were townies again. Mark had two letters from his mom. One had been mailed before they left for their Boundary Waters trip, so he read it first. In it, his mom thanked Mark for the postcard with the bull moose on it. It had been a big hit. He had sent it before the trip, so she would know where they were headed. All was going well back home, with good business at the fruit stand. She had hired Judy, a neighbor girl, to babysit the twins during the day. The other letter asked how their trip went, to be careful of wild bears and not to drown.

That was vintage mom, a sweet lady, but she always feared the worst. Mark chuckled as he returned to memory lane. He and his older brother Pete had hiked across backroads and fields to fish at Lake Antoine. They were sworn to stay in grandpa's wood rowboat and fish on the north shore. But they had sought greener pastures and sneaked across the bay to fish off the peninsula. They were fishing in forbidden water and feeling quite smug when a Michigan State Police squad car drove up on the nearby peninsula. A tall Michigan State trooper stepped out of his car and hailed them.

"Is one of you boys named Peter?" he shouted.

Pete answered, "Yes."

"Well, your mother was worried and called us," the trooper said. "You boys best get on home."

Lines were quickly reeled in and Pete rowed like a fiend to the north shore. The two truant youths tied up Grandpa Pete's rowboat and raced home in record time. It was the only time she ever turned them in "to the law" with chilling effect. They did win a reprieve when their mom saw their stringer of fish!

Mark's mom's letter also said that Pat (P.J.) had stopped by and reported that the bass were on the spawn beds and hitting anything. Mark and P.J. had caught some big bass in Moon Lake, but they threw most back. P.J. once caught a big walleye in Moon Lake. It was a rare feat and he was proud of it. It was a private lake with no public access. That kept the fishing pressure low and the fish population high.

Bob had a few letters from his folks so they shared news from home. Then it was high time to open their pay envelopes. It was all in cash! Their hands trembled as they spread the crisp new bills out on their beds. It was more money than either of them ever had at one time. The awestruck lads gingerly slid the stacks of greenbacks back into the envelopes. Quickly, they each broke the wax seal on their bonus envelope and glanced inside. Bob had "banjo" eyes and was speechless. With shaking hands they began counting their bonus.

"We're rich, my man!" Bob squealed.

"Amen to that!" Mark agreed.

They clasped arms Indian style and danced a jig.

"Look out, Ely!" Bob joked. "I'll get a money order tomorrow and send most of my pay home, but a townie needs bread, man!"

"We worked hard for it, but I wouldn't trade one hour for our normal summer grunt work at home," Mark said. "I'd have taken odd jobs and worked at the fruit stand for a lot less. I plan to send most home, also. School starts the first week of September, and it's a long, lean winter. I'll keep out enough for incidentals, such as replacing my filet knife and for expenses on our trip home."

They lay there for a while, lost in their thoughts. After a while they packed the money back into the envelopes and slid them into their front pockets. It was time to write a thank you to the good doctor. They completed their letters and sealed two envelopes that had "Doctor" marked on each. Next, they dutifully wrote letters to their folks, but left them unsealed until they could insert money orders. Even though most stores closed on Sunday, the drugstore and restaurants would be open.

Mark decided to celebrate the event by listening to the golden oldies. He kept the radio at low volume in case they both grew sleepy and dozed off. In fact that's just what happened. Mark had been chatting with Bob, but noticed Bob's responses came slower until all he got in response was heavy breathing. Mark realized he was having a wonderful one-sided conversation. He knew it was time to call it a night. He quietly turned the radio off, visited the bathroom and was soon back in his bunk and fast asleep.

Chapter Nineteen

Meeting Sigurd Olson

Dawn broke the next morning and all was quiet. Suddenly, their peaceful slumber was rudely interrupted by the kitchen bell that insistently probed the room. It caused bedlam. They both jerked upright but were barely awake. After a foggy stumble to the bathroom, they came alive. They broke out of the barracks and sprinted for the kitchen.

Pierre welcomed them with tongue in cheek: "Good morning, mes amis!"

They froze at the sound of his voice, then came to attention. "Sorry we're late, Pierre!" Mark croaked, then saluted smartly.

"At ease, hommes du nord!" Pierre laughed as he returned their salute. "You need strong coffee!"

"Mais oui," they cried in unison.

"Help yourself to pure Columbian brew," Pierre offered. "There be scramble eggs, ham toast – orange slice also! We are early. Take time, enjoy petit déjeuner."

Bob and Mark filled their plates and joined Pierre. Mark enjoyed the robust brew's burn going down.

While they ate, Pierre sipped his java and filled them in on the day's plan. "We leave for town soon, but need make short detour. We visit old friend. I introduce you. I phone him last night – briefed him on trip. He expect us – wants meet you."

Mark and Bob smiled and nodded their agreement. They were stumped by all the mystery, but trusted Pierre's plan. By 8 a.m. they were tooling down Fernberg Road in the old Dodge pickup. Pierre made a right turn at Falls Lake Road, then continued on a dirt road and stopped at a small log cabin. They piled out and followed Pierre to the front door. A gray-haired woman opened the door and welcomed them in. She escorted them through the modest cabin to the back "den," as she called it. It was paneled in knotty pine throughout. Big windows looked out on the surrounding forest. There, in the far corner, a slight, fit older man stood looking out the window. Next to him was a desk with an old manual typewriter and stacks of legal pads full of cursive writing. He heard them enter and turned to meet them. His ageless face broke into a smile as he shook their hands.

"Good morning, Sig!" Pierre said. "These be new guides I tell you about."

As he shook Mark and Bob's hands, Mark said, "You're Sig Olson! It's an honor. We are all in your debt, sir."

"Thank you, and welcome to our humble abode," Sig replied. "Now here's my dear wife, Elizabeth, with some of her fine cookies and coffee. Please have a seat, guys."

Mark settled into a comfortable leather chair and thanked Sig's wife for the refreshments.

Sig was pushing his mid-seventies. His face was well wrinkled and there was stiffness in his gait, but he had strong grip and his eyes still had fire. Sig raised his coffee mug to them and toasted their "bravado" and courage "beyond the call of duty."

Mark mentioned the lone wolf howl he heard during their last night in camp. He said it was an amazing first for him and it made his neck hairs prickle.

"Mark," Sig said, "I'm glad you heard a wolf howl. Most people will never hear one! Rarer still are those who see one in the wild. In the early 1900s, our well-meaning federal and state governments, with the cattlemen's approval, decided to declare war on wolves. Their flawed thinking determined that killing off these top carnivores would benefit the powerful cattlemen's herds from predation. It would also increase the number of deer and moose, thereby satisfying hunters. But it was a disaster. Herds of deer and elk overpopulated and overgrazed their range. Crowding created more disease and starvation with no predators to cull out the old and sick. Animals that were sick or deformed survived to mate. This weakened the herd's genetics and multiplied problems in future generations. I freely admit that I once felt that wolves were just bloodthirsty, wanton killers. But after doing some field research, I changed my mind and found wolves to be intelligent, efficient hunters. Wolves carry out a vital part of the forest ecosystem. They cull out the weak and diseased while being no threat to man. Wolves, coyotes and bears all prey on deer and moose, but one must remember that vehicular traffic kills more than all the predators combined."

Bob mentioned that their group had caught several smallmouth bass in the BWCA. He remembered hearing that Sig was instrumental in planting them. Sig took the bait and happily told the story that had become a legend among those who consider the smallmouth the best game fish in the wilderness. Sig recounted how forty years earlier, he and a friend had packed in containers of fingerlings. In the years since, the species proliferated and can now be found throughout the BWCAW.

Sig regaled them with stories about his years as a guide and teacher; but mainly he talked about his passion to preserve "Le beau pays" as a wild sanctuary where man and beast could escape the trappings and pollution of the "civilized" world.

He told of meeting with some of the most powerful men in the Federal Government, including President John F. Kennedy. Before the Boundary Waters finally received its Wilderness designation, tremendous pressure was brought to bear on federal and state government officials by powerful organizations who hated the very idea of "locking up" a million square acres of northern Minnesota. A giant consortium of varied commercial enterprises saw the proposed Boundary Waters Wilderness area as a gold mine for mining, lumbering, real estate development and other commercial interests.

Sig said he was disliked in his home by many, especially the mining and logging interests. They considered him a threat to their livelihood. The *Ely Echo* newspaper, which once was called the *Ely Miner*, railed against him and his wilderness proposals. He reveled in telling the group a story from the days when the designation still hung in the balance. A petition asking for the Boundary Wilderness to be enacted reached President Kennedy's desk. It was a complicated legal document that required his final approval or disapproval. He turned to a trusted adviser and asked him to simplify the petition. The adviser said that it came down to deciding in favor of the powerful logging and mining juggernaut or the beaver. President Kennedy, in his characteristic witty, cavalier style, said, "I think we owe this one to the beaver" and signed it into law.

Sig told them that it was officially designated a wilderness by the U.S. Congress in1964. But some resorts continued to operate illegally inside the Boundary Waters Wilderness. They continued operating in direct opposition to the Federal "interference" in their lives. They defied the law and thought they might be "grandfathered" in and able to keep their moneymaking business going. Renegade private floatplanes were still flying fishermen into the new BWCA. The planes and their fishing clients often returned with illegal fish catches. The FBI finally acted. They flew in teams of armed agents. They shortly shut down all the resorts and the floatplane activity by making arrests and confiscating planes. Eventually, the remaining resorts were forced to accept a government buyout and were torn down and burned. It allowed the land to gradually heal and revert to its natural state.

After they had visited for an hour, Sig's wife popped into the room and thanked them all for coming. She informed them that she had to limit his time visiting with his large numbers of friends. He loved to meet with everyone, but fatigued more easily now. It was her duty to see he got enough rest. After exchanging hugs and handshakes, the trio thanked Sig and Elizabeth for the nice chat. They walked slowly to the van knowing they had been in the presence of a great man. Once back in the pickup, everyone was quiet for a moment.

"Thanks, Pierre!" Mark said. "It was an honor and a neat surprise to meet Sig. Without him and other courageous men, there might be no sanctuary for us and the wild creatures to enjoy."

"D'accord," Pierre agreed. "I've known Sig for a long time and have much respect for him, as do Walt, Ray and the doctor."

"It was quite the auspicious beginning!" Bob said. "The day will go downhill from here. Let's go to Ely and live like a tourist!"

Soon they were pulling over at the Chocolate Moose. It was bursting with patrons, but they finally managed to sneak in the side door. Mark hailed a busy waitress and ordered coffee. They carried it outside and sat at a massive log picnic table. They cradled their thick stoneware mugs and watched an endless parade of vehicles transporting canoes. It was a mixed bag of campers, tourists, yuppies and locals. The locals' vehicles were easy to spot. They were the older rusted ones riddled with holes, were missing parts and were beat right down. It was a sure sign of proud, tough, over-wintering souls who loved their home, but struggled to survive in the rust belt. The tons of road salt used over the long winter were a blessing and a curse. The salt not only melts ice, but also eats fenders and frames. Used northern vehicles typically die with perfectly functional engines and transmissions. Used car parts from southern states are in demand to resurrect them. Rust never sleeps.

Pierre stood and said, "Merci, Mark, for coffee. I go now. You enjoy town. We meet back here – two p.m."

They found the drugstore and purchased the money orders. Then it was a short walk to the old brick building that was the Ely Post Office where they bought stamps from a machine and mailed them home. The carefree hommes du nord ambled back to the Moose. Each had reserved some cash for general needs, so they opted to check out the upstairs at Piragis store. There they found a marvelous bookstore. Its many shelves offered books on everything connected to the outdoors. Canoe camping and wilderness lore predominated with a good section by local authors such as Sig Olson and Bob Cary. They lounged and read on the comfy chairs that were scattered about.

Mark was especially drawn to the accounts of survival in the wilderness. He found himself looking forward to their trip with Ray Bond. He hoped they would spend part of the trip as a solo experience, similar to the Sylvania survival test. He did miss the solitude and wanted to try out his new bow drill. To make a fire as the Indians and voyageurs once did would give his campfire making a completely new meaning. It was an ancient process akin to magic. Nature provided all the materials and man applied wisdom and sweat. If he was alone in the wild with only a knife, could he create a fire to warm himself and cook food without matches? He would still secret away other types of fire starters as backups. Mark wasn't a purist, but he hoped to become proficient in making a friction fire. Mark also bought a new filet knife at Piragis' camping section.

After a few hours of relaxed reading, they needed a snack. Since the Moose was still busy, they sauntered over to the Pizza Hut and ordered personal pan pizzas with lots of olives, onions and meat. It had been a long dry spell since their last pizza. They ate with abandon and washed it down with pink lemonade. Bob splurged by feeding several quarters into the restaurant's jukebox. He found some "crossover" golden oldies hidden among the predominately country and western tunes. Mark took care of the tip, and with full bellies, they staggered out into the bright sunshine.

"Man!" Bob said. "This town life is so easy and tastes so good! I can see why the yuppies don't care to go roughing it in the wilds. We had better get back to work soon. I might be tempted to spend my money on a natty safari outfit and join the Ely yuppie crowd!"

Mark laughed and said, "It's normal to pig out and overindulge in creature comforts after a wilderness trek. Face it, Bob, a week of this decadent living, and you'd be chomping at the bit to be a sweaty, grimy wood rat again!"

With forty-five minutes left until their rendezvous with Pierre, they thought of all that handmade ice cream at the Moose and made a beeline back. The place had finally thinned out, so they took a seat at an inside table. Bob ordered a big turtle sundae while implying he was trying to honor Jacko's clan. Mark snorted and rolled his eyes. He ordered one of his old favorites, a fresh strawberry sundae. It was made with homemade vanilla ice cream and covered with a big scoop of fresh berries. As Mark savored the sweet-tart flavors, his thoughts returned home. It reminded him how the fresh picked strawberries tasted as he picked them. He always sampled a few, strictly for quality control, as he filled the quart boxes.

After chasing their treats down with some cool water, they paid up. They over tipped the pretty waitress and sat outside in the warm sunshine. As they leaned back and soaked up the rays, their eyes slowly closed. The townies were only seconds away from la la land, when a familiar horn blew and brought them back. Pierre parked alongside and sat happily grinning. They hopped into the truck and left town with a tinge of sadness. It had been sublime.

"Sorry, mes amis," Pierre said. "I not mean rob you of beauty sleep!"

Bob replied, "It's hard to improve on perfection!"

They all convulsed in laughter at that as they cruised by more canoes than one could count. Ely probably made more money off the canoe crowd than it ever had off mining and logging. It was ironic that the very land that so many wanted to assault with saw and motorboats was now drawing paying visitors from across the nation! They come and spend money just to experience the wilderness that almost wasn't.

Pierre said that he had phoned his wife and filled her in on their client trip. He also mentioned Mark's interest in making his own tipi. She hoped he could schedule a few days with them before returning to Michigan. Mark thanked Pierre and his wife, Clay Basket, for their kind offer. He promised to make time for the visit. It might work out perfectly during the last week of July, after the trip with Ray. It would be a grand way to finish up the month before going home. There might be a chance to work for Walt a few days as well. It would provide some traveling money for bus fare and maybe an excursion in Duluth.

Mark was content. It had been an amazing adventure. There were opportunities he never dared dream about. He felt blessed beyond belief.

They returned to the lodge by late afternoon. After thanking Pierre, they decided to wander down by the docks. The lazy day in town was a nice diversion of decadence, but they needed some outdoor exercise. The placid lake beckoned. They took a slow canoe tour of the whole lakeshore. The dinner bell rang a few hours later just as they were tying up the canoe. Supper was simple but wonderful. The entrée was a rich beef stew with sourdough bread, apple pie and coffee. They ate outside in the cool shade. Pierre had left a note for them. He reminded them of the early start for their trip to Winona in the morning.

It had been a relaxing, fun day. They had adapted to easy living rather well. All they wanted to do was retreat to their nice, quiet room and vegetate. Mark turned on the Zenith and kept the volume low. He used the oldies as mellow background music. Bob had opened the front door and the screened windows to let the light breeze cool the room. After a brief flurry of packing an overnight bag, they showered and lay about, reading and writing some letters. Mark paged slowly through the Herter's Co. Catalog while wishing he had kept more cash. He let the catalog close as his mind leaped ahead to tomorrow's trip.

"Bob, my main man!" Mark quipped. "Are you ready for a road trip?"

"Mais oui, mon ami!" Bob answered. "Pierre plans to depart right after breakfast for the trip to the Wenonah Canoe Factory."

"It sounds like a fun trip," Mark added. "We'll see some pretty country including Gitchi-Gummi and the Mississippi River which runs beside the factory. Our only real work will be to load the canoes on the trailer and unload them when we return. Walt said we'd get a tour of the plant so we can watch the canoe-building process. I plan to do a lot of dreaming and drooling, especially if there are solo canoes!"

"Not only that," Bob commented, "but Walt mentioned that Wenonah has been experimenting with some radical fibers. One is called Kevlar and something called 'Tuf-weave.' They use combinations of resins and fiber to create canoes that are light but strong. They are also experimenting with various hull shapes."

"I love it!" Mark replied. "Did you hear what Pierre said about taking us to see the Duluth Pack Factory? It's where the packs are sewn and riveted together. They also do custom work on packs or tents and guarantee their craftsmanship. It will be a nice break on our return trip."

"Mais oui!" Bob said. "I look forward to it all. Let's make sure we take along a pillow, a blanket and a book. We can switch off riding shotgun in front with Pierre and relax in comfort in the back."

"D'accord," Mark answered. "Good thinking. I'll try to rustle up some snacks from the chef and a thermos of coffee tomorrow. Our meals and lodging will be compliments of Wenonah's owner. Pierre said we'll stay over tomorrow night at his guest cabin and eat lunch, supper and Tuesday breakfast at the employee cafeteria."

"Now that's what I call the red carpet treatment," Mark said. Our employer and Mr. Bond are certainly well connected! Another plus is that Pierre plans to treat us to lunch at Grandma's Restaurant after we tour Duluth Pack."

"Oui, oui, monsieur!" Bob agreed. "That restaurant is supposed to make a mean chicken-wild rice soup and fantastic burgers. It's a popular eating spot, so we want to be there before the noon rush or we'll starve like rats waiting in line!"

They returned to their writing and drooling over Herter's catalog. The sweet sounds of '60s rock tickled their ears. WLS' famous D.J., Dick Biondi, announced a special tribute to the "British Invasion," including Brit groups such as Dusty Springfield, Herman's Hermits, The Beatles, Tom Jones, The Buckinghams, Petula Clark, The Byrds, The Animals, The Rolling Stones, the Kinks and more. As Mark listened to The Dave Clark Five sing, he realized how often he confused them with the Beatles, a credit to their mimicry. Mark was also of the opinion that the early years of the Beatles were their best. Later, as they came under the influence of drugs and their Maharishis, their music changed. But their public continued to worship them. As they listened to the "fab four" Brits' music while shuffling through the catalog, a sudden loud staccato hammering came from the tin roof! Mark jumped up, peered out the window and saw hail bouncing off the roof! The hail was marble sized and lasted only a few minutes before it turned to rain. He felt a wet spray through the screen. It poured down a deluge. He shut the windows. They watched the sheets of rain turn late afternoon into early dusk.

The storm's noise obliterated the music, so Mark shut the radio off. They lay there and let the storm lull them to sleep. Bob heard a loud thud from the lower bunk. He looked down and could see the Herter's Catalog lying on the floor. Mark was in a peaceful slumber. Bob climbed down, visited the bathroom and doused the light. Soon he joined Mark in oblivion.

Mark was lying on his back when he opened his eyes and saw daylight coming through the window. The roof eaves were still dripping steadily, but the rain had slackened to a heavy mist. Obeying an urgent call of nature, he headed for the bathroom. On his return, he heard the muted ring of the dinner bell. Bob sat up in his bunk and looked wildly around. Mark was trying to dress and glanced at him. Bob was bleary eyed with his legs still dangling over the top bunk.

"Daylight in the swamp!" Mark announced. "Hurry up and get dressed. Don't forget your boots and rain parka. We need to hustle if we want any breakfast!"

They splashed through the mist, arriving at the kitchen door in a dead heat. Pierre was waiting. He held out two mugs of hot coffee and waved them in.

"Bonjour, mes amis!" Pierre greeted them. "Enjoy strong java and sweet roll. We leave soon, long drive today."

They gratefully accepted two mugs of Pierre's coffee and the fresh sweet rolls. Before Mark sat down, he had a word with the chef. Just as they were finishing breakfast, the chef appeared with a smile. He handed Mark a sack and a full thermos of coffee. Mark thanked him and accepted the goodies.

He turned to Bob and asked, "Would you go to our room and grab a blanket, a pillow and maybe a book to take along? I'll run this stuff up to the van and see you there."

"Right," Bob replied. "I'll be there in five minutes."

"Allons-y, mon ami," Pierre said, as he left the kitchen.

"Right behind you, Pierre," Mark answered as they walked toward the van.

Pierre hit the ignition switch. The Dodge van's engine caught with a reassuring roar then settled down to a low purr as the engine warmed. Pierre switched the interior lights on as Bob caught up and threw the blanket, pillow and book into the back. Pierre hit the headlights, doused the interior lights and motored out to the highway. Mark busied himself with filling their coffee mugs and checked inside the lunch bag.

"Voila!" he said. "We have quite the little snack sack here! There are three big steak sandwiches with Vidalia onion slices, brown mustard and dill pickles, plus sweet rolls and big oatmeal raisin cookies."

Pierre smiled and said, "Très bien, Mark, we not starve when you along. We be hungry sometime after pass through Duluth – Superior."

The van had slowed as they traveled south of Ely on the "snake trail," as U.S. 1 was called. Mark and Bob knew how curvy it was and watched Pierre take his time, expertly threading his way through its many twists. The road was still wet with puddles in low-lying areas. It was nice to be taking a long road trip again. It was novel to cover such distances without having to expend any real energy. Soon their turn appeared ahead. They slowed and turned right onto Hwy. 2 and were in more open country, with a much straighter road. Just as Pierre commented that this marshy, open land was excellent moose habitat, a dark shape materialized on the right shoulder. It began to cross the road ahead!

Pierre warned them: "Hold on tight, mes amis, no want hit big fella!"

Pierre braked, then swung to the right as the moose, a big black bull, halted on the left side and glared at them. They missed him by a good margin. Bob and Mark released their white-knuckle grips on the van's safety straps.

"Mon dieu," Pierre said. "That be close call!"

"Amen," Mark agreed. "Did you see those massive antlers and how he looked at us? I guess when you're that big and powerful, you don't need to fear much except a hungry wolf pack or a hunter during moose season."

Further down the road, the open country became a dense forest of spruce, balsam and tall white and red pines that had escaped the loggers' axe. It was still mainly lowland. Occasionally, they saw a ruffed grouse moving through the underbrush or sitting on the shoulder where it picked up grit for its gizzard. A roadside sign announced a picnic area ahead on the left. Pierre tripped the left turn signal and the van slowed. They pulled off onto a woodsy little road that skirted a swamp and stopped at an opening that served as a parking area.

Bob and Mark climbed out, grateful for the rest, stretched their legs and began to look around. They stared at the quiet giants that stood like mute sentinels. Their eyes followed the massive tree trunks upward until they almost fell over backwards. The old growth pines had stood the test of time and weather. They had been seedlings when the Declaration of Independence was signed in 1776. They walked the guided path in rapt wonder through the big trees. Wind and electrical storms had wrought significant damage. Some of the giant pines had been struck by lighting and were missing their tops. Lightning had left its calling cards that split the tree trunks from the top to the roots. Forest fires had also left their mark. The bases of tree trunks were blackened; some were great charred stumps. The surviving behemoths stood mute, but still spoke volumes of the ravages suffered over time and of the vicious assaults of nature's fury.

The morning sun promised a warm day with high humidity, because of the previous night's rain. A breeze from the southwest whispered peacefully through the treetops. They soon completed the circular tour. After a necessary trip to the pit toilet, Mark poured more coffee and broke out the sweet rolls before they continued their trip. A half hour later, they left the forest and climbed through more open country with rolling hills, country homes and farms. The van soon began a descent towards Two Harbors and Gitchi-Gummi. Driving west on Hwy. 61, they took the bypass to Duluth and were there in 15 minutes. They passed the exit to the scenic route, as they entered Duluth's city limits. They crossed the bridge over the Lester River and passed the famous Glensheen Mansion. Many other old, pricey homes stood tall in all their palatial splendor. The mansions sit high above Lake Superior's North Shore. Mark and Bob were able to catch a few glimpses of the lake before entering Duluth. Turning left, they climbed above the harbor, where the steady stream of freighters steamed back and forth over what looked like a placid waterway. They soon dropped down off the bridge and stayed straight ahead through Superior on Hwy. 53 South.

"We take 53 to Spooner," Pierre advised. "Then we take Highway 63 to Minnesota. There be très jolie scenery."

Mark distributed the steak sandwiches near Spooner, WI. The grilled steak with horseradish mustard and Vidalia onion slices were followed by a big oatmeal raisin cookie and washed down with coffee.

"One thing's for sure," Bob said. "You never have to worry about starving if Mark's rustling up the grub!"

"D'accord!" Pierre agreed. "Our chef's grub is très bon. Mark be bon hunter and gatherer. We make exception on return trip – eat déjeuner at Grandma's in Duluth. We eat tonight's souper, Tuesday breakfast as guests at Wenonah Canoe. We meet Mike, Wenonah Canoe owner, today– stay over. Guest cabin overlook Big Muddy River."

A few hours later they crossed the Mississippi River into Minnesota and continued south on MN Hwy. 61. The highway paralleled the "big Muddy" right to their destination. Mark switched seats with Bob. He snuggled up close to the window on Pierre's side to watch the mighty river. Ray Bond once told his and Bob's survival class that he had jumped across its headwaters where it originates near Bemidji. Mark could see the vortexes and bulges ebb and flow on its surface. It was evidence of the turbulent water world beneath. The great river carved its meandering path from Itasca State Park in northern Minnesota to its end where it meets the ocean in Louisiana. It had always been a major trade route.

This great liquid highway bisects North America into east and west, forming several state boundaries. Samuel Clemens, the famous author, grew up in Hannibal, MO, on its banks. He was once a steamboat captain. He piloted a stern wheeler on the boisterous, ever-changing river he had loved since he was a youth. Later in his life he wrote his famous novels, *The Adventures of Huckleberry Finn* and *The Adventures of Tom Sawyer*. The books were based on his boyhood experiences along the river, written under the pen name of Mark Twain. Mark Twain was a term used when navigating the river. It meant that there was enough depth or "two fathoms," meaning there were twelve feet of water under the stern wheeler's hull. He became famous for his writing and his witty humor.

Mark had read both books and found them fascinating, especially when the characters, Huck and Tom, built a raft and floated down the "big muddy." Mark was always drawn to rivers, creeks and lakes since his boyhood. He fished brook trout, bass, pike and pike. He swam and explored their shorelines and had even walked an ocean beach where he played in its salty brine and picked seashells.

"Is after two now," Pierre said. "We be at factory soon. There be factory tour—three p.m. We load canoes after tour."

Chapter Twenty

Wenonah Canoe Factory

True to his word, Pierre pulled the van into the Wenonah Factory parking lot at 2:45 p.m. Mark and Bob climbed out gladly. They stretched and yawned while Pierre went inside. The two of them leaned against the van. It was good to be out in the sun and warm breezes. They took in the splendid vista that beckoned across from the parking lot. The river was a short walk beyond the parking lot. It was easily accessed via a paved walkway that led to a small landing for launching canoes and kayaks. Mark found the setting to be charming. It was a perfect blend of nature and canoe technology on the shore of an ancient waterway that still stood ready to test all comers.

"I'm looking forward to the tour, but even more important to meet the man who planned this," Mark said. "He has to love nature as much as he does canoes. It's easy to see the connection to Walt and Pierre. No doubt he has done considerable canoeing and is intimate with the Boundary Waters."

"Allons-y, mes amis," Pierre called. "Start factory tour in five minutes."

They both waved and scampered back up the hill to the front door. They entered right behind Pierre and their tour guide, a broad shouldered man named Ron. He mentioned that the owner was not there yet, but would meet them at the cafeteria for supper at 5 p.m.

The tour began at the research and development lab where canoes were designed. Technical designers worked at drafting tables which held large sheets of paper full of diagrams and specs. Every wall was covered with the fruit of their labor. Large glossy prints of canoes sitting amongst beautiful wild settings lit up the room. Some were being paddled into rough water while others sat in tranquil bays. Some floated before gorgeous sunsets and sunrises or raced ahead of storms. Quotes from Teddy Roosevelt to Sig Olson were emblazoned across the doorways and hall. They emphasized man's duty to be good stewards of the natural world. One quote by Sig Olson from his book, *The Singing Wilderness*, was especially inspiring:

> *The movement of a canoe is like a reed in the wind. Silence is part of it, and the sounds of lapping water, bird songs, and wind in the trees. It is part of the medium through which it floats, the sky, the water, and the shores..... A man is part of his canoe and therefore part of all it knows.*

Leaving the inspirational room of theory and design, they followed the manufacturing of the canoes that were showcased in the beautiful posters. They watched resins and fibers being combined in forms where heat and pressure were applied to create the various hull composites, styles and lengths. Last, the hulls were allowed to cool and cure before being stacked. It was a carefully choreographed operation that spit out a variety of models. Some were short and heavily braced with specialized seats and footrests for running white water. Longer three-seat tandems were engineered for touring big water while carrying heavy loads. Last were the beautiful solo canoes in several styles. They were fast, stable and perfect for a lone paddler. The paddler alone controlled when, where, and how far he paddled. Mark and Bob were intrigued and excited about the solo canoes. They whispered as they inspected the different styles and hull composites. At the end of the line, the finished product complete with trim, sat ready for service. There were also beautiful laminated paddles with layers of basswood, butternut, spruce, cherry and ash. They were covered with a tough clear finish and had "Rockgard" protection around the paddle's blade. The canoes would soon carry a new generation of present day voyageurs in much the same way as the dugout and birch bark canoes carried the Ojibway and the fur trade voyageurs.

After the tour, Ron returned them to the cafeteria where they were treated to coffee and a cookie while their canoe and gear order was pulled. Pierre explained that their Old Towne Royalex tandem canoes were aging and needed to be replaced. They would sell the old canoes to new owners who would still find them useful for normal service. The pounding canoes take over time from rough outfitter use and from the elements weakens even the toughest canoes. Hulls develop cracks and become brittle over the years. Delaying replacement could lead to tragedy when a canoe fails deep in the wilderness.

Pierre said, "Allons-y" and led them from the cafeteria to the entrance. They hopped in the waiting van. Pierre brought the van and trailer around to the loading dock. They first loaded the two mystery canoes, with their black plastic covers and amazing lightness. The Royalex tandems were next. They would take the place of the Old Towne canoes that would be sold. Last to be loaded were the paddles, life jackets and accessories. When everything was tightly packed and strapped down, Pierre signed the invoice. Pierre drove the rig around and parked in the front while Bob and Mark walked into the plant and back to the cafeteria. It was only fifteen minutes until supper so they had a seat and waited.

Pierre reappeared in ten minutes, walking alongside a man, presumably the owner.

"Bob, Mark!" Pierre said. "This man be owner. He be Mike, or Mr. 'C.'"

After the greetings were complete, Mike asked them to be seated and left to speak to the chef. In minutes, large covered trays and bowls were set before them.

"Welcome, hommes du nord," Mike said. "I hope you have enjoyed touring our canoe utopia! Please enjoy the meal we've prepared for your pleasure—bon appétit!"

Mark uncovered the tray nearest him. It was full of deviled eggs and six kinds of cheese. He scooped up a sample of each and passed it along. He found another full of warm bagels that cried to be chewed. There were five heaping trays including potato salad, pickles, olives and garden salad with seasoned chicken chunks. Carafes of fresh-squeezed lemonade and coffee completed the exquisite meal.

While they ate, Mike asked for details of their recent BWCA guide trip. As the trio took turns relating stories of the trip, Mike listened intently. He marveled at their courage, resourcefulness and toughness during the trip, especially during the bear attack. He found the details of the first aid treatment the campers provided to the injured man, Pierre's leadership and the subsequent mercy trip by Bob and Mark to be amazing. He hadn't heard of an outfitter taking a group of handicapped clients into the wilderness before. He asked several questions concerning it. Pierre suggested he contact Walt for more information.

Mike thanked them for their willingness to answer his questions. He also then answered some of their questions about his own experience and background. They were in awe of his successful venture to make some of the finest canoes in the industry. Mike was a regular visitor to the Boundary Waters and Quetico, as well as to other areas of Minnesota. He had grown up locally, held a love and deep respect for the land and had a strong commitment to make the best canoes possible.

The four of them did the food trays justice. After a final cup of coffee, they hauled their dishes to the kitchen. The factory was shutting down for the day, so they helped clear the table of leftover food containers and placed them in the walk-in cooler. The night watchman let them out and waved goodbye. Mike waited for them to start their rig. They followed him up the highway until he pulled off on a side road. It soon curved up into the bluffs. They stopped behind Mike's car. He stepped out and beckoned them to his guest cabin. He opened the door, showed them the layout, and then wished them a good night. He shook everyone's hand. Although he couldn't be around in the morning, he told them to drive to the factory for breakfast at the cafeteria before returning to Ely.

They thanked Mike for all his kindness and waved goodbye. Without further ado, they entered their snug cabin. It had a loft bedroom, two bedrooms on the main floor and a small, but complete kitchen with a fridge full of snacks and natural drinks. The fridge door had a sign that said, "Help yourself." The cabin had its own wind generator that provided the electricity. There were high efficiency fans, triple-glazed windows and solar light tubes that illuminated each room during the day. Mark was reminded of Cora's home with its minimal impact on the land. After touring the state of the art interior, they walked out on the front porch. Comfortable bamboo padded chairs and an old metal glider couch sat waiting. The view was fitting. One could watch the Mississippi River and its marshes beyond. The rich and varied parade of wildlife offered front row seats for their pleasure. It was an idyllic finish to a long rewarding day. They used the handy 10-power binoculars to follow an endless chain of creatures on the wing or swimming. It held them completely spellbound. After a while, hunger distracted Bob who left to check out the snack situation. He soon reappeared with a large tray filled with three big bowls of buttered popcorn. A tray of glasses and a pitcher of ice water followed!

"Très bon!" Pierre exclaimed. "It be perfect treat for ce soir."

"My pleasure!" Bob replied. He set his bowl down and turned toward them, saying, "There's a commercial grade popcorn popper here that makes it just like at the movie theater!"

Mark couldn't respond due to his mouth being crammed with popcorn. He merely smiled and gave Bob a thumbs up. The long road trip and factory tour had been nice but tiring. They all heartily toasted Mike for his exceptional hospitality. With possibly a campfire being the only missing ingredient to perfection, Pierre provided a good substitute by lighting up his clay pipe.

As the sun sank below the bluffs behind the cabin, its last golden rays glowed on the river and the marshes. Tall grassy hummocks studded with trees were illuminated. It was near dusk. Suddenly large flights of ducks came roaring by in squadrons. The feathered acrobats began pitching into the myriad of river channels and pools. It was their safe haven for the night.

"Bonsoir, mes amis," Pierre announced. "Time for all voyageur to retire!"

He knocked the ashes out of his pipe and began climbing up to his loft bedroom.

"Bonsoir, Pierre," Mark and Bob said in unison.

They collected the glasses and bowls and dumped the leftover kernels into the shrubs for the creatures. After washing dishes and toweling them dry, they replaced them in the cupboards and made ready for bed. Before Mark fell asleep, he set the wind-up alarm to ring at a quarter of six. That would be time enough for quick showers and still arrive at the factory for the appointed 7 a.m. breakfast.

The alarm's loud ringing forced Mark awake, but he lay still for a few minutes before he staggered to the bathroom. He showered, dressed and woke Bob. Pierre was already standing outside on the porch greeting the sunrise over the busy marsh. He stood with his arms outstretched, paying homage to the Creator for another day. Mark delayed joining him for several minutes. He quietly returned to pack up his overnight bag. When he again walked out on the porch, Pierre was sitting with his eyes closed. Pierre heard Mark's footfalls and looked up. He gave Mark a nod and spoke a soft, "Allons-y." Mark tipped his hat then stood beside his mentor and friend. Together they watched the marsh come alive. The night creatures slipped away as the sun energized the marsh.

As they prepared to leave, Mark knew Pierre would wait until after breakfast to have his first smoke. Mark appreciated his habit of not smoking inside the truck when others were with him. He understood it was an irritant to his and Bob's eyes and lungs in a confined space. Wood smoke from a campfire sometimes stung his eyes and made him cough, but it was unavoidable and a small price to pay for its warmth and comfort.

Bob appeared with his overnight bag in hand, wet-headed but chipper. Pierre and Mark greeted him with a brisk, "Allons-y!" Everyone loaded their bags and climbed into the van. They hit the highway and in fifteen minutes entered Wenonah Canoe's parking lot. Pierre led them to the front door where a secretary named Dee escorted them to the cafeteria.

Mark gave their guide the coffee thermos and asked that it be filled. The employees were gathered in small groups while enjoying coffee, muffins, bagels and cereal. Mark led the way to the breakfast buffet. They took a tray and filled their plates and coffee mugs. The large bowl of mixed fruit drew Mark's attention. He filled a cereal bowl with pineapple slices, muskmelon and orange sections. A toasted English muffin with raspberry jam completed his breakfast. It was filling and a fine start to the day. After clearing their plates and lingering over a second mug of java, they carried their trays to the kitchen. Pierre thanked the chef, waved at the workers and led them back out. Their guide handed Mark their full thermos. He thanked her and stepped outside. Mark carried the thermos to the van and poured their travel mugs full.

While Pierre enjoyed a quick smoke, Mark and Bob took a quick trip down to the river's edge. They watched it run cool and deep on a never-ending journey to the sea. Pierre said he had been at its headwaters, in Itasca State Park, near Bemidji, MN, where it was small enough to jump over. Many attempted to run its turbulent currents each year with everything from canoes and kayaks to rubber or wooden raft—some with little shacks. Those who were skilled and lucky successfully navigated the monster river and celebrated at New Orleans. Many quit part way after they swamped their craft and were injured or drowned during their attempt. As the river flowed farther south, it grows wider and multiplies its currents and dangers. Motorized barges and other boat traffic made it more hazardous for small, non-motorized craft. Nonetheless, the lure of running the Mississippi drew new participants each year.

Pierre soon blew the van's horn, prompting their scramble up the hill and into the waiting van. Once again they were on the road and backtracking their route. They drove parallel to the river until they reached Red Wing, MN, where they crossed the bridge into Wisconsin. Many deer stood in the woods and ditches grazing on fresh green grass, gorging on life-giving herbs and sedges before retiring for a mid-day nap in the cool shade. They were mainly creatures of the night and twilight. Their eye structure absorbed and intensified ambient light. Even in the dark, their eyes allowed them to move and feed with ease.

After several hours Mark and Bob switched places. It was neat to take turns chatting with Pierre and sipping coffee. Pierre's stories made them laugh at times and sad at others, but were always fascinating. He had been a woodsman for the past twenty-five years. Pierre had seen more strange happenings, natural beauty, and tragedy than most. He had fought men, beasts and storms, but never lost his spiritual connection with the land and his deep reverence for, and a love of, its wonders.

They passed through Spooner and made Duluth before noon. Pierre drove to the west side of Duluth where an old brick building had become the famous birthplace of all Duluth Packs. Entering the factory was a walk back in time. Once there were many places like it, where local craftsmen made a variety of durable goods. They worked with pride for their entire careers and raised their families, secure and stalwart. Unfortunately, cheap labor and corporate greed had conspired to close many shops. These venerable factories couldn't compete with low foreign wages and cheaply made goods. It was good to see that some American crafts still thrived, like this place. At Duluth Pack, heavy canvas and leather were sewn and riveted into historic, sturdy canoe packs by true craftsmen. These packs came complete with tump straps that the early voyageurs used to transfer weight forward. The straps were two-inch wide leather and extended from the bottom of a two or more 90 # trade bales and up to the top of their heads. The tough French Canadian voyageurs trotted off with their heads low to support the heavy load on their backs.

Pierre introduced them to the woman at the front window. When she learned they worked as guides for Border Waters Outfitters, she offered to give them a tour of the factory. One woman's job was to make heavy canvas tents. The unique tents could be configured various ways depending on weather and needs of their owner. Some employees cut canvas to be sewn on industrial machines; others riveted packs and canvas and leather bags. They also did alterations, made repairs and fulfilled special orders. It was an interesting tour. After thanking their guide, they left with a catalog and a new appreciation for the hard working, conscientious people who continued a fine tradition. It was also a nice chance to get out of the van and stretch the kinks out. But suddenly their stomachs were sending distress signals to their brains! Feeding was necessary. Soon! They set a course for Grandma's Restaurant at Canal Park, hoping that the lunch crowd would have thinned out. They arrived at 1:30 p.m., famished and glad to find a double parking place near the entrance.

Soon they were seated in a massive old wooden booth next to a window. The weather remained warm with fluffy cumulus clouds scudding by in a fair breeze. The menus featured way too many tempting choices, leaving Bob and Mark a bit bewildered.

Pierre smiled upon seeing their frustration at the wide range of eats and gave them a hint:

"Chicken and wild rice soup be très bon. Go with sandwich – warm belly," he said.

They took his advice. Both had a bowl of the chicken and wild rice soup. In addition Mark chose a toasted cheese on rye while Bob ordered a Bicycle Burger. Pierre ordered the same soup and a toasted cheese on rye. Mark ate slowly and savored the rich creamy soup. It had chunks of chicken and lots of luscious wild rice. He scanned the walls and ceiling which held tons of antique memorabilia. Mark had their server fill their coffee thermos for the last leg of the trip back to Ely. Pierre paid the bill and tip. He refused any help from Bob and Mark, saying, "It's been covered, mes amis."

They all piled back into the van to resume the trip home. Mark poured everyone's mugs full of coffee to help fight drowsiness. Pierre said it would be around supper time when they returned, so he and Bob should wait until morning to unload the canoes. It was OK with them since they were about knackered. They arrived back at the lodge, thanked Pierre and retired to their room for a nap that ended abruptly when the bell rang. After supper, which consisted of delicious Swiss steak and mashed potatoes with a garden salad, Mark returned the thermos. With a hearty "bonsoir," Bob and Mark saluted Pierre.

After retrieving their pillow, book and blanket from the van, they trooped wearily to their room. The room felt stuffy after being closed up all day. They opened the windows and front door and stepped outside to enjoy the air. A few hours of daylight remained. It felt good to walk after spending the day riding. The refreshing breeze lightly pushed them along. The sunset was fading. Its vibrant colors surrendered to the dusk. Their walk has worked out the kinks, so they headed for the bunkhouse. Once back in their cool room, they opted for a hot shower. Showered, warm and very relaxed, they turned off the light and lay in their bunks, chatting quietly until the room went silent but for their steady, comatose breathing.

A loud cry from a flock of crows flying over woke Mark from sleep. He sat on the edge of his bunk, stretched and rubbed his eyes. He traipsed to the bathroom. Splashing cold water onto his face and a good teeth brushing brought him back to the land of the living and even put a little spunk in him. As Mark entered the room, he decided Bob needed a wake-up.

"Bear in the camp!" Mark shouted. "Run for the hills!"

Bob jerked upright! He gasped and tried to run but his feet tangled in the sheet. He fell hard on the floor. Mark laughed as he helped untangle Bob's legs and got him seated on his bunk.

"Man, that was a shock to the system!" Bob groaned. "I thought we were still at our campsite and was just dreaming about chasing a bear with cubs!"

They had a good laugh after Bob accused Mark of trying to give him a heart attack. Mark didn't often pull a practical joke, but he sometimes found it hard to refuse his dark side.

"It will be time for breakfast soon," Mark said, "so get ready. I'll wait for you outside."

"D'accord," Bob answered, as he left for the bathroom. "See you there in ten. Maybe we'll get to see what the two mystery canoes look like! Whoever made the special order must be a real VIP."

As they approached the lodge, they noted some new guest vehicles in the parking lot. Pierre had mentioned some guests were expected and would be staying primarily in the lodge rooms. The guests were sightseeing and taking some day trips. Some might enter the Boundary Waters, but would return in time for supper at the lodge. Their short trip could be due to physical limits or just choosing to take the easier path. That was fine with Mark and Bob. The guests could visit the BWCA, but their day trip would keep the more popular campsites from becoming overcrowded. At least they had made an effort to flee the city and appreciate nature. Many urban dwellers fear venturing into the wild, whereas the artificial city is most frightening to others. Mark would much rather take on the dangers of the natural wilderness than the noisy, crowded and crime-infested cities.

Driven by hunger, Mark and Bob hustled to the kitchen and followed their noses to the enticing aromas. After tying into some scrambled eggs, ham, toast and coffee, they felt re-charged and left to meet Pierre and Walt at the trailer. Walt asked that they first unload the two tandem canoes and gear, leaving the two mystery canoes until last. They complied and unstrapped the two Wenonah tandem canoes. After carrying each of the shiny boats into the Quonset, they attached bow and stern to waiting carabiners and hoisted them up just beneath the rafters and tied them off. All the new gear, including paddles, life vests and miscellaneous gear were placed in appropriate bins or racks. All that was left were the two wrapped mystery canoes. Walt walked over to one wrapped canoe. He opened his pocketknife and cut open a yellow plastic envelope stuck to it. He reached in, pulled something out and turned to face them. He smiled at Mark and Bob as they stared at what he was holding. It was a familiar manila envelope, similar to the ones their paychecks had come from! Walt broke the red wax seal and extracted a sheet of what looked to be parchment. After briefly scanning it, he began to read it aloud:

> Dear friends at Border Waters Outfitters. We are Paul and Jerry, the two campers who were rescued from the bears at Horse Lake. We wanted you all to know that we are doing well, with a few scars and exciting tales to tell our friends and children. It is our distinct pleasure to make a special gesture of our thanks to Pierre, Bob and Mark. We first contacted Walt, who then suggested we talk with the good doctor, who in turn, guided us to Mike at Wenonah Canoe. Without your timely help to chase the bear, apply first aid, and escort us out, we might have been overcome. We were panicked, confused and would've been at a loss for sure. Your taking charge and ministering to our needs turned a disaster into a triumph. You shouldered most of our gear, listened to our ramblings and may have saved our lives. We talked with our families and friends about this and made our decision. Pierre has been thanked and

compensated for his quick first aid and directing our evacuation without delay. Mike at Wenonah Canoe was then contacted by the good doctor. When Mike, the owner, heard the story about the rescue on Horse Lake, he proposed a fitting reward. He mentioned that the company had made two prototype solo canoes designed with extra tough innovations. They were built using new combinations of fiber and resin to create tougher, lighter craft for rough use. Their staff put the canoes through a rigorous testing on the Mississippi River. They found them fast, tough and agile. The canoes handled well and passed with flying colors. The solo canoes have special features including: raised foot braces, sliding tractor seats and a special built-in sail rig that collapses and is controlled from the center by cables and pulleys. It gives you another advantage when the wind is in your favor. Mike said that the fur trade canoes used sails to speed them across lakes. We found out from Walt that Bob and Mark had no canoes of their own, so we made a deal with Mike. We gladly offer these canoes to you both with our undying thanks. We hope they carry you swiftly and safely for many years. They are scratched and gouged from their trials, but are sound. We hope this is a small payback. Bonne chance. Paul and Jerry.

Bob and Mark stood immobile, like two deer caught in the headlights! They stared at the canoes, still wrapped, then at each other. Slowly Mark's wide eyes narrowed. With a grin he reached for his new Rapala knife and began to cut away the plastic. Bob recovered also and followed Mark's lead. They feverishly sliced the black plastic sheets away and let it fall to the ground. Now fully exposed were two very rugged, prototype solo canoes! They did have some scratches and gouges, but they were beautiful works of art to Mark and Bob.

"Mon dieu!" Bob blurted. "What a gift!"

"C'est magnifique!" Mark agreed. "It's hard to believe. "Thank you, Paul, Jerry, and the good doctor. And thank you, Walt!"

"We're very happy for you both," Walt said. "Not everyone would have had the courage to act as you did. Paul and Jerry were most fortunate you happened by. Now why don't you take these babies down to the lake and put them through their paces. Don't forget your new paddles!"

Mark and Bob grinned widely, then set up the portage yokes and shouldered their new canoes. They set off for the beach at a trot. Mark estimated the canoes length at sixteen feet and their weight less than forty pounds. They were a natural marsh grass color. After being used to carrying the heavy Royalex tandems, these were a breeze. Once on the water Mark raised his butt off the tractor seat to adjust it before digging his paddle deep for several strokes. The solo was just what he had dreamed of. It was stable, fast and nimble. He closed his eyes and ceased paddling to enjoy the long glide. They put their new craft through a tough sequence of panic turns, reversals, and a general shakedown. The low center of gravity due to sitting near the bottom of the canoe gave one a secure feeling. Unlike most caned or plastic canoe seats which sat just below the gunwales, these were more like a kayak's with the option of sliding forward or back. Depending on how the canoe was packed, it allowed for trimming a load for optimum balance. It was a delight. He was excited, grateful and overwhelmed. Suddenly his eyes teared up and he raised his arms skyward as he thanked the Creator for the blessing. When his eyes met Bob's, he knew Bob felt exactly the same. They would send their sincere thanks to Jerry and Paul, as well as to the good doctor.

"Bob, my man," Mark said, "let's have a little race!"

"Très bien, monsieur!" Bob joked. "Let's raise the sails and use the wind to reach the island, then drop them and race back to the dock."

They raised the sail masts and pulled the cable that unrolled the square sail. The sails caught the wind and carried them swiftly to the island. They had never sailed before and had only had to use their paddles as a rudder to keep their canoes on course. The two prototype solos fairly flew across the lake in a dead heat. Just before they reached the island, Mark hollered, "Release your sail cable!" Bob complied and both sails rolled up at the bottom of the mast. A quick pull on another cable lowered the mast. Pierre had shown them how the sail rig worked. Mark was thrilled with the sail and now returned to paddling. As they rounded the island they faced the stiff breeze. With about a mile of water to the lodge docks, they pushed their canoes hard. It caused their bows to cut cleanly through the wind-driven chop. The two canoes were still tied as they glided into the pier.

"What a ride!" Bob shouted. "We owe that sow bear a nice big hug."

"D'accord," Mark said. "The generosity of the good doctor and Paul and Jerry is touching. These solos and our camp guide stories should surprise Ray when we meet with him tomorrow."

After the exhilarating shakedown cruise, they jauntily saluted each other. Then they triumphantly toted their new toys up to the Quonset hut. The rest of the day flew by as they checked and packed their gear. They soon discovered an alarming shortage of snack food for their trip! They quickly asked around to see if anyone was going to Ely. Pierre was having some java and a pipe smoke in the parking lot. He announced he was about to leave for Ely. Walt needed a few supplies, and they were welcome to ride shotgun! Pierre needed time to make out a list of supplies, but would be ready in "fifteen." That gave Mark and Bob time to make their own lists. They still had some cash left from their stash. They sat on the lodge steps and made out a short list of goods. Pierre walked up as they quenched their thirst with tall lemonades. Then they all piled into the trusty Dodge pickup and headed for Ely.

First stop would be at Zup's grocery. They bought a few summer sausages, chocolate, roasted nuts, dried fruit, jerky and lots of Mrs. Grass Chicken Noodle Soup. They knew that Ray Bond would cover the first few days' meals, so they leaned toward the simple eats. They added fish batter mix in hopes of catching their dinner. Bob reminded Mark about taking bannock mix, as well as jam and syrup.

Next stop was the Army Surplus store where Mark bought a new type of fire starter. It was a solid stick of magnesium with a flint insert. He also bought a few tough foil-faced emergency blankets that fit in a pocket. It could thwart hypothermia and might just be a lifesaver. It also worked as a fire reflector or a quick shelter. The main purpose of reflecting body heat was to prevent a person from going into shock and suffering exposure. Bob and Pierre also bought some. It was cheap insurance. Little did they know how soon they would find it useful. Pierre told of his past experiences where wilderness mishaps such as canoes being swamped in icy water or injuries and severe weather required fast action. Dry clothing, a hot fire, blankets and hot drinks saved lives. Mark and Bob decided to have one emergency blanket in their pack and one in their pocket.

"Well, mes amis," Pierre said, "allons-y, we go back!"

"D'accord," Mark agreed. "We're running out of cash and need to get this stuff packed."

After returning to the lodge, they thanked Pierre for the ride and found room for their purchases in their packs. After finishing, they wandered over to the lodge where they studied the large outfitter maps that covered one wall. The maps encompassed the entire Superior National Forest, including the BWCAW and Quetico Park in Canada. They still had no clue about the route they would take with Ray Bond. The wealth of options for a trip was mind-boggling.

After a supper of hearty beef stew and fresh baked bread, Pierre wished them a good safe trip. He was leaving to spend a few days at home, but would return to lead some day trips with lodge clients. He reminded Mark and Bob that their guide services would be required for several small groups of fly fishermen the last two weeks in July. It would involve positioning canoes so the clients could cast to fish along the shore. As Pierre waved goodbye, he suggested that they might like to watch the July Fourth fireworks. The Ely display would be visible after dark if the sky was clear.

"That would be fun!" Bob said. "But it would be better to watch from a higher point. Wasn't there a ladder that allows access to the top of the Quonset?"

D'accord!" Mark answered. "Let's climb up there and check it out."

After climbing up the ladder, they made a quick reconnoiter of the roof. It was curved with deep corrugated panels that wouldn't hold chairs. They brainstormed and climbed down. In the scrap pile they found a couple pieces of plywood. On one side they nailed narrow wood strips that were spaced to slide into the corrugations. They hauled them up and laid them over the roof. It made a sturdy flat base for their chairs. Mark sneaked a bag of corn chips and water bottles up in a daypack. Bob brought his binoculars. They hauled two headlamps, two folding chairs and a couple blankets to ward off the night chill. Dusk fell. The fiery sunset was followed by a starlit, clear night sky. They felt almost giddy about their new canoes and their secret perch. As they relaxed and waited for the fireworks show, they munched corn chips. Their high perch allowed them a commanding view. It felt good to relax and curl up in their warm wool blankets.

Mark had a flashback to his younger days and one of the precious few family outings after closing the fruit stand for the day. A rare treat was getting everyone into the Willys station wagon and driving to the Tri-City Drive In, near Quinnesec. It was on a Friday or Saturday when his dad was off work the following day. Sometimes a night swim at Lake Antoine Beach preceded the movie, but that was even rarer. Once at the drive-in, his dad paid the admission of two bucks per car. Then they drove along the dirt roads and found a space on the bermed area alongside a vacant speaker post. It was exciting to watch a steady stream of cars pick their favorite spots in a semi-circle facing the giant screen. His dad hung the metal speaker box with wire attached, over his window. The Willys wagon was now parked with the front end elevated up toward the big screen. His parents relaxed and waited until dark while they listened to the piped in music.

Mark and his siblings made a dash for the convenient playground below the huge screen. It had the usual slides, teeter-totters, swings and monkey bars. Mark's favorite ride was a round horizontal merry-go-round with seating on a plank around its outer edge. It was propelled by pushing a steel bar with one's feet while pulling back with one's arms on another bar. Mark always felt like he was using a railroad car. He had seen one fly by near the tracks that ran along the north shore of Lake Antoine. Two men faced each other and pumped the cart down the tracks. The drive-in ride held up to ten kids and could be pumped until it rotated to very scary speeds. Sometimes kids were frightened by the velocity and the centrifugal force generated. The ride threw some poor devils off and onto the ground! The place was wild with kids running and riding with abandon without adult supervision. It was heaven.

The fun ended when dusk fell and more cars with lights on rolled in and populated most of the ramp slots. If the sun was still too bright to allow the drive-in's film projector to produce a good picture on the massive screen, there would be advertisements for the concession stand at the rear, cartoons and previews of coming attractions. All the kids would abandon the darkening playground and run to their family's car. Before the first feature began, Mark's mom would bring out a big bowl of bruised but "perfectly good" fruit and another of homemade popcorn. There were also bottles of Dad's Root Beer from their fruit stand's cooler. It was a grand time, watching cartoons, snacking and having popcorn fights in back. Without fail, there was always the necessary trip with the twins to the well-lit bathrooms and snack bar. Teenage hoods stood around looking tough and smoking cigarettes, while moths and June bugs attacked the yellow fluorescent lights. Halfway through the first feature everyone in the back seats was fast asleep. The playtime, snacks and late movie start conspired so they never stayed awake for half the feature.

"Mark!" Bob exclaimed. "There's a dandy one!"

"Mais oui, that's très magnifique!" Mark replied.

The fireworks continued with more and more spectacular bursts of color, punctuated by loud booms following bright flashes that rivaled lightning and thunder. It reminded Mark of his family's annual ritual on July Fourth back home. They lived outside town and couldn't watch the city of Iron Mountain fireworks display. They would pack the Willys Wagon with folding chairs and take some snacks, blankets sparklers, caps, ladyfinger firecrackers, black snake smokers, and Black Cat firecrackers and head for Grandpa Pete's home. It sat on a hill with a clear view of Millie Hill, where the fireworks were lit. There was a wild and crazy time with their cousins. Kids lit sparklers and ran with them, set off firecrackers, exploded caps and committed other mayhem. It was inevitable that, while running around on the pavement, one of the kids either grabbed a hot sparkler or stepped barefooted on the hot wire. Loud screams and smartly delivered parental whacks ended that activity. First aid for burns was provided by grandpa's aloe plant leaves.

The Black Cat crackers were larger and more potent. The tiny ones, called ladyfingers, came in a long string and made a prolonged racket. Teenagers often lit these strings as they cruised the main drag.

Sometimes they exploded inside the car with disastrous results. The undisputed king of them all was the M-80, a fat, stubby cracker with a fuse in its center. It was a mean-looking device, almost in the military ordnance category. It packed a punch and was responsible for most of the lost fingers and eyes. Others were called Silver Salute Firecrackers which could be heard all over town. If things got out of control and a "hang fire" cracker went off near a child's hand or exploded under an adult's chair, Mark's mom would rise up and scream, "That's it, give me those things – NOW!"

When the bag of corn chips and the fireworks were finished, Bob and Mark lingered for a while. It was pleasant enjoying the return of the quiet. Overhead sparkled a spectacularly clear sky as the night cooled down. Mark pointed out the two constellations he knew. Bob spotted a shooting star. With regret they picked up their things, folded the chairs and slid the plywood off the roof. Tired but happy, they headed for the bunkhouse. Ray would be there early in the morning. Ray was pushing his mid-fifties and seemed to be in good health. It remained to be seen how strenuous a trip he could take. Their destination was in his hands. Wherever he led them would be good and in the best of company. Quickly, they slipped into bed, turned the lights out and succumbed to the near death.

Chapter Twenty-One

Camping With Ray and Ange

A robin's song drifted into the room. Mark was awake but still groggy. He remained in his bunk listening to the eaves drip and watched the false dawn gradually light the room. Soon, the trip with their friend, teacher and hero would begin. There was little left to do, so he luxuriated in his cozy bunk. It promised to be a good time of renewing friendships and entering new territory. He checked his watch. He saw it was past 6 a.m.! He dragged his body out to the bathroom where a hot shower brought him to life.

After donning shorts, river sandals and sweatshirt, he shook Bob's sleeping form, saying, "Rise and shine, mon ami, time for all good wood rats to hit the brush!"

"Allons-y, monsieur!" Bob drowsily replied. "Did you get the license number of that truck that ran me over last night?"

"Surely you jest," Mark chided him. "I'll wait for you outside while you grab a quick shower. The dinner bell should be ringing soon, so hurry!"

Bob jumped up and rushed off while Mark walked outside. He inhaled the fresh scent of earth and flowers after a rain. Night crawlers had been out on the grass during the rain. They left their telltale little castings. Mark marveled at how clear the sky was at bedtime, but had clouded over bringing a pouring rain. Nature was not predictable. It was part of the mystery and the primary cause of a weatherman's gray hair. Just when the experts think they have it all figured out, it's back to square one on the cosmic drawing board.

Bob appeared. He was clean, alert and ready to do battle with "rocks, roots and mud." They ambled off toward the kitchen. A tray of fresh-baked donuts, pecan coffee cake and a carafe of hot coffee awaited their eager grasp. With their hands full, they thanked the chef. They munched coffee cake and sipped java as they sauntered out to the Quonset hut. After finishing the last bite and swallow, they opened the big garage door. In no time, all their packs and gear sat ready alongside their new solo canoes. It would be fun to see what Ray thought of their lavish gifts. Bob returned to filch two more sweet rolls and java refills. They ate, sipped java and continued their vigil, patiently awaiting Ray.

Unknown to them, Ray and his wife had arrived the prior afternoon. They had stayed overnight in Duluth the day before after spending time shopping and relaxing. They slept in and didn't leave Duluth until after noon. A leisurely drive took several hours getting to Ely. After a little food shopping, they arrived at the lodge after supper. Walt had invited them to stay as his guest after making them a snack and enjoying a short visit. Walt told them that he had seen Mark and Bob watching the fireworks atop the Quonset building. All of them agreed it was best to let the guys enjoy the fun. Seeing them in the morning would be soon enough. The trip had tuckered out the two, but they slept soundly and were up early having coffee and sweet rolls. Ray and Ange left their cozy room, waved goodbye to Walt and drove over to where they found their star pupils.

All at once, there came the welcome sound of tires on gravel! Mark and Bob stood up and watched as Ray pulled up in his Toyota van with canoe trailer in tow. As soon as the rig halted, Ray limped slowly out. Bob and Mark almost bowled him over in their exuberant greeting! Numerous hugs and double handshakes commenced with Ray and his wife Ange.

Then Ray spied the Wenonah solos!

"Where did you steal these?" Ray exclaimed, his eyes wide, incredulous. "I've never seen anything like them! Seriously, are they rentals?"

"Nope, they're a gift!" Mark said proudly. "We'll tell you all about it on the way. Sure glad you brought a canoe trailer, Ray."

After all their gear was loaded and the canoes were securely strapped on the trailer, they all piled into the van and headed towards Ely. Bob could wait no longer.

"Can we please know where we'll be going for our camping, Ray?" Bob pleaded.

Ray's laugh boomed inside the van! He reached for a map and handed it to them. It had a route highlighted. Both recognized the area instantly. It entered the BWCA via the Mudro Lake entry. It was the same one they had used on their client trip! The difference in this route began by following Mudro Lake's north shore. It led to a shallow, rocky bay where they would make a few short portages and enter Fourtown Lake. It was simply incredible how Ray had outfoxed them.

"Well," Ray said, "I wanted a route that was relatively easy since I'm a bit out of shape, and Ange concurred. Numerous side trips are available. It's also fairly close to the van should an emergency occur. I looked at various routes, but chose this in the end. You were already familiar with the area and it would allow Ange and me to set up a base camp on Fourtown. We figured that after a day or so of you guys camping with us, exchanging war stories, and eating Ange's cooking, you'd move out to your solo camps."

"Perfect!" Mark agreed. "There should be plenty of options for our solo camps on Fourtown, Boot or even Horse!"

As they chatted and drove down the Echo Trail, Bob and Mark finally had the chance to enlighten Ray about the solo canoes. Ray listened to the story in wonder. He shook his head and laughed. He could only muster a garbled, "It's too much!" When Bob brought up the good doctor's gift of a cash bonus besides their guide pay, Ray nearly ran the van off the road. He and Ange cheered. Mark and Bob basked in the praise. It would resonate in their memories forever.

"My old heart can't take anymore!" Ray blurted. "I want to hear every detail of your client trip before you two leave for your solo!"

"Mais oui," Bob and Mark said in unison.

Ray smiled and said, "Well done, mes amis, or should I say hommes du nord?"

Ray pulled the van and trailer into the Chainsaw Sisters' parking lot and paid the fee while Bob and Mark began unloading. The three canoes—Ray's tandem Royalex and the two solos—went to the Mudro Creek landing first. Mark insisted he would portage the tandem. Next they humped the packs that were set directly into the canoes, which were tied off in the shallows. When everything was loaded and balanced, Ange seated herself in the bow of their canoe. Before shoving off, Ray compared his maps with those of Bob and Mark and gave the boys their permits.

Bob and Mark led the way down the small, twisty creek. After negotiating several tight bends and dodging boulders, they entered Mudro Lake. That's where their travel route differed from their client trip. They hung to the left shore. The first of three portages was on the right and a few were a bit tricky. The second was the longest and ran along a sheer rock cliff. The last was easier and short. They soon stood on the rocky southwest shore. Fourtown Lake was large with many bays and narrows. They pushed off into its widest end and followed the shore toward the north. A breeze blew out of the southwest. They passed an occupied campsite and continued until they paused at the boulder-strewn portage alongside a creek's mouth. The portage trail followed the creek upstream to Boot Lake. Then the trio continued along Fourtown Lake's shore and approached the campsite nearest the portage. It was unoccupied.

Ray made them a proposition: "Would you guys land here and see if it will meet our needs as a base camp? We'll sit in our canoe and await your evaluation, OK Ange?" Ange smiled and nodded.

Mark and Bob chimed in with, "Roger, wilco." They beached their canoes on the rare sandy shore and checked out the site. After a brief foray about the campsite, Mark called their findings to Ray.

"It looks like a go," Mark said. "The sandy landing is gradual. There are several good tent sites and trees for hanging a food sack. The pit toilet is a short walk and private. There is a nice high fire grate with good sunset viewing and firewood is plentiful. We give it a five-star rating."

"Très bien!" Ray replied. "It sounds good to us. Base camp it is!"

Ray brought their canoe into the sandy landing sideways so Ange could easily climb out. Bob gave Ray a helping hand because of Ray's sore back. Bob and Mark hauled all of Ray and Ange's gear up by the fire pit while they found their tent sites. Ange located a suitable tent site and let Ray set up the tent. She left to check out the toilet. Bob and Mark found decent tent sites further back. They set up the tents and stowed their gear. Their next job was to take their saws and cut enough dry firewood for the first few days. A dead, bone-dry spruce provided plenty of branches. After limbing it with the hatchet, they cut the trunk into chunks and split the larger ones. They hauled it all down to the fire pit and piled it inside the log square where it would stay dry under the rain tarp. Ray and Ange brought the tarp and helped to erect it.

Base camp was officially ready. Mark added a plastic bag stuffed with birch bark and then made a birch bark and twig fire starter bundle to simplify starting a fire. He had already dug out some excess ashes with a spare paddle. It made room to build a good fire under the grate for cooking. Bob hung Ray's food bag pulley and rope system and left the food pack hanging at waist level. That kept it out of reach of critters but allowed easy access at waist level. Bob also raised his and Mark's small snack packs up with a pulley and removed some jerky strips for a needed snack.

Ray decided some hot tea was in order. He fired up his white gas stove and put the pot on to boil.

"Well, guys," Ray said, "we will provide the meals as long as you're with us at base camp. Ange is quite the cook, as my waistline will testify."

"Much obliged," Mark answered. "We've been looking forward to some good home cooking!"

Ange said, "Tonight's supper will be thick steaks, baked potatoes with sour cream, steamed green beans and fruit cocktail for dessert. But for lunch, it's my chicken noodle soup."

"C'est magnifique!" Bob exclaimed. "Just what the doctor ordered."

While Ray poured them hot jasmine tea, Mark and Bob spread out their maps. They sipped the aromatic brew while plotting solo camp possibilities on the maps. The jerky strips were passed around and held off their hunger for a while.

Ray suggested that after lunch they could all take a short trip to explore the lake. Small streams connected Fourtown, Boot and Horse Lakes. The lakes contained good populations of pike, walleye, bass and some pan fish. It was like old times, studying maps before a camp out, as they did in Ray's class and on class field trips. Mark appreciated being so well taken care of, especially the gourmet meals prepared by "Chef" Ange. Ray and Ange had also brought very comfortable wood and canvas folding director's chairs, so everyone could sink into a comfy chair instead of sitting on log seats or little folding stools.

Ray put a pot of chicken noodle soup on the gas stove while Ange prepared the rest of their lunch. It was one Mark and Bob never tired of: piping hot chicken noodle soup with oyster crackers, jalapeño cheese, Zup's summer sausage and saltine crackers. There were Hershey chocolate bars for dessert. It was a tasty, filling lunch that would definitely hold them until supper.

Mark and Bob took turns answering Ray's and Ange's questions about their experiences, good and bad, during the client trip. They covered everything they could with detailed answers. The bear attack prompted the greatest amount of interest. Ray had seen numerous bear during his years of camping in the wild, but had never been bothered, much less attacked. When Ray had applied for their trip permits, the Forest Ranger had mentioned the Horse Lake attack, but emphasized there had been no subsequent problems or sightings of the sow and her two cubs.

Mark related how Jacko had prayed to the Ojibway spirits during the attack. He told how Jacko had implored Gitchi-Manitou and lesser spirits to remove the bear from where the campers were and to lead the bear and her cubs deep into the wilderness where they would remain. That led to a long, detailed discussion of Jacko and his Ojibway training by his full-blood grandfather. Mark told how Jacko's return to the old ways had enriched them all.

Another incident covered was their first night's sudden, violent wind and rain. Bob related how he had hustled Cora and Ruby to Mark's tent while Mark muscled the girls' tent to a safe place. Ray and Ange peppered them with questions that they thoughtfully answered. All the details were still vivid in their minds. Mark and Bob sometimes injected a detail that had escaped the other or offered a slightly different slant on a situation. This made for a lively discussion. Bob teased Mark about his habit of exaggerating the length of fish he caught. It was dismissed as "jealousy" by Mark.

Lunch was a delicious comfort meal. Their pleasant chat continued unabated between bites of lunch and sips of tea. The warmth of the noontime sun and soft breeze off the lake made it perfect. After the conversation died down, everyone agreed that a short nap was in order. Mark joked that taking a nap after a meal was part of the sumo wrestlers' routine to gain weight. Ray and Ange smiled, nodded and took a squat sumo stance. They then bowed and duck walked to their tent! Bob and Mark howled with laughter at their hosts' antics. They also assumed a squat stance, solemnly bowed toward Ray and Ange's tent and duck walked to their own tents.

An hour later, the "sumo" group was awake and seated. They sampled more of Ange's hot tea that cleared away the cobwebs. At Ray's suggestion, they all piled into their canoes and left for a bit of afternoon exploration. Ray waited for Mark and Bob to paddle up beside them, then asked for more details about the origins of their gifted solo canoes. They took turns telling the story of their trip to the Wenonah Canoe Factory with Pierre and the shrouded mystery canoes. The secret was exposed when Walt read the letter written by Paul and Jerry. Ray said he had no knowledge of it!

"I was sure out of the loop on that!" Ray said. "Walt and the good doctor had kept mum and never spilled the beans! I knew about the bear attack via a phone call from Walt, but I guess they wanted the gift of the solo canoes to be kept secret until now."

They plied the waters of Fourtown and stayed close to the shoreline. It was a leisurely paddle that followed the north shore to its shallow, boulder-strewn end where they had entered. They continued down along the far shore. Several campsites appeared at intervals. One had a steep rock face behind the campsite that intrigued Bob. It was unoccupied and would eventually be his choice for his solo camp. Further down the shore, they found a little bay guarded at the narrow entrance by large sentinel pines. Horse Creek began its run parallel to the portage to Horse Lake. After viewing the portage access, the group returned through the narrow "sentinel" opening and followed the shore into a large bay with many protruding and submerged boulders. After winding through what Ray called a "minefield," they continued on to base camp.

Once back, Mark and Bob were told to have a seat and relax. Mark lit a pile of duff and soon had a fire blazing. The pampered junior guides were presented with welcome mugs of hot tea. Everyone sat contentedly sipping tea while the fire crackled and the wind whispered through the pines. The lake surface changed from ruffled to calm as the sun's power waned. Ange got busy with supper prep except for grilling the steaks. That was Ray's expertise. Mark and Bob had ordered their steaks cooked medium well or seared outside with a hot pink center. Mark commented that he might eat raw meat in a survival situation, but so far had been able to avoid being a true savage. Bob countered with a remark about Mark's voyageur dream and his liking roobaboo! Mark blushed and had to agree that he was "almost a savage."

"Ray," Mark asked, "have you been to this lake before?"

"Yes," Ray answered. "It was a long time ago. In fact, it was a trip with the good doctor and Pierre. Walt and Pierre had just started their outfitter business, and we happened to be their first clients! We only passed through this lake twenty years ago. We headed north in a loop to Crooked Lake and back through Horse and finally to Mudro Lake. There were no Forest Service campsites. It was before the Wilderness designation. We were young and on the move every day. We camped at a new site every night. Age and wisdom tends to slow one down. We now choose to take time to smell the roses and consider the lilies."

"Ray, you can start grilling the steaks anytime!" Ange suggested.

"Yes, dear," Ray answered. He slowly extracted himself from his comfortable chair, but his lips and back protested. "Pardon my groans, guys, but age and Mr. Art Ritis team up on me," Ray explained.

Bob rose up to help, but Mark had already grabbed his arm and helped pull Ray vertical. Ray limped over to the grill. Once he moved about a little, he was okay.

"He still has his dignity," Mark whispered. "Ray once told us about his sports activity in high school and college, not to mention his time in the U.S. Army in World War Two. He gets stiff sitting and just needs to work the kinks out. My dad has a similar problem."

"D'accord," Bob replied. "I still remember Ray Bond beating you at Indian wrestling last year!"

Mark nodded and grinned at Bob. He well remembered that day when Ray took over the boys' physical education class at Quinnesec Junior High for Mr. Cummings. Ray had been a tireless promoter of competitive sports. He challenged the class to a run-off Indian wrestling competition in pairs. He would take on the class champion. Losers sat down. Winners continued competing with others still standing until only one was left. Participants stood facing each other and shook hands. Then, while gripping right hands with their feet planted in a wide stance, they waited for Ray's command to start. The object was to try to shove or pull your opponent off balance. When a competitor moved his foot off the floor, he lost. Mark and Ike were the last pair to face off. Ike was strong, wiry and taller than Mark. They shook hands and waited for Ray's command. It was a close match, but after a short fake left, Mark pulled hard to his right. Ike teetered, but began to recover, so Mark pulled hard to his right, and Ike fell. Mark stood still and tried to prepare for Mr. Bond.

The final match made Mark nervous. Mark was strong and big for his age, but Ray was still in his prime. He was built like a boxer and was too much of a competitor to ease back. Everyone gathered around. Mark faced Ray and spread his feet wide. He could feel the quiet power in Ray's arm as they shook hands and waited. At the count of three everyone shouted "Go." Mark made a quick surge forward, but Ray outfoxed him by pulling him forward and down. Mark wasn't prepared and lost his footing. Ray laughed and then raised Mark's arms up over his head like a fighter. Ray thanked the class for a "fine effort." He slapped Mark on the back and led everyone back to class. Later that year, Ray asked Mark to come to the front and to lie rigid across a desk. Ray lifted Mark first to his chest, then moved under him and pressed Mark over his head!

"Supper's ready!" Ray announced. "We'll bring your plates to you."

The steaks sizzled on the platter. They were served with steamed green beans and a big baked potato. After applying sour cream, salt and pepper to the potatoes, they were ready to dig in. Ray raised his hand and said grace.

"Très bien!" Mark gushed. "You sure do cook a supreme camp supper!"

"Amen to that," Bob added. "We may never go solo at this rate!"

After cleaning their plates and dropping them into the fire, Ray placed a few logs of dry pine on the fire. Everyone drew their chairs closer to absorb the fire's warmth. It was the end of a "très magnifique" day. They watched as the last rays of the sun lit the shore. Everyone shielded their eyes from the glare. After a few minutes, the sun dipped beneath the horizon. Its indirect rays caused the clouds to glow in a dazzling array of pastels. No painter could capture its essence.

The four of them laughed and told stories into the night while slapping at pesky mosquitoes. Ray filled Bob and Mark in on home news. Mark's mom was busy picking the row crops and said she missed Mark's help, but had hired some locals to help. Mark felt some guilt. Summer was very busy picking berries, beans, and tending the fruit stand. His mom also cooked and handled the twins. His dad and brother Pete helped on weekends. Pete had just graduated from Kingsford High and worked across the highway at a Pure Oil service station. Mark would regularly deliver a covered supper plate to Pete at the station. Mark was glad there were enough neighbor kids who were eager to pick crops for pay.

Bob's parents had been doing a lot of camping on the weekends. They said that they were planning to paint their house, but were waiting for Bob's help. Bob groaned at hearing that. Everyone had a good laugh. Ange served more hot tea. It was almost too comfortable! Ray and Ange's unmatched hospitality tempted them, but they were stalwart and ready to untie the fetters.

Their departure for solo camping would begin the next morning after breakfast. One last meal would propel them on their way. Ray requested he be allowed a short paddle in one of their solo canoes before they left for their solo camps. The tired group decided to call it a night and said "adieu."

Loon music drifted into Mark's tent as he lay on his back, awaiting sleep. The high-pitched hum of mosquitoes outside the tent became a symphony. A barred owl hooted. The last sound he heard was a loud splash, as if a horse fell in the lake.

Mark woke to a steady patter on the tent, while robins sang their thanks in the false dawn. It was high time for them to go into solo camp mode. Mark couldn't hear anyone moving about. He gladly slugged in his tent. He remained wrapped in his downy cocoon while slowly waking up. A roaring sound alerted him. A squadron of large ducks cruised by as their primary wing feathers ripped through the still morning air like cleavers. Another big splash caused Mark to peek out his window. He spied the culprit. A beaver had slapped the surface and swam serenely away. A light breeze sprang up, shaking rain off the pines.

Mark sighed, slipped quickly out of his bag and into his damp shorts. He pulled his rain parka over his red "river driver" shirt. After adjusting his boonie hat, he quietly exited his tent. He walked to the still quiet fire pit area where he found his bag of birch bark and duff. The fire pit and kindling were dry under the rain tarp. After arranging a nice tinder nest, he tried his new fire starter. First, he shaved magnesium filings into a little pile. Next, he struck the flint insert with his knife blade. It sent a shower of sparks into the filings that instantly erupted in a hot blaze. That ignited the birch bark, which licked hungrily at the twigs. Mark added larger sticks and fed it some split pine chunks that burned hot. The coffee pot was charged, and he put it on the grill to heat. He pulled his chair closer to the welcome heat. The fire dried and warmed him. He raised his arms up in thanks for the new day and life-sustaining rain.

The java pot began to perk. Mark moved it off the main flame where it continued a slow perk. The fire crackled and popped, radiating cozy warmth. He listened to the comforting sound of the coffee as it raced up the metal tube and burst against the glass top. A light breeze stirred. The first rays of sunlight poked through openings in a clearing sky.

Mark began to hear stirrings in the camp. A tent door zipper sang, clothing rustled, followed by more zippers. Someone stumbled and fell. Bob walked under the tarp first. He yawned and nodded his head. He managed a muffled "morning" before he pulled his chair close to the fire and sat heavily. Mark rose up and poured him a mug of joe that Bob grabbed hungrily. After pouring himself a mug, Mark sipped the freshly perked Columbian. The two friends quietly watched the changing scene. Various creatures passed by. There were chipmunks and red squirrels at ground level while raptors, ducks and crows cruised overhead as they hunted prey. A pair of loons swam into sight. Two brown, fluffy chicks rode on the mother's back. The male dove and caught small fish that he fed to the ravenous chicks.

Ray was next to enter the land of the living. He waved at them before staggering to the water bucket where he splashed noisily. He gargled, brushed his teeth and slicked back his hair before joining them.

"Coffee, please!" Ray grunted. He stood near while holding his free hand toward the fire. Mark poured his mug full of hot joe. Ray thanked him, took a sip, then filled another and delivered the steamy mug to Ange in her tent. When he returned, his mug awaited him near his chair.

Ray cupped the mug and said, "Good morning guys! It's starting to clear up and promises to be a beautiful day! No need for you two to rush away. Your gear should dry in a few hours."

"D'accord," Mark agreed. "A wet tent is a pain to pack and set up. Besides, we'll have time to savor the final 'pork eater' voyageur breakfast Ange promised, and you'll have time to test a solo canoe."

As Mark re-filled their mugs with java, Ange appeared looking chipper and poured the last of the java into her mug. Then she rinsed the pot and basket and made a fresh pot. After greeting them with a cheery "Morning, guys," she took a few sips of coffee and began assembling the ingredients for the "pork eaters" breakfast. Ray lowered the food pack to waist level. He and Ange could reach the food but it was out of reach of critters. From long experience, Ray found most damage to equipment and food was done by mice and squirrels. Mark and Bob chatted with Ray while trying to ignore what Ange was preparing. Mark noticed the carefully wrapped brown eggs and spied a slab of Zup's country bacon emerge. The drooling began in earnest. Hash browns sizzled in a fry pan while her homemade whole wheat bread was buttered and placed on the grill. Country style bacon fried enticingly. Mark saw Ange drop cheddar and Monterey jack cheese slices atop the big fry pan of scrambled eggs and cover it. Mark winked at Bob as he nodded towards the grill. The mélange of aromas was about to overload their senses.

Ange announced the meal was ready! She announced it would be served to them. Mark and Bob would be given VIP status and served first.

There was a gourmet tray with little bowls of hot sauce and salsa, sea salt and a black pepper grinder. When everyone had been served and java mugs were full, Ray said grace and they dug in. The cheese had nicely melted into the scrambled eggs and hash browns. The smoked, lean bacon was truly a pork eater's delight. The homemade wheat toast, jam and hot java made it a blowout breakfast. The fur trade voyageur would have thought he had died and gone to Heaven!

After munching their way through the decadent fare, they were full, content and resisting any serious exercise. Mark stifled a belch and reflected on their predicament. It seemed almost a diabolical plot to make them their food slaves forever. But Ange immediately dispelled that idea.

"Well, guys," she said, "we hope you've enjoyed the pork eater special! All we're having from now on is rice, beans and soup!"

"Très bien, merci!" Bob replied. "It's been wonderful to have our own personal chef, but we do have to cut the gourmet umbilical cord! It's high time to go find our solo camps!"

The light drizzle quit as they kibitzed about a range of subjects from gardening to the world situation. Ray summed it up as "It's gone to hell!" Mark decided to change the subject.

Mark filled them in on Pierre's canvas tipi and Pierre's invitation to visit him and his wife. Mark told them about their offer to help make him a tipi. Pierre's wife was a full blood Sioux and they had designed Pierre's camp tipi after their full-sized tipi that they called home in summer. Ray gave Mark a congratulatory pat on his back, then laughed and shook his head.

"I never would have believed this possible," Ray said. "You showed poise, practical understanding and courage. I'm as proud as I would be if you were my own sons. I envy your experience and can only imagine what the future holds for you both."

"Merci! We are very blessed," Mark added.

"D'accord!" Bob agreed.

They continued their chat. Ray mentioned that the iron ore cars continued to roll through Iron Mountain. He also said the South Vietnamese city of Saigon was renamed Ho Chi Minh City. It honored the man who outlasted the greatest military might in the world without an air force or vehicles – only bicycles. It was once again a flourishing city, entertaining tourists and trading with other nations, including the U. S. Ray said, "So much for the old 'domino' theory!"

"Enough talk," Ray quipped. "Let the adventure begin! I'm ready for my shakedown cruise in the solo canoe."

"Mais oui!" Mark replied. "You can take mine out. Just let me adjust the sliding seat. I'll have it waiting in the shallows for you."

"I'll be right beside you as your wing man," Bob offered to Ray. "Let's head over to check out the inlet that connects to Moose Camp Lake."

The sun threw a bright beam onto the camp. It was bathed in a golden glow as Ray and Bob were seated and paddled away. Mark and Ange stood watching them go. Ray and Bob sailed swiftly down the north shore, running with the wind. The onshore breeze at the camp began to dry out the tents. Mark helped Ange with the breakfast clean up. After that, he started packing his gear into his Duluth Pack. He let his tent stand empty so it could dry. If it failed to dry completely, he would stuff it on top of his pack and strap it down. He lugged his gear down to the water and piled it close to the shore.

Ange called to him as he finished and motioned for him to come up. He saw her pouring hot tea into mugs as he drew near. She was slicing her homemade bread. He thanked her and inhaled the fragrant tea. Ange offered him a toasted slice of whole wheat bread spread with homemade strawberry jam!

"Ange!" he said. "This is great."

"This is the last treat you'll get until you return after your solo," Ange promised.

As they munched their snack and sipped the tea, he was aware of what a fine woman and wife Ange was and how lucky Ray was.

They were still sitting there sipping tea and chatting when the two solo canoes re-appeared. The last hundred yards was a race. It ended with Bob leading by a canoe length. Bob hopped out on shore. He saluted Ray and ran up the hill to where Ange held out tea and bread. Mark could tell that Ray was in some pain and having trouble exiting the canoe. Mark helped Ray stand and step free of the canoe. He let Mark pull the canoe further on shore and walked while bracing a hand on his lower back.

"Thanks for the help," Ray said. "I think my old sports injuries and World War Two army service has finally caught up with me. I really overdid it when I challenged Bob to a race. I just might be getting too decrepit for this stuff. Maybe I have to re-think car camping! Confidentially, this may be my last year of teaching. Thirty years is a long time."

"Mum's the word," Mark answered. "It would be a grave loss to Quinnesec School, but you've taught a long time. We were privileged to have you as our teacher. When you do retire, Ray, what are your plans?"

"I'll write," Ray answered. "First my memoirs, then maybe prepare a manual for use in teaching survival and outdoor lore. Other than that, I'll take naps, canoe, fish and spend more time with Ange and our grandchildren."

They walked up to join Bob and Ange at the fire pit. They sat down and waited while Ange served them tea. Ray declined the bread and jam, so Bob and Mark split it.

"You sure can push water!" Bob said. "I thought we were going to tie until the very end."

"Your solo canoes are unique!" Ray replied. They are light, fast and agile, unlike me! I ran out of steam. I feel like a whipped pup. Thanks for a wild ride! It was an adventure."

After more talk and tea, it was time to depart. Mark bid everyone "adieu" then left to take his tent down. He was loading gear into his canoe when Ray walked toward him, limping.

"Mark," Ray said, "I'll come to check on you both every two days. Bob will be on my morning schedule and you'll see me in early afternoon. This back of mine has given me trouble before. It should be fine by tomorrow after applying a hot water bottle and a massage from Ange."

Mark shook Ray's hand and waved at them all as he turned his canoe northwest and made for the portage to Boot Lake. He saluted Bob who headed in the opposite direction.

Chapter Twenty-Two

Mark's Solo Camp

Mark followed the shoreline back to the Boot Lake portage. Its enormous boulders appeared, split by a fast-moving stream that flowed into Fourtown. It was a short portage of forty-eight rods alongside the clear creek. In less than an hour he was paddling toward the first campsite on the right shore. Fortunately, it was available. He landed the canoe and checked it out. It had everything he liked. A row of cedar trees bordered the shoreline, and tall pines provided shade and had good branches for hanging his food sack. A nice flat tent space was shaded in the afternoon and was protected by a rock wall. Another plus was the useful table rocks that were situated near the fire pit.

Mark unloaded the canoe and set up his camp. It was still early in the day with no rain in sight. He hung his rain tarp, gathered some birch bark in a bag and cut enough wood for a few nights. Once that was completed, he walked down to the water and peered through the curtain of cedar trees. He oriented his map with the top facing north. Then he found his location on the map and found an island almost directly across the lake. About a half mile north of the island was a small inlet creek with ponds and beaver dams upstream. He planned to explore and fish the ponds.

Mark's campsite faced west. Its elevation allowed him perfect sunset vitas. Hunger compelled him to light a small fire to cook some soup. He reached for his fire stick but had an idea and put it back. It was a good time to see if he could coax fire out of Jacko's gift. He dug it out of his pack and unwrapped its deer hide covering. After gathering some dead grass and frilly birch bark into a fuzzy duff nest, he gathered small twigs. These were stacked into a curved tipi with space to insert the smoking ember. He knelt on a bed of pine needles and wrapped the bow cord around the drill. In his left hand he held the drill cup over the drill's top and began sawing the bow using long strokes. The spindle spun rapidly in its base hole. As he applied more pressure and increased the bow speed, a thin line of smoke began to curl upward. Beads of sweat formed on his forehead as he again increased the bow stroke speed. Plumes of smoke began to billow and a black lump threw a spark! He stopped sawing and laid the bow drill aside. Very carefully he tipped the base and dropped the ember into the waiting duff nest. A breeze caused the bundle to begin smoldering. Mark waved it in the breeze until it gushed black smoke and then gently placed it into the twig tipi just as it erupted into a blaze! He quickly fed it dry twigs and branches until it crackled and burned hot. It was his first friction fire and a proud moment. He held his arms overhead giving thanks to the Creator and to Jacko for the wonderful gift. It was time to give a baptism of fire to his soup pot.

He filled a pot with four cups of water, added a handful of jasmine rice, wild rice and barley and brought it to a boil. A box of his favorite Mrs. Grass Chicken Noodle soup with the "golden nugget" was stirred in covered and left to simmer. Meanwhile, he sliced up some Zup's sausage and cheddar cheese and withdrew a handful of saltines.

The soft breeze was soothing to him as he surveyed his new domain. He was home. He felt at peace being alone without being lonely. Of course, he had to admit he missed the camaraderie at base camp. That had been a special time. Even the fabled Robinson Crusoe craved a companion after being shipwrecked and alone for many years on an uninhabited island. It was one of Mark's favorite reads from the old Quinnesec School Library. He often envied Crusoe's life there and his ingenious ways of survival.

Mark wondered if Bob was equally at ease at his new camp. Ray and Ange were unflappable and at home in the wild. The fire crackled, spewing sparks from the hot pine pitch that exploded with a bang. Some sparks bit hit Mark's bare leg! He jerked it away, then laughed while rubbing his singed calf. It brought to mind how the Ojibway and voyageurs melted this same pine pitch and birch bark every night around the fire to repair any damage to their canoes. Pine pitch could also be used as a healing balm on wounds. It was well known as a great fire starter, wet or dry. It was like birch bark: its resins burned fiercely.

He lifted the soup pot cover. The long simmer created a fragrant, thick soup that was almost a stew. He ate the crackers with cheese and summer sausage and sipped the rich soup. He consumed all of the soup. The soup carton suggested it made four servings. Mark was amused by that. The four people must have been anemic dwarfs! The combination of a full belly and the cozy warmth of the fire caused Mark to slump low in his chair and doze off.

Sometime later, a sharp slap on the water made him jerk awake. He calmed down when he found he'd been disturbed by a kingfisher! It had dived on a careless minnow in the shallow water. The kingfisher flipped its catch up above its perch and swallowed it headfirst. It scanned the water then dove headlong. The feisty killer suddenly dropped like a javelin. It struck and instantly rose with a minnow clenched in its beak. The expert fisherman then flew back to the same limb, swallowed it and was ready for more. Mark watched, entranced. The small blue-and-white-crested hunter never came up empty. The intrepid bird suddenly flew away while uttering its raucous cry.

The row of cedar trees along the shore partially hid Mark from view. It allowed him a veiled viewing of the passing parade of wildlife. At the fire pit he was more exposed but had a more panoramic view. It was now late afternoon and the breeze began to subside. Mark had lost track of time while being entertained by wild creatures. They ranged from tiny warblers to a family of otter and various ducks. White-throat sparrows and warblers worked the shoreline. They fed and hopped nimbly. Some flitted within five feet of Mark and were remarkably tame.

One white throat caught his attention. It seemed a bit unstable as it moved. Looking closely, Mark found the reason. It had but one leg! It flew as well as any other and made standing on one leg look easy. It was a wonder that endeared the tough little bird to him. Mark thought of the client trip and how well Glenn did after losing both his legs. In nature no artificial limbs were available.

A few hours of light were left. The lake was becalmed. Mark hopped into his canoe and took a leisurely paddle across to the island and circled its shore. He headed up the shoreline to where the creek entered the lake. He penetrated up the creek to the first pond where he had a look around before returning to his camp. After tying his overturned canoe to a cedar tree, he coaxed a fire from the ashes. Tomorrow he could fish for his supper. It was a quick paddle to cross the narrow section of the lake and up the stream to the beaver dam pond. He had seen a few rises on the pond's surface and hoped they marked fish.

It was almost dusk. He put two pots on the fire grate, one for tea, another for rice. When the rice was ready, he added butter, salt and pepper. The hibiscus tea was sweetened. It was a quick and tasty meal. The sunset was already fading into darkness when he awoke after nodding off. He swallowed the last of his tea. After quickly cleaning his dishes with the unused tea water, he raised the food bag high and brushed his teeth. It was dark when he reached his tent and snuggled into his bag. He lay on his back and listened to loons call. He was well fed and at peace. As his body began to relax and shut down, his brain finally saw its chance to play. It was time to pare down most of its duties and enjoy some free time. His body's sleep demands were far less strenuous. It merely required monitoring autonomous respiration, digestion and a complete multiple system renewal. It was now free to delve into more interesting areas like dreams and other fantasies. It allowed the unconscious free rein. Complex and superior to any man-made computer, his brain would continue essential life support functions, but it was capable of much more.

Marq swept the back of his hand across his forehead to wipe away the sweat that burned his eyes. The big birch bark trade canoe glided toward the portage with its upturned bow bobbing in the shallows. It had been a long sixteen-hour day of portaging heavy fur bales and paddling endless lakes and rivers. Now it was near dusk and time to make camp and supper. The brigade's voyageurs grunted, cursed and stumbled on the jagged rocks and roots. Their brightly colored waist sashes danced between muscled legs and massive torsos. Their strong, compact bodies bore countless cuts and bruises from the rough trails. The ninety-pound fur bales were handed from voyageurs in the canoe to others standing in the water. The bales were passed along until all bales were onshore and stacked high and dry. The heavy bales rode on long poles that distributed their weight and protected the birch bark canoe's hull.

If the canoe struck rocky shores, the hull could tear or break and would need to be patched before its next use. Marq helped hand the bales out of the canoe. His full name was Marquez Fisher, Marq for short. He winced if the bale slipped. If the heavy bale struck a voyageur in the water it could submerge him. He would surface with choice French curses, shake his head and be ready for another bale. When the canoe was empty, Marq hopped out and helped carry it to an opening. It was turned over, checked for damage and repaired. A fair-skinned, freckled young clerk with red hair, named Sean McTavish, carried his gear a ways from the main camp and set up his canvas lean-to. He was a Scot who had finished his apprenticeship at Rainy Lake and took a position as the new head clerk at Grand Portage. He spoke with a brogue that Marq enjoyed listening to. Marq and Sean were not regular conscripts like the voyageurs. Marq was working his passage to the fort at Grand Portage on the Northeast shore of Lake Superior.

It was near dark when the canoe had been patched. Each man was given a chunk of pemmican, which they all threw into a large kettle and cooked on the fire. Water, sugar and flour were added to the pot, and then stirred into a thick stew. When pemmican wasn't available, they used salt pork and dried corn or peas. The stew was called roobaboo. The voyageurs thrived on it and shared the potful until it was gone. Marq and Sean chose to take their share of pemmican to cook over a smaller fire. It was enjoyed along with the fat walleye Marq had caught on a hand line. Marq roasted the pemmican in Sean's personal frying pan while the fish was poached in a pot. It was infinitely better tasting, and healthier.

Sean was single, 25 years old, and was signed to a new contract with promotion to head clerk. He worked for the North West Company. He wore a plaid wool beret and wool knickers that ended just below his knees. He sported a gay colored sweatband around his forehead, like Marq's. Sean definitely stood out among the dark haired, squat, swarthy, French-Canadian voyageurs. Sean was a "company man." He was exempt from paddling and only was required to portage his personal pack. He earned a grudging respect from the crew by volunteering to paddle. Marq happily shared his spacious canvas shelter. The voyageurs slept under the overturned canoes. Each had a wool blanket as a cover. They did their arduous work without complaint, endured hordes of insects, heat, and cold and sixteen-hour days with enough spunk to laugh and sing chansons while they worked. They were greasy, dirty and a bit foul smelling. They never bathed until they neared a fort. Then they underwent a transformation. Before arriving, they stopped to bathe, put on clean shirts and even wove colorful feathers into their hair. As they neared fort, they made a fine display of their paddling while loudly singing a chanson. Voyageurs looked forward to the food, rum and available dusky Indian maidens at the forts. The fur trade voyageur camp grew quiet as the exhausted brigade fell asleep.

A loon sang a quavering tremolo that brought Mark awake with a start. He slowly opened his eyes. "Alors!" he said aloud. He was lying alone in his own tent and it was dawn! It had all been another dream. He chalked it off to the prior day's rigor. His dream was still vivid. He opened his eyes, looked around and found all was well. He had enjoyed the surreal experience of watching a fur trade voyageur brigade. Now he was back in his solo camp. He dressed and left the tent. Some embers were still alive in a big pine knot. He held some frilly birch bark close to it and blew until the ember smoked, then the bark burst into flame. Soon a hot fire blazed.

He started a pot of coffee. A cup of oatmeal, brown sugar and dried fruit were added to the water. Once the oatmeal began to boil, he added the dried fruit and let it bubble until it thickened. Mark sat back and enjoyed the sweet, rich oatmeal. He washed it down with pure

Columbian java while he watched another dawn come to life. The tops of the trees across the lake glowed golden as the sun's rays struck them. The lake surface remained calm while a clear blue sky fairly shouted, Halleluiah!

The kingfisher's chattering cry broke the stillness. It was answered by a solitary loon's plaintive cry. The sound was something he never tired of. Each new day was unique. It was never predictable but always a miracle. Mark stood and raised his arms heavenward. It was a gesture he had seen Pierre and Jacko make when praising their Great Spirit. After a moment he relaxed his arms, cleaned his dishes and made haste to explore and fish. This was his second day at solo camp and he needed to catch some fish for supper. He expected that Ray would be checking on him later in the day. He left a note by his chair in case he was late getting back.

With his fish pole, daypack, possibles bag and canteen loaded, he was off. In fifteen minutes he was at the inlet stream and was closing on the first dam. The spillway at the top center of the dam was only a few feet above the outlet stream. He paddled hard to gain enough momentum with the canoe. He slid up and over the top. Once in the beaver pond, he hooked a fat worm and cast it near a group of lily pads. The line twitched then slowly pulled away. He set the hook and was tied to a fish that fought like a demon. It finally yielded and came belly up to the canoe. Mark smiled as he landed the colorful, ten-inch brook trout. He placed it in a wet burlap sack. The next cast brought in a chunky bull bluegill as large as his hand. He worked his way around the pond, ending up with three of each. It was plenty for a meal. He filleted the bluegills and gutted the trout on shore, using his paddle as a cleaning board. Once again Mark vaulted over the dam and headed across the lake to his camp.

Arriving at camp, he decided to fry the fish for lunch. He rolled the fillets in seasoning and fried them in oil to a golden brown. It was a fine lunch. The sweet, pink brookie meat was a complement to the crisp bluegill fillets. He washed the last of the fish down with liberal amounts of hot hibiscus tea. For a final treat he enjoyed a Hershey almond bar.

With a full belly and no plans to leave camp, he decided to stretch out in his tent. It was nice to lay back, carefree and well fed. He intended to catch up on his reading. He opened a book on the fur trade in the early to late 1800s. After reading a few pages, his eyes closed and the book fell out of his limp hand. His left hand began making small twitching movements. His eyes moved rapidly under his closed lids.

> Men were shouting and swearing in French while being swept down the rapids, with equipment and bales bobbing along like corks. Marq looked up just in time to fend off a

menacing boulder. He fought to stay afloat and rode feet first through the four-foot standing waves. He caught one of the bales floating by. He held onto it to let it take the hits on boulders and used its buoyancy to keep his head up. He was taking some whacks to his legs on logs and rocks. He worked the bale towards an eddy near shore. As the current slackened, he pushed the bale towards the nearest shore. As he worked closer to shore he spotted a half-drowned voyageur gasping for air! He extended his paddle and pulled the poor voyageur over to where he could grab the bale. He coughed up water but held on, wide eyed.

"Merci, mon ami!" he gasped. "I was gone beaver, monsieur. No can swim."

Marq nodded at the thankful voyageur and grabbed another passing bale. He found he could touch bottom. With the voyageur's help they pushed and pulled the bales to shore. After beaching the two bales and helping retrieve other items floating by, he could see men struggling above and below. Not far downstream in a quiet eddy, men were pulling a big canoe out and turning it over. Marq could see a big hole in one side, but the canoe's framework was sound. The sun was shining. Men began carrying bales along the river to where the damaged canoe was. The bales of furs had been pressed tightly together and sewn into bison hide but the furs had to be separated and dried out and the canoe repaired. It would slow the brigade's progress, but it was fixable and there were no severe injuries or major loss of the precious cargo.

This would be their camp until then. Fortunately the cooking pots and food were intact. The voyageur brigade had dodged a bullet. Marq saw men weeping and hugging each other. The man he had rescued gave Marq a big hug and a kiss on his hand. Marq was touched and patted him gently. Together they approached the rest of the crew who crossed themselves as he approached. They all shook Marq's hand after hearing the semi-drowned man tell of his rescue.

Marq saw that Sean had just pulled himself up on the riverbank. He ran to help bring him out of the trees and into the sunny clearing. Sean stumbled and coughed up some river water but managed a smile while clutching his personal pack. Marq straightened Sean's soaked beret and gave him a double handshake. Then they gave each other a hug and laughed at their sorry state. It had been a scary ordeal that ended well. Sean had also found his tent floating nearby.

The brigade's guide was a stout, strong, French Canadian named Pierre. He directed some men to build a fire and others to find and mix pine gum to make canoe hull repairs. It would be heated and applied as a sealer on the new birch bark patch. Birch bark and pine pitch were carried in the canoe, in case they were not readily available enroute.

Dépêchez-vous!" Pierre shouted. "Hang up bales, furs. All must be dry!"

Marq smiled at Sean and asked what had happened since he had been preoccupied at the time. Sean said it all started with an honest mistake. They had tried to steer to shore before entering the rapids, but the current caught the stern and swung it broadside to a boulder. It struck it hard then capsized and threw everyone out. The other two canoes of the brigade collided while trying to avoid the damaged canoe and its struggling crew. One man suffered a gash to his head and another swallowed a lot of river water but nobody drowned. Most of their load was recovered and was spread out, drying in the blessed sunshine. A good hot supper, a hot fire, a shot of rum and a good night's sleep would renew the bedraggled voyageurs.

Most voyageurs were non-swimmers and were shaken but soon recovered. Pierre handed out some bison jerky and had hot tea and rum made available to all. Everyone understood they would soon be able to continue on to the fort. All was well.

Marq and Sean lay back and rested in the warm sun. They fell asleep, resting on their packs.

"Mark, are you okay?" A familiar voice called to him.

Mark jerked upright and answered, "Yes, is that you, Ray? I guess I dozed off, sorry!"

"It is!" Ray answered. "I'm glad you're here and doing well."

Mark moved slowly out of his tent. He stood and yawned before shaking Ray's hand.

"I lay down after lunch. Other than feeling groggy, I'm fine!" Mark said.

"That's good news!" Ray replied. "I just left Bob at base camp with Ange. He had an accident. He fell while climbing the cliff behind his campsite. He's doing fine, but has a nasty gash to his head. Ange cleaned, disinfected and bandaged it."

"Sorry to hear that!" Mark said. "Should we try to pack him up and get him to the clinic today?"

"That's a possibility," Ray agreed. "He was unconscious for a while after the fall. When he woke up it was near dark. He held cold compresses on his head, made a fire, took some pain killers and slept. I arrived at his camp at ten a.m. He was sitting by his fire having a hot tea and felt fine except for a headache and much soreness. I helped him pack up his gear and followed him over to our camp. Suffice it to say that this trip is basically over. It all depends on how Bob feels and whether he wants to spend another night here. Let's get your camp dismantled and packed up, then we'll see what gives."

"D'accord," Mark agreed. "You can take down my tarp and bear bag and I'll handle my tent and personal gear."

"Right," Ray replied.

Mark woke up as he hastened to pack his sleeping bag and other gear into his Duluth pack. As he broke down his tent and stuffed it into its carrier bag, he felt anxious about Bob.

"Almost ready, Mark?" Ray called out.

"C'est fini!" Mark replied. "I just need to make a final check."

After loading all his gear into his canoe, Mark shoved off. With a last look at his splendid camp, he joined Ray and paddled alongside him to the portage. An hour later they had reached base camp. Bob sat by the landing and waited for them. He waved and flashed a big smile as he and Ray approached. His head was bandaged, and he nursed a mug of Ange's hot tea.

"Sorry for the inconvenience, mes amis!" Bob said. "The pain is tremendous but it does have its perks! I get lots of attention, unlimited treats and all the hot tea I can drink!"

"I knew there was a devious reason for you doing this!" Mark teased. "You'd do anything for tender care and food!"

Ray laughed and walked arm in arm with Mark and Bob to the fire pit. Once there, Ange checked Bob's head bandage and gave everyone mugs of hot tea. Then they held a parley.

"We need to decide whether we pack up now and leave for the Ely Clinic or stay overnight and leave early in the morning," Ray said. "It's Bob's decision."

Bob said, "I vote to stay and stuff ourselves with the pasta dish Ange has been hiding!"

"I guess you're the doctor," Ray announced. "If you're hungry enough to eat, that's a sign you're on the mend. We leave tomorrow morning!"

The pasta with Italian sausage and garlic bread was a big hit. Ray and Ange placed an early curfew on Bob. Soon after supper and an hour of chatting, everyone headed to their tents.

Mark lay in his tent, knowing this was his last night in the wilderness for a while. He wanted it to last longer. He strained to hear and remember every sound and smell, etching them permanently in his memory. Loons called, ducks roared over and then everything went black.

Marq reached down and rubbed his sore legs. His red headband began to itch. He couldn't scratch it because a fur bale pulled the tump strap tight against the top of his head. He walked bent over and followed the line of voyageurs toting their own bales over the longest portage he ever wanted to see. He walked alongside Sean who happily carried his own personal pack. He was bound for his new job at the fort. It was Marq's last required portage for his passage.

"Hoot, mon!" Sean cried. "This be a rough trail! We must be halfway there, mon."

"Aye," Marq grunted. "This be nine tough miles." Marq struggled with his bale as he followed the line of sturdy, squat voyageurs. He thought he would never last. He feared falling and breaking a leg or suffering a rupture which voyageurs commonly suffered. It was a perilous profession and a strength-sapping way to end the long trip. After he dropped the ball at the fort, he would return for his own personal gear. It would require a thirty-six-mile trek with half the distance under load! Ahead of him, the voyageurs carried two bales or more and would make a second trip to earn extra pay. Just when he had given up hope of ever seeing the fort, they broke into a clearing on a hill. Cheers erupted from the sweaty brigade as the Grand Portage fort and Gitchi-Gummi came into view. He gratefully dropped his bale along with the others and immediately fell on his face! His body had been bent forward to balance the load, so that when it was removed, he collapsed forward. Whatever they paid these poor devils was not enough, he thought. As he massaged his sore back, he looked around and caught his breath. Sean waved as he continued on to the fort.

"Thanks for everything Sean. See you tonight!" Marq yelled. He sat against a big tree in the shade and drank long draughts from his canteen. The big lake looked like an inland sea. He had lived on its shore since his birth on Isle Royale, but never tired of its majesty.

A monster birch bark canoe forty feet long unloaded its cargo of trade goods. Everything that was needed to make the Indians trade for beaver and other furs was fresh from Montreal. It was the end of the annual rendezvous. A long line of half-breeds and voyageurs carried all the goods up to the fort. The big canoe was tied alongside a long wood dock so it remained afloat during the unloading. Other Montreal canoes were also being unloaded and more were already empty and were undergoing repairs.

Two separate voyageur tent camps were set up on the west side of the fort. One was reserved for the hivernants, or over winterers, the hommes du nord who would leave after the rendezvous and paddle a 1,000 to 1,500 miles back to the North West Company's distant forts with a full load of trade goods for the fall and winter. The other voyageur camp was separated from it by a creek. It was reserved for the "pork eaters" or voyageurs who paddled the Montreal canoes on the long trek to Grand Portage and returned after two weeks of celebrating their rendezvous. Their canoes, laden with the winter's fur bales, were returned to Montreal where the voyageurs spent the winter. These "pork eaters" were looked down at by the hommes du nord who sometimes taunted them and started fights.

It was nearly time for the rendezvous to end. These were the last few fur-laden canoes to arrive, and everything needed to be checked and made ready for shipping to Montreal and then to Europe. There was much noise with music provided by instruments that included flutes, drums and even bagpipes which entertained with an eerie piping so dear to the Scottish Highlander leadership of the North West Company. Feasting, fighting, dancing and debauchery prevailed; and rum flowed freely.

There was an Ojibway village a ways down the shore to the west. The voyageurs were kept a distance from the fort and could not enter. They were free to deal with an independent merchant outside the fort for their needs, but could purchase only on credit with the North West Company. It was a two-week annual rendezvous that featured bonfires, rum and dancing with Indian maidens dressed in their best-beaded buckskin attire. It offered time to relax and celebrate before returning to a hard, dangerous life. Inside the fort there was also feasting, drinking and dancing with Indian maidens; but it was also the time for partners, clerks and Montreal accountants to tally and send furs and trade goods packing. The company's leadership also transacted company policy and other business.

Marq quickly covered the distance back to the river and found his pack waiting. He bent down to shoulder his pack and noticed a metallic glint in the grass. He uncovered a trade medal that someone had lost. It featured the head of a French king on one side and an inscription on the other. It was a trade token given to Indian chiefs. It was date-stamped 1800. Marq shoved the shiny souvenir into his front pocket. He began the long trek back. He was happy to be toting his own pack and rifle.

It was almost dark as he once again reached the fort clearing. He dropped his pack and erected a canvas tarp over a low tree limb, well away from the noisy voyageur camp. He took out a few pieces of jerky and drank deeply from his canteen. After a short rest under the tarp, he felt much better. He obeyed a compelling need to renew his bond with the crystal clear water of the "inland sea." He soon stood at its shore and gazed at the great sea whose waters stretched to the horizon. Marq obeyed another compulsion—to immerse himself in its pure depths. He also needed to cleanse his sweat-soaked, grimy body and buckskin togs. He removed his belt knife and moccasins and left them on shore. With arms out stretched, he gave thanks and dove into its beguiling, sacred depths. The frigid water astounded him! He was freezing but forced himself to stay and thrash about. He cavorted, did barrel rolls and floated on his back until he began shivering uncontrollably. He walked out into the last rays of the day. It was amazing how refreshed and clean he felt despite being chilled to the bone. He sat for a while and drank in the dying sunshine while drying out. He patted his front pockets of his buckskin pants and found the trade medal had fallen out. As he warmed up and stopped shivering, he scanned the lakeside scene.

The Montreal canoe was finished unloading its cargo of trade goods. He saw a familiar figure walking away from the trade canoe and heading towards the fort. It was Sean! He was already at work checking each bale of trade goods. He carried a quill pen and a clipboard. He and his assistant clerks kept written records of all incoming and outgoing supplies and furs. Marq caught up with Sean. He was invited into the bustling, noisy fort and was treated to some hot tea in Sean's private office. He also accepted an invitation to dine with Sean as his guest! Soon, a platter of venison, baked potatoes, gravy and fresh-baked bread was brought in. Sean motioned for him to be seated and poured them both a glass of high wine, or brandy. It was the first fresh cooked meat either had tasted for a while. After stuffing themselves with the sumptuous fare, they drank coffee and talked for hours. After thanking Sean, Marq said goodnight and made his way through the fort using a pine knot torch, thanks to

Sean. He wove his way through the loud revelry and out of the fort to his tent. Falling on his blanket, Marq was out like a light.

Somewhere far away, a voice was calling his name! He was so tired and foggy, he thought it was only voyageurs celebrating and ignored it. Then there was a loud noise outside his tent. Thinking it was a drunken voyageur, Mark said, "Get away from me, bête noir (black beast)!"

"So, there is life in there!" Bob joked. "You sure did have a rough night! I'll just go my 'bête noir' way."

Bob began chuckling, which made his head hurt, so he just stood there with an impish grin and waited. Mark soon stepped out, looking a bit addled. He gladly took Bob's offered arm, and they stumbled toward the campfire giggling like schoolboys.

"Top of the morning to you wild and crazy guys!" Ray joked. "Rest your tired bodies in these chairs and warm yourselves by the fire. Ange will pour you some java that's guaranteed to warm your cockles."

Bob and Mark gratefully slid into their chairs and waited for the life-giving cup of caffeine to start their hearts.

"Here's your joe," Ange said. "There's a four-star breakfast coming: eggs, corned beef hash and toast with homemade strawberry jam. It is guaranteed to last until we reach Mudro Lake parking lot!"

"Man!" Mark said. "Très bien! This is great. But I still can't get over my vivid dreams, lately."

"Are we talking about a return to the fur trade era?" Bob asked.

"Mais oui!" Mark replied. "This last one was a dandy, but I think it's over now."

"Does that mean I won't have to hear 'Get away from me!' anymore?" Bob joked.

Mark blushed and replied, "Sorry, mon ami. I confused you with a drunken voyageur!"

Bob grinned, and said, "You're forgiven. Je suis un voyageur!" (I am a voyageur).

That broke the group up. Ray laughed so hard he spilled hot coffee on his crotch and fell over backwards! Mark hurried to his rescue and with Bob's help and despite their laughter managed to get him seated and brushed off. Ange refilled his coffee mug and put a "diaper" towel on his lap. Ray chided his "unruly crew" for trying to give him "scalded gonads!" Everyone laughed. They enjoyed more coffee and a good visit, but needed to tend to Bob's medical condition.

Soon afterward they packed up, loaded the canoes, paddled and portaged to the Chainsaw Sisters parking lot and loaded the van. The trip to the Ely Clinic was uneventful. Bob had an x-ray taken of his head and a fresh dressing put on. The diagnosis was a mild concussion. He was released an hour later with instructions to take it easy and get some rest. Ray insisted on first driving them to the Chocolate Moose. He treated them to a soup and sandwich lunch and then delivered them to the lodge where he helped them unload.

    Pierre was out guiding some lodge fishermen, but Walt appeared and invited everyone in for a chat and coffee. Ray filled Walt in on Bob's fall and the fine time they all had, despite it. Walt invited Ray and Ange to visit and stay in the lodge anytime, as friends not guests. Ray and Ange said their goodbyes, and Mark and Bob saw them to their van. After hugs and tears, Ray and Ange departed amidst much horn blowing. Mark and Bob waved as they watched them drive away with their new solo canoes on their trailer. They planned to spend a few more days in Duluth before heading home.

Chapter Twenty-Three

Going Home Again

The last few weeks were busy ones for Bob and Mark. They worked as guides for a few small groups of fishermen by taking them on day trips into the BWCA. It was fun, and their pay would come in handy for the trip back home at the end of the month. Mark took a three-day break to visit Pierre and his full-blood Sioux wife, where Mark learned how to make his own tent tipi like Pierre's. Mark also got to sleep in their full-size tipi and was treated like a king. Before he left, they had helped him cut and sew his tipi and ordered custom poles that would be shipped to his home in Michigan. It was a fine gift and something he would use with pride.

Before Bob and Mark knew it, the summer was over. Mark and Bob thanked Walt, Pierre and the staff and left thank you notes to be sent to the good doctor. It was a bittersweet moment.

The next morning they caught a ride to Ely with Walt. They shook hands warmly before he handed them their final pay envelopes. Then it was time for a final farewell. Their eyes were wet. Mark even saw Walt wipe his eye as he beeped and drove away. They carried their packs and duffel bags into the Greyhound Bus station at Britton's, put their gear near the door and sat down to await their ride. A pretty server brought them hot java in heavy stoneware mugs. It was time to open their pay envelopes. In each pay envelope were notes to them from Walt that commended their guide service and contained work contracts for guiding the next summer. Mark also found a piece of birch bark at the bottom of his envelope. It had a message printed in pencil that read: "To Mark and Bob, be safe. May wind always be at your back. Bonne chance, hommes du nord. I salute you. Pierre."

It was tough to leave their great bosses, cool bunkhouse and especially, Le beau pays. On the other hand, they had their pay and fat tips from successful fishing clients and more adventure ahead. They got up and purchased their tickets home and each ordered a ham, egg and cheese on a ciabatta bun to go.

As they sipped coffee and chatted about Duluth, a big, shiny Scenicruiser Greyhound Bus pulled up outside! They rushed out with their bags, checked them with the driver, handed him their tickets and staked out the front seat. It was the "catbird seat," as Bob referred to it. They had both called their parents from the cafe to alert them that they would be home in a few days. They had decided to take the liberty of stopping to shop and explore Duluth and the Lake Superior shore area for a while before going home. They would get around by foot and bus or taxis, cash their paychecks and spend some time being tourists. They could hike along the shores of Lake Superior, eat at Grandma's and shop the unique stores, including the Duluth Tent and Awning Store. Ray and Ange would drop their canoes at their homes.

Mark was looking forward to showing his solo canoe to P.J. It was a given that they would spend a day trading their summer stories and plying the fertile waters of good old Moon Lake. It would be a good time. That would be sandwiched between preparing for their freshman year at Kingsford High School. Mark would work at the family fruit stand. Mark and Bob hoped to try out for the Flivver football team. The physical contact and competition, championed by Ray, suited them. Mark planned to buy a light/horn combination for his old Columbia bike so he could travel at night, especially when returning from a long day of fishing at Moon Lake.

The short bus ride to Duluth was a blur. After eating the breakfast buns, they slept most of the way. They caught a cab and asked the driver if he would find a motel where they could stay cheaply for a few nights. Their short stay at Duluth was all they had expected. They stayed at a youth hostel and hiked Superior's beaches, ate well and bought a lot of stuff. It was a fitting end to an extended camping trip. They spent some pay on eats and gifts and generally indulged themselves. He and Bob had hours to talk, plan and reminisce.

They arrived home the first of August. Mark's reunion with his parents and siblings was an emotional, happy event. He had bought them all little gifts in Duluth and there were hugs, kisses, and a special supper. He could tell they were proud. Frank and Wendy, his twin siblings, were thrilled with their deer hide moccasins. Their eyes opened wide when he told them stories of his time in the wilderness. He presented his dad with a hunting knife and gave his mom a colorful silk scarf. Brother Pete's gift was a sack of Zup's jerky and a boonie hat. The family's fruit stand was showing a profit; the crops were all picked, except for the second crop of ever-bearing strawberries. It was good to be home. He called Bob and found him equally glad to be back. His canoe was on blocks under a big pine by the house.

Mark lay quietly in his own bed the first night home while listening to the oldies from WLS radio in Chicago. He felt his legs and arms begin to tingle as he slid into oblivion. The hairs on the back of his neck prickled as he closed his eyes. Scenes of voyageurs and birch bark canoes charging through rapids filled his mind.

Mark understood that, during his dreams of the fur trade, he was present only in spirit. The bearded buckskin-clad man through whom he experienced such vivid, rugged times was real. Somehow his life-long desire to live in the past had been granted. What he had observed of the voyageur brigade had seemed real. He once saw the other man's name written on a note that Sean held. It sounded similar to his name, but it read, Marquez Fisher. He was called Marq, for short. The wonderful but weird "wormhole" back in time had opened briefly but was rapidly closing. Mark watched from afar as the tall, bearded, buckskin-clad man stood on Gitchi-Gummi's shore. He was holding his arms upward, in thanks.

A sudden flood of emotions filled Mark's eyes with tears. He wept, then dried his eyes and smiled. He was finally at peace. He shut his eyes and fell into a deep slumber.

Marquez Fisher stood on the shore of Gitchi-Gummi. His fresh, new, Ojibway-made, birch bark canoe was loaded with fishing gear and ready to launch. He waved to Sean and shoved off to begin a new adventure.

THE END

Made in the USA
Lexington, KY
31 October 2017